CROSSED ARROWS

THE MOUNTAIN MEN BOOK 1

TERRY GROSZ

WOLFPACK
PUBLISHING
— EST 2013 —

Crossed Arrows
Terry Grosz

Paperback Edition
© Copyright 2015 Terry Grosz

Wolfpack Publishing
6032 Wheat Penny Avenue
Las Vegas, NV 89148

ISBN: 978-1629189031

CONTENTS

Epilogue   401

ACKNOWLEDGMENTS

I wish to acknowledge all those hearty souls from long ago who had the dream, curiosity, devotion, foresight, and the courage to wander west. West to the great American frontier when the land was savage, untamed, unforgiving, and belonging to other cultures who fought to hold their lands. The West was a harsh land for all those who historically ventured upon it but was also one of great beauty, having come directly from the hands of God. And, one not seen since those times in its natural state...

It is to those brave souls that I wish to acknowledge their efforts in the discovery, taming, and many times making the ultimate sacrifice in the building of one of the greatest countries on earth.

I only wish that I had been one of you...

CROSSED ARROWS

1

GENESIS IN THE FLIGHT OF
AN ARROW

ZZIP...THUNK WENT THE STEEL-TIPPED ARROW INTO THE middle of Lemuel's sweating back. He plunged against the plow handles. Then Lemuel felt the searing pain as the arrow lodged deeply into his lungs. The pain was so intense that he instinctively struggled to reach the arrow and tear it from his back. Quickly realizing he was struggling in vain, Lemuel reached for his Pennsylvania rifle hanging from the plow handles in order to face his attacker. He staggered forward while trying to cock the firearm. He turned slightly, then became aware of the fast approaching darkness at the edge of his eyes and the loss of strength flowing from his muscular arms. Seeing an Indian running towards him only a few yards distant with an upraised tomahawk, he vainly struggled to raise his rifle. The rifle now felt like an immense, heavy lead weight far beyond his lifting capacity. Making one last desperate effort to bring the rifle to bear, he helplessly felt it slip from his weakening hands.

———

THWACK WENT the steel-bladed tomahawk as it viciously split the farmer's skull. Bear Paw, leader of the raiding party, let out a primal yell as he cleanly snatched the rifle from the hands of the mortally stricken farmer. Bear Paw's victory scream was quickly echoed by seven other Indians from the raiding party as they raced across the plowed field for the white man's log cabin and its inviting open front door.

———

SARAH, hearing the frightened braying of the mules in the field, turned from her washing in time to see her husband's deathblow struck. She screamed and started to run to Lemuel's aid and then in the same instant, realized to do so would bring a like violent death to her and her infant son. Racing back inside the cabin terror-stricken and finding it difficult to breathe, she scooped up young Jacob from his cradle and ran for the back door. Once outside, she grabbed and turned over a wooden tub spilling the drinking water across the ground. She hurriedly shoved Jacob under the upside-down tub, then turned and ran back into the cabin. In a controlled terror bordering on panic, she grabbed the double-barreled, muzzle-loading fowling piece hanging over the fireplace. She turned just in time to observe the first fiercely painted Indian bursting through the open doorway of the cabin. She fired, barely having time to cock the hammers and shooting from the hip. A tremendous explosion and cloud of white smoke followed as did an ounce of lead pellets into the Indian's midsection. Blood and what was left of the Indian's cornmeal and venison breakfast explosively spewed out his backside, decorating the cabin wall with his essence. A second Indian rushed past his falling companion and met with the same fate; the second barrel from the fowling piece sent an ounce of lead tearing through his face and out the backside of his skull, crumpling him instantly.

Sarah realized she was now defenseless. She tried to escape out the cabin's back door. However, she ran head-long into another Indian, who knocked her senseless with the butt of his stone-tipped war club. The next instant, the cabin filled with madly yelling Indians victorious over their success.

———

CHIEF BEAR PAW arrived at the cabin and seeing two members of his raiding party bloodied and dead by the front door, flew into a rage. He grabbed the white woman by her long amber-colored hair and dragged her from the cabin and out onto an adjacent woodpile.

There, he ripped off her clothing in rage. It was then

he was surprised at the bright white color of her body except for her tanned arms, face and neck, which were normally exposed to the elements.

Not like the soft brown color of our women, thought Bear Paw.

Leaving the woman unconscious, spread-eagle and naked over the wood pile, he joined his companions as they tore the cabin apart looking for useful items. Guns, flints, powder, pigs of lead, fish hooks, brass pots, brightly colored clothing, knives and Dutch ovens fell prey to the still excited raiding party. Even the Dutch oven cooking a venison stew on the stone hearth had its contents dumped out on the floor so the pot could be easily transported. Cleaning out the last of the farmer's meager possessions, they exited the cabin. Then with live coals from the fireplace, the cabin was quickly set on fire.

———

As the cabin burned, the six remaining Indians took turns on the still unconscious woman lying on the woodpile.

Coming to, Sarah became aware of the burning indignity between her legs and the tearing of flesh on her back as she was violently raped over the woodpile. Her plight came into focus. She tried to ignore the pain and shear brutal agony of her violation. Indian after Indian forced himself on her as she quietly cried inside over the loss of her husband and the shame of the moment. She was also aware that if her infant son lying quietly under the wooden tub was to have any hope of survival, she must submit and pray her life would be spared. Only then would Jacob have someone still alive to care for him. Back and forth over the rough logs she was ridden, as the sexual appetite of the Indians intensified now that she was awake and wide-eyed. Looking skyward, she tried mentally to focus on the blue sky and white fluffy clouds drifting by as the latest Indian painfully chewed on her nipples at the height of his arousal.

DANIEL PAUSED from his labors of pulling oak stumps in his field upon hearing two shots. He looked up. He discovered a wisp of dark black smoke curling up over the treetops from the direction of his younger brother's cabin. To his alarm, he reckoned it was smoke from a burning building.

"Zeke, Jeremiah," he yelled at his nearby grown sons. When they looked at him, he pointed to the plume of smoke boiling heavily over the treetops. "Grab your rifles and powder, boys," he yelled as he raced for his rifle leaning on a nearby stump.

Within moments, the three men had stopped their work and, with rifles in hand, were racing for Lemuel's nearby farmstead some quarter-mile distant. Like the woodsmen and near "red men" they were, they raced silently through the forest. As they did, they swung their practiced eyes from side to side and looked for any signs of danger associated with the smoke rising over the treetops.

"Indians," thought Daniel. That dreaded word lent even more speed to his already flying feet. He silently prayed: "God, let us be in time."

Daniel raced to within forty yards of Lemuel's cabin, then held up his hand for caution. He motioned with a silent hand signal for the plan of attack. The three men spread out and grimly approached the burning cabin's clearing at a ground-eating but safer pace.

———

IT WAS NOW Bear Paw's turn as he settled down on the white woman. Still upset over her having killed two of his braves, he roughly forced himself deeply into the woman. He used so much force, he felt her flesh tear and was delighted when it elicited groans of pain from the woman. Pushing harder and faster, he smiled at the woman's obvious discomfort over his size as the other braves stood around yelling encouragement.

Suddenly, the woman rose up and tore at Bear Paw's face in desperation with her hands, opening up several long gashes on his cheek.

Roaring with rage, Bear Paw quickly stood up, drew his knife and plunged it deeply into the still defiant woman's chest.

Surprised at his reaction and the new searing pain, the woman grabbed at the knife handle. Then she gasped once and slowly closed her eyes on the final moments of her personal scene of horror.

Standing there, Bear Paw leered at his knife work on the woman who had the almost pure white body. Reaching down, he jerked his knife from her still quivering chest. As he did, the blood oozed from the wound, ran down her side and contrasted brightly against her white skin.

Bear Paw's head burst like a ripe melon as a speeding lead ball found its mark. Bear Paw crumpled to the ground never knowing what had hit him.

———

TWO OF THE Indians turned at the unexpected intrusion and the sounds of rifles fired from Daniel's direction as two other raiders received the heavy impact of lead balls hitting them in their chests. The lead balls tore through their lungs at the same instant as the one raping Sarah wriggled his last. No doubt all they ever saw were three puffs of white smoke dotting the tree line as they stepped into eternity. The remaining Indians quickly fired back at Daniel and his sons, hitting nothing but air. Daniel's father, having fought in the Revolutionary War with Roger's Rangers, had learned well the techniques and skills of frontier warfare. He also saw to it that his sons and grandsons had learned as well.

After carefully picking and each shooting an Indian, the three men swiftly moved away from the telltale puffs of smoke left by their rifles. To linger would only invite the same sure death they had just administered. They loaded on the run and were soon ready for the next round of action. Meanwhile, the three remaining Indians frantically reloaded their North West fusils, the poor quality trade muskets normally sold to frontier Indians.

Boom-boom-boom. Three deadly accurate Pennsylvania rifles bellowed almost at the same instant as their .40-caliber lead balls sped true. The remaining three Indians crumpled as if on cue. There they wiggled their last on the ground as their bodies' mechanisms for life slowed and then stopped. The light went from their eyes as the three violently angry frontiersmen plunged gutting knives deeply into their necks and chests.

Daniel left his sons to see if they could do anything for Sarah and to look for Baby Jacob.

He hurriedly reloaded as he ran to his brother's side in the field. Then he scanned the edge of the forest to see if the Indian raiding party held more unseen numbers.

Satisfied the raiding party was accounted for, he knelt alongside his brother and placed his hand on the lifeless body. Tears quickly welled up in his eyes. In deep anguish, he let out a primal moan filled with heartfelt grief. He rocked back and forth over his brother's body in the emotion of the moment, then he felt Zeke's hand on his shoulder.

Daniel raised his tear-filled eyes and asked Zeke, "Where is your brother?"

"He is back at the cabin, still looking for Baby Jacob,"

softly replied Zeke, respectful of his father's extreme grief. "We couldn't find him anywhere. Maybe he is still inside the burning cabin..." His voice trailed off into nothingness.

———

THE THREE MEN quietly dug a grave under a massive oak and gently placed Lemuel and Sarah together for the last time and forever. By now the small cabin, dry as it was, had pretty much burned itself to the ground. While waiting for the ashes to cool to see if they could find the body of young Jacob, they scalped the Indians. They also removed all the Indians' fingers from their trigger hands. That way—according to Indian lore—they could not enter the Happy Hunting Grounds because they were missing body parts. And if one were missing body parts, they had to wander forever looking for them. The fingers would later be fed to the men's hogs.

Then the bodies of the Indians were hung upside down in the surrounding forest around Lemuel's clearing —a warning to anyone else possessing a like mind of destruction when it came to the local settlers. As for the scalps, they were sold in town to a passing military contingent who were always looking for frontier souvenirs.

By then, the cabin's ashes had cooled and the men looked for Baby Jacob's remains. Nothing was found and Daniel began to wonder if the raiding party was bigger than he figured. Had they taken young Jacob as one of their own? That very mental picture quickly brought terror to his heart. The rest of the war party might now be at his cabin doing what had been done here.

With that realization in mind, he quickly yelled at the boys and started to run back to his clearing and cabin several hundred yards distant.

A low wail from under the overturned wooden tub brought him up short. He quickly returned to the cabin's remains and turned over the tub. There lay Baby Jacob, none the worse for wear.

Zeke stepped in front of Daniel, scooped up Baby Jacob and softly cradled him in his arms.

"We can do no more here," Daniel said quietly as he headed for the open grave.

Daniel and Jeremiah finished burying Sarah and Lemuel. They fashioned a crude wooden cross and placed it in the soft earth at the head of their grave. Then Jeremiah went back to the field, unfastened the plow and brought the valuable team of mules from the field of death. The three men sadly returned to their homes a clearing away to report the news to their families carrying Jacob and with the animals in tow. The news, as expected, was met with grief by all the families even though it ultimately meant a genesis for young Jacob.

2

AN OAK WITHOUT ROOTS

ZEKE AND HIS YOUNG WIFE OF THREE YEARS HAD BEEN unable to have children. It was decided among the remaining clan, since they all had children, that Zeke and his wife would take Jacob for their own. That way, each family would have children growing up to help as the men folk aged. Margaret, Zeke's wife, was beside herself with happiness at the new addition to their family even though the baby came to her in sorrow. Now, despite the everyday hard work and drudgery associated with frontier life, she would have a child and companion, especially when it came to brightening her long hours while Zeke was away hunting, plowing or clearing additional lands. And so it was into a household full of love and promise that young Jacob grew and learned the ways of the wilderness.

Years passed and the settlement of Salt Lick,

Kentucky, grew as more families moved into the area to settle and develop the rich, forested lands into productive farms. Soon a general store, several drinking establishments, a meeting hall, a barrel factory and a crude hotel —with a healthy population of bedbugs—graced the frontier community. That was soon followed by a water-powered gristmill nearby on Rocky Creek, a blacksmith's shop, and a livery stable to round out the rapidly growing settlement.

Young Jacob also grew by leaps and bounds. By his twelfth birthday, he possessed his dad's stout arms, bull neck, and powerful hands. He had also hardened his body from the labors on Zeke's farm, was a crack rifle shot, an excellent tracker, skilled horseman and common sense thinker. Well liked among his kinfolk and the townspeople, Jacob grew like the great oaks he felled as he cleared Zeke's lands for the plow.

However, there always seemed to be something missing in the young man. It wasn't his new parents. They were loving and as good as the real thing. But there were many times young Jacob would stand looking off towards the west for long moments at a time. Looking as if wishing he could leave this dark and bloody ground to follow an unknown, yet mysterious force found in the land of the setting sun, to leave for something else that could salve his yearning soul and fill the emptiness that he constantly carried inside. When he visited the grave of his parents, he would come home quiet and reflective, preferring to be by himself for a time. When he went into the field to tackle the ever present oak and hickory stumps with a vengeance, he'd not stop until his personal demons had left him for the time being.

By his fifteenth birthday, he was six feet tall and truly stout as the forest oaks. Yet, he was as common and quiet as the rich, dark earth he plowed. But those demons possessing his soul never left him. Even in learning from Zeke to read the weather, animals' life histories, tracks of every critter, and cultural history of nearby Indians, he still carried that faraway look in his eyes. That look was not something bothersome or crazy. It was the look of a Westering man—one looking towards new horizons and dimensions to further define his life, in order to satisfy the longing and emptiness living in his soul.

That look was furthered even more when the occasional traveling fur buyers came to town. These men would trade for furs that the local settlers could pull from the forests and surrounding rivers. They offered a little bit of the hard currency that was scarce in Salt Lick, and more often, goods in barter. On their day of arrival, many of the local Indians, farmers and townsfolk would gather to trade skins: elk, deer, beaver, river otter, wolf, bear, mountain lion and the occasional buffalo.

During those exchanges, the discussions ran from the quality of hides being traded to the rich fur-filled lands existing ever farther to the west. That talk was especially exciting about the fortunes to be made fur trapping in the area they called the Trans-Mississippi— an area lying north and west of a jumping-off place called St. Louis. A place where a man could be his own person, life was bigger than all get out, and if one looked he could see forever and a day.

Jacob's quiet and reflective moods were also apparent after travelers came through their settlement heading for the new lands to the west. Those travelers were full of hope and spoke of the many wonders awaiting those who ventured west. Tales were spun about the money to be made in the trade of animal skins and the fierce Indian tribes just waiting to lift one's hair. Those tales were often intermixed with stories about flatboats and keelboats moving trade goods up rivers so immense in size that in some places man could not even shoot across them. As if a young man needed to hear more, stories were often further intermingled with descriptions of the adventurous life awaiting those choosing to become free trappers in the booming fur trade. And for the benefit of the hard-to-convince farmers, accounts were told of the richness of the vast lands where corn grew taller than a man sitting on a horse. Yams wafted through the air like so many leaves blowing in the fall winds. There were stories of lands full of game of every kind, and rivers awash with many species of huge fish. Stories of such fish called sturgeon that were longer than two men were tall and weighed as much as a horse.

Many travelers spinning such yams swore by them because they had been there and seen such things of wonder for themselves. Now those travelers had returned and were bringing their entire families west to seek their fortunes based on the richness of those lands just explored or yarned about.

Every time Jacob listened to these accounts from folks staying at his parents' cabin or in town, he would come away with an even greater emptiness inside that he could not explain away. It was an emptiness that only seemed satisfied when he was in the quiet forests hunting game or just exploring with Martin, his long-time Delaware Indian friend of the same age. But even at that, that emptiness or restless spirit found itself only partially fulfilled.

On Jacob's sixteenth birthday, in 1829, he approached Zeke as they toiled in a new field with mules to pull stumps from the ground.

"Father, I've made my mind up. I need to go West."

Zeke turned, not as surprised as Jacob had expected, and nodded.

Jacob continued, "I need to see for myself what's out there. The traders, when they come, they speak of the West with such wonderful words and bright smiles. It's something I have to do." He waited for Zeke to show his displeasure.

Instead, Zeke quietly tied off the mule's reins to the oak stump he had been attempting to pull. The older man sat down on the stump, then drew in a deep breath and let it slowly escape as he seemed to be gathering his thoughts.

The mule huffed in impatience. Somewhere, a bird

sang. Zeke looked up once at Jacob and pulled the boy's childhood out of his own memory.

Zeke had expected as much from his adopted son at some point. But now that those times were upon them, he found himself unprepared. Zeke was aware of Jacob's lost moments in time and their increasing frequencies, especially during the great fall migrations of waterfowl and the annual bugling of the quickly vanishing elk in the forests. Those pauses by Jacob had harbored the look of wanderlust and adventure offering the potential of life-long fulfillment. That yearning was also accompanied with longer visits to his parents' grave and in the mean-ingful hugs he gave his adopted mother when he returned—meanings all pointing to a young man about to venture into the unknown to fulfill the vast unex-plained emptiness gnawing at his soul from within.

"Okay, Jacob," Zeke finally said. "But I will need your help in getting in this fall's harvest. After that, we can go to town and have you outfitted for whatever awaits you on the frontier. We can trade some of the cattle to the storekeeper, and that should be enough to cover your outfitting needs. Now, settle down, you've earned it. You've given plenty of years of loyal service to this family."

Jacob was about to say something, but Zeke grabbed his wrist and stared him in the eye, man to man. "Son, I am going to hate it, you going West. I have fears that you won't return from such adventures. But I know that's where your heart wants to be. I understand it, and I support your decision. But please, find some gentle way to tell your mother. And use words that will reduce her worries."

Zeke felt his eyes beginning to fill with tears of emotion, and he quickly looked away to the mule. "Now, let's see what we can do with this damn oak stump."

The rest of the afternoon the two men worked side by side without uttering a word as they pulled stumps so more acreage could be put to the plow. And for the first time, they worked as equals in a world made of hardy men possessing a vision. Be it as a farmer or as an adventurer looking for his place on the land or in his soul.

3

THE WILL OF THE WEST

"Martin," said Jacob, "The travelers from the West tell of rich farmlands, herds of buffalo that shake the ground and blot out the sun with their dust, and great rivers that are so wide one can hardly see across them. They also tell of beaver and river otter in every stream thick as the ants on the ground and every other kind of opportunity that abounds. I am leaving to go to those lands further west."

Martin furrowed his brow.

"My father said I can go after the crops are gathered in this fall and that I intend to do."

Jacob watched as Martin's eyes quickly began darting in thought.

"Would you like to go with me?"

Martin was almost as tall as Jacob and equally as strong, not to mention, very capable as a frontiersman.

He was a full-blooded Delaware Indian whose family had
been swindled and then forced from its home in Ohio by
land-hungry speculators—the product of a land swindle
aided by the United States Government after the Treaty
of Greenville of 1795. That treaty had opened up most of
the State of Ohio after the Shawnee, Miami, and
Delaware had fought hard against the United States
trying to save their lands from white encroachment.
Martin's family now peacefully farmed on Lemuel's old
farmstead, which they had purchased shortly after the
Indian raid that killed Jacob's parents. Martin came from
a large family of eight and, like Jacob, had been educated
in the town's small one-room school when not working
on the farm. That was a tribute to both of the boys'
mothers who had stubbornly insisted the boys get some
"schoolin'," so they could learn to read, write and cipher.

"Go where the sun sleeps?" asked Martin with a wide
open set of eyes. Then they filled with wonder, awe and
the pure, faraway look of adventure matching Jacob's.

"Yes, and maybe more. I want to see everything that is
out there to see. My parents never got the chance before
they were killed. Now that I have the opportunity, I want
to go and see for not only myself but for my parents as
well. If I go, it will first be to a place they call St. Louis
along the Mississippi River. It is a river settlement where
large boats bring in supplies and those venturing further
west leave from. This settlement is at the edge of what is
known to civilized man. I want to go not only to St.
Louis but farther west to see what is out there as well. I

would also like to go with a friend," said Jacob with a gleam of adventure in his eyes and a crowding of emotion in his voice.

Martin's brown face slowly pulled a wide, beautifully white toothed smile.

"I, too, would love to go and see what is out there. But I must first talk to my father and get his blessing. If he says yes, I will go with you and the two of us can make good medicine together," he replied with his character-istic trademark grin.

"Then it is almost done," said Jacob as he reached out and the two friends shook hands. They validated the deep abiding friendship and respect they held for each other.

Jacob raced home and burst into his family's cabin filled with the good news about his friend and the possi-bility of going West together. His mother was at the hearth fixing supper as his dad sat at the wooden kitchen table quietly smoking his pipe when Jacob shared the news.

"Father, I asked Martin to go with me. He said he would, if his father says it's okay. Martin's asking him tonight for permission to go. Martin thinks his father will agree. You see, Martin's three older brothers are still at home. They can help with the farming, so Martin thinks his father will say yes. After all, it's one less mouth for them to feed. Oh, I hope he can go, I really do. If he can go, we can go to the West together to make our fortune."

Jacob grinned at his father, who grinned back. In the last four years, Jacob had not felt this excited over anything. All his emptiness, his strange longing, had lifted from his shoulders with this decision to go West.

However, when his mother Margaret turned from her cooking, it was evident she had been crying. Jacob, seeing her emotion, was instantly touched out of the love he shared for his mother. In his excitement and haste, he had forgotten his father's earlier words of caution about his mother and her feelings regarding such an adventure. Jacob gathered her up into his powerful arms. Her body at first trembled and then openly shook as she broke down and sobbed. After a few moments, Margaret regained her composure and pushed herself out from Jacob's arms. Her tears left dark blotches running down the front of his buckskin shirt.

She said, in a quivering voice still filled with emotion, "Young man, I have a supper to finish. You go get washed up and just as soon as the Dutch-oven biscuits are done, we can eat." With that, she set the cast-iron pot of elk stew on the table and returned to the Dutch oven on the hearth to check the biscuits.

Jacob raced outside to wash up. He ran headlong into Martin on the cabin's steps. The collision put both of the young men on the ground in a swirling heap.

"I can go! I can go!" shouted Martin. "My father said after the corn is shocked and the winter hay is in the barn, I can go!"

Both boys wrestled around on the ground in glee

until Margaret interrupted from the cabin doorway to ask if she should set one more plate for supper.

The boys' imaginations ran wild as their thoughts swirled around the supper table that evening. Margaret, in order not to show her true emotions, joined in the conversations with many questions in an attempt to show support. However, like Zeke, she could barely hide her feelings that once Jacob left, she would never see her son again.

The discussions went long into the evening, as plans were made and then remade. Both boys even agreed if one father's crop was in first, that boy would help the other so they could be on their way before the winter snows arrived. That became a somewhat worrisome topic in those discussions; winter could be a hard time in their neck of the woods for any traveler, especially those who were young and foolhardy in nature. However, both boys tried to calm Margaret's fears—and those in themselves— by saying they would travel northwest to St. Louis, and as such, would pass through the many settlements dotting the way. They could hole up in one of them if the weather moved in. Plus, they planned to winter over in St. Louis if they got there in time before the heavy snows flew. Once there, they could work and earn some money for the next leg of their journey in the spring of 1830. Beyond St. Louis out in the Trans-Mississippi, they would be self-supporting. They would hunt the great buffalo for their hides, tongues, and meat, or trap the silky furred beaver, to sell to merchants back in St. Louis.

And so the excited talk went on into the night until Zeke reminded Martin the boy had to go home or his parents would start to worry.

Zeke leaned back in his chair as Martin said his goodbye and rushed out the door. The boys didn't say a single word about returning someday. Maybe it was an oversight...or maybe it was the intervention of fate.

4

ESSENTIALS

IN THE FALL OF 1829, JACOB AND ZEKE WENT INTO TOWN for those supplies they felt necessary for the great undertaking. Jacob still had his dad's Pennsylvania rifle and powder horn. It was tight as a tick and deadly in the right hands out to at least two hundred yards with its .40-caliber lead ball. Coupled with Jacob's almost uncanny shooting skills, the rifle had been named "Old Meat in the Pot." It was so named because every time Margaret heard him shoot, she would get out the cast-iron frying pan knowing it would soon be filled with chunks of fresh venison. He also had his father's tomahawk as well as his old skinning and gutting knives. However, his father's bullet mold, lead melting pot, and fowling piece had been lost in the cabin fire along with everything else.

Other than that and the clothes on his back, he would

need almost a complete outfitting for his travels. In Salt Lick's small general store, items deemed necessary for such a trip abounded in the eyes of one used to living on a hardscrabble farm and backwoods log cabin. Zeke had little trouble selling four head of his fattened cattle for top price in trade. Zeke and Jacob figured there was little use in carrying a year's supply of goods since the boys were only heading to St. Louis on their first leg of the journey. There they could re-outfit more appropriately for the times, travels and challenges that lay ahead of trappers in the Trans-Mississippi.

First on the immediate list were the essentials such as several small wooden kegs of powder, whetstones, pigs of lead, grease, spare gunlocks, a bag of flints, hatchet, coffee mill, and a spare skinning knife. These were followed with a good riding horse, packhorse and the necessary tack, including extra horseshoes, nails, file, and farrier tools. Then came the foodstuffs including a goodly supply of salt, hard sugar cones, coffee beans, cornmeal, flour, bacon, dried beans and pepper. Last came a large cast-iron legged skillet, bean pot, medium-sized Dutch oven, plates, coffeepot, cups, coffee grinder, and metal serving and eating spoons. The men figured their sheath knives and fingers would furnish the rest of the necessary eating tools.

Back in the forest, Jacob and Martin shot six rolling fat white-tailed deer and made jerky out of the entire batch. They also shot a large black bear getting ready for hibernation that was fatter than a pig. Margaret spent the better part of two days rendering fat from the bear for the boys to use on the trip for a variety of uses but primarily for cooking. The rest of the bear was processed in Zeke's smokehouse for winter use on the farm. Martin supplied his own riding horse, packhorse, tack, personal gear and "possibles." In addition, he brought a bale of tanned animal skins of deer, elk, and buffalo for the two boys' bedding and for replacing worn out clothing and moccasins. He also carried his dad's old Pennsylvania rifle and gear, along with his ever-present set of bow and arrows.

One week later found Jacob and Zeke saddling horses and loading gear in the cold pre-dawn hours. Margaret was at the hearth making a hearty breakfast of bear steak, fried cornmeal mush, scalding hot coffee, and her usual wonderfully light Dutch-oven biscuits. As the two men labored to make ready, they were surprised to see Martin quietly standing not ten feet away in the morning's darkness. He had "Indian typically" slipped up on them and stood quietly alongside his horse and pack animal waiting for Jacob and Zeke to finish.

"Just like a damn Indian," said Jacob with a grin once he discovered the presence of his close friend, "sneaking around all the darn time."

"Just like a white man, can't hear nothing or nobody coming," Martin responded with an even bigger grin illustrating once again the strong bond shared between the two young men.

"Breakfast is ready," said Margaret quietly from the cabin door.

With that and finished with their making ready, the three men washed up and entered the warm cabin. Little did the two young men realize, it would be many a day before either of them felt such household warmth and family life once they began this, their life's journey.

Jacob and Martin sat down to the table with Margaret and Zeke. The boys grabbed this way and that, clanking her favorite silverware and china without regard for ceremony. Martin managed a polite "This is so nice of you" and "This tastes good, Miss Maggie" between bites, but Jacob was too busy trying to fill and then clear his plate.

"Sunrise is almost here," Jacob said to Martin, as he placed his napkin on his empty plate. "We got to get going."

Martin mumbled something through his mouthful of biscuits.

Jacob rose and strode purposely for the door. Martin followed as the two of them once outside finished up with last-minute details. Finally they were ready just as daylight broke. A cold nip in the air foretold that winter was not far away. Both boys looked skyward. Jacob strode over to his mother and gave her a long and meaningful embrace that had to last both of them for a long while.

Jacob then turned to his father and shook hands without looking him in the eye. But when Zeke failed to let go, Jacob suddenly hugged him in a warm, strong embrace.

"I've never hugged you like this, Pa, but I'm glad I am. I'm so grateful for all you've done. You done right by my dad and me." Then he let go, and stood there, indecisive.

Jacob thanked his parents again and once more for all they had done for him. He lightly swung up into the saddle and, without looking back, headed for his folks' old farmstead. Martin rode closely alongside with the loaded packhorses in tow.

Margaret and Zeke watched the two young men ride off down the forest trail leading from their cabin to the land which one time belonged to Jacob's true parents who had been killed by Indians. Margaret returned to her kitchen and Zeke returned to feed his small herd of cattle.

———

JACOB AND MARTIN stopped first to say goodbye to Daniel's family, and then to Jeremiah's, both of whom lived nearby. Jacob made one last stop, at the gravesite of his parents, Lemuel and Sarah. Martin watched silently as Jacob paid his folks his last respects. Tears welled in Jacob's eyes, then cascaded down his cheeks. He got a grip of his emotions, straightened the cross one last time, and watched as the morning's sunlight spill over the tree-tops and on the gravesite at his feet.

Martin nodded. He always saw signs, The Way of Indians. "This is good," Martin said.

It was time.

Jacob walked back to his horse and swung lightly back into the saddle.

"Let's go."

5

ON THE ROAD

FOR THE NEXT THREE WEEKS, JACOB AND MARTIN SETTLED into the regimen of traveling and roughing it as they headed northwest towards St. Louis. They traveled old Indian traces, wagon trails, rutted roads, game trails and directions provided by the locals through the forests and glens as they worked their way ever westward. Day after long day with the cold moisture-laden air and even cooler fall nights surrounding them, winter weather was becoming their ever-present traveling companion. Winter came early that year and the boys had discovered they would be facing its icy blasts from out of the north-west on a daily basis. Yet their excitement at being on their own and seeing new country every day softened all weather-borne adversities.

Martin, the ever-efficient Delaware, spent his evenings by the light of the fire to work with knife, steel awl and freshly chewed sinew on some of the tanned hides. Soon he had fashioned heavy, three-quarter-length winter coats from tanned buffalo skins for both of them. Riding was ever a cold venture when riding horses. The coats covered their legs with its added warmth and, if necessary, could be used as a roll-up blanket of sorts when sleeping on the cold ground. As the miles and days passed, both men discovered that what had once been strong memories of home were now softening. It was now difficult to visualize faces of loved ones or remember the tastes of specialty foods prepared espe-cially for them by their families. Also lost were many of the sunrises and sunsets experienced with their loved ones in times past. Replacing those memories were now those new found experiences on the trail. Harder memo-ries than those of home softened by the passing of time. But life as the two young men now came to know it had been bittersweet, in those aspects needed for the soul and life that was to come.

———

JACOB AND MARTIN passed numerous small settlements and lone farmsteads along the way. Being the outdoorsmen they were, they chose to sleep in the forests by themselves come dark. They knew the forest to be friendlier, except for the occasional bear and panther, compared to the rough looking settlements and even rougher looking people. Besides, many on the frontier resented any white man befriending and associating with an Indian. That violent period of Indian fighting on the frontier provoked many bitter memories and feelings from the settlers—memories and feelings that died especially hard for those having lost loved ones during the many years of death and privation associated with the Indian wars.

Jacob and Martin journeyed through the Kentucky countryside, cold and wet from the latest November storm that had howled in their faces all day. They prepared to spend an evening in a heavy, protective stand of evergreen timber along the trail.

They built a small lean-to for sleeping and a simple pole corral for their livestock. Jacob tended to the horses while Martin started a large campfire to warm up, cook dinner and dry out. Martin had taken a nice fat deer earlier with his bow and arrow, a tool that was a constant companion and one which was always deadly in his hands. Now they would soon smell venison roasting by the fire on sharpened cooking sticks and have a frontier repast of the first degree. Jacob smiled at his friend's labors for a tasty outcome soon to follow. A heavy meal of hot fresh deer meat and coffee would be a welcome addition to their long, wet and cold day with only jerky for breakfast and lunch.

Jacob placed the saddles and saddle blankets over corral poles under a heavy forest canopy of branches to dry, then curried the tangles out from the thick winter coats of the horses. Care of the animals was something

Zeke had taught him well. Horses had to get you there and get you home. The only way that was possible was if they were cared for properly before you cared for yourself. Jacob had learned those words of wisdom well. He had just finished currying a second horse when he heard the unmistakable sounds of horses' hooves quietly approaching.

Jacob gave a low whistle to get Martin's attention. He pointed to his ears and then in the direction towards the sounds of the approaching horses on the soft damp forest floor. Jacob moved closer to his rifle that lay across a nearby saddle. Martin in turn picked up and cradled his rifle in his arms. Five burly riders soon rode into view and seeing the firelight, headed directly for the campfire.

"Hello the camp," hailed the apparent leader of the group who was a bear of a man. Standing at least six feet tall and weighing over two hundred pounds, he really was a bear of a man.

"Hello," responded Martin as he cautiously cradled his rifle in his arms at the ready. "Care if we light down and share your fire a mite?" asked the leader.

"Help yourself," responded the still very alert Martin. It would have been improper to turn anyone away in their time of need.

The rest of the horsemen pulled up short of the campfire and began quietly dismounting.

Jacob kept a sharp eye as well. The newcomers appeared encumbered under their heavy, full-length buffalo skin coats. When they dismounted, Jacob noticed in addition to their rifles, they carried large .69-caliber, single-shot horse pistols, tomahawks and knives as well.

"Got any extra of that?" one of the men with few front teeth asked pointing, to the deer meat happily roasting away by the fire.

"Help yourself," smiled Martin, never taking his eyes off the group as he nodded towards the deer's carcass laying at the edge of the light cast by the fire. It was then the group finally noticed Jacob standing silently by his horse watching the happenings.

"Hello," said another burly man with a bright red and still very fresh knife scar running from his lower cheek clear across the bridge of his nose, stopping as it narrowly missed his eye.

"Evening," said Jacob pleasant enough but still on the alert. With that many men roaming the forests late at night and the two of them being in possession of four fine horses, it made good survival sense that both he and Martin kept their eyes peeled for any signs of trouble.

For the next twenty minutes, the strangers talked and acted very friendly. In fact, almost too friendly, to Jacob's way of thinking. They pitched right in gathering extra firewood and dressing out the deer, hanging it from a tree limb to continue cooling out. From all intents and purposes, it now appeared they were preparing to stay not only for supper but spend the night in their company as well. While cutting and propping up extra cooking sticks loaded with some fresh cuts of venison around the fire, the small talk quickly changed and then darkened.

"Where you two fellas from?" asked the man with the fresh facial knife wound.

"Down near Salt Lick," replied Jacob, as Martin still on the alert, continued brushing up their lean-to for sleeping.

"Damn, that is a fer piece for a couple of young bucks to travel," replied the leader of the group, as he spit a long stream of tobacco juice into the fire. Jacob sensed an edge in the stranger's tone.

Jacob kept currying their last horse, all the while keeping a wary eye on the entire group. Jacob figured if anyone tried anything, it would first come from the burly one appearing to be the leader, since he continued verbally setting the tone for the group.

A tall man who had yet to speak said to Jacob, "What you doin' travelin' with an Injun?"

Jacob, without any emotion in his voice replied, "He is my friend." As he spoke, he looked the tall one dead in the eyes and quietly cocked his rifle unseen from behind the pile of drying saddles and saddle blankets.

"And a stinkin' Injun at that!" declared the tall one, now looking hard at Martin.

The air went instantly electric and silent around the group with the utterance of those words.

Martin just continued brushing up the lean-to as if he had heard nothing, in typical Indian fashion. However, Jacob could tell Martin was ready to go "native" the moment anyone so much as touched the frizzen pan on their rifles.

Jacob realized this group wasn't going to leave until they had his and Martin's hair, all four of their horses and anything else of value. He grimaced. Well, not without a fight, he figured as his eyes narrowed. Narrowed like they always did just prior to him killing a varmint that needed killing.

He had killed men before in his sixteen short years of life on the frontier and found it a very simple thing to do. Man, unlike most wild critters, killed or died easily, spoke the dark voices from his memory.

The leader slowly rose from his place by the fire and then in an instant whipped out his tomahawk from his belt and swung it viciously at Martin's head.

Martin just as quickly knocked the blow aside with his rifle barrel and then whipped the muzzle of his rifle around towards the assailant's belly and pulled the trigger. *Poo-foof!*

Flash in the pan! A damn misfire! thought Jacob as he quickly raised his rifle. One man was drawing a bead on Martin with his rifle. Jacob shot the assailant square in the face. The man dropped like he had been pole-axed.

In that instant, the mass of men confronted Martin and Jacob as one. They whirled with their rifle barrels clanking and poking every which way. They were so close to each other, they were getting in each other's way.

In one fluid motion, Jacob dropped his now empty rifle and vaulted the corral fence. He ran in a low crouch towards the center of the group of surprised men, yelling madly like an Indian on the warpath.

That had the effect of further startling the men for an instant, creating additional panic. An instant which coupled with Jacob's surprise attack to provide just enough time—Martin brained the leader of the group with the stock of his now spent rifle. And in that braining blow to the leader's head, Martin's hard maple rifle stock exploded into two pieces.

Martin hit the leader so hard, the man's brains spurted out over everyone close at hand, creating even more consternation.

Pow went the explosion from a horse pistol as the toothless man fired, hitting and knocking Jacob sideways as he continued his sprint for the group of milling and confused men.

"Ugghh!" went Jacob. The .69-caliber lead ball had skidded along his side, ripping and tearing at the hardened muscle mass covering the outside of his ribs. Fortunately the bullet glanced off a rib and exited harmlessly out the back of Jacob's buckskin jacket.

Jacob instantly saw red, but still quickly closed his distance. He sank his tomahawk into the toothless man's face who had just shot him. The tomahawk smashed into the nose and facial bones on the shooter's face with a loud bone-crunching thwack, followed by a blood curdling, primal scream from Jacob that pierced a simultaneous *kaboom*.

Another rifle bullet had creased Jacob's face. It left a six-inch-long bloody gash and a powder burn on his right cheek from its close range.

By now Jacob felt nothing but the hot-blooded urge to kill every man in sight. Jacob drew his gutting knife with a swift sure motion. He closed with the man who had just shot him in the cheek. In that fatal instant, the man tried to raise his rifle and use it as a club to still the onrushing Jacob.

Jacob knocked the rifle aside with his left hand holding the knife. Then he grabbed the now terrorized man by the throat with a right-handed iron grip—a steely grip that had made many oak stumps yield in Zeke's fields.

Down the two of them went onto the forest floor, both looking for an opening to kill the other.

Jacob finally got his knife hand loose from the man's hands and plunged its long blade deep into the man's throat with such force it severed the spine. A gurgling rush of fetid air from his mouth and a surprised look in the man's eyes was the reward for Jacob's savage attack.

Jacob leaped instantly to his feet like an enraged panther. He saw Martin tomahawk the last man of the group as he tried running for his horse to escape the deadly scene. A loud "Ugghh" accompanied the tomahawk's entry into the back of his skull followed by a soft sigh. He fell to his knees. Then—killed before he hit the ground—the man gently rolled forward onto his face into the leaf litter. The body kicked a bit with one foot and leg, then lay still as blood pooled around its head in the damp earth.

Both Jacob and Martin surveyed the scene with the

eyes of animals forced to the primal brink of survival. They had not wanted this altercation, but both had killed with a ruthlessness and sureness that surprised them. A ruthlessness that was never further discussed or questioned then or in the future between the two young boys rapidly growing into men. Sometimes violence was a way of life on the frontier and best approached in the way it was meant to be. When deadly circumstances were forced upon a man, he met them violently and then moved on or he himself became part of the soil.

The winter damp air now hung heavy with the pungent smell of freshly-fired black powder. There was another pungent smell now sharply rendering the cool night air. One of fear as the five men had soiled themselves during the quickness and ferocity of the attack by Martin and Jacob. This was a frequent occurrence with some men going into deadly battle with the mortal outcome present in one's mind, especially as it turned out in the case of these five strangers.

As Jacob's emotions subsided somewhat, he began feeling the pain in his side. He slowly sat down with a soft groan. Martin, upon hearing the moan, was at Jacob's side in an instant.

"How bad you hurt?" he asked with deep telling worry in his eyes.

"Don't know," responded Jacob as he pointed to his bloody right side with difficulty.

Martin lifted Jacob's blood-soaked shirt, then poked his fingers around the wound's edge with less than a gentle touch—but a touch guaranteed to ascertain the true extent of the damage.

"Maybe cracked ribs, plenty of blood but flesh wound only," Martin uttered with a look of relief flooding his face. "Face looks like hell though," he continued with another smile of relief.

Satisfied his friend would live, Martin walked around the scene of carnage to check all the men for any further sign of life and existing possibility of danger. "All dead," he said with obvious, yet stoic satisfaction.

Sitting on a fallen log next to the lean-to, Jacob tried to get comfortable, but the wound on his side now blazed with pain. In fact, every time he breathed it was like getting shot all over again.

While Jacob sat there trying hard not to move, Martin rounded up the dead men's horses. He put them into the makeshift corral with their own four horses. He removed their saddles and saddle blankets and stacked them alongside the trail for any traveler to take upon discovery.

Martin gathered up all the dead men's weapons and placed them within arm's reach alongside their lean-to, then sat down. He then determined their calibers and reloaded those fired in case other outlaws or kinfolk of the dead drifted by as well. Five rifles of different calibers and various makes, four horse pistols, six knives and four tomahawks graced the pile of weaponry alongside the lean-to when Martin finished his "gathering of the deadly sheaves."

"Yes," Martin said, "these men came looking for trouble and not just something to eat or a warm place in which to crap between a pair of moccasins."

Realizing his own rifle was now useless without a stock, he picked out another like rifle of equal quality from those laid alongside the lean-to. He quickly double checked to make sure it was loaded and kept it close at hand now as his own. He also stuck a newly acquired and freshly loaded horse pistol snugly in his sash, just in case. Then he helped Jacob over to a large granite boulder closer to the fire on which to sit. He cut off several pieces of cooked meat and handed it to his friend. Jacob ate slow, groaning and occasionally flinching at the movement of his cheek and side. Yet Jacob didn't turn the food away—the hot deer meat seemed to offer him an inner warmth that helped.

Apparently satisfied that his friend was eating, Martin walked over to a cedar tree and plucked some black moss off the bark from its north side. He returned to Jacob and laid the moss on a log. Then he walked over to one of the dead men and cut a long strip of cloth from the back of his shirt. Martin returned to Jacob and took out his moccasin needle and his remaining thread. Without a word, he took the flaps of skin left by the passage of the rifle bullet across Jacob's face and pulled them together. He squeezed the open wound until Jacob flinched, then forced out a mass of blood clots in order to clear the wound. Then with a deftness born from living on the frontier where open wounds were common, he sewed the flaps of muscle and skin together. Next, he packed the moss from the tree over Jacob's cheek wound to slow the bleeding. Deftly, Martin then tied the piece of shirt recently taken from the dead man around Jacob's head like he had a toothache. That move forced the wound closed. At first, Jacob objected, but then the moss began to work its magic as it softened in the blood. Soon, its healing properties began "melting" into the wound and deadening the pain.

The pain and bleeding soon diminished as a result of the medicinal properties of the moss and now Jacob found it was easier eating. But there was little Martin could do for the side wound at the moment. That meant a sharp pain followed every breath making it hard to move the arms or turn in place, which is typical of a rib wound. But eat Jacob did. "Damned if I'm going to let a little hurrah spoil my appetite," he said.

Then, as if they didn't have enough to worry about, another problem arose. The horses began to get jittery and started snorting and nervous hoof stomping. Soon a pack of wolves glided silently into view at the edge of their clearing. Within moments the camp was surrounded by a dozen sets of red eyes hungrily reflecting off the firelight.

The smell of fresh blood from the dead men must have brought them, thought Martin.

A few firebrands thrown their way made the glowing eyes leave but they soon reappeared at another point at the edge of the darkness.

Martin recharged his weapon with fresh powder in the pan, to prevent a misfire in the damp air. Then he walked over to the pile of dead men's bodies, took one by the arm and dragged it to the edge of the clearing. Leaving it there, he returned to the group of dead men. Martin continued dragging the rest away from camp until they were all at the very edge of the light of their fire. Backing away all the while facing the now growing, noisy menace in the woods, he returned to the safety of the campfire.

Martin inspected Jacob's wounds again, then placed a small stream of gunpowder in the tear of Jacob's side wound, along the ribs. "This will burn, but you need to have this wound cauterized," he told Jacob.

Martin set a small burning limb from the campfire to the gunpowder. This technique was common, and Martin had seen it used numerous times by his father. Jacob made a horrible face as the gunpowder burned, but made no sound. "You are pretty tough for a white man," Martin said, smiling. Jacob grimaced back.

The worst noises imaginable came from the dark at the edge of the clearing where he had dragged the dead men. So much so, and since the ripping, tearing and growling continued most of the night, neither of the men got much sleep. It was probably just as well, though— Jacob hurt so much, he couldn't sleep but fitfully.

Come the next morning, Jacob was stiffer than a new pair of soldier's leather boots. His face was puffy and bright red looking, but felt better thanks to Martin's frontier medicinal knowledge of things natural. However, his rib cage was as sore as a boil. Martin soon had the fire going and put more slabs of venison on the cooking sticks to roast along with a pot of steaming coffee. Next he saddled up their two riding horses and packed the remaining two. Then he bridled the five horses from the dead men but left them barebacked. He planned on leaving their five saddles and saddle blankets stacked along the trail for whomever came along needing them. But horses were another matter. They were very valuable on the frontier and would be better used somewhere down the line to help the two of them on their trek west.

However, when going through the saddlebags of the deceased leader, Martin discovered a large sack containing many U.S. silver fifty-cent pieces along with several handfuls of Spanish gold and silver coins. Martin checked the other men's saddlebags and discovered more of the same.

A small fortune, to say the least. The previous owners won't need the money. Martin figured he would include it into their own small stash of silver coins. As he stood there holding the bags of heavy coins, it was obvious someone else had not been so lucky earlier in meeting the five men as had he and Jacob. With difficulty, Martin stuffed the bags of coins into his and Jacob's saddlebags, with the rest being put into their packs. He returned to his friend without uttering a word of his find.

The two young men finished their breakfast of half-raw sizzling deer meat and black coffee, then Martin dressed Jacob's rib wound once more, this time adorning it with fresh moss along the edges of the running sore and wrapping it as well with a soft piece of tanned elk skin. Martin examined the wound one more time before he covered it with the pain-killing black moss, and found it to be clean of any bone chips.

That is good, he thought. That means only a very sore flesh wound, one that will quickly heal. Aside from two small places, the gunpowder burn has done its work well. The wound has pretty much sealed and Jacob can ride without bleeding every jarring step of the way. It will be painful, but he can ride if we take it slowly.

Martin helped Jacob to his feet, and they walked over to Jacob's saddled horse. "Here, let me help," Martin said as he cupped his hands for Jacob to step in.

Martin hefted his friend into the saddle.

"Oof!" Jacob grimaced and moaned softly, but stayed put in the saddle.

Martin tied the outlaw's horses to their own horses in two short strings. "I think that should prevent a horse wreck," he said as he inspected his handiwork. Jacob only replied with a grunt of approval.

Then Martin looked over the remains of the five men in the timber. He clenched his mouth tight to keep his fortitude. The bandits' clothes had been torn from their bodies, and their bones glistened white where meat had been just hours before. Their intestines had been strung out all over the ground and it seemed the only things not touched were the bones of their skulls—skulls, not heads, for the wolves had chewed off the meaty soft parts of their faces, and not one had remained recognizable.

The wolves, meanwhile, lay all around the pile of dead men. The animals were gorged and wore potbellies. They were too lazy to get up even at the men's departure.

"That is good," Martin told Jacob. "The wolves will stay until all of food value is consumed. Then those bears not hibernating will eat the rest. Any kinfolk examining the scene will be hard pressed to determine the causes of death, thereby reducing the chances of pursuit."

Jacob nodded slowly in agreement, and Martin continued. "Plain and simple, it will look like the five men had set up camp, had been attacked, killed and eaten by a pack of wolves, and their horses run off. Any remaining equipment like firearms were picked up by strangers passing this way and one has a clean explanation for the men's disappearance. Yes, today is going to be a good day!"

———

THEY CAME to the Ohio River the next day. When the ferryman looked over the two of them and their horses with a practiced eye, he said, "That will be fifty cents per horse and a dollar each for the two of you. I know that is high but this is the only ferry for miles and I have a family of twelve little ones to feed."

Jacob reached into his saddlebag looking for his small

bag of coins brought from home. Doing so, his fingers "clunked" on many larger sacks of the same. He realized what was at his fingertips but did not want the ferryman to see the hoard of coins for fear of being charged more. He looked over at Martin for some sort of an explanation. Martin's expression and eyes advised nothing more than a pay the man expression.

Typical Indian in his explanation. Jacob returned Martin's smile, painfully.

It took two trips on the small ferry to transport all their gear and horses across. Jacob and Martin agreed it was worth it.

Once on the other side and out of earshot of the ferry operator, Jacob asked, "What the hell? Where did all this money come from?"

"I found it in the bandits' saddlebags. They didn't need it, and I figured we earned it, seeing as how we put an end to their sinful ways."

"If my face and ribs didn't hurt so much, I might not agree, but they done near killed me, and perhaps you're right, we should get some kind of reward. Thanks, for taking the money, and for keeping me alive."

"Do you think the money will be missed?"

"Not rightly," Jacob said thoughtfully. "But we should put more ground under us before the night is through. Just might be key to our survival if those fellows had any kin in hot pursuit who see through our ruse back at camp."

Martin agreed, and they once again headed northwest.

After several days of riding—slowed because of Jacob's injury—they came upon another river, the Wabash. Again, a ferry and more pieces of silver gained access to the west bank. In the small burg of Maunie, Jacob sold one of the five men's horses that was starting to go lame. It brought in exchange several large bags of freshly ground cornmeal, two heavy Hudson's Bay Company blankets, another small sack of coffee beans, and some ear corn for the horses.

"A good trade for a gimpy horse," Jacob told Martin with a smile. A quick look over at his stoic partner's face revealed the same satisfied look over the transaction.

———

BY NOW, the winter of 1829 had set in with all its fury. Their journey was slowed even though Jacob was healing up and getting better by the day. Several times they holed up alongside small streams with dense brush cover to avoid biting winter blizzards and wet snows. The cover also provided shelter for the horses in which to rest and provided much welcome feed. That, plus the occasional feedbag of corn and their heavy winter coats, made life for the horses livable.

Martin finally said, "There is much mud, and the snow and cold is bad."

Jacob replied, "I suppose it's time to hole up some-where. How about the next settlement we come to?"

Martin nodded in agreement.

That afternoon, they came upon the burg of Mt. Vernon, Illinois.

They rented a hayloft in a nearby farmer's barn and moved all their gear in out of the weather. In addition for helping the farmer with his chores, they were allowed to winter their horses with his livestock free of charge. In their spare time both men hunted elk and deer for the farmer's larder and themselves. They made their share up into jerky. In so doing, they also provided for their "found" as well.

It was a couple of months well spent, especially for healing up, equipment repairs, repairing footwear and re-shoeing horses. Eventually the horses were well rested; in fact, they were growing fat. The same could be said for Jacob and Martin who had been eating well of the good German farmer's wife's cooking. But both longed for the spring traveling weather of 1830 so they could go to St. Louis, "see the elephant" and start their journey into the Trans-Mississippi.

6

ST. LOUIS

WHEN THE FIRST VESTIGES OF THE 1830 SPRING ARRIVED, both men were more than ready to continue their journey. They said their good-byes to the gentle farmer and his wife the night before their departure. Then Jacob and Martin retired to their comfortable, clean smelling hayloft. However, not being able to sleep because of the excitement of discovering new places in the morrow, they arose long before daylight and headed out. Dawn found them miles from the winter farmstead and facing new country and adventures.

The road from Mt. Vernon to St. Louis was clearly marked and well-traveled. As the days progressed, they passed many people walking, riding in wagons, on horses or in stagecoaches. All seemed to be in the same general direction and most were in a hurry.

After several weeks of traveling in improving weather, they stopped one night near the settlement of Shiloh, Illinois. The town was nothing more than a collection of mud and log huts with some of the poorest looking people either of them had seen. It was obvious making a living in that area was pretty hardscrabble.

They bunked down a few miles out of town, a lean-to was again constructed, the horses cared for and dinner of fresh venison started. Soon the soft spring night enveloped them. Over steaming tin cups of coffee and the incessant hum of mosquitoes, both men's thoughts quietly returned to loved ones back in Kentucky, a place and time that now seemed so far away that even the memories were becoming more faint and distant.

Whinny! Suddenly the horses started pulling on their picket ropes and acting crazy as loons. Both men quickly jumped up with rifles in hand looking for the cause of the uproar. Then Jacob saw it: A huge bear was trying to get at the horses. However, between their collective flailing and kicking with their rear hooves, the bear was having a hard time trying to make an evening meal out of horseflesh.

And it's going to get a whole lot harder in the next few moments if I have anything to do with it, thought Jacob as he quickly shouldered his rifle.

Boom-boom, went Jacob and Martin's flintlock rifles in unison. The bear, roaring in pain, left the horses. It stood on its hind legs, turned and started walking towards that which it figured had caused its discomfort.

Martin raced for the stash of extra rifles from the men who tried to rob them last autumn as Jacob stood his ground with his drawn horse pistol. *Pow* went the handgun in a cloud of white smoke.

This caused the bear to whirl and bite at its flank. Jacob had misplaced his shot in the poor light, and had hit the bear too far back.

Jacob drew his knife and prepared for the worst. He heard *boom...boom* as Martin shot once from each of the two flintlocks he had brought back to the fight. Both shots hit their marks.

The bear moved slower and forward toward its assailants. It roared with a determination that did not speak well if it managed to get hold of either of its antagonists. As the bear shuffled closer, Jacob smelled the fetid, moist breath and looked at the small but angry-looking red eyes.

Pow went Martin's horse pistol, this time at close range, with staggering effect.

The bear slowed, lowered its head and then laid down, groaning all the way to the ground. Both men hurriedly reloaded their rifles and shot the bear each once more in the head before it finally expired.

Never had either of them seen a bear take so much killing. However, upon closer examination, the bear turned out not to be a black bear but a grizzly bear—a species they had heard took a tremendous amount of killing but one which neither of them had ever seen before. Grizzlies had originally lived in the Salt Lick,

Kentucky area and had been a problem to the farmers. But by the time the boys were of age, they had been all but exterminated.

They carefully examined the carcass and found an old wound in the lower jaw of the bear. It had festered and the animal was in poor condition. Even at that, the bear still weighed at least four hundred pounds.

Jacob leaned against his spent rifle and considered the giant beast. "Martin..."

"Yes, my friend?"

"That is one big bear, and it took quite a bit of killing."

"That it did," Martin said.

"I'm beginning to think that our rifles are not the guns we need for what lays ahead in the West. What we got is for smaller game like elk, deer and black bear. But where we are going, there's the mighty buffalo, the huge-bodied moose and beasts like this grizzly bear. Or so the traders keep telling us. These guns, they just won't do in the Trans-Mississippi."

"I agree. Our friend the grizzly has given me doubts about our flintlocks, too. They've served us well so far. But only so far." Martin and Jacob stared more at the grizzly laying in a heap, lifeless teeth still snarling in death. It was as though the grizzly was telling them of the immense power of the western wilderness and its vicious unconcern for human life.

Then Jacob broke the silence. "Martin, when we get to St. Louis, we need to get better rifles with bigger bores if we're to survive. I also think we also better get newer pistols and two apiece if we can afford them."

Martin didn't say anything. He didn't have to. Neither man slept very well that balmy Illinois spring night and every rifle and pistol they possessed was loaded and "ready for bear," in a manner of speaking.

Days later, as the two men and their horses plodded along the forested trail leading to St. Louis, they heard a loud, unknown sound. *Whoo-whoo-whoo* went the new sound thundering through the trees. It scared the hell out of the horses as they almost ran off with the men. If the two of them hadn't been alert and hanging tightly onto the reins and sitting well in their saddles, they would have ended up on the ground. Thanks to the hoards of mosquitoes causing them fits, they were alert and when the great noise went off again, this time they were ready and the horses held.

As they continued towards the strange sound, log cabins began dotting the landscape more frequently. Soon, the silhouette of a town could be seen through the trees on a high bluff in the distance, and beyond that, a wide, slow-flowing river.

"The Mississippi River!" they both shouted.

Both men kicked their horses in the flanks and picked up the pace to see what they had ridden so far to see all these many months through bad weather and wild times.

Riding into the town of Wiggins Ferry, they were greeted by streets of mud, garbage, piles of horse manure, hoards of people, scampering barking dogs, and hogs running loose. With all that came a constant din of sounds. Huge paddle wheelers, the first steamboats the boys had ever seen, quietly belched smoke while tied to a cobblestone levee along the Mississippi River below the town.

As for the Mississippi River itself, the boys had never seen such a thing

"Martin, look at that river. It's huge!" Jacob said.

"It ain't no creek by a long shot," Martin replied.

"You sure are right about that. It's easy to see why people back in Kentucky said it was so big one could not even shoot across it. A long shot indeed."

LOOKING down the street on which they were riding, they observed filthy mud huts and log cabins jammed side to side alongside many places of business. They found the ferry dock, and took one of Samuel Wiggins' ferries across the river with several other travelers, for a considerable price. On the Missouri side of the great river, the passengers trampled off in a chaotic group, Jacob and Martin included.

So this is St. Louis, Jacob thought. Martin, too, stood agog at all the activity, the businesses, the warehouses, the heavy wagons, the merchants and traders and steamboaters and river workers and painted ladies and teamsters and coopers and porters and...and everything.

Then they saw the homes that were brightly painted

and so beautiful, it made both of them shake their heads in wonder.

There were white people, people who were black—the first they had ever seen—and dozens of gaily clad Indians from unknown tribes everywhere.

Oxen teams led by swearing teamsters and cracking bullwhips crowded the streets; all with creaking, straining wagons loaded with merchandise from the boat docks. Then they observed dozens of men with black skins hauling great loads of boxes and sacks on their shoulders to the places of business and warehouses dotting the streets. That was followed by more kids, barking dogs and ladies wearing brightly colored dresses —all muddy on the bottoms because of the unkempt streets.

There was so much motion and commotion it hurt their eyes and ears after so many months of quiet on the trail. Even their horses acted as if this was far more than they had bargained for, if the wild looks in their eyes and jumpiness on their parts meant anything.

They found a livery stable and paid the liveryman for the keep and care of their horses and security of their equipment. Then with saddlebags heavy with coins thrown over their shoulders and rifles in hand, they walked the wooden sidewalks in wonder. That is, when sidewalks were present in this place called St. Louis.

Soon they observed hotels, places to eat, a Chinese Joss house—a place of worship, opium den and meeting hall—

liveries, and blacksmiths with their ringing hammers and smoke belching from their furnaces filling the air. The scene continued with wagons and teamsters making noisy of their work, riders on horses, gun shops, military personnel parading by in columns of two, and boot cobblers. That was followed by wheelwright shops with large piles of wagon wheels, and butcher shops with animal carcasses covered with flies hanging outside for the buyer to view. And the likes continued greeting them at every turn. It was almost more than a body and their backcountry senses could take. Never had either of them heard so much noise and seen so many people in one place or time in their lives. But the excitement continued as many new things unfolded at every turn in the streets and doorways. Even exotic excitement that included "Ladies of the Night," the first they had ever seen, added to their wonderment.

For the next six hours, the two men were lost in the exploration of their new home. Every turn produced more and more sights until their heads were swimming as the day grew long in the tooth. Not wanting to sleep outside with the hordes of mosquitoes another night, they decided they would stay in a place that advertised sleeping quarters for rent.

Inside a sleeping emporium, for ten cents a night, they were directed to a long room at the back of a clapboard building. There, strongly smelling of sweat, vomit, whiskey and stale cigar smoke, already laid about a dozen men on straw sleeping mats. Some were snoring and others obviously sleeping off a drunk. Still, it was better than having a hovering cloud of hungry mosquitoes buzzing overhead all night in the woods.

Hungry and still excited over what they were seeing, they decided to eat first and then come back to sleep. Walking down the boardwalk, they stopped in a place advertising: Louie's Emporium, The Best Meals in St. Louis. They both ordered steak dinners and sat back into real chairs for the first time since their winter stay at the farmer's barn in Mt. Vernon. They continued watching in awe the happenings around them. There were men in suits and glistening beaver top hats carrying silver-headed canes, and ladies in all manner of clothing that included hats covered with strange bird feather plumes and billowing dresses that rustled softly when they walked. Then there were Celestial men waiting the tables and the tinny clanking of something called a piano in the back room. All of which was accompanied by clouds of cigar smoke, men in muddy clothes, fur trappers in their backcountry garb and more black men waiting on their masters. It seemed that—and everything else—continually challenged their awakening senses.

When their meals arrived, they discovered the steak was tougher than the old grizzly they had shot back on the trail. However, they were hungry and used their hunting knives to cut off slabs of meat so they could eat it in proper style.

"The beans are good but not as good as if Margaret had cooked them, but these homemade bread and biscuits are a treat," Jacob told Martin.

Martin in the meantime was on his tenth biscuit loaded with a slather of wild honey.

Later, a fresh homemade apple pie between them and six cups of steaming black coffee finished off their first commercial meal in fine style. One silver fifty-cent piece covered the entire meal for the both of them. They each carried a full gut as they grabbed their gear and headed for their sleeping quarters.

Arriving, they found the place packed with snoring men, all smelling like a little of Margaret's homemade lye soap would have done all of them a great deal of good. Locating two straw mats alongside a wall near a window, both men tossed their gear in between their sleeping mats for safety, lay down and soon were fast asleep.

"Hey! Hey! Hey!" yelled Jacob as he awoke to find a man leaning over him reaching for his saddlebags. Jacob jerked the man over the top of himself, then slammed the scoundrel face down on the floor between Martin and himself. In an instant, the two friends had a strong grip on the unknown thief.

"Let me go! Let me go!" screamed the thief in terror.

By now the whole sleeping area was an uproar of yelling men. Grabbing a lit sleeping candle off an overhead shelf, Martin held it over the face of their thief for a better look.

"I didn't do nothin'," he yelled. "Let me go!"

Jacob stood up and dragged the terrified man to his feet. The Kentuckian looked about and saw that he had caught the man before anything was taken. He tossed him like a rag doll against the wall with a resounding, bone-rattling thump.

"Get out of here or I will cut you from ear to ear," snarled Jacob.

With that, the man bolted out the nearest open door. Thereafter, Jacob and Martin slept with one eye open and their hands on their horse pistols the rest of the night.

Come dawn the next day, the two men went back at the eatery from the night before. Once again, both men were boggled at the humanity they observed coming and going. For breakfast, both had huge stacks of griddle-cakes with wild honey, slabs of salty cured ham and cups of scalding hot black coffee. Fifty cents once again paid for both of their meals.

They gathered up their gear and slowly walked back to the livery stable, taking in the sights. Walking under the windows of a two-story building, Jacob almost had the contents from a foul-smelling chamber pot sloshed onto his head. Only the sharp eye of his friend and Jacob's quick reflexes kept him from smelling rather poorly the rest of the day. However, it didn't take long for a nearby hog running loose to discover the contents of the chamber pot and make quick work of its delightful lumpy contents.

Back at the livery, they gathered up the rifles taken from the band of outlaws who had tried to rob and kill them earlier back on the trail. They also picked up the ones belonging to Jacob's father and Martin's old broken one with the blood and dried brains still on the remnants of the stock. They also collected their old pan-and-flint-style horse pistols. The two of them walked down Laurel Street to where Jacob had seen the gunsmith sign, still taking in the sights, smells and sounds of a "civilization" still very much foreign to their senses and comprehension.

Jacob and Samuel Hawken read the top part of the sign. *Gunsmiths & Gun Repair. Pistols, Knives, Axes and Rifles for Sale or Trade* continued the wording on the bottom of the sign.

Jacob looked at Martin with a "Let's try here" look. They both entered the store. The air inside the store smelled of stale cigar smoke, gun oil, wood smoke from a leaking stove in the comer, and coffee from a pot that had boiled far too long.

"May I help you?" asked an older man from behind a counter who was carefully filing down the comb on a maple rifle stock.

"Yes, you may," replied Jacob. "My friend and I plan on moving out onto the plains come this fall and doing some hunting and trapping."

"Who isn't?" replied the gunsmith with a timeworn grin.

Jacob, caught unawares by that salty response, hesitated and then continued. "We would like to trade in some older rifles and purchase several modern rifles of a heavier caliber if they be available. Maybe even purchase some good pistols if you have any of those as well," he added, almost as an afterthought.

"Well, that we have, lad, and you fellows came to the right place. What kind of hunting you plan on doin'?" asked the gunsmith.

"We are looking at trapping some beaver and in the interim, taking some buffalo for meat and hides, plus defending ourselves if necessary."

"Oh, you will find it necessary to defend yourselves alright. The country you are talking about is full of cutthroats, white and red, wanting to steal your plews and horses or lift your hair. Between the mean-assed river men and the hair-lifting Lakota, Cheyenne and Blackfoot Indians further north, you had better be armed, and I mean well armed! In fact, from the looks of that fresh scar on your face, I'd say you already know what I'm talking about." The man spoke in a rather straightforward manner as he looked at Jacob's scarred face.

Jacob ignored the gunsmith's comment about the ugly scar on his cheek and said, "Would you show us what you have that would meet our needs, please?"

They laid their multitude of rifles and pistols down on a front counter, then followed the gunsmith into a side room full of rifles hanging on wooden pegs along one wall. Underneath and off to one side of the wall of rifles, a glass-topped showcase full of pistols, knives, steel-bladed hand axes and tomahawks sparkled as well.

"Where do you want to start?" asked the gunsmith.

Looking over at Martin, Jacob said, "If that is alright with you, let's start with some heavy-caliber rifles."

Martin nodded in agreement, at which time the gunsmith turned and took down a heavy octagonal-barreled rifle hanging from a set of wooden pegs on the wall.

"This is the newest of our line and made right here in the shop by my brother and me. It will more than meet any needs you and your friend will have out on the plains. It is a .54-caliber Hawken, which when fully loaded and primed, will shoot a four-hundred-grain bullet clear through a buffalo at two hundred yards. It will also stop a mad-as-a-hornet griz in his tracks if you hit him right. If you notice here, this rifle does not utilize a pan and flint system like your old-style rifles, but utilizes the new percussion cap."

"What is this thing called a percussion cap?" asked Martin.

"Here, let me show you," replied the gunsmith. He dug out a small round brass tin from under the counter. From it, he produced a small copper cap looking like the upper part of a gentleman's beaver top hat.

"You take this cap after you have loaded the rifle and place it on this here nipple of the firearm like this. Then all you have to do is cock the hammer and pull the trigger." *Pop* went the cap loudly as the gunsmith pointed the barrel away from the two men and pulled the trigger.

"With this kind of device, you don't have to worry so much about misfires like you did with a rifle possessing a flash pan, especially in wet weather. Plus you can load this one on the run and not worry about spilling your powder all over the place trying to prime the pan," he continued with a look backing his statement.

He handed the rifle to Martin and took another like rifle off the wall for Jacob to heft and examine. Both men, born of outdoors experience, carefully hefted the new rifles weighing between ten and twelve pounds. They were much heavier than their old flintlocks. They discussed among themselves how stout the rifles were, especially the stocks.

"This is so unlike our Pennsylvania rifles. A much heavier and sturdier stock," Jacob said.

"This rifle has a big bore," Martin added. "This new primer ignition system is very smart."

Both men hefted the rifles to their shoulders and smiled their satisfaction.

"Martin, feel this balance. Feel how it handles."

"Yes. And the stock, being heavier, should take the rough and tumble wild much better than the Pennsylvania flintlocks. The heavier trigger guards will help as well."

However, both men were new to a double-set trigger combination that was present on the Hawkens. They required some further explanation from the gunsmith. The gunsmith took the Hawken from Jacob and commenced to show the two men how the new system worked. Then he handed the rifle back to Jacob and watched in pleasure when Jacob set the back trigger. Jacob smiled at the smoothness of the release when he pulled the front trigger.

Martin did the same and that was followed with a huge smile advising he was more than pleased with the new rifle. "These sights, they are much lower than I am used to," he said.

The gunsmith replied, "The low-bladed front sights are designed for the backcountry. By making them lower, they are less likely to break off."

"And the barrel," Jacob said, "is what, only about a yard?"

"Thirty-five inches in length, son."

Jacob laid the new rifle across his thighs, as if to imitate carrying the firearm on a horse's saddle. "I like that. It's short but hefty. Good for cutting down on snagging and breaking in the mountains, I would think."

"Exactly." The gunsmith grinned.

"Well, sir, your Hawken rifles appear to be as advertised and just as bit good as everyone in town's been sayin'."

Jacob looked at Martin and seeing the acceptance in his eyes, said, "We would like four of these rifles in .54 caliber. We will also need powder, lead, bullet molds, extra ramrods and a bunch of those ignition caps. Enough for at least five years in the outback for the two of us."

"I can do that but you will also need several sets of nipples because with repeated and heavy use, the nipple stem will eventually deform under the heavy fall of the hammer. You will also need a special wrench so you can change out the nipples. I would also suggest several spare sets of locks, small files and extra flat springs which you will need over time. Last, but not least, you will need a 'worm' bullet-puller in case of a misfire for each rifle and some picks so you can clean out the flash hole running through the nipple."

Hawken tapped the glass. "Now, how about a set of pistols? Most plainsmen carry at least one pistol and many two because of the Indian threat with the close-in fighting that is so common." Then the gunsmith looked up abruptly at Martin, then faltered and blushed over what he had just uttered. "Sorry, my friend. I didn't mean to imply..." His voice dropped off in embarrassment over the "Indian" remark he had just made to a potential Indian customer.

"That is alright," replied Martin with a smile. "We have the same problem back home in Kentucky with our Indians."

That broke the awkwardness with chuckles all around, and the three of them began arranging for the needed items. In addition to the rifles and needed accessories, they purchased four new pistols of .69 caliber and a twelve-gauge, double-barreled fowling piece. All of those weapons were fitted with the new cap and nipple system as well. With them came all the needed accessories in case something broke down once in the outback. Soon, a small mound of supplies began to stack up on the counters as the weapons, parts and accessories were assembled. With that came five thousand primer caps in waterproof tins, six twenty-five-pound sacks holding bars of soft pig lead, and three small cast-iron lead melting pots in which to melt the pig lead down into a liquid by the campfire so new bullets could be molded. That was followed by four .54-caliber bullet molds, four twenty-five-pound wooden barrels of powder and four twenty-five-pound bags of shot for the fowling piece. The gunsmith also threw in four metal powder horns for free since the men were making such a large purchase, along with a bolt of cloth for gun wadding.

Then Jacob had the gunsmith look over the rifles, pistols and rifle-specific accessories they had brought into the store as trade items. For the longest time the gunsmith carefully looked over their offerings including Martin's rifle with the broken stock. Seeing dried blood and brains on that rifle's stock did not even make the gunsmith show any kind of emotion other than a quick knowing look at the two men; he acted like blood and brains on a rifle stock was an everyday occurrence. "Living on the frontier can be like that at times," he commented.

Putting pen to paper, he wrote out some figures as to the values of the firearms offered for trade. Then he wrote out the costs of the new firearms, parts, accessories and supplies that had been selected on another piece of paper.

"For the items you fellas want to trade, I will give you one hundred and sixty dollars in credit against your new purchases. The new purchases will cost you right at three hundred and sixty-five dollars. With the difference, you owe me two hundred and five dollars," he said.

Jacob looked over at Martin and Martin's look told him that appeared to be fair.

Jacob turning to the gunsmith said, "You have a deal."

Taking the saddlebag off his shoulder, Jacob began counting out two hundred and five dollars in U.S. and Spanish gold and silver coins. The gunsmith smiled largely at the wonder of coins spilling over his counter in shiny profusion. So many times, even in St. Louis, deals depended on the barter system because of the scarcity of the coin of the realm. Hence his look of pleasurable disbelief at the coins stacking up on the counter.

"We will leave our gear here with you for the moment if you don't mind, with the exception of the pistols," said Jacob quietly. "I feel the need for us to carry two of those while we are in town. Would you please show us the proper load and include a leather pouch with a few extra bullets and caps? A small horn of powder would be good to have along as well."

The gunsmith, pleased over his huge sale, agreed and headed off into the back room to start supplying the rest of Jacob's request. Jacob picked up his father's old Pennsylvania rifle and fingered it lovingly.

Martin looked on, knowing what Jacob was feeling but said nothing. Out West, firearms would be a necessity and a tool to keep them fed and alive. If a rifle doesn't do the job, one must get rid of it and acquire another that does. That is just the way it is and both of us know it.

Reverently taking the old Pennsylvania rifle from Jacob and laying it back down on the counter, Martin helped Jacob break from his "old life."

That afternoon, Jacob and Martin looked around in a mercantile that supplied those heading out West with the items they would need for their venture. That included such staples for at least a year on the trail as coffee beans, cones of hard brown sugar, salt, pepper, pinto beans, cornmeal, flour, fire-making steels, iron buckles, fish hooks and line. The two also found sewing needles for clothing repair and sewing minor wounds shut. That was followed with wooden spools of thread, several heavy flannel shirts each, buttons, Hudson's Bay Company three-point blankets to replace theirs, which had just about worn out, and four square axes.

The supplies began stacking up, yet they added more: files, shovels, fourth-proof rum, moccasin awls, hatchets, and six extra whetstones, which had a tendency for being broken, lost or stolen. Then sixteen New House No. 4 beaver traps—four extra to cover losses incurred, in addition to the six normally carried by each trapper—extra saddle blankets to replace those already worn out from their long trip, four extra packsaddles, eight "mannies"— tarps to tie over the packs once loaded to keep the rain and snow off—and a small spool of one-inch halter rope.

"Now," said Jacob, "let's get the necessaries. If only you weren't such a big eater."

Martin grunted at the friendly jibe.

Jacob grabbed another large coffeepot, extra knives, forks and spoons, a large camp kettle, another large Dutch oven, and two cast-iron frying pans

"Don't forget some plates and cups," Martin said. "We can use ten pounds of those blue glass beads for trading. Get some cuds of that James River chewing and smoking tobacco for us and for trade."

Jacob obeyed and their inventory grew some more.

The merchant made more suggestions to the two would-be trappers. "You'll want to procure some brass wire for repairs, and you'll certainly want horseshoes and horseshoe nails, and about one hundred extra feet of halter rope. A few simple iron rings are always good as trade items."

And so Jacob added the suggested goods.

Anything else they needed and had forgotten, they would have to forego or make due from the materials at hand in the wilds until they could be replenished at a rendezvous.

The two adventurers then headed back to the livery stable with armloads of supplies and a loaded, small rented horse-drawn cart in tow. They stopped back at the Hawken Gun Shop along the way. Jacob asked the elderly gunsmith if they could store the recently purchased supplies as well in his back room, along with their new guns and other accessories. The gunsmith agreed and for the time being their supplies were safe. The gunsmith also agreed to return the horse and cart to the livery that afternoon once he got his "colored" back from running another errand.

The two men left the gun shop and again visited an eatery. They partook of the best civilization had to offer. Then off to their sleeping quarters they went for the evening.

7

FREE TRAPPERS

THE NEXT MORNING, AFTER ANOTHER HEARTY BREAKFAST of flapjacks, side pork, coffee and apple pie, Jacob and Martin walked the city streets. They chanced on a group of men standing on a sidewalk. The men were looking into a newspaper shop's window and reading a posted article with rapt attention. Curious, they waited their turn until the crowd thinned, then read the newspaper article from the *St. Louis Gazette* posted in the window.

It read simply:

NEEDED, *eighty enterprising young men to join me, Jedediah Smith, David Jackson and William Sublette. Travel in the largely unexplored Trans-Mississippi west, trapping and trading. Hiring now for an expedition to leave on April 7, 1830.*

If interested, meet one Clayborn Jones at Hickory and First

Streets at ten in the morning daily until April 4, 1830. On April 7, the brigade will leave St. Louis at five in the morning. Travel will be on the Mississippi and Missouri Rivers north by boat until the Platte River is reached. From there the expedition will proceeded westerly by horse along the Platte to the junction of the Laramie River. After a final supply of the parties, brigades numbering twenty men per group of contract and free trappers will move off into the northern reaches, trapping and pelting out beaver throughout winter and spring.

Once a year trappers will return to a designated rendezvous site in the summer to outfit and bring in their furs. At the end of the annual rendezvous, trappers will return to their trapping areas until the following year's rendezvous. Interested parties must initially supply their own rifles, pistols, horses, knives and other essentials for the trip. Supplies may be topped off at field prices prior to leaving the main party once the jumping off place is reached.

Signed,

William Sublette, Jedediah Smith and David Jackson March 10th, 1830

MARTIN TURNED TO JACOB, smiled, and said, "This seems like the answer to our dreams."

"It sure does! Trapping and hunting. And right there: 'The unexplored Trans-Mississippi west.' Such an expedition would let us travel through the hostile country in the company of armed men who know the ways of beaver trapping. We could learn the trade while safely traversing the country. That's our boat." Jacob stabbed the article with his fingertip. "We have to be on it."

"Then why are we standing here?"

Jacob laughed. "You are right. Let's go sign up and get this adventure underway!"

Jacob extended his hand, and Martin grasped it warmly in the Indian fashion.

They asked directions to Hickory and First Streets from a passing citizen, then off they went. As they approached the location advertised in the paper, they observed a crowd of men already gathered around a tall, thin individual representing himself as one Clayborn Jones. The closer they got, the more they could hear all kinds of excited talk among the crowd. Moving in closer, they stood at the outside edge of the crowd listening to what was being said. Many of the hopefuls wanting to sign on to the trapping expedition lacked any kind of good horseflesh or other necessaries. As such, they were turned away. Eventually, Clayborn worked his way through the hopefuls to Martin and Jacob standing quietly at the edge of the crowd.

"How about you boys? Interested in becoming a contract trapper for Messieurs Sublette, Jackson and Smith?"

"No, sir," replied Jacob. "We would like to sign on as free trappers. We have our own equipment and goods, and wish to remain free in our business dealings as well as independent in our work as trappers."

Clayborn looked the men over closely through a

narrowed set of eyes based on his knowledge and years on the frontier. "Either of you ever been up north in the Trans-Mississippi before?"

"No, sir," replied Jacob.

"Well, I am here to tell you this is not for those without a bucket of guts, a lot of sand, a feedbag full of luck and a damn good shooting eye. Living is hard, food is sparse and long in-between eating, and the winters are murderous. There is an Indian behind every bush looking to lift your topknot, steal your horses, firearms or plews. There is no medical help out there 'cept yourself and your own good common sense unless you hook up with a good woods-wise squaw. You won't see another white man for a year at a time and many times if you do, he could very well be out there to kill you and also take your valuable plews. And the only women out there is a red one crawling with lice, stinking of rancid bear grease, and one who knows how to use a knife if you get out of hand or mess with her honor. Still interested?"

Jacob and Martin grinned back.

"Life's not all that easy where we come from, either. And sure as hell even less so on the trail. This is what we want, come hell or high water," Jacob said. "This is meant to be what is ours."

"Where and when do we form up with the rest of the brigade?" asked Martin.

Clayborn smiled and said, "Come over here, boys and sign up." Jacob and Martin moved over to a small table where several pieces of paper, an inkwell and several goose-quill pens lay.

"Sign here and you are part of an adventure of a lifetime," stated Clayborn with a smile.

"What do these papers say?" asked Jacob as he looked Clayborn directly into his eyes.

"They say you will sell your catch of furs to Messieurs Sublette, Jackson and Smith at the rendezvous, and purchase your needed goods at the same time from those same gentlemen. That is as long as they have the supplies you need. Barring that, you can trade with anyone else you are of a mind and as the need arises."

Martin and Jacob looked at each other for a few moments as they thought over Clayborn's words. That meant possibly selling their furs low and purchasing needed goods at higher prices. But, it would also get them into the country of their dreams and give them a start.

They picked up the quill pens and signed their names with a flourish, as if to emphasize the significance of the moment at hand.

Clayborn picked up the contracts and looked at their signatures. "You boys know how to cipher?"

Both men nodded affirmatively.

"Well, I'll be damned! You two are the first in several days of recruitment who made something other than a mark for your name. Keep in mind however, you will kill off just as easily and get dead as all the rest who have gone before if you are not careful as a raven. For your information, since this type of fur trapping has been ongoing, we are losing about a quarter of the men who go north every season. At least since we started this method of trapping and commerce in 1822, that has been the case. Don't know where or how, but the trappers just up and disappear. Injuns for the most part I reckon, and then everything else gone bad in between from a mean-assed bear bite to a horse wreck," he continued as if discussing something as simple as the time of day.

Jacob looked long and hard at Clayborn and then with a smile said, "Man has to have a little pepper on his meat as well as salt to make it taste good."

Clayborn smiled back. "We will meet on the north end of the boat landing docks and be boarding the paddle wheelers Jeremiah O 'Brian and the General Slaxton on the seventh of April at five in the morning. They will take us upstream to where the Missouri and Platte Rivers meet. There we will be offloaded at the wooding station and proceed westerly along the Platte until we reach the Laramie River. From there we go north into the fur country and whatever awaits. Don't be late or you will be left sucking hind tit if you get my reasonin'. Also watch out for roving bands of thugs and crooks along the docks and city alleys after dark. They will approach you as friends and before it is all over, will steal everything you have, kill you or both."

With that, Clayborn shook their hands and moved on to the next candidate who clamored for a chance at losing his topknot in the hands of a savage or having a bite taken out of his hind end, as Clayborn was wont to say, "by a mean-assed bear."

Jacob and Martin walked back to the Hawken Gun Shop after renting another small horse-drawn cart to carry their firearms and supplies to the livery. Once all their gear was loaded, they drove the cart to the livery stable where their livestock were being kept. They unloaded their gear into an empty adjacent stall for safe-keeping, then threw down their bedrolls alongside in the straw. They ate in shifts so their property would always be guarded, then they finally settled down for the night.

Visions of high and dangerous adventures ran through both men's minds like a dose of the salts as they lay in the bedrolls. What would they discover in their travels; how would they fare as trappers; would they be killed; and would they ever see Kentucky again? Finally a welcome but fitful sleep overcame the two soon-to-be adventurers and Mountain Men.

For the next four days Jacob and Martin tended to the examination, inventory and care of their equipment and livestock. They made a few last-minute purchases at the nearest mercantile such as files to float the teeth on their horses. Horses were examined by the livery man for their overall health as the blacksmith checked their shoes and replaced those as necessary.

Extra shoes were also made by the blacksmith for those horses acquired from the deadly fight on the trail. The new Hawkens were tested out back of the livery stable and found to be excellent in shooting and handling qualities. The same was discovered for the four Hawken single-shot horse pistols.

However, Jacob did return to the gun shop to procure five hundred extra primer caps for their weapons. He figured numerous years in the outback would use up what they had already purchased and wasn't sure on their resupply under rendezvous conditions. Packsaddles were custom fitted to those animals so designated as the pack string, and extra halter ropes created for each horse. Mannies were constructed from sheets of canvas by Martin to cover the packs against the bad weather certain to follow. Jacob saw to it that tanned, soft, buckskin-leather fringed sleeves were made to cover and protect the valuable Hawken rifles against the elements.

By the fourth day, the men were more than ready to head out. Still eating in shifts, they finished their last meal. Afterwards, they sat on a couple of old barrels outside the livery stable and chewed some of their newly purchased chewing tobacco. Jacob had purchased a small barrel full, containing four hundred cuds of tobacco the day before, figuring if they didn't chew or smoke it, they could swap it with the Indians for furs. Both men found satisfaction in the chew and their recent dinner as they sat there watching the life of St. Louis going by.

They finished with the packing and loading of the horses around four in the morning on the day of departure. Then they saddled up and headed with their pack strings towards the docks. Once they arrived, they took their places at the edge of the milling crowd of trappers and other soon-to-be Mountain Men. Much mayhem mingled throughout the crowd of trappers: braying mules, swearing teamsters with their cracking whips, and creaking wagons loaded with hay for the horses while on the boats. Sweating black men loaded cords of firewood for the paddle wheelers' always-hungry steam engines that belched smoke and hissed steam continuously from the two vessels, dotted with the ever-present, always yelling deck hands. As final dressing, men dressed from head to toe in furs and buckskins were announced to St. Louis the day of departure, for the newest fur company was at hand.

As the sun peeped over the horizon, it found the General Slaxton loaded and the Jeremiah O'Brian getting there. Jackson was on hand to smooth out any wrinkles and give last minute instructions to the expedition leaders. Finally, the appointed time arrived and the mooring lines securing the paddle wheelers to the docks were cast off. As the General Slaxton drifted back in the current a short distance to clear the dock, she gave two long blasts on her steam whistle. Then the great paddles commenced their rhythmic swish-swish-swish as the boat slowly headed upstream into the current of the murky Mississippi. The Jeremiah O'Brian fell in behind the General Slaxton and the trip into the Trans-Mississippi, and a new and exciting life, was underway.

8

THE TRANS-MISSISSIPPI

JACOB AND MARTIN HAD BOARDED THE PADDLE WHEELER General Slaxton. They had quickly secured their horses near the bow of the vessel and had unloaded their packs and sleeping gear alongside. With some fresh hay meant for the livestock, Jacob and Martin quickly made a bed next to the rail where they could watch their horses and gear during the trip. Having nothing else to do, they both watched the countryside roll gently by as they enjoyed their first paddle wheeler ride, up the mighty Mississippi and into the mouth of the Missouri River.

For the next several days, the two paddle wheelers plowed upstream, dodging the many sand bars while avoiding the numerous floating snags and numbers of dead buffalo floating downstream—dead buffalo that had earlier broken through the spring ice and drowned while trying to cross the Missouri. Some of the men onboard, to avoid boredom, took great sport shooting the feeding ravens and crows off the floating buffalo carcasses as they bobbed their ways downstream alongside the vessels.

"A real waste of powder and shot," Jacob told Martin.

In the two men's eyes, the food or swill served onboard the paddle wheeler was really bad, especially when Martin discovered Camel-Backed Crickets in his watery soup and white worms throughout his hardtack. The jerky the men had purchased for the trail was soon put to use to keep "the big guts from eating the little guts."

Soon the geography began changing from the heavy green forests of Missouri to the drier short-grass prairies of the lands to the north. Several times the men observed herds of buffalo swimming the river or grizzly bear looking for food along the shoreline. In the river itself were flocks of ducks, mostly of the fish-eating variety. Bald eagles and osprey soared overhead constantly. With the changing geography, everyone had something new to observe and enjoy.

Friendships were made or rekindled, and there was much talking and teaching regarding the trapping of beaver, muskrat and river otter. Then the talk turned to the dangers of the mighty Lakota, the horse-stealing ways of the Crow Indians, the dangers of the grizzly bear, the ever-killing Cheyenne, and the merits of the different firearms. Once discovered, many trappers who sported the tried and true Pennsylvania rifles stopped by to admire Jacob and Martin's unusual and prized St. Louis Hawken rifles; so much so, that Jacob and Martin kept an even tighter watch on their gear, especially their state-of-the-art firearms.

However, in the process, Jacob had to smile. Both he and Martin had only been able to purchase their new firearms because of a lethal encounter that had occurred along the trail to St. Louis—a fight where men had planned on taking Jacob and Martin's lives and property, but in the end may have saved them. As a result of the coins taken from the outlaws' saddlebags after the killing was over, both men were able to procure the finest and heaviest of firearms newly available—firearms that would not only provide for them, but would save their lives and those of others many times over the ensuing years. And unbeknown to everyone onboard the paddle wheeler, there were still two very full saddlebags containing coins remaining from that fight—more than enough for the two men to buy some land and settle down if they so desired once this trapping and exploring thing was out of their systems. That is, provided they survived.

There were two heavily bearded men that took a particular interest in Jacob and Martin's rifles. "Who are those two men?" Martin asked one of their fellow travelers.

"Don't know much more about them 'cept they ain't ones to be company with. They used to be free trappers, but they weren't much good at it, and the others say they went bust spending more than they made at rendezvous. They signed on as contract trappers, 'bout the only way they are gonna get by."

"Hmm," Martin replied. "Thanks."

Later, the two bearded men came by again.

"Hey!" said the larger of the two.

"Can I help you?" Jacob asked.

"Yeah. Howdy. My name's Bear, at least, that is what they call me, on account I got this here bear-claw necklace." Bear pulled on a large set of bear claws strung onto a necklace. "You like it?"

"Mighty impressive."

"Well, my pal Wentz and I are kinda bored. We were thinking of playing some cards. I'll put our buffalo robes up against one of your fancy rifles, make it interesting." Bear pointed to a nearby pile of buffalo hides.

Martin shook his head as Jacob said, "No, thanks. Not interested."

Bear was not swayed. He asked again, taking the tack of "Be men and show some courage." To no effect.

"Do you think we are cheaters?" growled Bear after Jacob and Martin declined the invite to gamble with their new rifles for the second time.

"No," replied Jacob not wanting to start a hurrah. "We just want to make sure we have good rifles for the chores ahead."

"Well, hell, you have four of them there new Hawkens. Missing one of them won't cripple you or cause a great deal of gas," grumbled Bear as he continued to press for a card game.

"Yeah, why not give your hand a chance at luck," chimed in his partner Wentz. "You could win this here pile of fine buffalo robes and our rifles," he continued with a smile that said here was one not to be trusted.

"Sorry, we are not interested, now or ever," said Martin as he stretched out on his straw bed watching the far shoreline drift by.

"Who the hell is talking to you, Injun?" snapped Bear through a vicious snarl.

Martin slowly rose from his bed of straw, only to be held in check by Jacob's hand. Martin was a fury when aroused, and Jacob sure didn't want to have to clean Bear and Wentz's blood off the deck after Martin let these pesky trappers leak their life's juices out all over the place.

Jacob said, "Gentlemen, we aren't interested in your game of chance or anything else that would jeopardize our ownership of these firearms," said Jacob. This time when he spoke, instead of being polite, there was a ring of steel in the tenor of his voice.

Bear and Wentz, picking up on the tonal change in Jacob and observing the deadly look in Martin's flashing dark eyes, backed off like the cowards they were. Still grumbling, they ambled off but not without some mighty vicious looks back over their shoulders at Jacob and Martin.

"You boys sure didn't do yourself any favors by

pissing off that pair of skunks," said a quiet voice from a man richly dressed in beaded buckskins standing by a nearby rail.

Jacob and Martin turned and discovered a tall thin man of obvious Indian descent looking intently at the two of them. Martin got a huge smile of recognition on his face and said something in Delaware to the man. The man replied in the same tongue and soon the two of them were chattering away in the Delaware language like long lost friends. Jacob saw this was a private conversation between Indians from the same Nation and just politely watched.

Martin stopped speaking in Delaware. "Jacob, this is Ben Bow. He is also a Delaware. He is going West as a free trapper as we are doing."

"Pleased to meet you," said Jacob as he warmly shook Ben Bow's hand.

Like Martin's handshake, Ben let you know there was a real man on the other end of it.

"What brings you to join this here particular expedition?" asked Jacob.

"Lived in the Knife River Indian Village for three years past before I returned to St. Louis this spring. I missed the people, the trapping and the brand of living in this here part of the wilderness. So just figured I would earn my way north once again. After a few years trapping and watching my earnings, figured I would return to Knife River, get myself a good woman and then settle down." He flashed Jacob a wide, beautiful, toothy smile like Martin's.

All three men smiled, not at Ben's statement but at the mutual thought of a possible friendship among the group when it came time to trap their way north.

That evening, Ben moved his sleeping gear and packs alongside that of Jacob and Martin. That move turned out to be the beginning of a strong, enduring friendship and bond among the three men.

For the next several days, realizing he was with "greenhorns," Ben taught Jacob and Martin the Indian sign language so commonly used on the plains. Both men picked it up rapidly and soon all three were conversing in the universal "tongue" of the plains. Ben also spent time with Jacob and Martin on the history and mechanics of the fur trade. That included the art of not only trapping beaver but the skinning, grading and care of the plews as well. His several years living and trapping on the frontier and among the Indians on the Knife River had served him well. It warmed his soul to share such knowledge with his two new friends, who eagerly absorbed it all.

Sitting near the bow of the paddle wheeler, the three of them talked about the country, the Indians and beaver trapping in general throughout the daylight hours. Ben was a vast storehouse of information and Jacob and Martin found themselves hanging onto his every word.

"Best time to trap beaver is in the fall and early spring. That is when their pelts are prime and generate the highest prices. When we leave the Laramie River, we will probably be in a larger group of twenty trappers or more. Then, as we pass through prime trapping country, small groups of up to four will leave the brigade and begin trapping in those beaver-rich areas. The rest of us will move on to the next trapping grounds and again another small group will be dropped off to trap those waters. This process is continued until the last group is left to find their own area to trap. Once in our trapping area, a small camp will be set up so as not to cause the local Indians any interest or concern. Those trapping will carry and set only six traps each. Trap weight is one factor and the other is, if the trapping is good, bringing back six beaver each to camp for skinning and dressing is about all one wants to handle. The trappers will set out their traps each day in the morning. Then we will scout out new areas that same day for later trapping, especially once we clean out the first area. Then the traps are checked again in the afternoon as we return. Once caught, the beaver are skinned, fleshed and dried on a hoop built for the size of the pelt. We will make our hoops from the many willows growing along the streams and beaver ponds. Then once the plews are dried, they are folded in half with the fur side in. As you get more and more of them, you will need to compress the folded hides into a bundle of about fifty or sixty pelts depending on their sizes. Using rawhide ties, you will compress those bundles with your body pressing down on top while another man does the tying." Ben bent over with arms wide to demonstrate.

He continued. "Those bundles will pack perfectly on a

horse, with a bundle attached on each side of the pack board. A smaller one can also be tied on top of the pack board to fill the bill. But before we do that, we will tie around and cover each pack of plews with a tanned deer hide. That will make it easier to load and offload when traveling and keep them clean."

Ben waited for the two young men to nod in understanding, then he said, "Part of the reason for such poor relations with the Indians is the competition for the furs and fur trade. Another bone of contention is that of firearms and our earlier trade practices. Some bands of the Lakota and the Blackfoot don't want other tribes to receive the white man's goods. If they can keep the other tribes from the white man's goods, especially firearms, they can rule the other Indian nations. Trading with everyone as we are wont to do has loosened those Indian's powers and now those tribes are mad at just about every white man. Another reason they don't like us is because this is their land. The Indians just don't want us here. That is why we must be very careful in everything we do. That is also why we must stay in pairs so if we are attacked we can help each other to survive." Ben touched both men on the shoulders.

"Most trappers use a liquid from the beaver's glands, called castors, located at the base of their tails. That liquid, called castoreum, is used to lure other beaver to the set. Other liquids are used to extend the volume of the castoreum so it will go farther as will we. I have a special potion I make and will teach both of you how it is made. Once it is placed in the vicinity of the trap on a lure stick, we will have a beaver in the trap within hours. Even small bottles of this liquid cost up to ten dollars in St. Louis, so trappers usually choose not to purchase it there. We will get our own from the beaver we trap and save the ten dollars. The way to do that is once on the trapping grounds, we will locate some beaver dams. We will create a small break in one of the dams and set our traps in front of that hole. When the beaver come to repair the hole, they will step into the traps and we will have the start of our supply of castoreum. However, most of the liquid we use will be collected as we continue trapping other beaver."

Jacob and Martin fastened onto every word.

The next morning, Ben brought three of his traps. "Setting the trap will take some learning and practice. But, I will show you. The way I do it is as follows. First, I cut a thick willow or aspen stick about four feet long. Then, I cut that stick in half.

Next, I set the trap in shallow water, about ten to twelve inches from the bank. With my hand I swirl the water around the set trap until it is covered with silt from the bottom of the pond. You don't want the beaver to see the metal of the trap and that is the best way for concealment that I have found. Then I extend the chain on the trap out into the deep water. Taking some cord which I always carry, I will tie my trap ring to the stake. That way if the beaver is a large one and manages to pull up my stake, I can later find the trap still tied to the stake. There

I drive in one half of the stake with my hatchet, fastening the ring on the end of the trap's chain over the stake driven deeply into the mud. I take the other half of the stake, and I drive it into the mud of the bank over the trap at an angle over the water. On the end of the stick hanging over the water I place several drops of the castoreum. When the beaver smells the castoreum and comes to investigate, it is almost over. The beaver will swim to the stake with the castoreum sticking out of the water. Standing up on its hind legs, he will grab the stake for a better smell. When they do that, one false step and one of their feet will be in the trap. Struggling to get away, it will swim out into deep water until it hits the end of the trap's chain. There it will stay, trying to swim away until it tires and eventually drowns. That is why keeping a tight chain on the trap short of the bank is so important. It can't allow the animal to reach land because, if it does, it will chew its foot off and escape. It also can't allow the beaver to swim to its lodge. It has to be set just right so the animal drowns," he continued.

And so the lessons continued, hour after hour and mile after mile traveling on a river "too muddy to drink and too thin to plow."

In another lesson, Ben explained how the trappers played only a small part in the trapping trade.

"The Indians play the biggest part," he said. "When it comes to the overall volume of furs, the Indians contribute the most. That's only natural, as there are more of them than there are trappers."

"But then why do they trade with the trappers for simple beads and knives?" Jacob asked. "Why don't the Indians ask for more valuable things?"

"Indians use furs and hides for everyday living items. Hell, they wipe their asses with them. But they consider the White Man's goods to be of greater value. In their minds, they are trading the waste skins of readily trapped furred animals and easily killed buffalo for items they consider of real value."

"Like what?" asked Martin.

"Anything they consider of necessity. Steel knives, iron pots, beads. And liquor. Firearms, certainly, and all that goes with them like gunpowder, lead and such. Fish hooks, too. They love tobacco, and salt."

Later, Ben taught them about the White Man's side of the trade. "There are quite a few fur companies working in the wilderness. Most of the trappers work for fixed wages. What those trappers collect in furs, they give to their companies in exchange for the annual supplies they need. I hear they make about four hundred dollars a year, not much. And those trappers are forever broke because the fur companies charge them high prices for needed supplies every rendezvous."

"But what of the free trappers, men like us?" Jacob asked. "Believe it or not, they're considered the elite of the trapping community. Once the trapping season is done, free trappers trade their furs at the trading posts, or at rendezvous, or some trappers will take their furs all the way back to St. Louis. I believe that because a free trapper has to live by the quality of his furs, he's more likely to go after the finer furs. Furs like beaver, and otter, fox, mink, and pine martin. The contract trappers, they take whatever they can get their hands on to make their quotas."

"So, how many beaver does a free trapper usually catch?" Jacob asked.

"Oh, I figure, on average, a good trapper can trap and pelt out somewhere between one hundred and one hundred forty beaver in a year. Good thing, 'cause any less, and you won't be able to sustain yourself when it comes time to trade. You'll have to go into debt to the fur company to get what you need."

"Don't sound like there's much money in fur trapping," Jacob said, with some worry in his voice.

Ben laughed. "Not many get rich, that's for certain. The only men getting rich in this business are the St. Louis merchants who supply the goods for the trappers. Me, I just want to make enough money to go back to the Indian villages at Knife River, settle down, marry, and raise a family. Ain't looking to be a rich man. But to make enough to do even that, I figure being a free trapper is the best course of action."

The training continued every day without let up, until they arrived at a location where the Platte joined the Missouri River. There the General Slaxton slowly pulled into a pole dock at a wood camp, on the north side of the entry point of the Platte River.

"Not much of a river," Jacob said to Martin and Ben,

"compared to the Missouri River." The Platte was fairly wide, maybe forty yards or so, but seemed sandy and shallow at the mouth and as far upstream as Jacob could see. Willows and cottonwoods abounded along the Platte and everywhere he looked, he saw small herds of buffalo seemingly uninterested in the presence of the humans as long as they didn't get too noisy or active.

Several river men jumped off onto the dock and tied the paddle wheeler's bow lines snugly to a large post that had been driven deeply into the stream bottom. Then the paddle wheeler was allowed to slowly drift back with the current until it comfortably rested alongside the dock. Its sister ship did the same, tying off directly behind them. Then, all hell broke loose.

Yelling, bellowing of orders and counter commands flew through the air like so many leaves in a November prairie wind. Men were scrambling everywhere lowering gangplanks and walkways for the livestock and the "anxious to get the hell off the boat passengers." Trappers pushed to be free from their smoking, whistle blowing, spark throwing, newfangled traveling devices so they could get their feet back on solid ground. Many of the trappers couldn't swim and were especially nervous in deep waters. So many had a bad case of nerves being on a deepwater riverboat, and now they couldn't wait to get off. It seemed ironic that they were willing to take chances at the point of a lance or speeding lead ball, but when it came to deep waters, many quaked at the thought.

Jacob had anticipated the boat's landing. He worked with Martin and their new friend Ben to pack their animals and be ready to go. He and his team fell in behind the confusion of the other disembarking men when their turn finally came. There was little trouble offloading the horses and pack animals. However, once on shore, confusion reigned. Closely grouped men and their pack strings moved in every direction.

Jacob winced when he saw that his own pack animals had tangled up with those belonging to Bear and Wentz.

"Git yer mangy mules out of my way!" Bear roared.

"You sons a bitches," Wentz added. "You bunch of greenhorns."

Jacob kept his tongue silent, and much to their credit, Martin and Ben did, too, as they worked through the tangle of horses.

The barrage of epithets from Bear and Wentz continued, which only spooked the horses that much more. The nervous horses had all intertwined their halter ropes, and it took a few moments to square things away.

"Ben, you're right about those two," Jacob said. "We've got a couple of human skunks in Bear and Wentz who are right pissed at us."

Skunks that bear watching the whole time we are in country and they are close at hand, thought Jacob with a leveled gaze at the two still yelling and swearing men.

That night the trappers celebrated their first time back on the ground after the lengthy river ride. The resident woodcutters had killed several large cow buffalo

and were cooking great slabs of the meat over a hot bed
of coals. Several barrels of whiskey on hand—supplied by
the fur company for the occasion—beckoned the horde
of trappers. Then there was a special treat, one most
trappers found hard to refuse—several barrels of rum
cake from a St. Louis bakery were broken out, awaiting
the trappers' palates and sweet tooth. It was a meal fit for
a king after the wormy, sour food served on the paddle
wheeler. Soon singing and guns fired wildly in the air
disturbed the pleasant evening and numerous critters
along the rivers.

However, the ever present frontier mosquito was not
put out by the noise and revelry, especially when making
hay on those trappers who drank more than they should
have, passed out and made slow-moving targets for the
clouds of biting pests. Come daylight, such unfortunate
men were a mass of red welts beyond description.

A minor mishap among those making poor decisions
that would likely magnify in later days when poorer
choices were made and a serious "debt" was claimed.

9

UP THE PLATTE

By FOUR THE NEXT MORNING, THE TRAPPERS' HUGE hangovers made for a little more subdued and quieter camp. Nobody wanted to move very fast or very far for fear their heads would simply fall off after drinking so much cheap, trade whiskey—trade whiskey that was made many times from cheap whiskey, gunpowder and sometimes a dash of coal oil.

Jacob and company had refrained from heavy drink and were glad for it. Besides, the whiskey tasted like no other drink of "old tanglefoot" any of them had ever previously drunk.

"Witness the result of the trapper's brand of cheap whiskey," Ben said as he swept an open hand across the panorama of the camp. Many men staggered about trying to round up their livestock and pack them for the trip. Others puked up the remains of last night's dinner in big, partially digested chunks of almost raw buffalo meat, or just laid where they had fallen from their over-indulgences. Almost all scratched at the many angry red welts left behind by the aggressive mosquitoes.

"This bodily disregard and drunkenness will be repeated at many a rendezvous in the years to come," Ben said. "That is, for those trappers who live through the rigors and dangers of the land."

Jacob, Martin and Ben put their pack strings together, then breakfasted on remaining buffalo from the night before. As they stood quietly in the cool of the morning at the ready, Clayborn, the company's main man, selected them to lead the contingent of men. Ben cracked a wide grin and told his friends, "This is quite an honor because being farther back in the mile-long string of trappers and their animals would mean to eat a lot of alkali dust from those traveling in the front."

Meanwhile, Bear and Wentz were back in the pack. They seethed over their placement and the preferential treatment given those at the head of the pack.

Clayborn had four scouts far out in front of the column. About eleven in the morning on that first day, several shots were heard far in advance of the main company as they dustily plodded along the dry sandy soils on the banks of the Platte. At first, Jacob figured there was Indian trouble brewing upon hearing the shooting. He figured they were in Lakota country as they traveled up the Platte River and was now decidedly very alert. They had seen several bands of Indians sitting on their horses at a respectful distance during the morning watching the trappers' long column and that was all it took to remain more than alert.

Soon over the rise to their front galloped a lone rider. Pulling his horse up short alongside Clayborn, they had an animated conversation that Jacob strained fruitlessly to hear. Then, the rider galloped back from whence he came. Clayborn rode over to Jacob and said, "Pass the word down the line: the outriders have killed several cow buffalo along the river. They are now preparing them for the men's midday meal."

Jacob relayed the news to Ben, and Ben rode back to the next group of riders, passed the word, and they did the same in turn. Soon Jacob could see the riders far back in the column picking up the pace in anticipation of the feed to follow. It seemed many hours on the trail under the hot scorching sun made for clearer heads and emptier stomachs than he had realized, especially since many had puked up their dinners from the evening before at the wood camp and most basically had nothing to eat since two days previously.

At the cook site, four men were butchering out several buffalo a few yards distant. Several roaring fires had been made with driftwood from along the nearby river, creating great beds of coals. Alongside those coals were numerous green willow sticks sunken into the earth. Great slabs of buffalo meat hung from the sticks and were merrily cooking away, filling the air with many good smells waiting for a hungry taker.

The first few men rode up, dismounted and deep staked their horses so if the Indians tried to stampede or run them off, the stakes would hold them in place. Happy for the break from the stiffness of riding horses long distances, other riders soon dismounted, staked their mounts and headed for the great smelling fires as well. However, in so doing, each man carried his rifle, just in case. The men squatted and removed the stakes from alongside the fire holding the huge slabs of buffalo meat and commenced cutting off the semi-cooked portions with their knives. When the meat was too raw for the eater, he simply returned his stake to the fire's edge for more roasting. However, because of abject hunger or what they were used to, many men ate their meat warm or just raw. The men butchering the buffalo continued bringing more slabs of meat to be cooked by the fires. As more trappers moved into the area, they, too, took their places around the fires. Soon noisy eating, laughing and belching was the word of the day as the men gorged themselves. Then, after wiping their greasy hands on their pants and shirts, they relaxed by lying or sleeping on the warm, sandy soil alongside the Platte. However, their rifles were kept at a close distance and one never really slept too soundly while in Indian country.

Day after day, this routine continued until the men reached the North Platte branch of the Platte River. Taking the north fork, the men hardly paused as their adventure continued.

This plodding travel continued for the next ten days

as the trappers trekked towards where the Laramie River ran into the North Platte. All the while they moved deeper into a country beautiful in its wildness yet grandly stark in much of its geography. They constantly observed great herds of buffalo, elk, deer, pronghorn antelope, and even greater numbers of curious, ever watchful bands of Indians. There were also numerous flocks of sage grouse, sharp-tailed grouse and prairie chickens spooked up at the trappers' horses' feet at almost every turn in the river, especially in the mornings and evenings when the birds came to the river to drink. Beaver were seen frequently swimming in the quieter pools of the North Platte, but none were trapped or shot —they were out of prime. River otter and muskrat were also frequent visitors in the river and wetlands found along the way, as were many species of waterfowl. It truly was a wildlife paradise, one unlike any Jacob or Martin had ever seen.

Ben, having been in this type of country before and having previously witnessed such abundance and diversity of wildlife, just smiled at the wonder on the faces of his two new friends. He knew before their lives ended, the two newcomers would see many of God's wilderness marvels. Marvels that abounded throughout this beautiful land and were there for all to see and enjoy. Yes, he thought, these two have just begun what will be a wondrous life...if they live to see and enjoy it.

10

BUFFALO CALF, SINGING BIRD

THE TRAIN OF TRAPPERS TOPPED A LONG RISE, AND THERE it was down below and off in a distance—the junction of the much sought Laramie and North Platte Rivers, dotted with numerous tepees. In reality, the junction didn't look like much, and it wasn't. But it was a form of civilization the men had not seen in many days of travel across the almost endless monotony of the Great Plains, travel that had brought the trappers nothing but bouts with dust from the long column, dust storms, winds, heat, hoards of mosquitoes, more heat, more dust, and bad water.

"Regardless what the junction of the Laramie River with its collection of tepees represents, it had to be a damn sight better than the rest of the short-grass prairie we've been traveling," Bear told Wentz, with a trace of St. Louis still running in his veins.

With their goal now in sight, the train of men and

animals picked up the pace. That only created more dust for those in the rear of the caravan. Bear and Wentz were still at the very end, partly out of their laziness but most of all because the other trappers didn't want to put up with their foul tempers and abusive words for their comrades.

Clayborn swung the contingent of trappers onto an unused grassy plain with plenty of feed for their livestock near a shaded bend in the North Platte near the Laramie, then signaled a stop. Trappers soon scrambled for those flat, shady places without the ever present prickly pear cactus in which to make their camps. As it turned out, those flat places were quickly staked out by those fortunates in front of the column; they enjoyed a camp along the river's slow-moving waters under the shade of huge cottonwoods. Being last, Bear and Wentz found themselves camping out in the blazing hot prairie sun in order to camp near the rest for the protection such numbers offered.

Soon, friendly Indians from the sixty or so tepees scattered around the confluence of the two rivers straggled into the trapper's camp. Talking, begging, trading— they came in almost oppressive waves. Clayborn quickly set up shop on some open ground covered with buffalo skins for tables. Soon the trading for furs and buffalo hides was in full swing while many of the tired, first-time trappers looked on in amusement and interest. Several kegs of whiskey were broken out and soon the camp was swirling with merry Indians, barking dogs and happy trappers.

Jacob, Martin and Ben watched from a distance as they kept a sharp eye on their own goods. It would have been nice to circulate around the trading action, but to do so would find themselves without a stitch of gear left for the coming years of trapping due to light-fingered Indian opportunists and their less-than-honest trapper "friends."

Just then, a young Indian man strode into the three trappers' camp and with a yell of recognition, walked over and threw his arms around Ben. Both men seemed to know one another and after a few minutes of jabbering excitably in the Lakota Indian language, Ben brought him over to meet Jacob and Martin.

"Jacob and Martin, I would like you to meet my old friend, Buffalo Calf. He is from the Knife River area where we spent many hours hunting and fishing together. I saved his life one spring in a bullboat—a round boat made from buffalo hides and a willow frame —when the ice went out on the Missouri and he got caught on an ice flow. We have been friends ever since."

Jacob and Martin welcomed Buffalo Calf with wrist-grabbing handshakes. The Lakota was not as tall as the three other men, but was stout in build. Like the other Indians, Buffalo Calf smelled of sweat and bear grease that they smeared liberally on the body, to keep the mosquitoes and other stinging insects at bay.

He seemed friendly enough and soon the four men

were having a great time getting acquainted. Jacob and Martin soon learned that Buffalo Calf spoke broken but understandable English as well as Lakota and the language of the Mandan Tribes.

"Buffalo Calf," Jacob said, "it is good to meet a new friend in this land."

Buffalo Calf strained to follow the white man's Kentucky accent. "I much like seeing friends of my friend, Ben Bow."

"Are you here with your clan?" Martin asked.

"I do not know this word, 'clan.'"

"Are you here with your family?"

The Lakota straightened up with pride, clearly understanding the rephrased question. "My squaw is Singing Bird. She is here with me. We not have child. Are you with family?"

"I have no wife," Martin replied, despite Buffalo Calf's slight misunderstanding of the question. "My friend, Jacob, has no wife. Our families are back in Kentucky—back in the White Man's camp in the land where the sun rises."

Buffalo Calf clasped Martin and Jacob by the shoulders. "May the Great Spirit provide you family in these lands, to keep you warm."

Martin and Jacob both shifted uncomfortably as they thanked Buffalo Calf. Ben just chuckled.

Soon the talk turned to beaver trapping and all four men became animated on the subject. Buffalo Calf was familiar with much of the country to the north having lived there and tried to explain its trails, passes and the best trapping grounds to the eagerly listening men. He also explained to the three men who had never been to this part of the Rocky Mountains before about its many and constant dangers. He considered the Blackfoot Indians and their allies from the Algonquin Nation the biggest dangers to the north. But he also spoke of the difficult winters, grizzly bears, always aggressive and hungry gray wolves, and clever horse-stealing tribes of Crow.

Then, Buffalo Calf asked, "May I come with you? I wish to travel the land and trap the beaver. I know this land and can show you where the beaver live. I have hunted all the animals that live in this land, and I know how to make beaver trap." Martin looked to Jacob, who shrugged. Then Martin replied. "We did not plan on another member for our party. Perhaps we do not have enough supplies?"

"The Great Spirit gives Lakota all they need, not like White Man. With more trapper, you trap more beaver. You have no squaw to make meat. Singing Bird can make meat and make beaver hide."

Buffalo Calf began signing as he spoke, to emphasize his argument: "Many Indians, not Lakota, make war on trappers. Mountains dangerous to trappers. I am brave Lakota, I fight strong against Blackfoot and Snake and Crow. I will defend my friends, if you will make me friend."

The offer caught Jacob and Martin by surprise, Ben

noticed. He stepped in and said, "This is a surprise to us, my friend. But I would be pleased to have another trust-worthy member in our trapping party who has much to contribute. I know that you are strong and wise with knowledge of these lands. You are right, you are a good friend. I need time to speak with Jacob and Martin so that we can speak as one and give you our answer."

Buffalo Calf smiled, then Ben continued. "We will have a hard journey, and there is much work to do. I ask you to speak with Singing Bird about this. She, too, must agree. I cannot bring your squaw into danger and hard work unless I know she wishes it, as well."

"I understand." Buffalo Calf reinforced his grin and glided away in the direction of his tepee.

When Buffalo Calf was out of ear shot, Martin said to Jacob, "It would be alright with me. Ben likes him and he seems to fit in well with our group. We could certainly use another hand to help out with the trapping and defense against surprise attacks. Especially since we haven't found anyone else in this group of trappers that we would like to add as a fourth partner."

Jacob thought for a minute about his friend's words and then looked at Ben. "What do you think, Ben? Can Buffalo Calf and his woman add to our travels or just slow us down?"

"I have known him for a long time. He is a good worker, excellent hunter and has a strong heart. He is Lakota and acceptable to most other tribal cultures we will run across with the exception of the Snake, Crow and Blackfoot. His woman is also a good worker, a happy person and a very good maker of meals and clothing."

Jacob thought to himself for a moment and said, "Well, I like Buffalo Calf as well. I doubt he will be able to bring much in the way of equipment to the venture, but I like having someone around knowledgeable of the area and skilled in several languages of the other Indian tribes. That, plus we have some extra gear and traps he can always use. If he is as good a hunter as you say, that would serve us well. I also say we include him as a member of our party if his wife is willing and that may just give all of us an edge we could use."

All three men nodded in agreement.

When Buffalo Calf returned, Ben said, "Welcome, my friend. I have good news to tell. Jacob, Martin and I would be happy to have you as a member of our trapping party so long as Singing Bird is in agreement."

Buffalo Calf flashed a toothy grin. "Singing Bird say she agree to go with trappers, if she can be with her people when her people are close to trapper camp."

That being acceptable, the four men shook on the deal. They were now a foursome in a team that not only knew the country in which they were going but fast becoming a band of brothers. A quality that often times was in short supply in the wilderness.

Bear and Wentz, on the other hand, cussed at every "damn Injun" that came near, and chased them off with drawn horse pistols.

CAMP

CLAYBORN AND COMPANY TRADED WITH THE INDIANS FOR four days, then closed down the small trading festival. Then those trappers needing additional supplies were topped off from the company's stocks. Many trappers' marks were made in the books as they additionally purchased a portion of their year's supplies on credit. Credit that was to be paid off during the next year's rendezvous to be held in Cache Valley.

The group's eighty trappers were formed into four smaller twenty-man brigades and sent to points northwest into the Rocky Mountains. As it turned out, Bear and Wentz were assigned to the same brigade as Jacob, Martin, Ben and now Buffalo Calf. With that, Clayborn took the remaining men with his pack train to intercept William Sublette's pack train—a pack train that was already heading for the Wind River Basin for the upcoming trapper's rendezvous in July of that year. Sublette's supply caravan consisted of more than eighty men with packhorses and several wagons heavily loaded with trade goods for the trappers already afield. At the end of that rendezvous, the supply caravan would head back to St. Louis with furs valued in excess of $80,000—a monstrous reward for those merchants in St. Louis who had the conviction to invest in such a risky venture.

Soon the four smaller brigades went separate ways as they moved north into the prime beaver trapping regions of the central Rockies. Then Jacob's brigade broke up into even smaller groups as they staked out individual trapping territories. Buffalo Calf just kept Jacob's crew pointed north as they ventured into the Bighorn Mountains. On they went, day after day, followed by Singing Bird riding one horse and leading another that pulled a travois loaded with buffalo hides for the tepee and other family items. A third horse pulled a second travois loaded with tepee poles and sleeping skins.

My God, this country is absolutely stunning, Jacob thought. Mountain grasses were belly high on the horses. Cold, clear creeks rushed about everywhere. So did buffalo, elk, deer, pronghorn, moose, bighorn sheep, and grizzly and black bears. Blue grouse were often underfoot, spooking the horses with their sudden and unexpected "rises" on a daily basis. Ten minutes hunting with the fowling piece or fishing with hand lines produced more fish and grouse than could be eaten at an evening meal. The big Hawkens were everything Jacob Hawken had said they would be. A single shot behind the shoulder brought great beasts such as buffalo, moose or elk down quickly. Then the work began as everyone pitched in to butcher the animal before it was fly blown or spoiled in the late summer heat. No two ways about it, God has truly smiled down on this land Buffalo Calf has brought us into. No wonder the local tribes of Indians fight so fiercely and in such a deadly manner to defend their lands.

One afternoon, as they approached a small lake nestled up against a ridge covered with lodgepole pine, Buffalo Calf signaled a halt. Jacob watched as Ben rode forward and carried on a discussion with Buffalo Calf, who pointed out things of interest as they talked.

When Ben returned to the group, he said, "This is home until the next rendezvous. Buffalo Calf suggested we dig into that small hillside and make a cave for storage of our valuables. That way they will be harder to steal than if left outside. Plus those items will be out of the damaging weather. Then we could build our cabin and several lean-tos directly into the base of the ridge, facing the lake. That way we will miss the deepest of the winter's snows and winds. Plus we will have a constant supply of firewood close at hand, have plenty of good water nearby in the lake, and it will be a good place to fight off any attacks with our backs to the ridge. Buffalo Calf also says many elk and buffalo winter in the adjacent valley to the east and there is plenty of high quality mountain hay in the nearby meadow for our horses."

Jacob took a quick look around the area to make sense of what Ben had said, then watched as Martin did the same. Martin then nodded to Jacob in agreement. With that they moved all their horses into a close-at-hand, quickly made pole-and-rope corral to prevent a stampede in case of the ever-present threat of an Indian attack. Then the packs were lifted off the tired animals and stacked next to a deadfall of pines. In effect, this made a small defensive firing position against any roving war parties.

In the meantime, Singing Bird offloaded her horses' packs and commenced putting up the tepee in a small clearing immediately adjacent to where the rest of the trappers were working. Ever mindful of The Ways, she positioned the opening of the tepee to the catch the sun's morning rays from the east.

Buffalo Calf rode off to investigate the surrounding area while Jacob, Martin and Ben put their backs to their shovels and dug a sizeable cave in the hillside. The cave was eventually roofed, floored and walled on the inside with green logs. Once the cave was completed, the men began cutting a large number of pine logs.

In several days, the walls of a large cabin began to take shape adjoining the newly dug cave. After erecting a log roof over the walls of the cabin, it was then covered with cross-timbers, which were then deeply covered with chopped sagebrush. Then with their shovels, they covered the roof with three feet of fresh earth, which had been set off to one side when the cave had been dug.

Afterwards, the men offloaded barrels of gunpowder, primers, spare parts, extra axes, blankets and other valuable items from the packs. They stacked the boxes and barrels on the raised log floor of the cave, to keep them high and dry. Then they placed their dry foodstuffs on the shelves dug into the back and side walls of the cave, which had been lined with flat rocks to keep those valuable items out of harm's way.

About then Singing Bird spoke to the men in Lakota, and when they turned, they observed Buffalo Calf entering camp.

"Where have you been?" Jacob asked. "You've been gone for several days."

"I have been hunting, to bring food. I have bighorn sheep ewe for us to eat."

"You've been ducking out on what you think is 'woman's work' of cutting wood and building a cabin," Ben said.

Buffalo Calf gave a sheepish grin. He patted the sheep carcass laid behind him on his horse and said, "I bring bighorn sheep to eat."

"That will be some good eats," said Ben with a hungry grin as he moved to help Buffalo Calf unload the animal, ignoring the man's long absence in the process.

The two men removed the animal from the horse and took it over to a smiling Singing Bird. They left it next to her campfire for preparation, then Ben returned to building the trapper's winter quarters. However, Buffalo Calf still found it difficult to get involved in the hard and dirty work. He was not into this shoveling and chopping thing because in his Lakota culture, women did much of that kind of work. Buffalo Calf sauntered off again with his horse, going out of sight into the dense willows and brush lining the many creeks next to camp.

Ben just grinned at his Lakota friend as he and Jacob and Martin got back to work making a solid post and stringer corral for the horses. Singing Bird, true to her work ethic and reputation, was making her hands fly as she carefully dressed and skinned the bighorn. Doing so, she worked carefully because bighorn sheepskin, when properly tanned, made some of the most supple clothing imaginable, especially ladies' dresses.

The men had just finished their horse corral with heavy lodgepole pine logs sunken into the earth and lashed with smaller side poles when Singing Bird walked over to them. In her beautiful singsong language, she told Ben supper was ready. The three tired and sweaty men washed, picked up their rifles and walked over to her tepee. They got there just in time to see Buffalo Calf once again riding out of the willows with a big smile on his face.

The Lakota stepped off his horse lightly. "I ride one-half of one-half of valley, down along creeks below our camp," he said. He spread his arms as wide as he could. "Beaver more than my arms can hold and they are everywhere!"

A ripple of anticipation and excitement spread palpably

CAMP   119

throughout camp. Soon everyone was talking all at once through large mouthfuls of delicious bighorn sheep stew, laced with aromatic sage, pepper, salt, wild onions freshly dug from a nearby rocky hillside and starchy tubers from a nearby marsh—tubers none of which the men recognized but all enjoyed for their potato-like flavor. Then the thick, spicy gravy from the stew was sopped up with Singing Bird's wonderful Dutch-oven biscuits. With that kind of a repast in the evening high in the wilds of the Rocky Mountains, what else could one ask for?

Well, maybe less mosquitoes, thought Martin. Before the evening was done, the group had eaten most of the small bighorn sheep.

"I can't believe we finished off that entire animal," Jacob said. "Oh," said Ben, "it's not unusual. I figure that trappers will often eat between seven and ten pounds of meat in one sitting. After all, their meals may be few and far between."

The next morning, Martin and the others awoke to find a frosty dew on all their sleeping furs under the lean-to. For certain a sign of what is soon to come, thought Martin, ever the woods-wise individual.

The men hung their bedding furs on the sides of the horse corral to dry and let the hobbled horses out to graze around camp. Buffalo Calf provided horse guard while the other three continued building permanent lean-tos for the harsh winter weather to come. That even included a large lean-to for their horse herd, now numbering twelve. This would give them shelter when blizzards descended over the land.

As for the cabin, there were still lots of cracks between the wall logs. That problem was soon remedied. Singing Bird started mixing grasses from the meadow and mud of the nearby lakeshore. Carrying a load of the mud and grass mixture in a hide basket, she attacked the cracks in the logs with her flying and skillful hands. Soon the cracks were filled with bark chips from the log cuttings, moss, and the mud-grass mixture from the lake. The men cut window openings on the ends and front of the structure, and shooting ports in the walls in case of attack.

Then it was done! A log cabin with a dirt floor measuring twenty by fifteen feet in size and seven feet in height. No ordinary little fur trapper's cabin, this one. It had a porch over the stone front step and a long porch overhang extending the full length of the front wall. Here one could sit and watch out over the geography of the land. And from under the dry cover of the front porch, flesh out and hoop animal skins. At the north end of the cabin stood a stout mud, log and stone fireplace for heating and cooking.

Then they covered the window openings with soft deer hides that allowed in some light but kept out the weather. These drapes could be rolled up in the summer to allow in the breezes, and lowered in the winter to keep out the snow and cold. Additionally, they had interior log shutters over the windows with firing holes that could be closed and locked in case of an attack.

The back end of the cabin butted right into the hillside in front of the cave where their most priceless supplies and furs could be stored. On either side of the cabin stood a large, well-built lean-to. Close at hand and under the covering fire from several windows stood a very stout log corral for the horses. Twenty feet distant in the clearing stood Singing Bird and Buffalo Calf's tepee, close enough so they could safely and quickly run to the fortified cabin for protection if need be.

Then Jacob and Martin constructed log tables, chairs, benches, and sleeping and storage platforms for inside the cabin. It was then Buffalo Calf finally realized that if he wanted to be warm and have his food cooked, he would have to help in gathering the winter's supply of firewood. Apparently not happy about it, he began helping in the cutting and hauling of firewood in preparation for the upcoming winter.

Once they finished the inside of the cabin with a hearthstone for the fireplace and all the needed sleeping platforms, benches, and storage shelves, Jacob and Martin turned their creative talents to the outside. Soon pegged wooden benches and tables graced the outside for those who would be skinning and fleshing out the hides. Much bantering and good-natured talk flowed back and forth between those working in the house and those cutting wood.

After Jacob and Martin were finished with the furni-

ture, everyone tried and retried those household furnish-
ings, declaring they were more than fit for the life of a fur
trapper.

Then all four men fell to gathering up even more firewood to see them through the worst kinds of winter.
Once that feat was done, off to the surrounding rocky
hills they went to harvest the bighorn sheep for the meat,
jerky, tallow and fine hides they offered.

That was followed with the cutting of the iron-hard
mountain mahogany for the special kind of wood needed
for their Dutch- oven cooking. To use the local and plentiful lodgepole pine for cooking would smoke up the
sides of the Dutch ovens, and to use cottonwood would
take a mountain of wood to get the necessary bed of
coals. Hence, much effort was put into procuring a
winter's supply of the dense mountain mahogany
hardwood.

The work did not stop there. Hay from their meadow
was cut, cured and gathered by Singing Bird. That hay
was then secured in a lean-to for those times in the
winter when the snows drifted so deeply the horses could
not forage for themselves. At that same time, Singing
Bird gathered curing Indian rice grasses from the nearby
sagebrush flats to put between the inside liner and
outside wall of her tepee. Soft grasses were also gathered
and placed in leather bags, for her man's winter footwear
to act as an insulator when he came home wet and cold
from trapping. Seeds from those grasses, especially the
Indian rice grasses, were carefully thrashed from the

plants, ground into flour or stored in thick buffalo hide containers called parfleches to be used for thickening in stews.

Lastly, the men put an edge to all their knives, axes and shovels, then double-checked their rifles and made sure their traps were in working order. The traps were then smoked over an open fire to eliminate the "man" smell and hung on wooden pegs inside a lean-to.

The summer of building their base of operations was nearly done. With a fast-approaching fall, Ben and Buffalo Calf went out to open a beaver dam and trap those beaver who came to repair the damage. In so doing, they would get some of the much- needed castoreum for all the men to use trapping beaver. Come the evenings, Ben spent time carving and hollowing out wooden containers from Douglas fir limbs to hold the foul-smelling castoreum mixture. A wooden top or plug finished out the item that was hung about the neck by a leather cord for easy access during the trapping process.

Meanwhile, Martin and Jacob went out to the nearest buffalo herd to "make meat." Knowing Ben and Buffalo Calf would be through with their work before the buffalo hunters were theirs, they left directions as to where they could be found. Singing Bird, on the other hand, stayed behind to tend camp, build meat- drying racks and make final preparations for the start of trapping season.

Careful to just shoot the edge of the buffalo herd, Jacob and Martin each dropped a fat cow with their first shots. Then they took the extra Hawkens and dropped two more cows before the first two had quit kicking. Quickly reloading, they dropped another pair of plump cows. In a matter of minutes, they had dropped ten buffalo before the animals spooked and lumbered off. That was enough anyway, the two men agreed—any more than that and the meat would spoil before it could be processed. They rode out to the animals, then began gutting, skinning and boning out the meat as fast as they could. Both men had built travois for their riding horses and packhorses and soon they fairly bent under the weight of the great slabs of bloody meat.

By nightfall, the two men had boned out much of the meat and loaded it on the travois or stacked it on the skin sides of the fresh hides laying on the ground. A yell from the timber soon told the tired men help was on the way from the rest of their group.

The four men built a huge fire in among the remaining buffalo to be processed to keep the wolves at bay and provide some light, then hurriedly removed the rest of the meat and hides from the last of the dead animals. With overloaded horses, they slowly made their way back to camp. Behind them, the wolves made many gruesome noises over their still-warm gifts of guts, heads, bones and meat scraps.

They arrived back at camp well into the evening. The men tiredly sat down to the serious business of eating another great meal prepared by the ever-faithful Singing Bird. This time, it was cooked beaver meat and cornbread.

That was topped off with great spoonfuls of honey piled high on the remaining pieces of cornbread. The repast gave the men the needed strength to continue and that they did until the morning light. Come daylight, half the meat had been cut into strips and hung on wooden drying racks under a smoldering fire of willow, aspen and cottonwood. Finishing up the meal from the evening before, the men continued until noon. By then all the meat was cut into strips and placed on the smoking and drying racks.

With that, they turned in while Singing Bird tended the drying fires under the racks, making sure they were not too hot and not too cool for the job. She also kept the nearby coyotes and magpies from snatching pieces of the drying meat in between all her other duties.

The men woke to the delicious smell of frying buffalo meat in bear grease. They ate like they hadn't eaten for days. Then, after having occasionally turned more meat on the racks, brined some of the cuts for winter use, cleaned many feet of fresh intestines in the lake's waters for later consumption and kept the fires smoking, Singing Bird finally rested up.

Several days later, the meat processing was completed and hung from the cabin's ceiling rafters in many soft deerskin pouches. On the ropes leading from the rafters to the bags of jerked meat were wooden "plates" with a hole cut into the center for the rope to go through. That way the wooden plates could be placed over a knot on the rope halfway down, to stop any varmints from going further down the rope to get at the valuable bags of dried meat.

Much work went into "making meat," However, if not done correctly, terrible times would be the consequences come winter. Meat was the main food staple for the trappers and backwoodsmen in the wilderness, and without such high-energy foods, it was doubtful they could survive what awaited them, especially when the winter winds howled and temperatures dropped below zero.

With that necessary work behind them, the men made ready for the much-anticipated fall trapping season with all its "warts."

SETTING A TRAP

A CHILLED DAWN HERALDED THE TRAPPING SEASON.

The four men had finished saddling their horses. Then they breakfasted on fresh venison, cornbread and steaming hot coffee. They stuffed the rest of the cornbread into a soft deerskin pouch in their saddlebags, along with some jerky, and they were ready to go.

Each man carried a rifle: a Hawken each for Jacob, Ben and Martin, and a flintlock by Buffalo Calf. Each carried a horse pistol tucked in his sash, a tomahawk, and a gutting and skinning knife. A hand ax hung from each saddlehorn as did six beaver traps in a sack. A rolled-up blanket over the rear of each saddle contained extra pairs of moccasins and some James River chewing tobacco.

Each man sported a gray flannel shirt and a Hudson's Bay Company blanket coat with a powder horn hung over the shoulder from a leather thong. Blanket cloth leggings over a pair of leather breeches with dressed elk moccasins comprised the lower wear and a sack of "possibles" hung from their off shoulders to complete the outfit. The "possibles" sacks contained flints and steel for fire making, spare rifle locks and picks to clean the nipples, worms for pulling bullets, extra tins of primers, cloth patches and spare lead balls.

Everyone had long hair and Jacob sported a full beard, while his Indian friends remained essentially beardless.

They left a loaded double-barreled fowling piece and two pistols with Singing Bird for defense before they moved off into another of life's adventures.

Ben and Buffalo Calf took the northwestern side of the extensive creek-dotted valley while Martin and Jacob took the southeastern side. In short order, the trappers made their sets along the beaver-populated streams and ponds. When they finished setting out their six traps each, both teams continued exploring the valley further to the north and south, scouting out additional trapping sites. The valley was heaven-sent for fur trappers if the numbers of beaver present were a measure. Six large streams cluttered the valley, which were loaded with moose, willows, numerous beaver ponds, cutthroat trout and muskrat. Everywhere in the waterways showed evidence of the use by beaver: evidence such as mud runs, half-cut trees, beaver ponds, beaver houses, green limbs jammed into the mud at the bottom of a deep pond that were underwater beaver food stashes, tracks, numerous beaver dams ... and the animals themselves.

Jacob and Martin just grinned at their luck and were thankful for the land's lay and geographical knowledge of their Lakota Indian partner, Buffalo Calf. It was he who had led them to this place of plenty and come the rendezvous, they would be loaded with the land's riches.

After an exploring ride of about four hours, Jacob and Martin returned to their first sets of traps. They could not believe their luck on their first outing—every trap had a dead beaver. Ben's teachings had not only been very definitive back on the paddle wheeler but they had also learned their new trade well, as their traps so displayed.

They reset their traps and applied more castoreum to the lure sticks. They headed home with the heavy beaver carcasses draped and swinging along the packhorse's front shoulders and sides.

When they arrived back in camp, they were surprised to find Ben and Buffalo Calf already there. They were already skinning and fleshing out their catches as Singing Bird fixed another beaver stew heavy with ham chunk meat. They, too, had caught six large beaver each and couldn't be happier.

"I don't think this could have been a better day," said Jacob as he and Martin lighted down. "Trapping beaver here is like taking candy from a baby."

"The same with the western side of the valley," Ben said. "I've never found it so easy to trap beaver, and as near as I can tell, the same prosperity awaits up the individual streams, up into the surrounding drainages as well."

Skinning out the beaver, minus the legs and tail, the men had fresh hides that were left in a round pattern. Singing Bird had cut the men an armload of fresh willow limbs from the adjacent stream and to that they turned for material to make hoops to stretch the green beaver hides. The willow limbs formed hoops to fit the size of the pelt, and they cut thin strips of elk hide to weave through small slits cut along the edge of the beaver hides to tie around the willow frames. This kept the hide stretched and allowed for easier drying.

With that, the men finished fleshing out any meat or fat still hanging from the hides and then lined them standing up alongside the cabin and on the porch roof to dry.

The men split and placed the beaver tails on the smoking racks for drying. They would make a great tasting, fat-heavy soup during the winter months when their bodies were in need of high-energy fuels. Then they loaded the carcasses on two pack- horses and delivered them to a draw at the end of their valley for the critters to eat.

Dinner was ready and the men fell to as if they hadn't eaten in a month; they had been so wrapped up in their trapping routines, all four men had forgotten to eat their cornbread and jerky that they carried in their saddlebags.

The next day and what seemed like endless fall days thereafter, everything ran smoothly as the traps were filled many times with beaver from the rich waters of their trapping grounds. For the next several months, the men raced winter's icy blast as they trapped the seemingly never-ending supply of beaver. The men found that the plews got better and better in quality as the days shortened and the nights grew colder. With that, the men realized they had a bonanza in their valley that would soon make them economically well-off at the next rendezvous. Back at the cabin, safely tucked away in the cave storage area, they already had over four hundred beaver plews. If this success kept up, they would soon decimate the beaver's numbers and would have to move on to new trappings. But the bounty continued and their thoughts of wise use were lost in the value of their ever-increasing hoard of pelts back at the cabin.

One morning Martin checked his first trap only to discover it was empty. Next to the trap in the soft mud was a partial human footprint. Martin looked all around quickly to see if he had been observed or if someone was drawing a bead on him. He was relieved to see Jacob slowly riding his way.

Reining up, Jacob quietly said through a set of tightly drawn lips, "I have someone robbing my traps!"

Martin held up his empty beaver trap as their eyes knowingly met. Looking all around one more time for anyone laying in ambush and seeing none, they closely examined the footprints.

"Not an Indian," stated Martin flatly. "He walks the wrong way for an Indian."

Martin grabbed his rifle and commenced to track the small scuffmarks and impressions in the damp earth left by the trap robber. Jacob rode behind him on his horse with his Hawken at the ready. Soon Martin tracked the culprit's footprints to hoof prints made in the earth by that of a tethered horse.

"Hoof prints that were made by a shod horse," Martin whispered over his shoulder, "which in this wilderness must be ridden only by a white man."

Both men just looked hard at each other. Neither had seen any sign of anyone, not even an Indian, for the last several months. Now they had a stranger in their midst and a thief at that.

Martin mounted his horse and then the two of them followed the suspect horse's tracks until it entered one of the valley's many streams and disappeared.

Both men rode up and down that stream's banks for a ways, with neither of them finding where the horse tracks exited the stream. They now realized they had a very woods-wise thief in their midst. *Why else would one go to such bother to cover his tracks in such a fashion if he isn't an outlaw trapper?* thought Martin.

They returned to check their remaining traps and confirmed their worst fears. All had been picked clean by the thief. They reset their traps in the beaver-rich waters once again, then headed back to camp.

Singing Bird's quick look at their absence of beaver flashed into a look of surprise. An hour later, Ben and

Buffalo Calf also arrived in camp without a single beaver carcass swinging from their pack animal.

Both alighted from their horses and Ben said, "Someone is in the valley robbing our traps and doing a right good job of it, too."

"Us, too," said Martin grimly. The men just looked at each other for a long moment and then Martin added, "Whoever is doing it is not an Indian."

"Ours neither," said Buffalo Calf. "He not walk or ride like Indian. His horse is shod and with loose shoe on the left rear foot."

Martin just grimly stood there for a long moment with the other men, mulling over the problem. "Our thief's horse has no loose shoe," he said.

It was a high crime in the wilderness to take one's beaver. It was like stealing a man's horse. To deprive a man of his transportation or living was a killing offense to the trapper way of thinking.

And now they had an even bigger problem—they had two thieves in the valley robbing their traps and both appeared to be sneaky white men.

The next morning, long before daylight, Martin and the three other men left camp for their trap lines. Only now there was a seriousness in the air he had not felt since they had left the Platte River. Beaver was now secondary in his thoughts. All of them were out to catch the thieves and deal with a rather seamy issue.

Martin quietly sat out of sight in a thick stand of willows with Jacob and watched one of his traps set in a beaver pond full of the creatures. His trap had a huge beaver in it, one probably weighing at least seventy-five pounds. This pelt would be called a "blanket" due to its extreme size and would be of high value at any trading post or rendezvous. Shortly after daylight but with some darkness still remaining in the dense stands of willows, Martin thought he saw the shape of a small bear approaching his trap. Then the "bear" turned slightly showing an obvious white man's features.

This is the man they call Bear, Martin realized. The same man earlier on the paddle wheeler who tried to get them to play a card game for their Hawken rifles.

Martin, without a thought of more than killing a varmint, quickly raised his rifle to end a life.

Jacob placed his hand across the barrel and pushed it downward. He motioned that they should dismount and stalk the trap robber.

Martin nodded and shortly thereafter, both men silently walked in behind the trap robber as he intently tried to remove the heavy beaver from the trap. Once Bear finally wrestled the huge beaver out of the trap, he turned with a big grin on his face and about jumped back into deeper water upon seeing the two stern-faced trappers quietly standing there watching him from just a few feet away.

"What do you two pieces of crap want?" yelled Bear— yelling partly at being surprised finding Jacob and Martin standing there and partly out of fear for being caught red-handed in the serious act of trap robbing.

"We was meaning to ask you the same," mumbled Jacob through set teeth and narrowed, cold flashing eyes.

"Step aside. This here is my beaver and I mean to take him. If he was caught in your trap, that is too bad because you are trapping in my waters," snarled Bear through an equally tight set of lips with an animal-like sneer crossing his face.

"I don't think so, Bear," spoke an equally tight-lipped Martin. "We have been in this here valley since summer and call it and the beaver trapping our own."

Bear grinded his teeth, a sound that could easily be heard over the gurgling of the creek over the beaver dam. Jacob tightened up as well. Make a move, Bear, Jacob thought.

Ka-poof! went Jacob's coonskin cap boiling off his head as a speeding lead ball lifted it cleanly into the air like it was a goose- down feather in a draft. That was followed by the loud boom of a nearby rifle.

Man! That shot came from behind me and up on the side of the hill, Jacob instantly thought. He whirled and looked for the white telltale puff of black powder smoke. Jacob saw a man struggling with the reins on two nervous horses while hurriedly trying to reload his rifle.

In that same instant, Martin and Bear wrestled each other off the bank and into the beaver pond with a loud splash.

Jacob raised his Hawken, set the double trigger and touched it off in one practiced, fluid motion. He aimed at the man who had just shot at him. Boom went his

Hawken as the report echoed loudly throughout the valley. The man being shot at did not have to worry about reloading anymore.

Jacob looked around quickly, but saw no one else on the hillside but the nervous riderless horses. Then Jacob whirled to face the struggling Martin and Bear. As he did, he reached for his pistol.

Bear had his knife out and was about to plunge it into Martin.

Martin's gutting knife in a flash found Bear's midsection. Martin's long knife slid deeply into the stomach and then was jerked violently upward into the blood-rich area of the heart and lungs.

"Ugghh!" screamed Bear as the knife blade drove deeply into his vitals.

Martin jerked the bloody knife out, then with a quick backhanded swipe, slashed it deeply across Bear's throat. A spew of bright red blood sprayed forth. That was followed by a gurgling sound from the stricken man's lips.

Bear dropped into the knee-deep cold water face first, wiggled some and then went still in death. The normally clear water flowing through the beaver pond now turned bright red below Bear's body, then faded away to pink as it raced along.

Jacob reached out for his partner's hand and helped him up the slippery bank. Apparently without an afterthought, Martin took Bear's knife from his lifeless hand and then removed the beaver trap from this place of death. Martin then bent back down and lifted the spectacular grizzly bear necklace from Bear's neck, washed the blood off and handed it to Jacob.

"Maybe we will have a use for it somewhere down the line," Martin quietly said.

I can't imagine what for, thought Jacob as he placed the necklace in his saddlebag.

Jacob and Martin left Bear where he fell for the crawdads and varmints. They walked up the hill to the two thieves' horses. Wentz, Bear's partner, lay on the ground at the feet of the nervous animals. The .54-caliber ball from Jacob's rifle had entered just below Wentz's nose and blown out the top of his head with unbelievable force. There were brains and bright red blood blown all over Bear's horse, the ground, and the surrounding trees.

Martin smiled with pride at Jacob's shooting ability.

However, Jacob wasn't smiling. "Well, I just killed a mean-assed varmint that needed killing!"

Without another word, the two men rolled Wentz over and took his rifle, powder horn, possibles sack and knife.

"No use in leaving such valuable things to another varmint," thought Jacob out loud.

They left both bodies where they fell for the ever present and always hungry critters. The two men rode quietly back to camp after checking, emptying and resetting the rest of their traps. Each man now led an extra horse and carried an extra rifle.

On the way back, they crossed paths with Buffalo Calf

and Ben riding like the wind towards their partners' side
of the valley. They had heard the shooting and must have
figured Jacob and Martin found the culprits. With that,
they came just "a-hellin'" to see if they could help.

Jacob and Martin explained what had happened and
both Ben and Buffalo Calf grunted their approval.

"Bear and Wentz have been pure poison from the start
and best they're now bear bait," said Ben, as a smile
crossed his weathered face. "The life of a trapper can be
tough but can get a whole lot worse if one does not
follow the trapper's code of honor."

Back at camp, the men examined the two dead men's
tack. Their horseflesh was good—although one needed
his left rear shoe fixed—and their rifles were top notch.
Both rifles were .54-caliber Hawkens. Surprisingly. Since
neither Bear nor Wentz had a Hawken in their possession
on the boat months before, the men surmised they had
recently killed their two partners from the fur brigade
and had taken their rifles. After that discovery and
deduction, Jacob felt no remorse for killing Wentz.

Martin on the other hand, rather enjoyed killing Bear
up close and personal like.

The men looked for two days in a vain attempt to
locate the dead men's camp. They were unsuccessful.
From then on, no one stole from their traps as they
continued their trapping successes. They gave one of the
recently acquired Hawkens to Buffalo Calf to use; the
other they kept in reserve for any of the men to use in
case a Hawken was lost, stolen or destroyed in a horse

wreck. Buffalo Calf's flintlock was then left with Singing Bird for her defense when the men were out trapping. Singing Bird just smiled. She knew how to shoot and now had four firearms in her tepee.

Lord help anyone going after her if she got the chance to get to her arsenal, Jacob thought.

BUFFALO HUNT

THE MEN WORKED HARD IN THE VALLEY TRAPPING BEAVER, river otter, fox and some muskrats as winter and its icy blasts blew more and more. Icy cold wet feet and legs were now becoming a problem. Many a morning, the men had to vigorously rub their feet in front of the fire in order for their limbs to loosen up enough for them to be able to even walk normally. However, the trapping was good and the men worked hard realizing downtime was coming with winter's ice and snows. At first, the ice was not much of a problem as the men busted through it with their hand axes and continued setting their traps. They were catching less beaver now but still enough so that it paid for them to be out and about.

Then one morning after the icy wind had blown hard all night, they awoke to a vast and deathly quiet white wilderness. The air temperature was probably ten below zero but the men ventured forth just the same for beaver once again with high hopes.

When they returned home that evening, they had one beaver between them to show for all their frozen feet and water-numbed hands. They pulled their traps as the ice formed right in front of their eyes in the intense cold. Beaver trapping to their way of thinking was now done for in the winter of 1830. Sure, they could trap them under the ice, but that was a lot of hard, ice-busting cold work for small returns. As they sat around the fireplace that evening, they decided it was time to hunt some buffalo for the fresh meat it offered. That plus their hides would bring a premium during the up and coming rendezvous in Cache Valley.

Ben reminded them, "Buffalo hides are thicker in the winter and bring the highest trade premiums. Winter hides also make the best machinery belts in England. And, the British Army believes buffalo leather makes the best marching footwear for its soldiers."

With the hunt close at hand, the men recharged their powder horns, cast bullets around the fireplace, added more balls to their "possibles" bags, and checked the mechanics of their Hawkens.

Singing Bird moved about excitedly with the change in plans from beaver trapping to buffalo hunting. "She is hungry for buffalo meat, especially liver, fat and intestines," Buffalo Calf explained.

They figured their camp was safe since they hadn't seen any Indians for months, so they decided Singing

Bird would accompany them to help "make meat" for their winter larder.

Dawn the next morning found the trappers on the hunt as they trailed every horse they owned. For about five bitter cold miles across the country in knee-deep snows, they discovered nothing in the way of fresh tracks, droppings or anything indicating buffalo in the area. Then in the next valley over from their camp, they discovered great clouds of steam rising into the freezing air. Clouds of steam from their breaths that only a large herd of resting buffalo could make.

They tied off the horses in a draw out of the way downwind from the herd and left Singing Bird to guard them. The men crawled up over the snowy sagebrush-covered rim and looked. There below them were about five thousand buffalo some fifty yards distant, quietly feeding and resting. The four men spread out along the rim so each team of shooters could shoot the edge of the herd. They made ready. Soon the resonant booming of the heavy Hawken rifles filled the frigid morning winter air. Being as cold as it was, the sound of the firing rifles loudly cracked through the dense, moisture-laden winter air.

BUT THE SHOTS flew true and soon the snow was dotted with many dark and lifeless mounds of bison still emitting steam from their cooling bodies.

Still the heavy lead balls flew through the air and

more of the great shaggy beasts toppled over and dropped onto "Mother Earth" for the last time.

Jacob and Martin rose from their snowy beds, their rifle barrels steaming hot to the touch. Ben and Buffalo Calf rose almost as if on the same cue as well and the four of them looked over their morning's deadly but life-giving work. The remaining buffalo, upon seeing man for the first time, moved off to the east in typical fashion, grunting and shuffling out of sight with their tails held high. But not without leaving thirty-nine of their fellow travelers on the cold snow, to move no more.

The men and Singing Bird moved to the first buffalo. With several quick cuts from a very sharp and heavy bladed gutting knife, Jacob removed a large steaming liver. He then cut open the gall bladder and sprinkled its green liquid contents over the outside of the liver for the mineral salts it possessed.

The five of them greedily cut off and ate great chunks of the steaming hot, raw delicacy until it was no more. With their lips and chins smeared a ghoulish red, they moved to the next buffalo and did the same until all had their fill of the rich "bile salted" liver. Then the butchering work began in earnest.

Singing Bird returned to the draw and soon had a roaring fire going. The men in the meantime skinned the buffalo and removed great slabs of meat from the carcasses. Placing the meat on the clean snow for cooling, they continued their hard work for several hours.

Then a special whistle from Singing Bird snapped Buffalo Calf to instant alert.

Looking around, Buffalo Calf saw fifteen mounted warriors some hundred yards distant quietly looking on.

"Rifles!" A sharp word directed at his companions.

All four trappers filled their bloody and tallow-coated hands quickly with their Hawkens.

They are just watching and not attacking, Buffalo Calf observed.

Jacob hurriedly reloaded and primed his second Hawken as did Ben. Between the four of them they now had six loaded rifles and four pistols.

Not much of a match against fifteen mounted and well-armed Indians if trouble was brewing, Buffalo Calf grimaced, but far better than nothing.

Singing Bird walked right by Buffalo Calf with a purposeful stride towards another group of Indians who stood and observed the scene from off to one side of the first group of mounted warriors.

Seeing her go with such purpose, Buffalo Calf made no move to stop her. He sensed her purpose and he motioned to the others to stand their ground.

Singing Bird strode right by the mounted warriors without so much as a glance their way and walked directly into the group of Indians standing behind them in the timber. When she arrived, there were greetings and lots of friendly talking and gesturing.

Buffalo Calf let fly a great grin, then interpreted the

scene for his partners. "These are people of clan of Singing Bird. She has joy to see her mother."

———

SOON THE GROUP of women and children with Singing Bird came over the hill to examine the recent buffalo kill site. The warriors relaxed and with that, Buffalo Calf beckoned to Lame Deer, leader of the hunting party, to come forward.

As Lame Deer came near, Buffalo Calf grasped his arm and spoke in Lakota. "It is good to see you again, my friend. It is good to see more of the Lakota people. I did not expect you would travel to this valley."

"We were hunting the buffalo," Lame Deer replied. "We heard sounds of gunfire and came to see who was here. I also did not expect to see you here. It is good that you are. We are low on powder and ball, and we cannot fight our enemies. I am glad we do not find our enemies here. But who are these men you hunt with?"

Buffalo Calf pointed to each trapper in turn. "Ben Bow is my friend. He saved my life, and I owe him much, but he is generous and has let me be his partner in hunting. That one is Martin, a friend of Ben Bow and an Indian from the east. The other one is Jacob, a friend of Martin since they were children. He is a good hunter, and kind and strong."

"And these friends of yours, they do women's work?"

Buffalo Calf laughed. "Yes, they do women's work.

They also hunt very well, and shoot straight. I have never met better hunters."

Lame Deer stared at the trappers and their camp for a few minutes. Clearly, something was on his mind. "Buffalo Calf, you have taken Singing Bird as your squaw, with my blessing. I see that you and your friends have more buffalo than you can eat. I would not ask, but we are low on powder and ball for hunting, and we have not enough meat to eat. Will you share some of your kill with us, the people of your squaw?"

"I will ask my friends."

———————

BUFFALO CALF WALKED BACK to his partners, who had been watching on in curiosity. He explained, as best he could in his broken English, that the tribe was low on food and ammunition, and had asked if the trappers would share the buffalo meat. "Ben, what do you think?" Jacob asked.

"We have more than enough to eat. Twice more than enough."

"And you, Martin?"

"We should keep the hides, but the meat they should have." Jacob turned back to Buffalo Calf. "We are happy to share the meat. They can half of the meat, if they wish. However, ask them if we can have the hides from the buffalo they take in return, for our generosity."

"I will ask Lame Deer. I do not know if he will accept."

Jacob raised his brows in indignation as Buffalo Calf turned away, but Ben touched Jacob's shoulder and whispered, "Relax. It is the Lakota way."

————

BUFFALO CALF WALKED BACK to Lame Deer and relayed the offer. Lame Deer considered it and said, "To trade buffalo skins for buffalo meat is not an even trade. We get more from this trade than your friends get."

"Do not worry," Buffalo Calf replied. "My friends trade furs with the White Men in the cities of the east, and buffalo skins to them are very important. To my friends, the buffalo skins are very valuable, more valuable than the meat. They will believe that you have given them something worth more than the meat, and so it will be a fair trade, each of you getting something very important."

Lame Deer thought on Buffalo Calf's wisdom, then shrugged. "If the White Man needs buffalo skin so much, I would be honored to give them for buffalo meat which we need so much, And the Great Spirit will be pleased that all of the buffalo is used." The two Lakota men made the sign of a fair deal. Buffalo Calf returned to his trapper friends to tell them it was a good trade, while Lame Deer beckoned his group to come forward and start butchering their generous share of the fallen animals.

————

FOR THE REST of the afternoon and into the evening, they all butchered the buffalo until there were no more. Then the Lakota band moved together into the same draw, away from the biting wintery blasts, where they set up camp. Soon great slabs of fresh meat were cooking around many roaring campfires, filling the air with many great smells. With the cooking and eating, a lot of visiting went on and Jacob and Martin got to practice their sign language once again.

"This is Singing Bird's family and not the savage Blackfoot or the horse-stealing Crow," Buffalo Calf told Jacob. "This is...how do you say...lucky?...very lucky. And we have more women's hands to make meat."

The celebrating went on into the early morning as many ate until they could hold no more and then in an hour or so after eating, gorged some more. There were huge mounds of meat by camp ready to be loaded on the travois, not to mention great amounts still remaining next to the cooking fires for immediate consumption.

In the valley to the east, the killing area unfolded into another unusual macabre scene. Slinking wolves pulled and tugged on the gut piles and buffalo carcasses for the food they offered. From the number of wolfpacks and fights, there was no shortage of hungry mouths in the valley vying for the carcasses and scraps left behind. And, as usual and out of pursuit range, numerous bunches of the clever coyotes roamed, ever ready to snatch anything left behind by the wolves. All of which was governed over by the ever-present crow, magpie, gray jay and raven awaiting their turns at the "dinner pail." The next morning after another great bout of gorging and a lot of defecating around the camps, both parties made ready to move on. And then a surprise of surprises occurred—the group of Indians had unwittingly decided to move into the little valley in which Jacob and his party had their winter quarters.

Ben was delighted. He said, "Well, it's certainly a change in the neighborhood. But I can't say there is any problem with it. This valley sure has plenty enough of camping room, a lot of hay meadows around the lake for all of their horses, and we sure could use the greater safety in numbers, don't you think?"

Jacob and Martin readily agreed, much to Singing Bird's delight.

"Besides," Jacob replied, "any group of Indians other than a very large one will think twice before attacking a camp the size as ours will soon become."

The rest of that day, the group moved slowly back to winter camp. Travois groaned under the loads of fresh and now quickly freezing meat, as much joy was made over the good fortune of the group by everyone.

Back at the trappers' camp, the Lakota Indians camped about one hundred yards from Jacob's cabin in order to have better access to the hay meadows for their many horses. Soon the little valley was filled with tepees, campfire smoke that drifted lazily into the cold air, racks of drying meat, barking dogs and the happy voices of many men, women and children. However, with the good came the hard work. Jacob, Ben, Singing Bird and Martin found themselves fleshing and hanging out to dry almost forty buffalo hides in the sub-zero weather. Buffalo Calf on the other hand true to the Lakota way of men, spent his days visiting and renewing old friendships. It was still not his job to do women's work such as buffalo hide and meat preparation.

Thus the winter and the early spring of 1831 passed: Buffalo Calf visited old friends, Jacob and Martin studied the Lakota language, all the men hunted buffalo whenever the fresh meat supplies ran low, and the complement of trappers prepared for the spring trapping season just months ahead. Jacob and Martin also made good use of the ten pounds of blue beads purchased so long ago in St. Louis the previous winter. They traded strings of beads for the Indians' beaver and otter pelts to add to their own hoard of furs in the cave, and they added to the copious bright blue beads that adorned Singing Bird's neck and the dresses that she made from her tanned bighorn sheep skins.

Yes. This year to come has the spirit of happy and interesting times, Buffalo Calf thought, *especially with the peaceful arrival of Singing Bird's people to our winter camp.*

14

THE BIG SANDY

COME LATE SPRING OF 1831 AND ICE OUT, THE FOUR MEN were more than ready for the trapping season to begin. Daylight on the first day of trapping found the men hard at work making their beaver sets. Since the beaver's numbers close to camp were nonexistent, they now found themselves moving farther and farther up and down their great valley in order to fill their traps. For the next two months the men returned every day with beaver across the packsaddles as proof that the valuable furry bounty still remained.

During those heady spring days, Singing Bird, in addition to her other duties, often helped the men flesh out and hoop the pelts. Soon the cave fairly blossomed with the fruits of their labors. By now, the men had removed the willow hoops and had folded the hides in half with the fur to the inside. Then with the weight of a man on top of a stack of loose furs, another tied and made compact bundles weighing about eighty-five to ninety pounds each. Each processed beaver pelt weighed about one and a half pounds—about sixty hides to the pack. Soon, ten tightly wrapped packs covered with a tanned deer hide for protection, adorned the floor of the cave. A remarkable haul for the four trappers in such a short period of time. But the bounty in the valley was soon to end.

The Snake Indians who lived in their area were also trapping in anticipation of the upcoming trading season. Doing so, so they could trade the white man for powder, shot, brass wire, cast-iron cooking pots, beads and the like. With that kind of trapping pressure, it was only a matter of time before the valley, even as large as it was, soon held few beaver. Fortunately, there were other unexplored valleys lying nearby with numerous water-courses and a promise of more of the furry bounty to come.

Then rendezvous time was now upon them. It was time to gather up the gear, close camp, load their trap-pings and head for Cache Valley. However, much work remained in getting their horses ready for the long trip and their tack up to snuff. For a full week final prepara-tions were made as the men and Singing Bird made ready for another adventure. Singing Bird's family and tribal band were going to remain in the valley for a little longer to hunt buffalo, but they agreed to meet the trappers at their present camp if they returned to the Bighorn

Mountains after trading their furs and hides. If not, they would meet later somewhere along the trail. But for now, they were planning on heading south to trade at Fort Saint Vrain.

Come the day of departure for the rendezvous of 1831, the Mountain Men and Singing Bird were up early and excited about going. Their activity roused the Indian encampment and soon dogs were barking as the children ran about playing. Singing Bird, on the other hand, met with her many relatives and friends as best as she could.

Soon the trappers were loaded and ready to go.

Once on the go, they made quite a caravan. Four gaily dressed Mountain Men riding horses, leading nine other horses loaded with packs of beaver plews, buffalo hides, camp gear and spare equipment. Behind that string of animals rode Singing Bird on her horse, leading two packhorses pulling travois, each loaded with tepee skins, camp gear, more buffalo skins and bedding. After many goodbyes and tears on the part of Singing Bird, the little caravan was off to the rendezvous. Buffalo Calf led the expedition since he knew the way and the rest fell in behind.

For several days the group rode southwest out of the Bighorn Mountains, a place of many memories for the trappers that would soon translate into wealth and material things once at the rendezvous. The June weather remained warm during their trek, with late-day thunderstorms being the norm in the high country. They continued southwest and made good time. They

managed to avoid horse wrecks, run-ins with Ephraim—
the Mountain Man word for the grizzly bear—and
hostile Indians. Along the way, they saw more and more
evidence of large bands of Indians on the move. That
reminded the men every time they crossed the local
natives' tracks that they were leading a treasure trove of
trade goods and furs welcome in any Indian's camp. As a
result, all kept their eyes carefully peeled for any signs of
trouble and they kept their powder dry. They traveled
through South Pass, stopping only to kill the occasional
buffalo for fresh meat. To mind the travois being pulled
by Singing Bird, they required a trail at least three feet
wide, so the men kept to existing game or Indian trails so
she would have easier traveling. But for others using or
watching the same trails, it also become an open invite
for trouble if the locals were of such a mind.

One morning just before dawn, Jacob awoke with a
start. Not one in which he jumped up to meet the danger
close at hand, but one in which his eyes and ears were
now instantly alert to something out of place. He sensed
the kind of danger brought on by something unknown,
deadly or hostile.

And, close at hand.

His horse had snorted an alarm and was standing
looking in the direction of the willows alongside the Big
Sandy River where they had camped the previous
evening. A camping area full of mosquitoes but one out
of the wind and out of sight from prying eyes.

Jacob quietly nudged Martin, then very slowly

reached for his pistol so as not to arouse any suspicion, should someone be watching to see if he was awake. Martin, ever the Indian, then quietly nudged Ben. As it turned out, Ben was already wide awake and alert to the unknown danger.

As the men quietly armed themselves wondering if they had a bear or human visitors, a screaming yell followed by many others rent the early morning air. Down upon them showered a cloud of arrows, immediately followed by a rain of screaming savages.

Jacob rolled out from under his buffalo robe, now stuck full of arrows, and shot an Indian not two feet away in the face with his horse pistol. The impact of the big slug hitting the man caused him to just fold and collide with Jacob like a human cannon ball. The ensuing collision knocked Jacob off his knees, bringing both men to the ground in a human tangle.

Two more explosions rent the air near Jacob's bed as he rose from his collision with the dead Indian—explosions telling him Ben and Martin had used their pistols at close range as well.

Neighing horses, screaming Indians, thuds of tomahawks, more explosions from the trappers' extra pistols and rifles firing along with yelling, greeted the dawn. The sun peeped over the mountains only to witness a mass of men and one woman locked in deadly close-quarters combat of the most primal sort. Snot flew from the thudding impacts of tomahawks as men groaned and slid to their knees for one final mortal slide. Combatants wet themselves when skinning knives tore into their guts with soft rendering sounds. That action was intermixed with bones loudly crunched under rifles and pistols used as clubs, crashing violently into twisted faces or close-at-hand skulls.

Just as quickly as it started, it was over.

Jacob stood among his bedding furs, surrounded by four dead Indians at his feet. Two had been shot at such close range that the shooting had burned their faces black. Another knifed in the forehead still had the gutting knife sticking up to its handle in the brain case. The last one under his feet had a crushed skull from an empty horse pistol violently slammed up against the side of his head.

Blood ran from Jacob's right shoulder in streaming rivulets from a knife wound as evidenced by the knife still sticking in place. Another slash ran almost the full length of his left side across his ribs—not a deep wound, but painful from the near fatal swipe of a tomahawk.

Inspecting the wound, Jacob thought, *It will soon heal with the proper application of gunpowder poured into the cut and touched off with an open flame.* Jacob winced at the thought.

Martin stood next to Jacob, still shaking with a raging fury born from mortal combat. A deep tomahawk slash wound across Martin's cheek was so deep, the skin hung loosely in a bloody flap, and so wide that Jacob could see his chipped white teeth and jaw bone glistening in the early morning light even through the torrent of blood.

At Martin's feet the blood from his facial wound dripped without favor on the bodies of four more dead Indians. Two had been shot at close range by pistols. One had been knifed in the throat and one had a deathly bruise on his neck, apparently killed with Martin's strong hands in a violent fit of raging fury.

Ben had fared a little better. He had had his little finger on his right hand shot off at the palm. The shooter was still moving slowly at Ben's feet as he held in his guts. Ben's knife dripped with blood. Two more dead Indians laid at his feet as well, with crushed skulls—one had the pistol barrel still stuck in the skull, it having hit with such force.

Then all three men, as if one, swung their eyes towards Buffalo Calf and Singing Bird's camp a few feet distant. No one was standing.

Buffalo Calf laid in a pile intermixed with four of the attacking Indians; none of them were moving. Singing Bird, on the other hand, was kneeling over Buffalo Calf and rocking gently back and forth. She emitted a low sounding wail. Off to her side lay three more dead warriors. In the fury of the fight, she had shot one with her pistol, had knifed another and had sunk Buffalo Calf's tomahawk into the face of the last attacker.

Jacob ran to Buffalo Calf and felt his heart almost stop. There was a dark purplish-blue hole and powder burns in Buffalo Calf's forehead, from a musket ball fired at close range. A gaping bloody hole. A hole mixed with fragments of glistening white bone at the back of his head.

Before he was killed, Buffalo Calf had made sure someone paid dearly for the ill-fated morning's attack, if the dead at his feet were any evidence.

Ben stepped around Jacob and tenderly lifted Singing Bird up from Buffalo Calf's inert form. She did not object but just cried harder over the loss of her husband as she was lifted from him and held tenderly by Ben.

Martin, now coming back from a short jaunt into the willows, carried the still-bleeding head of a young Indian boy. Martin must have gone into the willows to see if any more attackers still lurked.

Jacob could just imagine the scene. Martin must have surprised a young boy, probably on his first raid. Such boys would often be holding the attackers' horses. No doubt, running into the boy, Martin still felt the fury of the earlier attack. Martin would have grabbed the boy by the hair, and in one savage swoop with a gutting knife, lopped off the boy's head.

"This boy was the last," spat out Martin. He threw the head into the slow-moving waters of the Big Sandy, its wide-set, dark brown eyes still showing great surprise. Within moments, live minnows in the waters tugged at the boy's exposed bloody flesh.

Singing Bird, in shock and yet with typical Indian stoicism, reached up and removed the knife sticking in Jacob's shoulder with a quick jerk.

The pain blinded Jacob. He let loose a sharp yell and

almost fell to his knees, but managed to recover his senses as the pain settled in.

Singing Bird undid Jacob's buckskin shirt and pulled it over his head, then dressed his wounds. Then she tended to Martin which took a whole lot more doing.

With needle and thread from her possibles kit laid to one side on a rock, she carefully washed out the facial wound and then sewed back the flap of skin—but not before expertly placing and sewing the many facial muscles crudely but firmly back into place. Martin said nothing of the intense pain during the operation. When Singing Bird finished, Martin silently nodded to her in thanks.

Then Singing Bird stoked up their fire. She took her always-sharp knife and placed the blade into the flame. After a few moments, she took Ben's hand and removed the hot knife from the fire. She pressed the flat side hard against the remaining portion of his little finger. In so doing, she cauterized the still-bleeding wound against further infection.

Once she had tended to the men's wounds, she partially pulled up her buckskin dress to reveal a broken arrow shaft sticking deeply into her thigh.

That woman is completely selfless, Jacob mused. *I have never known anyone to be so brave, to treat others while she herself is in great pain and having just lost her man.*

Blood trickled down Singing Bird's brown leg and onto the sand in which she stood but not a sound did she make. She took the still-hot knife blade and cut out the arrowhead, which had hit the thighbone and stopped.

Again, not a sound did she utter!

With that, she dug into a pouch she carried at her side, removed some moss and healing herbs and pressed them over the furiously bleeding wound. She quickly cut a piece of tanned elk leather strapping from her possibles kit, bound up her thigh, and then dropped the dress with the bloody arrow hole over her leg as if nothing had happened.

Jacob stood there in amazement at what he had just observed, and finally realized it was all over. Now they had work to do.

Ben, with tears of grief freely rolling down his cheeks over the loss of his close friend Buffalo Calf, took his ax and rifle and disappeared into the brush and trees along the river. Soon chopping sounds could be heard.

Singing Bird went back to her husband; she kneeled down and began a low wail of grief once again from her very heart and soul; as she wailed, she dressed Buffalo Calf's body in his finest buckskins.

Jacob and Martin, hefting their Hawkens and reloading their pistols, walked up the adjacent river bank above camp. From there they took a long and careful look out across the short-grass prairie for any other signs of danger. No other riders who might have heard the shooting and come to investigate were in view. Jacob was satisfied they were alone and not in further danger, and Martin agreed. They returned to their bloody campsite.

Ben identified the attackers as a raiding party of Crow. "I also think they thought our camp was Lakota and attacked. That mistake cost all of them their lives, and almost ours."

The west is certainly beautiful, thought Jacob, but it can be bloody and deadly as well if one is not careful or is unlucky. And even if one is careful...

They dumped the Crow's bodies into the Big Sandy to let nature work its magic. But not before mutilating the bodies so that entering the "Happy Hunting Grounds" would not be an option for the attackers.

Jacob and Martin then painfully assisted Ben in building a burial scaffold on the bluff overlooking their campsite. When completed and satisfied that the wolves could not get at the body, they wrapped and tightly bound Buffalo Calf—dressed in his finery—in a buffalo robe. They then tenderly laid the body on top of the burial scaffold. Alongside the body they placed his skinning and gutting knife. His bloody tomahawk was also placed at his side and his bow and arrows were laid at his feet. His old flintlock was laid along his right side with powder and shot—his Hawken being too valuable to leave. Food was also laid with him as well as under the burial scaffold.

A great silent sadness came over the group as they returned to camp to fix something to eat, load their livestock and be on their way. Singing Bird had already started breakfast as the men moved through the willows gathering up the attacking Indians' horses. Now they had nineteen additional horses to add to their livestock—a sure-fire attraction for every Indian group that chanced their way because of the great value horses held in the wilderness.

Jacob tried to break the pervasive silence. "The horses will be great trading material if they can make it to the rendezvous. So will the eleven extra rifles we took from the Crow. I know they are old flintlocks or North West fusils of poor quality, not really great guns at all. But Indians without any firearms at the rendezvous will happily trade away most anything they have to get a 'fire stick.'"

The three men finished breakfast, then loaded up their livestock and tethered the raiders' stock into two long lines.

They left the Big Sandy for the trip to Cache Valley and the rendezvous. Singing Bird now led the way since she was familiar with the lay of the land. But before they left, all said goodbye to their late friend laying quietly on the burial scaffold in the Rocky Mountains wind.

Ben said a few last words in Lakota, then quietly explained to Jacob: "Buffalo Calf is now waiting for his Maker to carry him off to the 'Land of Eternal Sunrises and Unending Herds of Buffalo.' Buffalo Calf was a good friend and knowledgeable frontiersmen. He will be sorely missed by everyone."

For the next several days, Singing Bird wore ashes on her face and made many small cuts on her arms—her people's tradition to show the grief she felt. Ben rode near her throughout those days as she continued her low wail and singing to the Great Spirit over the loss of her husband. From then on, when camp was made, Ben always made it a point to be near her side. She was still her own woman, but Ben just felt she still needed someone else around close at hand.

15

THE 1831 RENDEZVOUS

SINGING BIRD AND BEN HAD STOPPED LEADING THE caravan, and were looking from the mountain range on which they sat into the distant valley below. Singing Bird pointed and then made sign that this was Cache Valley, the site chosen for the 1831 rendezvous. Jacob and Martin tenderly rode up to have a gander for themselves —rode tenderly, because they were ever mindful of the still oozing wounds on their bodies slowly trying to heal. And riding on the hurricane deck of a horse cross-country wasn't the best way to feel good and heal quickly.

They slowly worked their way off the mountain range and soon reached the valley floor. It was deep in grasses and small clear streams abounded underfoot. They rode to a small shallow lake with heavy stands of willow and cottonwood alongside a stream. There, they stopped and surveyed their surroundings. The area where they sat was easily out of the wind and out of sight of anyone passing by. There was also firewood aplenty and grass in abundance for their growing herd of horses. A depression in the ground at a potential campsite also made for a natural defensive position.

Jacob decided there they would stay until they located the rendezvous site. For the rest of that day everyone pitched in and constructed camp. They soon discovered an old corral among the trees near their campsite made by earlier visitors. With a little work, it held their entire herd of horses. Not familiar with the Indian nations in the area, Jacob made sure all their riding stock were hobbled when they were let out to feed or water. That way, if the herd was stampeded by Indians, their riding horses would at least not be far away. Then several shelters were constructed under the trees and covered with green cottonwood boughs to keep out the afternoon rains and glaring midday sun. They dug out a central, rock-lined fire pit, with several logs dragged to its edge for sitting. Singing Bird soon had a fire going and supper cooking as the men dragged in more firewood with their horses, enough to last for several days. After supper and not fully realizing just how tired they all were, they turned in. But not before laying multiple firearms within arms' reach in case another hostile surprise came their way.

———

DAYLIGHT CAME. The sounds of Canada geese rising into the air in alarm erupted from the lake next to the camp. Quickly they honked their way out of earshot, but not before everyone in camp was instantly alert—without moving to give away that fact.

"Hello the camp," came a sonorous voice from the twilight dark. "We are friends heading for the rendezvous. We smelled the wood smoke from your evening's fire. May we enter and sit a spell?"

Jacob and Martin were up, armed and ready, as was Ben. Singing Bird had scuttled out of the way but was armed with her trusty fowling piece and two horse pistols, just in case.

"Come on in," yelled Jacob, "but don't touch a lick of iron unless you want to part with it and your hair as well!"

From the early morning darkness, three trappers slowly emerged with five mules in tow. Singing Bird must have sensed that all was well, for she commenced building her cooking fire from the previous evening's coals. She signed, Six men in the morning must be famished. She hobbled around in the process.

Jacob was more hesitant. He kept his Hawken directed at the feet of the stranger who was taller than the others, who had an eagle feather perched at an angle in a wolf-skin cap. He sensed that Martin had his gun pointed directly between the other two.

The strangers held their empty hands up at shoulder height, to show they came in peace, but all three looked towards Singing Bird, whose bloody dress and leg wound were apparent to see.

Ben instinctively moved between the strangers and Singing Bird, and aimed his rifle from one to the next. Jacob knew the meeting had come to a decision point, so he used the tip of his rifle to wave the strangers into the camp.

"Man!" said the taller one with the eagle feather in his cap, "I'd say you fellas was in a recent scrape. And from the looks of you folks, I would hate to see those who started the 'hoo-rah.'" Extending his hand, the man said, "I be Jim Bridger. This ugly one here is Hugh Glass and the squinty-eyed one is Tom Oliver. We was free trapping up on the Fire Hole on the Yellowstone. We was damn lucky to get out alive with all them red devils from the Blackfoot Nation behind every tree. Fact is, I am still carrying an arrowhead in my shoulder that I cain't dig out from one of them encounters. So who might you folks be?"

"My name is Jacob. These are my friends Martin and Ben. The squaw is Singing Bird, a Lakota. Her man was just killed in a fight on the Big Sandy several days back. We all were involved but those starting the 'hoo-rah' didn't make it to the next sunset."

"How many was they and what kind?" asked Bridger with a questioning look of interest on his grizzled weather-beaten and bearded face.

"They was Crows and nineteen of them," said Jacob.

"How many?" asked Bridger with the look of disbelief spreading across his face.

"Nineteen," repeated Jacob in a quiet but matter-of-fact tone of voice.

"Whoo-whee!" uttered Bridger. His two partners just shook their heads and clucked their tongues in amazed disbelief. The group just stood there looking at one another regarding the previous information involving the number of attacking Crows for a long moment.

"Normally, they ain't bad Injuns. Just up to their horse stealing ways. But that bunch must of had their 'red' up," said Bridger with a thoughtful look on his face. "They normally ain't this fer south either. If that was the case, I will be more careful in the future around that tribe in these here parts," he mused. Then with the Indian thing explored enough to his way of thinking he said, "We have a fresh hindquarter from an elk we killed just last evening. If you boys are willin' and iffin' your squaw can cook, we would be glad to stretch our legs and sit a spell. Hopefully that be followed with some palaverin' and eat some good meat for breakfast," Bridger continued.

Martin gestured with his hand and said, "Grab a log and pull it up. We would be glad to make your acquaintance and eat with you boys since you brought the grub."

With that, Glass and Oliver removed the elk hindquarter from the last mule and laid it down on a bed of firewood near the fire pit. As Singing Bird went to work gathering green willow cooking sticks and deftly butchering the hindquarter, the men sat around the fire with their weapons at hand and began visiting. Talk centered around the beaver trapping and trade, but they also shared information about the fierce Blackfoot Nation to the north. That talk was followed about griz and the problems they caused, especially at close range, and the price of plews, and on it went, until Singing Bird advised breakfast was almost ready. The meat was cooking away on roasting sticks and soon even better smells came from the two Dutch ovens sitting in a bed of glowing coals baking sourdough biscuits. Soon the men were wolfing down great chunks of almost raw meat, steaming hot coffee and Dutch-oven biscuits almost too hot to hold.

"Mm-mmm," Bridger said amid the lip-smacking sounds. "I guess your squaw can cook after all."

Singing Bird stood off to one side as the men ate. Then Ben suddenly motioned for her to join in and sit by him. Singing Bird took some meat and a biscuit, then demurely took a seat behind the men and out of sight. Jacob and Martin said nothing.

It had been obvious since they met Buffalo Calf and Singing Bird, that Ben was partial to her. Jacob had paid it no mind since Buffalo Calf and Singing Bird were married and happily so. However, Singing Bird would bury her husband's bones when they returned from rendezvous, according to Lakota tradition. With that accomplished, she would be free to do as she saw fit in her culture, or so Ben had told them. And to help her make that transition, all three men had already decided that Singing Bird, because of her hard work and having been married to Buffalo Calf, would get his share of the trappings.

"What do you fellas think about the three of us making camp next to your'n?" said Bridger through another mouthful of meat and biscuit. "That way, we would have more guns in case trouble was a-brewin'."

Jacob, Ben and Martin just looked at each other for common agreement. Once they decided with their "eyes," Jacob said, "That would be fine with us. We could use the extra rifles if needed and the good company goes without saying."

"Then it's done," said Bridger. "We will camp in that there adjacent grove of trees up yonder if that meets your fancy. That way we will be out of the way of your camp but close enough to lend a hand if the shootin' gets fierce and the killin' good."

With a grin over the newfound friendship and a wave of the hand, the men fell to the meal at hand until the entire hindquarter of elk and all the biscuits were consumed.

————

EVERY DAY THEREAFTER, two men from each camp rode out to hunt in different directions and replenish the meat supply. The valley was full of elk, pronghorn and deer but skimpy on the buffalo. However, "pickin's" were good as was the killing of many of the species, and so each camp member waxed fat under Mother Nature's bounty.

However, that was not the main reason for venturing forth each day. Both camps were loaded with the results of their last winter's and spring's trappings. They needed them at rendezvous, to be supplied with all the necessities for living in the wilderness the coming year.

Ben began his lessons again, teaching Jacob and Martin about what to expect at rendezvous, ticking off items on his fingers as he spoke: "With rendezvous comes a whole lot of hell-raising, trading, shooting, wrestling, foot racing, eating, drinking and visiting. Rendezvous also lets us see who lost their hair, and who didn't. If you listen to the loose tongues and boasting conversations, you might discover the location of some new trapping grounds. This will also be our only chance to hear the latest news of the civilized world, even though that news is going to be months old. Some of our more vulgar comrades will whore around and trade squaws as if they were merely livestock. But most importantly, pay attention to any discussions about where next year's rendezvous is going to be located."

No matter how hard the trappers looked, there was no evidence in sight of the supply train in the valley. As the men cast far and wide, they ran across other trappers and friendly Indians looking for that year's rendezvous site and supply train as well. Word had been let out at the last rendezvous that Cache Valley was the site for the next one and everyone was now responding. That is, those who were still left alive to do so. Soon tepees and lean-tos dotted the valley along the many waterways in anticipation of being supplied.

Come the first of July however, no supply trains were on hand in the valley to begin the trading.

————

ONE DAY, Glass and Oliver rode into camp late one evening, just a yellin' and a hellin'. "They're here, they are here!" yelled Glass.

The two camps came alive as everyone quickly gathered around the men for the news.

"I saw the pack strings and wagons gathered along a creek just south and west of here. There must be eighty mules loaded from stem to stem. They also brought five wagons heavily loaded, by the looks of the wheels sinking into the dirt. Henry Fraeb is leading the pack and says he will be ready tomorrow to trade so bring your plews, an empty gut and your drinking cups." Glass gushed out the words with a twinkle of anticipation in his eyes.

The rest of that evening was spent wolfing down great slabs of a freshly killed elk and making ready for the magic of the morrow that the rendezvous would bring.

————

DAYLIGHT FOUND JACOB, Ben, Martin and Singing Bird

packed and on the move. Jim Bridger and party, having less gear to assemble, had left earlier. By noon the rendezvous grounds were in sight. Approximately one hundred gleaming-white Indian tepees dotted the green meadows near a small creek. Pack strings of trappers and their pelts streamed into the area from all points of the compass, making the meadow come alive with the noises made by happy humanity.

Getting closer, Jacob's team could see the company's wagons in a rough semi-circle with buffalo robes scattered around on the ground and draped over quickly made wooden tables. That year's trade items and necessaries were laid out in gay profusion on the robes.

There were brass pots, frying pans, Dutch ovens, trade muskets and a few of the new Hawkens—which really hadn't yet hit their stride in the backcountry. On another side of the trade circle were coffee mills, bags of gaily colored trade beads, flintlock rifles, fowling pieces, Hudson's Bay Company two-and-a-half and three-point blankets. Near where the blacksmiths assembled, there were bridles, brass wire, fourth proof rum, spurs, horseshoes and shoe nails. Loaded on the hastily assembled tables were tin pans, ribbons, shot for fowling pieces, scarlet cloth, looking glasses, flints, copper kettles and stacked bars of washing soap. Closer to the fur-grading stations, laid out on more buffalo robes, were steel bracelets, iron rings, gunpowder, pigs of lead, spare rifle parts, the newest pistols and everything else in between. Off to one side of the main trading area stood small mountains of coffee beans in cloth bags, bags of salt, hard brown cones of sugar, flour, cornmeal, dried fruit, raisins, hard candy and other items vital to a quality of life in the wilderness.

The word was that Henry Fraeb was the man in charge of the merchant company's trades. And apparently, he had a convoluted excuse for being so late to rendezvous.

Thomas Fitzpatrick, it seems, had returned to St. Louis for backing and supplies for the Cache Valley rendezvous, without success. Then Smith, Sublette and Jackson, who were new owners of the company, were responsible for providing supplies to the current rendezvous, but they had traveled clear to Santa Fe to check out the trapping and trade opportunities in that area and to procure supplies. In route, Jed Smith was killed by the Comanches on the Cimarron River.

Seeking out and outfitting Fitzpatrick in Santa Fe, Sublette and Jackson dissolved their partnership.

Realizing many men depended on the supplies getting through, Fitzpatrick quickly headed north for the rendezvous site with his supply train. He met Henry Fraeb just east of South Pass, where he transferred his supplies to Fraeb. Then he turned around and headed back to St. Louis to make sure next year's supplies arrived on time.

Fraeb, now with the supplies, headed for the rendezvous site. Due to the number of delays, the general summer rendezvous in 1831 had been missed. Now, only a shortened later version could be held because the trappers had to get back and make winter camp before the snows fell, making trapping and travel difficult or impossible at best.

Henry Fraeb's buyers were already sorting through and grading beaver, elk, muskrat, deer, wolf, grizzly bear, gray fox, coyote, martin, river otter and buffalo hides. Pointed haggling filled the air as the trappers tried to sell high and the buyers traditionally bought low. The haggling became even more intense as the "firewater" slammed into the bottom of empty guts with predictable results.

The bottom line was always the same. This was the only store in town and if a trapper needed supplies for another year, it was either get them here or nowhere. Ultimately, transactions were made and in most cases the trappers found themselves breaking even or in the red to the trading company. Few trappers got rich, but the merchants bankrolling the rendezvous did very well because of the one hundred to seven hundred percent— or more—profits the trading companies were making. Most of the trappers were learning that living in the beautiful and wild West had its price, in more ways than one, be it on the end of a speeding, round lead ball, the point of an arrow or lance, the cold steel of a knife, the killing force of a tomahawk, the death hug of a grizzly, or the quick moving hands of a rendezvous fur trader hell bent on making a killin' off his fellow man.

Jacob and company moved their packs of furs into the

trading zone shortly after their arrival. Henry Fraeb himself, after looking at the numerous packs being offloaded, came over to personally get involved in trading with Jacob and company. Breaking down a few of the packs, he began sorting the beaver pelts from the smaller sizes to those larger-sized pelts called blankets. The more he looked, the more excited he became over the quality of the offering. Jacob and his partners' hides had been well cared for and showed it. Jacob looked over at Singing Bird and could tell she sensed her hard work on fleshing and stretching the hides was paying off, if the greedy look on Henry Fraeb's face meant anything. The pile of "blankets" grew until even other trappers had to stop and admire with envy Jacob's party's success.

Henry Fraeb finally contained himself and said, "Jacob, you and your'n have done very well. Especially for first-time trappers. I would say this hoard of furs will bring..." He cupped his chin in calculation, "...about four thousand in credit. That is giving you a price of three dollars each for the buffalo hides, four dollars for the beaver, three for your otter and thirty-three cents a pound for the deer skins. I can only give you twenty-five cents for each coonskin and twenty cents each for the muskrats though. " With those words, Fraeb stood back and intently looked at Jacob for his reply.

Without a word or hesitation, Jacob slowly shook his head no.

"That is a fair offer, Jacob," retorted Fraeb.

Jacob looked at his partners and they all agreed with

Jacob if the looks in their eyes meant anything. Jacob knew that except for salt, sugar, coffee beans, cornmeal and flour, they were in pretty good shape supply-wise. Having really stocked up in St. Louis the year before, not really knowing what they would need, was now paying big dividends. Nonetheless, they did need those few staples.

Shaking his head once again, Jacob said, "No, nothing less than five thousand in trade. Those furs are nothing but excellent quality and in a quantity guaranteed to bring you a handsome profit back in St. Louis. Less than that and we keep what we have. We can always trap our way south to Santa Fe, sell our furs and then overwinter there in comfort. Or we can make our way to Bent's Fort on the Arkansas River and sell them there for a higher price as well."

Henry Fraeb looked hard at Jacob. Then his eyes darted about to the other fur trappers intently looking on and listening with great interest to their dickering conversation.

If he gives in to me, thought Jacob, he will have to give in to the others with higher prices as well.

"I can't go any higher, Jacob. I made you a fair offer and it will have to stand," said Fraeb, but without a whole lot of conviction in his voice, Jacob thought.

"Please repack our furs. We have some horses to trade with the Indians along with some rifles, and when finished, we will return to claim our furs. Since the Indians have already traded with you, we can get in trade with them for the goods we need to see us through." With that Jacob turned and walked away, followed by Martin and Ben. Not a further word was spoken as none were needed.

Leaving the trading area, Jacob remembered the papers he and Martin had signed before leaving St. Louis with Clayborn: To sell to the company and purchase your stock from the same company at the going rate. There were also the words that they could trade with anyone else if the contract trader did not have what they needed. Jacob figured the extremely low price offered met that part of the escape clause. He also figured when he signed those papers it would cost some, but he didn't figure on taking such a big a loss and neither did his partners. If they had to, they would head for the nearest trading post or Taos—Ben knew the way—and trade their furs. Being a free trapper did have some benefits he reckoned.

Jacob, Ben and Martin returned to their herd of horses. They were being kept off at a safe distance by Singing Bird so they wouldn't co-mingle with other trappers' newly arriving horses. Jacob had heard from a fellow trapper that the Northern Ute contingent of Indians at the rendezvous were looking for a number of horses to help them pack back to their winter quarters all the supplies they had accumulated in trade from Henry Fraeb.

If that is the case, Jacob thought, maybe some good trades can be made in their camp. Jacob suggested to his partners that maybe they should explore that avenue of trade with their excess horses. They agreed and soon the three of them with the Crow horses in tow were en route to the Northern Ute camp, gaily set up in the meadow some half-mile distant.

When the men arrived, they were soon swamped with angry Ute Indians once the Indians saw and recognized fifteen horses being brought into their camp adorned with Crow markings. A riot almost ensued. The trappers were accused of being Crow lovers among many other words and taunts hurled their way that were even less civil. Soon Ute warriors surrounded and began threatening the men because of their affiliation with the hated Crow.

The chaos was soon stifled with the approach of Bull Bear, honored Ute war chief. Bull Bear walked gracefully up to the men and through sign language, asked who owned the horses belonging to the hated Crows. Jacob explained to Bull Bear that the horses had been taken in battle on the Big Sandy by his trappers.

Continually mindful of the problems that would follow if Bull Bear did not believe him, Jacob stressed that ownership of the horses had rightly passed to him and the other two men sitting on the horses behind him since all the Crow had been killed in hand to hand combat.

With those signed words, Bull Bear looked very surprised and a little amazed as did the other warriors standing around him watching the conversation. Bull Bear counted the horses, then signed his astonishment that Jacob and his men had been hugely outnumbered and yet somehow had survived.

Jacob could see the wheels turning in Bull Bear's mind over the bravery of Jacob, Martin and Ben. That bravery brought a warm smile to Bull Bear when he saw Martin's freshly damaged face, Jacob's sensitivity sitting in the saddle at an angle from unseen but obvious wounds, and the fresh absence of Ben's little finger on his still-swollen shooting hand.

"Come," Bull Bear said in English. "We will talk about trading our goods for these horses."

With that, he turned and walked towards a brightly decorated tepee at the center of the Ute camp. Pausing at the tepee flap, he made a gesture with his right hand of welcome and then entered the tepee. The three men dismounted but before heading for the tepee, Jacob, on a second thought, unrolled his saddle blanket.

Jacob picked out Bear's massive and very impressive front-claw grizzly bear necklace. Wrapping the many strands around his hand and forearm, Jacob led the way with Ben and Martin in trail into Bull Bear's tepee.

The three men entered and moved to the right, where they sat down facing Bull Bear. Jacob studied the older man. He was tall for an Indian and built like a small bull. His hands were almost ladylike as were his features. But his eyes spoke of a fierce pride and bravery honed by many moons of living, fighting and surviving in the wilds of North America.

Bull Bear examined the three men before him. "You

are strong men. You, Jacob, are tall, even for White Man. The horses are fine horses. They are Crow horses, and you have many wounds from battle. You must be very brave and have good fighting spirit. You are welcome in my tepee, and we will talk of trade of horses for goods now."

Now that Jacob was sitting down with Bull Bear, Chief of the Northern Ute Indians of the Bear Claw Band, he laid the magnificent grizzly bear-claw necklace at the chief's feet.

Bull Bear's eyes widened with very obvious surprise and amazement. He apparently had not expected such a gesture from a white man he did not know. In fact, everyone who had pushed their way into the tepee to view the proceedings looked at the necklace lying on the tepee floor and gasped in astonishment. Jacob knew that the size of the claws and their numbers meant that the necklace had been taken from at least four of the fearsome bears and large ones at that.

"It is yours!" said Jacob. An onerous hush overcame the crowd of Utes.

———

BULL BEAR PICKED up the necklace and frowned. *Does this man come to my tepee to insult me? This is a tremendous gift; I am not able to give anything of equal value. The Great Bear is our sacred spirit. A necklace of so many large claws is too great a gift.*

Bull Bear's thoughts moved quickly. If he could not come up with something of equal or greater value, he would lose face. *My warriors will see me as a weak chief I cannot be dishonored. I may have to kill this white man and bury him with his gift.*

The Ute Indian chief let the necklace's claws slowly clatter dryly through his fingers and back onto the tepee floor. *I have never seen such a necklace.* Bull Bear recalled the faces of his two sons who had each tried to take the Great Bear. They were of the soil now, as were many of the warriors who had tried to take the Great Bear. Those warriors who had returned from a hunt had been terribly disfigured.

Bull Bear noticed that his lesser chiefs were looking at each other in amazement at the gift. *They are wondering what I will give the white man in return. They are watching me to see if I am weak.*

———

INNOCENT TO ALL the consternation he had just caused but aware of the ripple of talk the necklace had created, Jacob just sat there waiting for Bull Bear's response. In fact, all Jacob wanted was to trade some of his horses for some much-needed supplies. He had figured the bear claw necklace would break down any existing barriers for what they had to trade, they being Crow horses and all. Nothing more and nothing less.

Before Jacob could compound his error by opening

up horse-trading talks, Bull Bear brusquely stood up towering over him. The chief said something to one of his warrior sub-chiefs standing inside the tepee loudly in the Ute language. The sub-chief hurriedly left the tepee.

Confused, Jacob continued sitting there in front of Bull Bear trying to figure out the meaning of the reaction he had just observed as a result of his gift.

The sub-chief returned shortly afterward with a large parfleche, a buffalo hide container used for storing items. Bull Bear signed that this was to be his gift to the white man in return for his great gift of the grizzly bear necklace. Then he took the parfleche from his sub-chief with great fanfare, and handed it to Jacob.

Because of its heavy and unexpected weight, Jacob almost dropped it.

Regaining his composure, Jacob slowly untied the leather thongs holding the top flap and looked inside. There inside were at least sixty ingots of gold, each stamped with the Queen of Spain's seal. Jacob was floored, as were Martin and Ben when they looked in as well.

This was a small fortune, worth far more than the four thousand that Henry Fraeb had offered for their furs. There must have been sixty pounds of gold ingots in that parfleche, probably collected in battle many years previously from the Spanish miners and explorers that the Utes hated so much. Jacob smiled in amazement at the chief who, with obvious relief at Jacob's surprise and pleasure, smiled back. Bull Bear made the sign of "Good trade." Jacob replied in kind, and the awkward cultural moment passed.

Earlier, Jacob and company had decided to trade fifteen of the nineteen horses captured from the Crows on the Big Sandy. They had kept back four of the best horses for packing their soon to be acquired goods from the rendezvous, and so they had entered Bull Bear's camp with the intention of trading the remaining horses for items they needed. Horses were always in short supply with the Indians and Jacob was now met eagerly with potential traders. Receiving the chief's blessing after the grizzly bear claw incident in the tepee, the air had been cleared and the trading began in earnest.

The entire party moved to the outside, and Utes began running off to find things to trade for the Crow horses. The reorganization gave Ben a moment to whisper to Jacob in a conspiratorial hush. "You are one lucky son of a bitch!" he said. "You have no idea how close you came to getting us all killed and starting a war between Bull Bear and the rest of the rendezvous."

Jacob gave him a quizzical look, not yet understanding. "When you give a gift to an Indian, especially a chief, he has to give you something in return of equal or greater value or he loses face. He would appear weak in front of his people. Rather than lose face, they will kill the gift bearer. This is what they mean by 'Indian Giver.' And boy, did you stumble in a pile of buffalo shit. This is the Bear Claw Clan, get it?"

Jacob rolled his eyes as the realization settled in. The

grizzly bear was sacred to these people. To them, it was like a holy relic from the white man's cross of Christ.

"Well, it got us all this gold," Jacob said, sheepishly.

"You lucky son of a bitch!"

"Well, I won't try my luck again. Next time, I'll know better and I'll stick with beads."

The horses were soon quickly exchanged for tanned buffalo hides, baskets of eared com, bags of salt from the Great Salt Lake, a new and larger tepee for Singing Bird, and tanned bighorn sheep hides. From previous trades with Henry Fraeb, the Utes had numerous sacks of corn-meal, flour, pepper, pinto beans, horse blankets, horse-shoes, powder, lead, trade beads, cones of sugar and coffee beans, which they traded for the trappers' horses.

At last, there were only four horses left. The Utes had run out of items they freely wished to trade or that Jacob wanted, but they still wanted the remaining four horses, mainly because they had at one time belonged to the hated Crow. After much haggling and discussion, the crowd of Indians parted and two battered, white teenage boys were pushed forward.

The boys wore little clothing and looked not only half-starved but mistreated as well. They were about the same age, just become men. One had blue eyes and greasy blond hair, the other, brown in eyes and mane. A well of lost youth lay buried in both their eyes.

Jacob looked over at Martin. Disgust was written all over his face. A quick look at Ben showed the same degree of displeasure. It was alright to trade in nature's abundance but human trade was not to their way of liking.

One Indian took a tree limb he had been holding and struck the closest boy because he was not walking as fast as he wanted. The lad, even though scared to death but still full of spunk, grabbed the limb from the offender's hand and broke it in half. That got him a quick beating with a horse quirt until Jacob stepped in and stopped the whipping.

"That will be a fair trade! Four horses for the boys!" Jacob said, looking sharply at the Indian who had brought the boys forward from the crowd. Ben stepped forward and quickly translated Jacob's harsh words into sign.

The Indian's smile at such a deal for two sullen spawn from a white man showed the transaction more than met the Indian trader's fancy. In sign language, he accepted the deal.

Ben handed the Indian the reins of the four horses and it was apparent that this Indian instantly became the talk of the tribe for coming out on the better side of the exchange.

Martin and Ben led the two young men away from the crowd of Northern Ute Indians before they changed their minds and wanted them back. Jacob now realized the tribe was out of other items his group might need. Because of that, and because he no longer had the stomach to trade with the savage Utes, he did not mention the guns taken from the dead Crows that they still had to trade.

That would be just all we need, he thought. The Utes wanting the rifles but having nothing left in which to trade. All he could foresee were hard feelings all around and maybe even violence. Thanking the chief for his hospitality, Jacob excused himself from the Ute Indian village.

When Jacob caught up with Martin, his longtime friend said to him, "These boys are in bad shape. I asked them for their names, but they only tremble in fear. I cannot get them to tell me where they came from or what happened that they became captives of the Utes."

Jacob looked to the boys. They shirked in fear, afraid of what they would be forced to do as slaves of the Mountain Men.

"You are safe now," Jacob told the boys. "We'll get you fed and cleaned up."

It was as if the boys did not understand English. They huddled together, pure fear in their faces.

"Martin, Ben, take these boys to Singing Bird. Have her feed them, and see if they'll clean up. Then let's meet at the other Indian camp over there and see what we can get for the Crow rifles."

The boys shuffled off with Martin and Ben, while Jacob waited. He watched the boys go, then realized that he had a heavy parfleche full of gold to care for. He followed his friends, carrying the heavy bag. By the time he reached camp, the boys had already eaten voraciously and fallen fast asleep.

A BAND of Northern Cheyenne at the rendezvous that were friendly to the Lakota and Singing Bird's band were given the opportunity to trade for the fusils taken from the Crows. In that trade, Jacob got a large cast-iron cooking pot, two Dutch ovens recently traded from Henry Fraeb, and one twenty-five pound keg of powder —the big Hawkens could kill anything but they ate powder in large gulps. He also acquired a dozen of the new Green River skinning knives, two military saddles— one of which had the blood of the trooper who had previously owned it still spewed across the pommel— several new Hudson's Bay Company three-point winter coats, and a stack of beautifully tanned elk and grizzly bear hides as only the Cheyenne women could tan. Singing Bird in that trade also arranged for eight parfleches full of cake pemmican and ten pair of buffalo-hide winter moccasins, decorated with as fine a set of blue and red glass-bead work Jacob had ever seen.

By the time Jacob finished trading with the Cheyenne, Martin and company had re-loaded the packs of furs Henry Fraeb had broken down and examined earlier back onto their pack animals. Fraeb was standing by the pack string with a long face as the finishing touches were added to the ropes holding the packs in place. It was apparent he was somewhat downcast at losing his opportunity for such a large and quality acquisition.

"Jacob, wait. We need to talk. I want those furs and you know it."

Jacob just nodded. He could sense Ben and Martin perking up their ears at some good old-fashioned horse trading between two white men now that Henry Fraeb's bluff had been called.

"I will throw in two brand new .54-caliber Hawkens like the kind the three of you carry. I will also throw in some primers, nipples, nipple picks, and give you forty-five hundred in trade from the rest of my goods for those furs," Fraeb quietly squeaked out.

"Only if you also include in that trade two additional twenty- five pound kegs of powder, ten pounds of those English glass beads of Singing Bird's choosing, and a bolt of that red calico cloth she favors as well," flatly stated Jacob.

Singing Bird had always been stoic and silent when the men were making deals, but now, this once, she squealed in delight. She collected herself quickly, though, and told Jacob "Thank you" in a quiet voice.

Jacob's lingering pain dissolved for an instant. Singing Bird's smile cheered him; for too long, she had been grieving Buffalo Calf's brutal death. Jacob knew she liked the English beads, but for some reason, probably some Lakota "Way" he didn't know about, Singing Bird had held back from asking for them. The smile was the first step to healing her heart, and hadn't she been promised a full share of the profits? Beads were such a simple thing, but like the gold, the boys, the grizzly bear-claw necklace,

Indians found a different value in things than white men did.

"Jacob, you are killing me," exclaimed Fraeb, "but you have a deal."

Jacob grinned and, with affirming glances from Ben, Martin and Singing Bird, nodded acceptance. With that bit of business done, the four men set about unloading the furs for the second time, this time for good.

In addition to the goods Henry Fraeb had thrown into the deal for their furs, Jacob, Martin, Ben and Singing Bird used their forty-five hundred in credit to replace their much needed goods and yet have some left over to trade with any friendly Indians they met on the trail over the next year: four additional twenty-five-pound kegs of gunpowder of the first quality, six North West fuzils that were in better shape than the Crow rifles traded to the Cheyenne, four square axes, a bolt of gray com- mon-quality cloth and twelve New House No. 4 beaver traps. Martin selected four pounds of thread, four gross of iron finger rings for trade, ten pounds of assorted red and blue glass beads and four pounds of vermilion. Ben selected twelve iron files because he was always losing the old ones, five gallons of fourth proof rum, two bolts of assorted colored ribbons for trade, eight dozen flints for their new trade rifles and twenty assorted iron buckles which he used in tack repairs. The group also selected twenty fire steels good for Indian trades, thirty pounds of first quality James River tobacco, thirty pounds of lead pigs for the Hawkens, a new coffee mill...and on it went.

When they finished with their shopping, as it were, the partners led their groaning horses and the two boys back to their camp with their rendezvous acquisitions. They had brought in high-quality furs and had done well in their trade with the fur company representative. They had paid high prices for their goods but out here in the wilderness that was the way it was and the goods received were of quality.

More importantly, they had come away from the rendezvous with their trade goods and had not blown it on women, gambling or liquor. This was something many of the rest of the trappers had not done. Most of the trappers had to leave their marks on the "paper" for the needed goods in order to work and survive the following year because they had lost the value of their furs on a few days' foolishness at the rendezvous. In so doing, they found themselves in debt to the fur company before they had even trapped one beaver for the coming season. A common financial position most contract trappers found themselves in year after year, Ben remarked. This was a situation many never got out of until they were killed or they just disappeared into the mountains never to be seen or heard from again.

"However," Ben chuckled, "many consider it a small price to pay to live in a land next to the hands and face of God."

Last but not least, Jacob's party had done well by the

Indians even to the point that they now possessed at least sixty pounds of gold ingots as well. An item that could potentially lead to many comforts once they were worn out physically or the fur trade had passed them by in its trek into history, comforts in the form of land acquisitions for a farm or cattle ranch or just retirement in a town once that point in life had been reached.

And then there were the two rescued captives. Back at camp by the lake, Jacob took a long, hard look at the two kids he had acquired in the horse trade. Singing Bird was feeding them again and they were eating like they hadn't seen a square meal in a month. In fact, they were pretty scrawny as well and covered with sores and bruises from being abused by the Utes.

When they had eaten their fill, Jacob sat the boys down around the campfire, with Ben and Martin standing alongside. He tried to unravel the mystery of their lives prior to their rather fortunate meeting.

"Where do you come from?" Jacob asked. "Do you have any family?"

The taller boy began blurting out some words. Something about being brothers from Ohio, settled on the Western Slope of the Rocky Mountains, a father and mother and three sisters, a raid by the Northern Ute that killed their parents and the other settlers and split their sisters up among other tribes, know not where...

That was all Jacob could make of the babble before the boy, and then his brother, broke down sobbing uncontrollably.

At that moment, Singing Bird told the men to pry no further. She took the boys to the lake and had them wash off the months of dirt and dried blood from their bodies. When they returned to the camp, she gathered up and provided two Hudson's Bay Company blankets so they could cover themselves as they stood shivering by the lake. She took them back to her old tepee and told them it was their home now. There were plenty of sleeping furs inside and soon the two boys had cried themselves to sleep once more.

Walking over to Ben, Singing Bird told him in sign that she needed to erect her new tepee recently acquired from Henry Fraeb. Soon the men had it up and staked out so the wind would not blow it over, but having used the parts of at least twenty buffalo skins to construct the structure, being blown over was a minimal concern. Without a word, Singing Bird moved her remaining things into the new tepee, taking the fowling piece she now considered hers, a new bag of glass beads and a bolt of bright red cloth.

After the boys and Singing Bird went to bed, the men gathered around the parfleche full of golden ingots. Jacob spilled them out on the ground by the fire. Their gleam dancing in the fire light was almost devilish.

Where had they come from? How old were they? How many men had died before they were given up? These were just some of the many more questions swirling through Jacob's mind. Jacob fingered through the ingots, then started dividing them into four piles. As it turned out, the numbers came out evenly.

Jacob pushed one pile towards Martin and another towards Ben. He said, "Those are your shares. I will take one share and give the other to Singing Bird. I suggest each of us hold on to these so when the beaver trade gives out or we get too old to continue trapping, we will have a grub or land stake in whatever we choose to do."

The men looked at Jacob and heard words of wisdom. Soon each of them had hidden the golden ingots among their most cherished items. Jacob took Singing Bird's share and placed it back in the parfleche. He walked over to her new tepee and placed her share in front of the entrance flap. He thought that he would explain in the morning. He headed for his bed and some much needed sleep. His old wounds received at the Big Sandy were still aching and to lay down and rest would help ease the pain.

The next day, Jacob, Ben and Martin returned to the rendezvous to pick up the rest of their trade goods. That included more kegs of powder, tins of primers and pigs of lead because those damn Hawkens shot through a lot of lead as well as powder. They purchased goods that would now be needed more than ever with the addition of the two boys to the flock, if that was their choosing. Always needed were whetstones because of the high breakage and loss rates. So, eight more whetstones were also added to their goods. That was followed with the addition of ten additional New House No. 4 beaver traps now that they anticipated the boys would become new members to the group. Additionally, new halter ropes, four new packsaddles, bits, halters, horseshoes and two pounds of horseshoe nails joined the increasing pile of goods. Lastly, two shovels, a package of heavy leather sewing needles, another coffee mill, tin plates, spoons and cups rounded out their needs. They loaded all those items on their four new packhorses from the Indian raid back on the Big Sandy and their own riding horses, then they slowly walked back to their camp.

When they arrived, they were surprised to see Jim Bridger and Hugh Glass asleep back in their old camp. Both were pretty hung-over but alive and well. They, too, had brought loaded pack animals back to camp with trade goods for the coming year. One look told the three that these men were in poor shape from too much whiskey and by the sounds of their snoring, lost to the world. Jacob, Ben and Martin went to their own camp and unloaded the packs off their animals so the mules could feed and not lose the trade items in the process. Bridger and Glass found solace in their beds for the rest of the evening, not moving a lick as they snored off a good drunk.

———

BULL BEAR ALSO FOUND SOLACE. He held the Great Bear necklace the White Man had traded him for the gold. He chuckled to the night breezes outside his tepee.

I have swindled the great white swindler. I am now rid of

the gold that has caused my people much grief and harm. Little do they know the gold is cursed. And I did not lose face in front of my people, who have no understanding of why so many of us have died or have been mauled by the Great Bear, or why we have so little food.

Bull Bear placed the bear claws around his neck. *Both the White Man and my people will believe it was a fair trade. This sacred necklace will keep us from harm, I know it, and with the cursed gold gone from my people, we will have plenty in moons to come.*

The Ute chief remembered the day the cursed gold came into his possession. They had come upon a Spaniard holy man, with his tribe of weak-willed men digging in the Earth, stealing from her the gold metal that makes the White Men crazy. His warriors quickly killed all the rest, and only the holy man was left. Because Bull Bear spoke the Spaniard language, his people had brought the gold and the holy man to him.

"WHY YOU DIG FROM MOTHER EARTH?" Bull Bear had asked. Instead of a reply, the Spaniard spit in his face and called him a spawn of the Diablo, no doubt an unholy spirit.

When Bull Bear told the holy man that he would be scalped and his skin cut from his body, left in the desert to be eaten by scorpions, the holy man showed much courage and began to sing a holy song in a strange language. Then, when he finished his song, he turned to

Bull Bear and said, "This gold, may God curse it, and may he curse anyone who possesses it." He spit again in Bull Bear's face.

In rage, Bull Bear had cut the Spaniard holy man's throat and left him to bleed, never to say another word.

The gold was cursed, though. All these years, my people suffered, but no more. Now, the Great Bear is with the people again, and no Diablo can best the medicine of the Great Bear. Bull Bear put his hand to the necklace and felt its spirit course through him. For the first time in as long as he could remember, he slept peacefully.

16

THE HUNTER BROTHERS

THE NEXT MORNING, JACOB, MARTIN AND BEN WENT BACK to the rendezvous to pick up additional supplies. When they returned to camp, they were surprised to see the two teenage boys each wearing an altered set of buckskin shirts and pants, clothing that had originally belonged to Ben. Additionally, they each sported a new Hudson's Bay Company blanket coat for winter travel, and they each wore a new pair of moccasins that Jacob had received in partial trade for the Crow's rifles. Each boy had a smile a mile wide to match.

Those two young men may not have had a family for all intents and purposes but they sure were dressed up fit to kill and now looking like family, Jacob thought.

Jacob asked the two boys to sit with him on a log by the fire. He loaded up his pipe and—mindful of the ass chewing he got the night before from Singing Bird's eyes for making the boys cry—he tried a different approach to understanding the boys' life history.

"My name is Jacob. That tall one here with the scar on his cheek is Martin, a boyhood family friend. My other partner is Ben, a friend Martin and I met on the boat that brought us to this land from St. Louis. They are both Delaware Indians from back east of the Mississippi River who lost their homes just like you boys. Only in their cases, to crooked land-thieving speculating white men. Me, I came from a faraway land called Kentucky where I, too, lost my parents in an Indian raid. We are fur trappers now, and with the exception of Ben, have been so but for a short time. But we enjoy the wilderness and plan on making it our home unless we cripple up from a horse wreck, meet the wrong end of Ephraim, get stuck with an arrow or just roll over and die. Hostile Indians looking to lift one's hair or crooked thieving white men always being a problem out here makes for a concern if one is to see the next sunrise. So much so, that one has to learn to stand on his own two legs. Otherwise, he will become wolf, bear or vulture bait. So with that in mind, can either of you boys shoot?"

"Yes, sir," they both uttered quickly in the same breath. "Our Pa taught the both of us to shoot and shoot straight when we was young," said the one with deep blue eyes.

"What are your names?" asked Jacob as Ben and Martin moved closer to the fire in order to hear better.

"My name is Jeremiah Hunter," said the one with

deep, piercing blue eyes. This was the same lad who had defiantly taken the switch earlier from the Ute Indian and broken it, only to be rewarded with a thrashing from a horse quirt before Jacob stepped in. Jacob smiled at the name, as it brought back memories of his uncle Jeremiah living in Kentucky.

"And yours?" he asked, pointing the stem of his pipe at the boy with dark brown eyes and heavy thatch of hair to match.

The lad sat up straight as if to emphasize his size saying, "My name is Leo Hunter."

"How old are you boys?" Jacob asked.

"Sixteen, sir," responded the boys in unison.

Jacob had to smile, as did Martin. The two of them were sixteen when they left home to venture west and make their marks. Jacob, Ben and Martin all looked at each other over the boys' easy and correct manners with a smile. That kind of behavior went a long way in the frontier and in their camp.

"Well, Jeremiah, Leo," said Jacob, "I've told you our story. I know you've had a hard time of it, but I'd like to hear your tale, orphan to orphan. Tell me where you come from, and if you have family, and how you came to be captives of the Ute Indians. Pretty much the same questions I asked yesterday, but now that you both have a belly full of good eatin' and a decent night's sleep, perhaps you can buck up and give me an account I can follow. You were so upset and darn exhausted yesterday, I could barely understand a word."

"Yes, sir," Leo said, sitting up straight with renewed vigor. His brother Jeremiah added, "And sirs, please don't think we don't appreciate being rescued and sharing your gracious hospitality. Your buying our freedom, well, it came so sudden that we didn't know what was happening to us. I guess we gave up hope."

"Yes, sir," Leo repeated. "And Ma always said the Bible tells us, never give up hope, God will take care of us."

"That, and a few Crow horses," Ben chuckled. The boys were too gratified to get Ben's little joke.

Leo continued. "And thank Miss Singing Bird for us, sir. She does cook good food, the best we have had in a long time."

"Call me 'sir' one more time," Jacob growled, "and I'll take you back to them savage Utes. I told you, my name is Jacob. I'm hardly much older than you are." Jacob extended his hand. First Leo, then Jeremiah took the hand, and they all shook in the way that says a boy is now a man among men. "So, I'm waiting, what's your story?"

Leo and Jeremiah looked to each other. Leo nodded to indicate Jeremiah should tell the story:

They had come from Ohio with their parents and three sisters some years earlier. They had settled on the Western Slope of the Rocky Mountains, not far from Antoine Robidoux's trading post at Fort Uncompahgre. Their father and two other families had banded together and were beginning to farm the rich Colorado River valley. A large band of Northern Ute Indians swooped down, and killed or captured all three families. The Utes burned their home, killed their parents and split up their sisters among several other tribes; they knew not where.

"Leo and I, we're all that's left of our family, all we have is each other." Jeremiah smiled at his brother, a smile that apparently been dormant for some time.

Leo and Jeremiah were enslaved by Bull Bear's band for about eight months, since just a few weeks before Christmas. They had been made to do the worst jobs and often pulled travois when there were not enough horses, switched and beat for miles a day.

"If it wasn't for Jeremiah, I would've given up a long time ago," Leo added. "He always said a time would come when we would escape, and we tried a few times, but trying to outrun a Ute is like trying to outrun a grizzly. They just don't give up."

"We had been thinking the rendezvous would be a chance to make a run for it," Jeremiah said. "But them filthy Indians must have been thinking the same thing, because they kept us apart and tied up, out of sight. You, sir, ah, Jacob, then traded us for those horses. And we are so grateful."

"Well, here is where we are, boys. We will spend one more day at the rendezvous carrying on and having a good time. Then we are heading back into the Bighorns for another trapping season. It is getting late in the season and we must head for our winter camp and lay in some meat, hay and wood before the snow flies. Hence the need for an early departure from this here shindig. Since you boys don't have nobody, you have two choices to make, to my way of thinking. We can outfit you with our extra horses and gear and let you ride out so you can try to get back to Ohio to your kinfolk, or you can join up with us to become free trappers," said Jacob.

Both boys looked at each other and then Jeremiah said, "May we join up with you? Since you four are all we have now and neither of us remembers much of Ohio nor where the rest of our kin went with the Indians, we want to think of you as our family. Plus, we don't want to go back to those Indians ever again!" Jacob turned to Ben and Martin. "What do you think? Keep them or skin and pelt them out for sale at the next rendezvous?"

"Well, if they can ride, shoot and skin, we might as well as keep them," said Martin with his twisted form of a smile. "After all, extra hands in this country are like good meat, never goes to waste," he continued.

The looks on Ben and Singing Bird's faces told it all.

You would think Jeremiah and Leo were the children Singing Bird never had. *I don't think she is of the mind to lose them entirely to a bunch of raggedy fur trappers who think of nothing but eating, belching and beaver trapping,* Jacob mused.

———

THE NEXT DAY, the men, including Bridger and Glass, stood at the edge of a nearby copse of trees that sheltered their camps with rifles in hand.

"That staub on that stump out there about seventy

yards is your target. Think you can hit it?" Jacob asked Leo.

"Yes, sir," he replied as he hoisted the heavy Hawken to his right shoulder.

Ben had spent about ten minutes going over the rifle and its workings with both of the boys just moments before so they would be ready for this. It was obvious from their questions and demeanor that both boys were skilled in the use of rifles, especially older-style flintlocks.

Ka-boom rolled out the roar of the Hawken along with a cloud of white smoke. The staub on the stump exploded and was no more. The men looked approvingly at Leo as he slowly lowered the rifle with a big grin of satisfaction on his face.

Then it was Jeremiah's turn. "What do you want me to shoot at, Jacob?" asked the boy.

"Take that thick limb on the log to the rear of where your brother just shot," Jacob replied.

Jeremiah reloaded the rifle and then hoisted the heavy Hawken with ease. He set the trigger and, taking less time than his brother, touched her off. The limb did a cartwheel into the air ten feet above the log before sailing off into the sagebrush and landing in a puff of dust.

The men looked at each other in amazement.

These kids can shoot! Jacob thought approvingly.

Even Jim Bridger just nodded his head at the exhibition the two boys just put on.

"Well, I've certainly seen enough," Jacob said. "I sure

can't see any reason why we need to waste any more powder or balls. You two certainly know your way around a rifle. Let's go back to camp. Singing Bird is waiting for a report on your abilities. She's a full partner in this operation, so she has a right to have her curiosity settled right away."

Singing Bird went to meet the group of men as they returned and, after taking one look at the men's faces, realized the boys had just passed muster. And from the looks on the boy's faces, they shot circles around anything the men had thought possible. She flashed a huge grin at that revelation. A short time later, she quietly approached Jacob when he was alone with the horses.

In sign, she asked about the yellow metal that made white men mad that Jacob had laid at the flap of her tepee the night before. Jacob explained in his broken Lakota what he had said to the others the evening before about the golden ingots.

"We traded bear-claw necklace for...yellow metal. White Men say 'gold.' It is very valuable. You are partner, you get equal share."

Singing Bird was taken aback by Jacob's explanation. Slowly, she remembered that the men said she was an equal among them. She blushed, and signed "Fair trade." Then she walked back to her tepee where the parfleche of gold still lay.

Still smiling at being considered a full member of the group— something very unusual for any Indian woman

—she picked up her share of the golden treasure and put it into her tepee. She had never experienced her own wealth before, and she found the new feeling of being an equal much to her way of liking.

Singing Bird cooked dinner. She realized, for the first time, that merely by cooking, she contributed to the success of the trapping party, a party that had grown. When everyone finished eating by the campfire, she watched as Jacob asked all the men to come with him to his lean-to. Even Bridger and Glass were invited.

Tom Oliver had left his two friends, Bridger had said, to head out with another group for the Sierra Nevada Mountains, in California. Singing Bird did not know where this was, and she missed Oliver, because he had always been the first to compliment her on her meals. But Bridger was always quick to outdo Oliver's compliments, and tonight had been no exception.

As she collected the tin plates and started to wash them, the men returned. Jacob and Martin carried the extra two Hawkens they had purchased from Henry Fraeb, and a bundle of other items she could not see.

"Singing Bird," Jacob said, "please put that down. We have a special occasion and the need of all partners to agree." Singing Bird, knowing the importance of being part of the company of trappers, set the plates on one of the logs and approached the others.

"As you all know, Jeremiah and Leo Hunter have asked to be partners in our trapping company. They have demonstrated the ability to shoot keenly, and they are brave in the face of adversity. Martin, Ben and I agree that it will be advantageous to include them in our company. We need all the partners to agree, so what say you, Singing Bird."

Singing Bird almost burst out with laughter. Certainly, she wanted the boys to join them, they so needed a new family. Jacob's official manner, like an Indian chief divvying the parts of a buffalo, seemed silly. But this was important company business, and this was, she suddenly realized, the first important decision she had ever been asked to make.

"Yes, I welcome Jeremiah Hunter and Leo Hunter to this company." She reached out to the boys as she had seen the others do, to shake hands. Instead, Jeremiah and Leo hugged her while Bridger led the others in three cheers of "Hip, Hip, Hurrah!" Jacob picked up both Hawkens and continued the ceremony. He handed a rifle to each of the brothers. "Jeremiah and Leo Hunter, these rifles are yours to use in what lies ahead. Take care of them, and they will take care of you."

Jacob opened the bundle and brought forth several new Green River gutting and skinning knives. He handed these to the brothers as well and said, "These are yours, as well. You will discover that next to your rifle, the knife is your best friend. Care for them well, and learn how to use them, because they just may save your lives someday."

The two boys examined the weapons in their hands and then thanked all of the company.

Jacob continued, "Tomorrow, each of you can pick

out a horse not yet claimed from the herd, and you can use the military saddles we got in trade from the Cheyenne."

Martin reached out to the boys with a bag of possibles, with ammo and powder and tools for the Hawkens. "Now that you are part of our family, you should look the part."

"Welcome to the family," Ben said.

Singing Bird watched the two boys intently. She could feel that they felt happier than they had ever been in a very long time. She also caught the instance of Martin calling the company "family." She silently agreed with the term.

In a rare display, Martin, Ben and Jacob in turn clasped the Hunter brothers, slapping each other hard on the backs. Singing Bird snuck another round of hugs in the latest "Hurrah."

———

THE MEN TOOK the boys to the rendezvous the next day. They all chuckled at the looks on Leo and Jeremiah's faces. It was obvious neither boy had ever been to such an event as a participant. While there, the company traded some of their remaining credit with Henry Fraeb for several more powder horns, bullet molds and extra ramrods for the boys' Hawkens.

Many of the other trappers found themselves enviously looking upon those young men and their fine rifles.

Flintlocks were good and in abundance with the trappers in general. However, the new heavy-barreled Hawkens were in a class all of their own and admired as such.

That was soon born out when the boys entered several shooting contests with the old-guard trappers. Soon piles of beaver pelts were wagered as the boys shot the "eyes" out of every target put before them.

When they returned to camp that night, Jacob told Martin that he couldn't have been prouder if the boys had been his. They had won two excellent riding horses and a pile of pelts in the shoot offs, and in the process, besting some of the finest shooters at the rendezvous. That ability to shoot well and accurately would soon be put to practice, in the most deadly and lifesaving of ways.

The next morning as they broke camp, Jim Bridger came over to say goodbye.

"I will be going west out Pacific Ocean way," he declared. "Which way you and the boys be agoin'?" he asked.

"Back to the Bighorn Mountains. There is still good trapping there to be had and we mean to catch what we can while the trappin's are good," replied Jacob.

"Well, manage to keep your hair so we can meet next year at Pierre's Hole." With that and a firm handshake, Bridger mounted up. With a wave of hands from both he and Glass, they meandered westward to new adventures of their own.

After Bridger and Glass left, it took another hour to

get Jacob and company loaded and ready. With Martin in the lead, followed by Jacob, the boys, Ben, Singing Bird, and their pack strings, they strung out pretty impressively. They now had seventeen horses both for riding and packing in their strings. Every pack animal was carrying a load as well, as were the two horses pulling the travois.

Martin pulled back to Jacob and told him, "It is a good feeling to have done so well from our labors and have so many goods to show for our work. Without a doubt, we have enough supplies for a good year, and if necessary, two, before we need to resupply. And we are now a group of five men who are more than capable of caring for ourselves, and with Singing Bird as the camp boss, that makes it all the better."

They retraced their steps back to the Big Sandy where they had lost Buffalo Calf. They approached Buffalo Calf's resting site, only to find his burial scaffold gone. Riding up to the spot, they observed that Buffalo Calf's bones had been picked clean and were scattered about by flesh-eaters of every kind. Closer examination revealed that buffalo had used the vertical scaffold timbers as rubbing posts and knocked the whole thing down in the process. Once on the ground, the scavengers had picked at Buffalo Calf's remains.

Singing Bird gathered up his now dried bones and buried them by a large boulder overlooking the Big Sandy with the appropriate Lakota ceremony. The Lakota ritual and reason for their return was completed and now she was a free women to choose any man for a husband if she so desired or was of a mind.

For the next several weeks, Jacob and company steadily traveled back over their earlier route to their winter quarters. All along the way, the three men took turns teaching and training the boys in the ways of the trapper, of survival and how to read the wilderness. That included the use and care of a knife and rapid reloading of their Hawkens.

Singing Bird seemed happier than she ever had been, especially with the attention from the two boys who took to her as their own mother...and from Ben, who now never left her side.

They found their old camp little used and not badly rundown after the several months of neglect. Someone had been inside after they headed out for the rendezvous and had left the front door ajar, but other than that, the place was like they had left it. The men placed their horses in the corral and started unpacking the horses. Jacob lifted a pack heavy with four kegs of powder for storage in the cave and staggered into the cabin under its awkward heavy weight.

"Oof!" Jacob cried. A surprisingly strong smell, almost a stench, had met his nostrils as he entered the darkened interior.

"Ugghhh!" *Wham.*

Jacob was knocked flat on his back.

Stunned for a second, he became aware of the fetid

breath of an extremely mad boar grizzly bear tearing at the pack of gunpowder kegs lying on top of him.

Jacob rolled back and forth underneath, all the while trying to keep the protective pack between himself and the grizzly's savage front claws and snapping teeth. "Help!"

The bear finally ripped the heavy pack off Jacob like it was light as a feather, then reached down and grabbed Jacob by the front of his shirt with its teeth.

Jacob, in his defense, grabbed the bear's face with his hands and tried to poke out its eyes with his fingers.

All that did was to push the bear into a monstrous, towering rage. It lifted Jacob up off the floor effortlessly and with a vicious head swing, the bear hurled Jacob into the back wall of the cabin.

Crunch. Jacob heard his almost inert body as it hit the solidly built wall.

Stunned but still in some sort of mental command, Jacob went for his knife and pistol only to feel the bear bite down hard on his left shoulder. Then he was lifted once again by the bear's front paws as he went for the dreaded "bear hug" and head-crushing bite.

Boom-Boom. The inside of the cabin exploded in flame and white black-powder smoke. With that Jacob was hurled to the cabin wall once again as the grizzly fell back and crumpled alongside another wall.

Jacob strained to shunt aside his pain and reassess his situation.

The boys, Leo and Jeremiah, stood at the open cabin

door. They had shot their Hawkens simultaneously. The heavy lead balls had flown true, and had struck the huge grizzly squarely in the head, and killed it instantly. The explosive force of the bullets' crushing impacts from such a short range is what must have hurled Jacob to one comer of the room and the bear to the other.

Stunned but still alert, Jacob staggered to his feet in an attempt to get away from the still-twitching bear.

It was all over. Jacob staggered out of the cabin on his own adrenaline and sat down heavily on a log bench to recover from the most recent deadly scare of his young life.

THE BEAR MUST HAVE TAKEN up residence in the cabin. When I walked in on the giant, I must have roused it from sleep. I bet it thought it was in danger. That's why it attacked me in true grizzly fashion! Jacob loosed a soulful sigh. Thank God I had the packsaddle loaded with bulky kegs of powder between me and the bear when I walked in. Had I not...

Leo and Jeremiah both stood in front of Jacob, worriedly looking him over to make sure he was all right. The looks on their faces spoke to more than just considering Jacob as a friend. Then they were quickly pushed aside by Singing Bird.

Singing Bird took Jacob's ripped buckskin shirt in her hands and lifted it over his head.

"Jacob," Singing Bird reported, "you have four bite

wounds. Very ugly, very deep. From canine teeth. Down to the shoulder bone. You are lucky shoulder not broken."

Jacob grimaced. "Still dangerous enough of a bite to take in the backcountry." His shoulder was now beginning to stiffen up but Singing Bird was right on it. She opened up the puncture wounds slightly with her knife to the depth of canine teeth's penetration, then washed out the furiously bleeding wound. Into that she poured some evil-smelling, oily looking, black liquid that burned like all hell. However, Jacob had come to trust Singing Bird and her medicinal remedies as he bravely put up with the stink and searing pain of her doctoring.

Meanwhile, the other four men dragged the grizzly out of the cabin with difficulty and laboriously hung it on the big-game skinning pole between two aspens adjacent to the cabin. It was a very large male grizzly, probably measuring at least nine to ten feet in length and weighing at least nine hundred pounds. The pelt was not in its prime but the bear was rolling fat and much good bear oil was in store once they rendered it out. That would go double for good eats with the huge hams and shoulders once smoked.

"How ironic," said Martin. "The bear tried to kill and eat Jacob. Now the moccasin is literally on the other foot."

With the bear's smell heavy in the air, the horses began to get a little uneasy. Seeing that, Martin and the boys reinforced the corral poles so the horses could not spook and escape no matter how nervous they got.

Singing Bird, in the meantime, was quickly cleaning out the cabin of the refuse and offal the bear had left behind. Soon everything was shipshape in the cabin and the men began to unload the rest of their precious supplies into the cave, cabin and lean-tos. That completed, they set about erecting the tepees for Singing Bird and the boys.

When the horses settled down a little, the boys hobbled all of them and herded them into the nearby meadow so they could graze and water. However, as everyone worked, they kept their firearms handy. That episode with the bear bespoke of the many dangers at every turn in the wilderness and if one was "to keep his hair or the meat on his bones," he had to be ever vigilant.

Ben and Martin finished their unpacking chores, then commenced gutting and skinning the bear. He was fatter than all get-out and that pleased Singing Bird very much as she stood by watching.

Soon Singing Bird had great slabs of fat stripped from the intestines, back and sides merrily rendering away in one of her big cooking kettles. Bear fat was the mother of all answers to many of life's problems on the frontier. From cooking to smearing the body when the mosquitoes got bad, bear fat was Nature's treasure.

It wasn't long before Singing Bird had the cooking fires going along with great chunks of fresh bear meat smoking away on the drying racks erected the year before. All the men were abuzz at her work ethic and speed in getting the whole thing done. In short, she was recognized as the camp boss for all but very few instances.

The next morning Jacob awoke to a shoulder that was stiff and sore. But not as stiff as it might have been had the boys 'aim not been so quick on the scene and deadly accurate, he thought. Singing Bird's quick aid and native medicine has once again done the trick.

In fact by noon, Jacob took to working with the others as they dragged in logs for the winter's wood supply. Not the heavy work, but leading the horses down the hill with their logs in tow. By the following morning when Singing Bird checked the wound and added more of her evil smelling liquid, Jacob felt pretty damn good.

The wound was still swollen and flushed with red color, which he knew meant that blood was moving to the wound and healing was taking place. Once again, he was lucky when it came to surviving in the wilderness. Luckier than many in his trade, especially when it came to crossing swords with Ephraim.

For the next several weeks, the company stayed busy getting camp ready for winter and the upcoming trapping season. They cut emergency hay for the animals and stacked it into one of the lean-tos after it had dried— backbreaking work but necessary, if past experience had anything to do with the necessity of such actions. The men killed numerous elk for the meat, jerky and hides, which Singing Bird tanned, another never-ending task.

Hunting the elk was a chore the men undertook with much happiness because of the freedom of movement it offered, along with the great meals and the adventures it brought. Elk supplied nowhere near the amount of meat of a buffalo, but elk were close at hand and would have to do until the men could venture forth later to hunt what they needed for winter from the great beast of the plains.

Ben taught the boys, "We hunt the buffalo for their hides, but during this time of year, the buffalos' hides are not in the best shape. They are better in the winter, when the hides are four or five times thicker than in the summer. It's a lot of hard work to make meat from a buffalo, but you'll find that you enjoy it, and hell, if you don't, you'll be hard pressed to survive the long winter months this far north."

The lessons continued with the finer points of hunting buffalo whenever the boys were skinning and gutting the elk as Singing Bird showed them how to smoke and store the processed, rich meat in parfleches that hung from the cabin rafters.

In addition to work around the cabin, Martin and Ben were often off exploring for new beaver waters to trap come fall, winter and spring. The valley in which they trapped the previous year still had not recovered in numbers of beaver. In fact, one scared more mallard ducks off the decaying beaver ponds than beaver because of their earlier over-trapping. This was mute evidence that their trapping season the year before had been very effective. However, one low ridge over in the mountains to the east provided another rich find. That valley was not as big as the one next to camp but almost as rich with beaver, with even more feeder streams coming down from the nearby mountains. Both Martin and Ben returned from their travels to the new trappings speaking in glowing terms of what they saw. Additionally, they saw no fellow trappers or Indians and few grizzly bears to compete with or muck up their day.

———

COME TIME TO TRAP, the men were more than ready. It was decided that Ben would take Leo as his trapping partner and teach him the trade. Jacob, Martin and Jeremiah would form the other trapping team. They would trap the upper streams in the new valley and Ben and Leo would trap the lower valley floor.

Singing Bird would again be left in camp by herself since no hostile Indians or other trappers had been seen in the area. That way she could help with the skinning and fleshing of the hides as well as stretching them when the men were off trapping. If she got behind, several of the men would also stay behind to help in order to keep up with the demanding but necessary work. That would also give Singing Bird time to tend to other camp chores, such as mending clothing and footwear as they gave out from the constant wading in the gravel of streams and the mud of beaver ponds.

Come daylight one day in the fall of 1831, it was decided the beaver were coming into prime. Singing Bird was up early and fixed a hardy breakfast for the men.

They loaded their gear and six beaver traps per man, and off they went into their newest set of trapping adventures.

Soon a steady flow of trapped beaver plews streamed into camp at the end of each day. Because of the distance now traveled to the trapping areas, the men skinned the beaver out in the field and brought back only the fresh hides. That way the packhorses didn't have so far to go carrying heavy carcasses. Work was hard but the new trapping grounds were rich and everyone "fell to" with joy in their hearts. The pressure of winter's approaching downtime and thick ice kept them full of energy.

Soon, almost too soon, winter's frigid breath arrived. This forced the men to break the ice daily with their hand axes and make their sets under the ice. But no snow came with the icy blasts so everyone kept trapping.

Finally the day came when the ice became too thick to trap with much hope for success. With that, the men pulled their traps and headed for their winter camp for the relief it brought from the daily wading and immersion in icy waters. But the work didn't stop there. There were still more buffalo, elk and deer to hunt as well as gathering and processing of those hides.

Then winter arrived in all its fury. Howling winds, sub-zero temperatures and drifting snow became the conditions of the day. Like Buffalo Calf had said earlier when he was alive, "The valley could be miserable in the winter and then even worse come spring."

Singing Bird had made sure the tepees were prepared

for winter and that she and the boys never had any worries when it came to the cold. There was plenty of firewood close at hand, water was made from melting snow and meat was aplenty—having been smoked, hung to freeze or jerked earlier. Times were good and maybe about to get better come the spring of 1832.

PROSPERITY

AWAKENING EARLY ONE MORNING, JACOB STOKED THE embers in the cabin's fireplace with some pine knots until a fire merrily blazed away. As he carried a large pot out the front door to fill it with snow to melt for water, he came smack dab onto a Lakota Indian warrior quietly sitting on his horse, looking at him from ten feet away. Jacob dropped his pot in surprise and quickly went for his pistol, only to quickly recognize Singing Bird's brother, Standing Elk.

Standing Elk smiled at seeing his friend Jacob, apparently amused that he had surprised him. With a big grin, Standing Elk then signed, "You jumped like a bug on a hot rock."

Jacob smiled back and signed, "I was surprised and jumped because I have never seen such an ugly Indian on a horse before."

Standing Elk chuckled and dismounted lightly, born from years of riding horses.

The two men embraced like the close friends they were and then Jacob scooped up some fresh snow for coffee water. As they entered the warming cabin, Ben and Martin immediately stood up in happy recognition at seeing Standing Elk. The cabin filled with excited conversations and flying hands making sign. Soon the water was boiling and the coffee was ready. Standing Elk, par for the course, poured his cup half full of coffee and the rest of the cup full of crushed, hard brown-sugar granules.

"MAKING HONEY?" signed Jacob with a big grin. Standing Elk ignored the jab at his coffee-making as he swilled down the cup of black, thick liquid. After finishing in one gulp, he signed for more. Jacob refilled his cup halfway and then watched more precious sugar disappear into the coffee.

It's a good thing we have a small mountain of that sweet stuff in our cave, Jacob thought. *But for a great warrior and good man like Standing Elk, I don't mind.* Jacob shared a warm smile with his friend. *He is the type of friend everyone needs in this country.*

Standing Elk signed, "The rest of the band is an hour or so away from your camp. They had a late start because of the surprise snowstorm the evening before. But soon there will be an additional twenty tepees in the meadow keeping you company during the winter." He punctuated the news with his typical wide grin.

"That will be very good," replied Jacob. Not only would Singing Bird be happy around her clan once again, but the trappers could trade some of their recently acquired goods from the rendezvous to the Indians for the animal pelts the Indians had acquired during their winter trapping.

Breakfast consisted of great strips of buffalo meat cooked over the hearth, fried cornmeal mush with honey, and many steaming cups of typical trapper's thick black coffee. The wafting aroma of breakfast soon brought Singing Bird and the Hunter brothers to the cabin.

Singing Bird greeted her brother in the usual, stoic Lakota fashion, but she managed to make a pest of herself as she fussed over her brother. She made sure Standing Elk had enough of the meat and cornmeal mush, and more sugar for the coffee she refilled. The rest of the company simply stayed quiet lest they interrupt Singing Bird's happiness.

About one hour later, a great commotion could be heard approaching the cabin. Barking dogs, yelling children, neighing horses, braying mules, and every other kind of sound in-between, announced the arrival of Singing Bird's band of Lakota.

After the usual joyful greetings, the band moved over to the edge of the meadow by the lake, where they had stayed the previous summer, and began clearing snow off the same spots with buffalo-shoulder-blade shovels. They used many of the same stones marking the old tepee rings. Then the support poles were quickly erected in the chilly air and the buffalo-hide portions of the tepees pulled and wrapped into place. The travois and pack animals were quickly unloaded before it snowed again and soon smoke rose in happy, lazy, hearty-smelling twists from the tops of the tepees. Horses were left free to roam in the meadow as the trappers and Indian women gathered dried, beetle-killed lodgepole pine fire-wood from the adjacent hillside. The trappers, with Leo and Jeremiah cutting, dragged the logs down to a central area in the Indian camp. By noon, there was a small mountain of dried wood for the Indians to use throughout the winter.

That afternoon, preparations were made for a great buffalo hunt on the morrow so all could lay in an additional supply of fresh meat before the snows became too deep.

The Lakota had made meat earlier that fall but many old women in camp advised a hard winter was coming. With that, the tribe decided to lay in extra supplies of buffalo meat if it was possible.

Excited over the prospect of so many helping hands, the trappers returned to their camp and made ready for the next day's hunt. Ben and Martin cast several pounds of heavy lead bullets for the big Hawkens. Jacob laid an edge to every knife they had because the coarse, knife-resistant buffalo hair always dulled knives rapidly during gutting and skinning. Singing Bird made sure all the powder horns were filled with fresh powder and that each possibles bag held plenty of primer caps, bullets, patches, a nipple wrench, nipple prick and bullet screw. She paused a moment to handle the bullet screw, a wondrous, beautiful work of White Man's technology. It was a corkscrew-like device that attached to the end of a ramrod, to be inserted into the barrel of a rifle after a misfire. The screw twisted into the soft lead bullet so it could be extracted from the rifle barrel. The old powder could be poured out and a primer cap could be fired into the now empty rifle to clear out the flash hole. The barrel could then be swabbed out with a fresh patch, then new powder would be poured into the rifle, followed by a cloth patch and lead ball. Once a new primer cap was placed over the nipple, the rifle would be ready to fire again.

That evening a great bonfire was built in the middle of the Indian camp and the two groups, sharing what they had in the way of foodstuffs, held a great welcoming feast. There was roasted elk, antelope and buffalo meat. Singing Bird and her mother made great mounds of fried cornmeal mush with honey and everyone fell-to with huge appetites. Even the camp dogs fed well that evening as the bones—cracked open and the marrow removed— were flung over the eater's shoulders to the eagerly waiting dogs. Everyone it seemed had a great feed and a good time.

When the meal was done, the men gathered around the hot fire, smoked and got reacquainted. The women and children in the meantime gathered behind the men and caught up on the latest gossip with Singing Bird and the happenings at the rendezvous. Leo and Jeremiah, being new to this kind of event, just sat there on several logs around the central fire learning, listening and adding another chapter to their lives—a chapter that included learning about an Indian culture other than that of their earlier captors, the Utes, as well as making and better understanding sign language.

The next morning, the men quietly sat on their horses several miles from their camps. They observed a great herd of buffalo feeding off in the distance from a hidden, downwind position. Steam rose from the horses' bodies and nostrils to announce that winter had indeed arrived with Jack Frost and all his minions.

Jacob seemed to get an idea and moved his horse over to Standing Elk. Jacob said, "Maybe we five Mountain Men with our heavy rifles should sneak closer to the buffalo and use our heavy firepower to kill those buffalo we need to make meat for everyone."

Standing Elk chewed over the proposal for a moment and then translated the suggestion to Lame Deer, chief of the band.

Lame Deer said nothing for a long time. So long in fact that Jacob thought he might have taken offense to the suggestion, especially in light of the cultural thing with the reputation of his warriors as the tribes' providers at stake. Then Lame Deer turned to Standing Elk and responded in Lakota.

Standing Elk repeated back to Jacob in English: "Lame Deer says we will watch how the white men kill a large number of buffalo. When the white men are finished, our warriors will ride into the herd and show the white men how we hunt buffalo with our bows and arrows."

Jacob smiled at Lame Deer's clever wisdom and looked up at the chief, who nodded in stoic agreement.

Jacob led his company and soon the five of them were lying in the light snow cover on a windblown sagebrush ridge some eighty yards from the great herd of feeding buffalo. They laid out their Hawkens alongside their possibles sacks and took their extra Hawkens in hand. They quietly laid out their plans: They would shoot the edge of the herd, cows if possible for starters because bulls made for coarser and stringier meat than the females. If any animals became alarmed and began moving off, they would kill them next until they had the entire herd in a confused stand. Then they would continue to kill those on the outside of the herd until they had all they needed.

Jacob figured one hundred buffalo would do the trick for their winter's meat. Besides, if the snow didn't get much deeper, they could repeat the hunt on a later date since they now had so many hands to help in the butchering, transporting and processing.

Boom. Boom. Boom. Boom. Boom. Five rapid gunshots started the killing as the Hawkens broke the cold morning's stillness. At first, the buffalo were nervous at the sounds of shooting, but, not seeing anything to cause them great alarm other than a little smoke from a distant ridge, they continued to paw up and graze in the valley's lush, dried grasses slightly covered by the snow. The guns continued their deadly work as the men's aiming proved accurate and true in the placement of the heavy lead bullets. Buffalo after buffalo dropped as if pole-axed. Soon the first guns became too hot to hold or to shoot. The men placed them sizzling in the snow alongside where they lay to cool and grabbed their extra Hawkens. The bullets continued to fly true and in a matter of less than thirty minutes, one hundred and six buffalos' dark bodies dotted the snow-covered valley.

Jacob determined they had plenty of meat. He turned and waved to the thirty or so mounted warriors patiently sitting on their horses below the ridgeline.

With a whoop from Lame Deer, the Lakota warriors streamed up over the ridge in a long fluid motion of horseflesh and humankind. The snow muffled the thunder of so many horses' hooves, more than matched by the rumbling of the buffalo that began swiftly moving away from the now realized threat. Soon the Indians and buffalo were in a swirling dance of death, illustrated by emotion, commotion and motion. Arrows thumped into the sides of the great running beasts, with many of the shaggy buffalo hitting the ground in loud sliding crumps. Within moments, the white valley floor had many more dark and bloody bodies littering its once pristine winter landscape.

Then it was over just as fast as it had happened. The buffalo rumbled off into the distance and quiet descended over the land once again, except for the excited squeals of delight from the onrushing Indian women and children heading for the nearest inert life-giving forms.

The five trappers rose from their concealed positions on the ridgeline, reloaded their Hawkens, picked up their equipment and headed for the horses they had tied off in the adjacent ravine.

After that, they loaded their excess gear onto the horses and led their pack animals towards the dark forms now cooling in the morning cold, with Singing Bird keeping the pack string in line. In just moments, everyone fell to the huge job of gutting and boning out the great beasts. Jacob worked with the boys to show them the proper technique of quickly sharpening the gutting and skinning knives as they dulled. Then, he made each boy responsible for one-half of the company's knives as the blades dulled. By the end of the day, both boys had the knife-sharpening skills down pat. Then Singing Bird and the boys each took a pack string of three horses loaded down with great slabs of still bleeding and steaming meat back to camp to begin the lengthy job of processing.

Ben, Jacob and Martin, however, continued skinning out the beasts and laying the fresh hide hair-down in the snow, to pile more buffalo meat high on the "mountain rug." The tongues, hearts and some of the intestines favored by Singing Bird, along with a number of livers, were carefully set off to one side in the snow to cool. All the men took a few moments to recover those lead balls that had not passed clean through the buffalo bodies— used lead bullets were so valuable that they would be melted down once again at a later date for reuse.

On and on the work went without stopping until around two in the afternoon. Then a group of women began a hot fire and slabbed a mountain of meat on roasting sticks near the coals. It didn't take long for the hard working men and women in the meadow to drift towards the good smells coming from the fires. Soon gangs of Indians polished off huge mounds of steaming meat alongside their sharp-shooting trapper friends.

During the wolfing-down session, Chief Lame Deer came over to Jacob. In the universal sign language of the Indians, he praised the shooting skills of the trappers and thanked them for their generosity in sharing the meat. He also asked that when they had a moment of time back at camp, he, Ben, Martin and Jacob needed to sit and smoke the Sacred Pipe of Friendship. Jacob nodded and with a smile accepted the offer. Then Jacob and Lame Deer happily "fell to" on several more slabs of smoking buffalo hump ribs

Jacob took in the cold, clear air and looked out at the majestic mountains. To nature in general and no one in particular, he said, "Now this is a moment I will never forget."

All day and into the evening pack strings and Indian

travois snaked back to the winter camp loaded with huge loads of still steaming buffalo meat. Many times Jacob saw the Lakota utilizing even their dogs to pull smaller travois loaded with meat as well; the hunt had been so abundant, much work still remained in processing the meat, but it had to come off the valley floor before the coyotes and wolves began filling their stomachs. By midnight, the work in the valley was done. They stripped all the readily useable meat from one hundred and thirty-one buffalo and carted it back to the winter camp. They also stripped off all the hides to bring back to camp. Behind them lay a bloodied, trampled snowfield littered with buffalo carcasses and many skulking wolves and coyotes silently slipping around the remains. Come the dawn, the air would be full of eagles, ravens, magpies, jays, and crows gathering in their fill as well. Not much would be wasted.

For the next ten days, the trappers and Indians processed the meat to their way of choosing and lifestyle. Great racks of meat were smoked, much was made into jerky, some was salted down, some covered with hides to keep the birds away and hung in the trees to freeze, and much eaten on the spot around the many campfires. Even the Indians' dogs, normally thin and always hungry for a meal, waxed fat over the next several days as they fed on the scraps thrown their way.

Back out on the valley floor, white buffalo skeletons glistened like the newly fallen snow. Wolves, gray fox, coyotes, ravens, crows, magpies and jays continued feasting on the remains until many could only walk around with full bellies and crops. Life was good as Old Man Winter laid claim to the valley once again with a vengeance that covered the recent killing field with another white blanket of snow as if to hide the scene of death and destruction from the Maker's eyes.

————

WINTER SNOWS SWIRLED around the two camps off and on for the next few months but everyone was happy. The winter camp was out of the wind and shielded from the path of much of the driven snows. Food was plentiful and in great quantity, thanks to that buffalo hunt and others that followed. There was still a mountain of firewood in both camps for the really cold days and nights, and visiting between the camps occurred daily. That made Ben, Jacob and Martin very happy for it gave them a chance to trade with the Indians. They traded mounds of extra glass beads, coffee, beaver traps, blankets, tobacco and pigs of lead for beautifully tanned pelts from elk, deer, beaver, river otter, martin, fox and now freshly processed buffalo hides that they added to their small mountain of hides and pelts, stored away for the next rendezvous.

Singing Bird, more than anyone else in the valley, was happy. The men in her company were dealing fairly with her people, and the people in turn had been telling her of their good feelings towards the trappers. And the spring beaver-trapping season was still to come. *And Ben Bow has my heart.* Ben and Singing Bird began sharing her tepee, on a regular basis. She had moved on from the loss of Buffalo Calf, and being with Ben Bow made her smile more and more.

Trappers are strange men, she often thought. *Ben Bow is like a little child when he is around me.*

As the winter progressed, she watched Ben Bow continue to teach the Hunter brothers the various lessons of survival and prosperity in the high country. She came to think of Ben Bow and the two Hunters as her family. "Thank you, Great Spirit," she often sang, "for bringing me Jeremiah Hunter and Leo Hunter, boys for a Lakota Sioux who has no children of her own." Jeremiah and Leo could often be heard singing their praises as well: "Lord, we thank you for the blessings of life, and for the freedom you have granted us, and for the friends of Jacob and Martin. We thank you, oh Lord, for our new father and mother, Ben and Singing Bird, who have taken us into their hearts," Jeremiah would pray, and Leo would add, "In Jesus's name, Amen."

Life was good. If only it would stay this way forever, everyone thought.

18

BLACKFOOT

JACOB KNEW THE GOOD LIFE WOULD NOT LAST FOREVER.

The spring beaver-trapping season of 1832 was just around the comer. The trappers stayed very busy getting ready and it seemed that the needed preparations were never done. They filled their days with shoeing horses, repairing bridles, rebuilding packsaddles, creating new halters, making bullets, putting edges on knives, wood hauling, repairing guns, making new clothing, mending old clothing and continued trading with the Indians. The days were getting longer and the winter snows were becoming a thing of the past with the advent of each warming day. Even the grasses in the meadows were poking through the semi-frozen ground and the horses were getting rolling fat on the new feed. It was also a time for young colts to be born, bringing happiness whenever an owner's horse herd was increased with the new additions.

Wham! With that noise, Martin and Jacob awoke with a start and went for their rifles. The door of their cabin was flung open with a tremendous crash, as Singing Bird and the two boys flew inside. *Boom-boom-boom...boom-boom-boom* sounded the thundering of rifles in their meadow.

"Blackfoot! Blackfoot!" screamed a frantic Singing Bird.

It didn't take long before everyone was awake, dressed as good as they were going to get, and armed to the teeth. The alarm was no small thing; simply the word "Blackfoot" brought fears of the fierce tribe from the north. Wherever Blackfoot went, a wake of tragedy, burnings, and the dead of all sexes and ages always seemed to follow.

Jacob raced to the open door and peered out at the Lakota camp some hundred yards distant. It was nothing but a swirl of tomahawk-swinging, fusil-shooting, knife- and spear-wielding Indians intermixed with the screams of running women and children. Fifty barking and howling Indian dogs added to the chaos.

To join that swirl of humanity with only five men will hardly provide any positive measure in the outcome. Jacob made a fast decision.

"Singing Bird, you stay here in the cabin behind locked doors. If the Blackfoot kill us and then break through the door, you have the fowling piece and your two pistols. You know what to do in that instance. The rest of you come with me," yelled Jacob.

Out the cabin they stormed, running around behind and out of sight of the fighting Indians in the meadow below. It was obvious to Jacob that the Blackfoot had not seen the trappers' camp or they would have swarmed all over them as well. They apparently only had "eyes" for the many tepees in the meadow, for the bounty they potentially offered and their large horse herd whose value on the frontier was beyond measure. Seeing that, they had attacked the Lakota camp right at daylight.

Jacob knew the Lakota and Blackfoot were mortal enemies, so there could be only one lethal outcome to what was now playing out beyond them on the other side of the ridge. But the Blackfoot hated the white men as well. No matter how you look at it, this will be a fight to the death for all concerned!

Jacob scurried behind the cover of the ridge—away from the cabin but towards the sounds of battle. Jacob kept looking for one thing—the Blackfoot raiding party's horses. They had to have ridden this far, being so many miles south of their usual territory. Horses had to be close at hand somewhere, since the attack was just over the ridge.

JACOB and the other trappers spread out and silently made their ways through the timber behind the ridge. I knew it! There they are! About forty horses were attended by three young Indian men.

Martin held up his hand. Jacob and the three others slid to a stop behind the cover of a dense stand of willows alongside a frozen creek. Martin handed his two Hawkens to Jacob and Ben, then took off silently through the trees with only his bow and arrows. Within moments, he soon disappeared into the darkened timber.

Zzip...thunk. Jacob watched as an arrow flew from Martin's position into the back of the closest Indian horse-handler's skull. The killing force of the arrow's impact toppled the Indian youth face first into the snow. He was dead before he hit the snow.

The second Indian horse-handier turned at the surprising sound of the arrow hitting his partner, only to have the next arrow hit him dead center in the throat. He grabbed at the arrow in his neck, struggled a little and then pitched forward into the frozen earth next to his already dead companion. In the fall, the arrow was driven clear through his neck upon impact with the ground. The third Indian boy guarding the horses viewed the demise of his friends, took off running and disappeared into the forest.

Jacob's team then ran forward and tied the Indians' nervous horses to nearby trees to prevent their escape. Then they quickly followed the tracks of the raiding party in the snow, over the ridge. This effectively cut off the raiders' escape route. The five trappers ran up and over the small ridge in a crouch and positioned themselves down the far side at the edge of the clearing just inside the tree line.

A few yards distant laid the Lakota camp and the scene of a fierce battle. Jacob considered the distance as his compatriots laid out their firearms alongside for hasty retrieval and use. They each chose a tree for cover and to help steady their deadly aim with the heavy Hawkens.

"On my cue," said Jacob quietly. He aimed at a very large Blackfoot warrior who was about to tomahawk a Lakota woman being held by the neck.

"Now!"

Boom...boom-boom-boom-boom went the Hawkens in rapid succession, and five Blackfoot warriors dropped instantly.

Just as instantly, the fighting paused as Blackfoot and Lakota alike looked around for the hidden shooters.

Boom-boom-boom-boom-boom went the reserve rifles in rapid succession and again five more Blackfoot warriors kissed Mother Earth for the last time.

Consternation reigned within the ranks of the attackers. The Blackfoot had attacked in barely superior numbers at the onset of the fight using surprise as leverage. Now, Jacob thought, in addition to the numbers they've already lost in fighting with the Lakota, ten more of their number lay dead, killed by unknown assailants from their rear!

The tide of the battle had swiftly turned. Now the Blackfoot raiding party is in double trouble. Their numbers have been dangerously depleted and we are between them and their horses!

———

Buffalo Heart, the leader of the Blackfoot war party, instantly realized their plight. Fighting the Lakota any further was sheer folly, so he yelled for his remaining warriors to break from the battle and follow him in a sprint for their horses. Within seconds, his warriors disengaged from the Lakota and were running right at the little group of shooters, howling like a band of banshees.

The first five Blackfoot—including Buffalo Heart—tumbled to the earth as heavy lead bullets tore gaping holes in their chests. The remaining Blackfoot kept at a dead run to hit the shooters head-on.

Stepping out from the timber as one, the trappers leveled their horse pistols at the nearest charging Indians. In an instant and in a blinding-cloud line of white black-powder smoke, the Blackfoot were upon them. Five pistols burned holes in the flesh of those unfortunates closest to the end of their muzzles. The big .69-caliber slugs fired at such close range flung those five Blackfoot into their fellow warriors who closely brought up the rear.

The collisions of the dying and the living gave Jacob and his friends time to draw their second pistols from their sashes.

Nothing more than pure varmint killing, Jacob thought as the heavy slugs from those pistol volleys tore into the Blackfoot still standing or running at them from some six feet away.

Jacob and Martin, and then Ben and the boys, drew their tomahawks and knives and lunged into the now stunned, smoke cloud-enveloped Blackfoot. The remaining Lakota Indians closed on their enemies from the rear.

In seconds, it was all over. Every Blackfoot warrior in that large raiding party lay dead in the stand of tepees, at the feet of the trappers or among the Lakota at the base of the ridge.

Jacob and Martin watched as their Blackfoot opponents, their throats slit, furiously wiggled and trembled to the ground. The raiders' lifeblood spurted hotly over everyone within reach.

Jacob looked over at the rest of his party. He was relieved to see all were standing with only Ben being slightly wounded over the eye by a close and almost lethal swing of a Blackfoot's tomahawk. The wound bled furiously like a stuck hog, but he would be alright under Singing Bird's care, Jacob thought out of relief for his friend and the moment just passed.

Jacob stepped over the many dead Blackfoot warriors now being scalped and savagely mutilated by the Lakota. He walked down from the ridge and into the Indian village as he reloaded his pistol. The cost to the Lakota has also been high, he observed. The main battleground in and among the tepees was littered with bodies from the Blackfoot raiding party and with men, women and children from the band of Lakota. Lame Deer and Singing Bird's brother Standing Elk lay dead, killed in the first savage onslaught. Singing Bird's mother and sister also lay dead at the opening of their tepee. Apparently they had been brained by Blackfoot tomahawks as they attempted to flee their tepee.

Jacob signaled to Ben who was holding the wound shut over his eye with his hand, and they soon met next to Singing Bird's family tepee.

Ben, after seeing that Singing Bird's entire family had been wiped out, grimly strode back to his guns at the edge of the trees. He picked them up and reloaded, then moved off swiftly to where Singing Bird was still holed up in the cabin.

Better that the bad news come from Ben than for her to discover her loved ones dead on the field of battle, Jacob thought. Still, her grief will be horribly intense.

Of the entire band of Lakota, over half had been killed during the first minutes of the rare winter raid by the Blackfoot—rare, because come winter, most western tribes stayed next to their camps in the face of the tough traveling and foraging required to make raiding forays. Most of the Lakota hadn't had a chance. They were killed as they slept or as they stepped from their tepees to defend their families. Wounded were everywhere and it took the rest of the Indians and the trappers all day to render aid. The next morning and into the day following, many burial scaffolds were erected on the small hillside down from the trapper's cabin. The spring season, usually a time of new life, was now a sad time for all.

Afterwards, the remaining numbers of Lakota moved their tepees closer to the set of lean-tos and cabin for the protection the structures and trappers afforded. Only eleven Lakota families or parts of families remained. Singing Bird, true to her stoic nature in the face of adversity, was everywhere among the survivors. She tended to the wounded and motherless children, saw to feeding those who needed such care, and helped the rest with their resettlement closer to her tepee. The remaining tepees from the deceased were burned as were their remaining possessions not sent along with those on the burial scaffolds. The Blackfoot were left where they fell and were soon consumed by the always-hungry forest critters. As for the raiding party's horses, they were taken by the remaining Lakota as the spoils of the "victory." They were now a band poor in numbers but rich in horseflesh.

There was still a perceived Blackfoot threat: one of the horse handlers had escaped to possibly tell the tale. To protect themselves, numbers in the spring trapping parties were increased. Additionally, there were always men left back at camp for defense. Jacob, Martin, Jeremiah and a Lakota named Broken Foot formed one trapping team. Ben, Leo, Stepping Crooked and Spotted Elk Calf formed the other trapping team. It had been worked out that the spring beaver taken would be split equally since sharing was "The Way." Thus, remaining band members would have furs to trade at the rendezvous or a trading post to fetch those needed necessities for the coming year.

That spring was one of the best for trapping the men had ever seen. The valley they trapped was just four miles distant from camp but full of beaver. Soon the beaver were pouring into camp and with an abundance of women to process the furs the men could devote more time to the actual trapping. Beaver pelts as well as furs from river otter and fox seemed to grace every drying hoop and hanging facility.

The cave was taking on a look of richness of its own as well. Furs from their earlier trappings, furs traded from the Indians and now the pelts flowing in from their recent although shared trappings provided a cabin full of bounty. However, the Mountain Men needed to trap everything they could, not only because it was a means to an end for those much-needed supplies, but because they were leaving this area for good after the spring trapping season.

They made such plans because of the bad memories and the fact that the beaver would mostly be trapped out and gone by late spring anyway. By the end of trapping season in the spring of 1832, the cave and parts of the cabin were full of furs. Trapping equipment was carefully packed away for the rest of the year and the men began to pack the furs in bundles for travel to the rendezvous in Pierre's Hole come summer.

Everyone was looking forward to the annual trappers' get-together and it had now been decided that Singing Bird's depleted band of Lakota would accompany the trappers to the rendezvous. Once there, the Indians would trade their furs for much needed supplies and then move on to Pa-Ha Sapa, their word for the Black Hills. There they could be closer to larger and more protective family bands of Lakota. That, plus the lure of hunting buffalo with their own kind, provided a very strong pull back to their roots, especially among the remaining young men in the band. The rendezvous at Pierre's Hole in 1832 would provide needed supplies for the small band of Lakota and more of the mad chaos between trappers that Jacob and Martin had witnessed the year before.

19

THE 1832 RENDEZVOUS

ON THE MORNING OF THE DEPARTURE TO THE RENDEZVOUS, the survivors said their goodbyes to those who had passed in the fight with the Blackfoot and now lay upon burial scaffolds on the hillside. Then, in a caravan with men equally distributed along the line of travelers for the protection it afforded, the trek began. Many good as well as bad memories were left behind by Indian and white men alike.

Jacob turned in his saddle as he led a pack string of horses loaded with plews. He looked back over an area he had come to love because of all the adventure and life changes that occurred while there. His eyes met Martin's eyes as his friend led a following pack string. Those eyes also spoke of mixed feelings that came from change. But like Jacob's, his look spoke of thinking forward towards those adventures yet to come—adventures neither of the close friends could yet imagine but would participate in as they moved through this event called "life."

As they traveled through the magnificent Absaroka Range, the group came into daily contact with herds of buffalo, the grand moose, elk by the score and dainty mule deer at every turn in the trail. Every night because of this bounty of wildlife, the party feasted on many kinds of fresh meat of the choicest cuts. The waters were clear and cold and the mountain grasses high and nutritious. Soon the horses were not pleasant to follow because all those rich grasses they ate were turned into clouds of foul-smelling methane gasses as they labored along under their pack loads of furs. But life was full and thoughts of the raid by the Blackfoot were dimming daily. However, because they were now in Blackfoot country, vigilance remained high. If the Blackfoot came this time, all would be ready with an ugliness in their hearts that bespoke of only violence to their enemy.

Up they climbed, using the many animal and Indian trails over Togwatee Pass and down its backside. In front of the caravan in all her mountain majesty now lay the spectacular Tetons, spiritual home to the Mountain Men. Skirting to the south side of Jackson Hole, they camped at the edge of the great valley and intertwined hills. The hunting continued to be exceptional and soon sounds of shooting from other rendezvous-bound trappers could be heard daily. By the second day in the valley, Jacob's group was joined by several other groups of trappers and large numbers of friendly Flathead Indians. By then, the collective group was so large it wasn't considered a likely target by raiding Blackfoot or Gros Ventre who, when observed, kept a safe watchful distance. The group then continued up over Teton Pass and down the back side to Pierre's Hole, which to a Mountain Man was another place of outstanding beauty.

The area identified as Pierre's Hole was about twenty-five miles long and anywhere from a few miles to fifteen miles wide. On one side of this valley rose the majestic Teton Mountains and on the other but not quite as spectacular, the Snake River Mountains. In between, there was grass belly deep to a buffalo, watered areas from the mountain ranges everywhere around and camping places aplenty. Even though the trappers lived in God's paradise on a daily basis, they always appreciated another of His great masterpieces and Pierre's Hole was one fitting such a bill: lush meadows, clear streams, abundant game at every turn in the trail and enough space to satisfy any man with a wilderness bent. That was topped off with soft blue skies and pleasant evenings so full of stars that one found it hard to close his eyes because of their numbers and magnificence.

The only negatives were the ever-present clouds of mosquitoes driving one to distraction. For the trappers and Indians alike, an extra slathering of bear grease kept the biting insects like the moose flies, no-see-ums, white sox and mosquitoes somewhat at bay. As for the horses, an ever-moving tail seemed to be the only defense—that and a good roll in the mud alongside a handy stream when the opportunity presented itself.

Sublette and Campbell were there to supply the trappers at the 1832 rendezvous with supplies for the coming year. And, as before, they and their American Fur Company did not arrive until the rendezvous was basically over. For once however, that was a small thing. Representatives from Hudson's Bay, the Rocky Mountain Fur Company plus others from independent companies such as Gant, Black-well and Nathaniel Wyeth showed up at the annual get-together with the much-needed supplies. With their input, the trading sessions went on without delay. In fact, that rendezvous turned out to be one of the largest on record. Over four hundred Mountain Men, two hundred Nez Perce and over a hundred Flathead Indians were in attendance.

Jacob and company with their small band of Lakota headed for a small copse of cottonwoods in the center of the valley alongside several fast-running mountain streams. Soon barking dogs, laughing children and tepees dotted the verdant meadows. The horse herd was safely positioned to the north and soon the smell of fires heavy with aroma of cooking buffalo meat dominated the scene.

Jacob and the men erected their two tepees and then pitched the rest of their camp close at hand under several massive cottonwoods. Soon Singing Bird had her cooking fire blazing as the men continued hauling dry firewood into camp. Their horse herd was posted with double hobbles and soon the men settled down around their fires with their backs against the packs full of plews. Relaxing, the men were soon to appreciate the smell of freshly crushed grasses underfoot along with the usual great smells of sizzling buffalo meat and coffee. Life at that moment was pretty special.

About a half mile to the west lay the camps of those fur companies that had arrived and were setting up for the business of trading. Already there were mobs of fur trappers and Indians gathered around to trade, drink and share news not only from the outside world but about each other as well. Especially about those Mountain Men who were conspicuous by their absence.

After supper, Jacob and the men decided they would let the initial charge of trappers and Indians have their run at the traders. Then when things ironed out and quieted down a bit, they would venture forth and trade their goods. In the meantime come the morrow, they would join their fellow man, hoist a drink or two, tell some tall tales and see who made it through the winter.

As expected, Leo and Jeremiah were wound up tighter than one of those newfangled Swiss watches that the traders had brought from St. Louis. In a way, this was the boys' very first rendezvous. The one they attended in Cache Valley in Utah the previous summer had some good and bad memories still attached: memories of captivity and then being rescued and taken in by their "current family." So in truth, this one was their first as

honest to goodness fur trappers, and they couldn't wait
to join the festivities.

In the damp and cold of the dawn, Jacob and party sat
around the fire feasting on fresh cutthroat trout fried
crisply in bear grease that Singing Bird had caught the
evening before. That wonderful smell was joined with
that of her always-fluffy Dutch oven biscuits.

The pink meat of the chunky cutthroat trout tasted
pretty good after all the jerky and buffalo meat Jacob had
been eating. By the way the others were wolfing down on
Singing Bird's crispy pan fried fish, bones and all, they
must have thought so as well.

After the morning meal, the men saddled up their
horses and without fanfare headed for the rendezvous
with its swirl of gaily-dressed trappers and Indians.
Singing Bird told them she would stay at the camp and
watch the plews and horses as well as get in some more
visiting with her Lakota band. They arrived at the center
of organized confusion at the rendezvous, then just sat
on their horses for a few moments and drank in the swirl
of events. There were shooting matches, foot races, heavy
trading and drinking of the questionable trade whiskey,
squaw swapping, and merchants repairing firearms or
selling new ones. The ringing of the blacksmith's
hammer repairing iron items of any kind added its
distinctive sound to the event as well. Great fires roared
throughout with the inevitable slabs of buffalo meat
hanging from green cooking sticks for anyone passing by
to partake. Indians, their kids and all the noise they

brought to the rendezvous were just another set of instruments in the mountain meadow's music.

As the afternoon wore on and the whiskey began to take its toll on common sense, fights broke out. Some were meaner than a snake as knives flashed and bright red stains decorated many a trapper's beautifully beaded buckskins. But generally, everything moved right along at a controlled crash. Soon, these men would re-enter the deadly world of a trapper for another long, hard year of isolation, so if one was going to "let her rip," it was now or never.

When Jacob and the others arrived back at camp that first evening, they found Singing Bird dutifully preparing supper. They dismounted and cared for their stock, then approached the cooking fire looking to see what was for supper. Singing Bird said little and went about her business quietly and with a lot less looking at the men than Jacob had ever remembered. Jacob looked askance at Ben as to why the quiet treatment. In response, Ben shrugged his shoulders with an "I don't know why either" look.

As they ate that evening in a manner quieter than usual, Jacob noticed that Singing Bird had a large bruise on her right arm and a reddish rubbed area on her left cheek that he hadn't noticed before. In sign, Jacob asked Singing Bird how she got the bruise.

Singing Bird just looked at Jacob, turned from her work around the fire and strode back to her tepee, obviously upset. It was then both Jacob and Ben noticed she was walking in a funny manner and not in her usual pronounced way. Jacob was glad to see Ben rise and follow Singing Bird into her tepee.

Soon Ben emerged from the tepee with a clouded and angry look on his face. He strode purposefully towards his horse and saddled up. Jacob sensed big trouble in the air, so he stood and walked over to his friend.

"What is the problem, my friend?" asked Jacob, ever mindful that Ben was now on the prod and when he was in such a mood, a killing was not far away.

Ben turned and gave Jacob a look meant to kill. He said, "Singing Bird was raped by four trappers coming into the rendezvous this afternoon. They stopped in camp and asked if she would fix them some food. When she did, they grabbed her from behind, took her into the tepee and had their way with her, many, many painful times. She is very bruised all over her body and still bleeding from being so brutally treated. I aim to go to the rendezvous, find those varmints and kill every one of them," he quietly added with a tone of finality and under-lying rage.

Jacob found himself rising into a towering rage as well. Not only had the newly arriving trappers done wrong, they had come into his camp and took the gentle and loving little Singing Bird against her will. He, too, found himself wanting to head into the main trapper's camp that night and kill everyone who had been involved with the violation of such a beautiful and caring person. But his survival instincts installed by his step-dad, Zeke, took over.

"Ben," he said, "we need to wait until daylight and then go together into the Rendezvous. That way we can be sure of who they were and take care of business in the manner as necessary."

Ben kept saddling his horse until Jacob put his hand on his arm to get his attention.

"We must wait until it is light enough to see and shoot. Going into the main trappers' camp in the dark and starting to shoot will do nothing but have every one of them returning fire in our direction thinking the Blackfoot are on the prod. Besides, we need Singing Bird to identify them. I don't want to kill anyone unless he needs killing and then, I want to do it right," Jacob said.

Ben must have realized the wisdom of Jacob's words. He just went limp and hung onto the saddle. Then he let his extreme rage and frustration register in his fiercely glaring eyes.

Jacob returned to the fire and shared with Martin, Leo and Jeremiah the words spoken by Ben about what happened to Singing Bird. In unison, all three men rose as if to make ready to leave and take care of four varmints that needed killing.

Jacob sensed the seriousness at hand and the need for cooler thinking. He said, "We will go into the main camp in the morning when we can see and be seen. Singing Bird will go with us and point out the culprits. Then, we will kill them. But I don't want to do so until Singing Bird has had her say. Then, I want to make sure all the other trappers are aware of what those four did. If we do it that way, we will have to shoot fast or the rest of the trappers in camp will take care of our snake killing business for us. Now let's make ready with our gear for the morrow, because we are going to need it for the serious business at hand."

The next morning found Singing Bird dressed up in one of her finest bighorn sheepskin dresses, one decorated beautifully with dozens of elk ivories and red and blue beadwork. Her long black hair was freshly washed, brushed back and glistened fairly in the sun. On her face, she wore a determined but noble Indian look. She was beautiful.

As she rode into the trappers' main camp with an examining and searching look on her face, every head turned to observe her riding gracefully. Behind her rode five heavily armed trappers with sullen looks in their eyes that needed no explanation. A confrontation was in the offing. Many of the trappers had sensed a deadly purpose for this armed display, and soon formed in behind the five men as they rode their horses slowly through camp behind the beautiful Indian woman.

Then all of a sudden, Singing Bird stopped. As she sat there in her saddle, her flashing dark eyes leveled a gaze towards a small camp of men.

The four men whom Singing Bird stopped in front of put down the breakfast they were eating, slowly rose from their campfire and faced her. Every one of them never took their eyes off her, nor she them. Their eyes showed a recognition of lustful times with Singing Bird and hers, a dark-eyed deadliness from a time past not to ever be repeated.

Those trappers who had followed the mounted men pushed in around Jacob and his horsemen to look on the scene before them with questioning looks among themselves.

"That squaw for sale?" mouthed a tall trapper among the suspect four, sporting a necklace with a brightly beaded shell disc resting in the center of his chest.

Boom went Ben's Hawken with an unexpected roar and white cloud of smoke. His .54-caliber soft lead bullet flew true to its mark, striking the shell disc dead center in the trapper's chest, blowing the ornament to pieces, not to mention destroying the man's heart and lungs behind it. The impact of the heavy lead bullet at such close range flung the man backwards ten feet like a rag doll, crumpling him into their roaring breakfast fire. He was dead before he hit the coals in the fire pit.

The quickness of the shooting and the violence of the bullet as it tore through the man's chest momentarily froze everyone looking on. The remaining three accused trappers quickly scrambled for their weapons, which lay on a log behind them. As for the horde of trappers innocently looking on just moments before, they found themselves scattering like a covey of disturbed sage grouse.

Boom-boom-boom-boom-pow went the almost simultaneous explosions from four Hawkens and Ben's .69-caliber horse pistol. The three remaining trappers, center of Singing Bird's rapt attention, spun violently around from the bullets' impacts, falling into a lifeless pile.

Jacob, Martin and the boys quickly drew their remaining unfired pistols. They and Ben whirled their horses around to confront the amazed trappers who started demanding what the hell had brought on such a deadly confrontation and finality of events. Holding up his hand for attention, Jacob got the silence of the multitude as well as those rushing from nearby camps to the scene with rifles at the ready.

"Yesterday, these four men rode into our camp and asked to be fed. Our squaw here commenced feeding them, whereupon they descended upon her. Then pinning her to the ground in her tepee, they ravaged her body. Not only once, but many times. When they finished they beat her in such a manner as to make her reluctant to tell anyone what had happened. Last night when we returned to our camp, it was obvious she had been brutally attacked. Today I asked her to identify the men who defiled her so we could kill them. That we have done. If anyone feels we were wrong and wishes to continue this fight on behalf of those four dead men, let them so speak. But I am here to tell you, no squaw deserves to be treated in such a manner," spoke Jacob. He maintained a tight set of lips, highlighted by narrowed, angry blazing eyes.

The only sound heard in reply to Jacob's words was that of a western meadowlark singing from the top of a nearby tepee pole, happy that all the noise from the shooting below had abated. Then there was some low talk among the trappers relative to Jacob's statements. Slowly at first and then in mass, the trappers walked away from the bloody scene satisfied that justice had been done, as the one dead trapper continued smoldering away in the fire pit stinking up the clean, crisp mountain air.

Besides, there was free whiskey to drink at many of the company trading sites and to tarry there at the killin' ground would not fill their cups with the free fiery liquid.

Ben dismounted from his horse and with a singular determination, gathered up the dead men's rifles, knives, beaver traps, tomahawks, pelts, hatchets and possibles bags. Once he had an armful of such goods, he would hand the items to each man on horseback. Soon, all such wealth from the four dead men was distributed to the men in Jacob's party. Then he rounded up the dead trappers' riding horses and pack animals, loaded them up, and tied them together on one long lead rope.

Turning from the deadly scene, the men with Singing Bird rode to the first traders in the area. Ben handed one trader all the gear, beaver plews and horses from the four dead men, then said, "Take these and figure what they be worth in trade. When that is done, give the credit to this woman so she might acquire the trade items she fancies. However, be careful mind you on how you figure out the credit due on this equipment and horses. She is one of us and deserves to be treated like the lady she is and I will stand for nothing less."

The surprised traders nodded in agreement at Ben's words as they looked over the dead trappers' goods and horses. There would be a fair amount of credit due because of the value of this trade and the trader was more than happy to do so. Singing Bird, mindful of the painful feeling in her thighs and the shame she still felt, managed a slight smile at the strength and conviction of her man. There were many things she would want from the traders to help her people decimated by the fight with the Blackfoot. And now she would have them, although a high price had been extracted from all sides in order to do so.

Meanwhile, the dead trapper still smoldered in the fire pit and the ever-present magpies and crows had discovered the remaining lifeless three and were investigating their potential for breakfast.

Just then, a trapper raced into camp on a lathered-up horse. He yelled "Injuns! Injuns! Hundreds of them! Blackfoot by the hundreds and coming this way!"

In the next few seconds, the entire camp was in an uproar. The rider gave directions along with the information that the Blackfoot had just been forced to ground in a dense stand of timber and downfall by some other trappers and he had been sent for more help. Jacob sat there as hundreds of trappers and Indians sprinted for their rifles and horses. Just as fast as they could arm themselves and mount their steeds, they were off in a cloud of flying clods of dirt from their horses' hooves towards the battle site. Jacob watched them go.

"Are we going?" asked an excited Leo barely able to contain himself.

Jacob just sat there thinking life was tough enough on the frontier without going and looking for trouble. But he also had to smile at Leo. He was becoming a savage fighter like his brother and not scared to try his hand at anything.

Then Jeremiah chimed in not wanting to be left out from the action. "Are we going to give them a hand? After all, they are Blackfoot and we still owe them some for what they did to Singing Bird's band awhile back."

Jacob looked over at Ben and Martin. Both had heard the questions and were now reloading their Hawkens after the shooting at the dead trappers' camp.

"No, we aren't going looking for trouble. The way I figure, it will find us soon enough. I say let's return to camp and load our horses with the pelts. Then let's return since most of the traders now have little to do because everyone else has run off to fight the Indians. That way, we can get our trading done with a minimum of squabbling and fuss."

With that, he turned to look at Martin and Ben for approval. They both grinned. Neither liked killing Indians unless they had to and, this was not one of those "had to's."

Leo and Jeremiah, ever mindful of Jacob's wisdom and leadership, settled for his response to their questions and without further ado, they all rode back to camp to load up their furs. However on the ride back, Jacob thought about the two boys rapidly developing into men. They had turned out to be excellent Mountain Men. Hardy, not foolish, wise in their youth and ways, yet possessing of an inner streak like that of a maddened grizzly, a streak that bode an end to one's life if the boys were crossed or hurt was brought to their loved ones.

The mass of Mountain Men from the rendezvous were clearly engaged in a stiff battle. As Jacob and company stayed in camp and did business with the traders, combatants would return from the battle, wounded, or in need of powder, shot, or just plain thirsty for whiskey, and they would relay the latest news of the fight.

Once the battle had been joined, the Gros Ventre Indians— not the Blackfoot as had been originally announced—dug in behind timbered downfalls and defended themselves fairly well. A few Gros Ventre were killed, as were some trappers and friendly Indians. Then the Gros Ventre managed to sneak off in the dead of night after a few days of battle without the trappers being aware of their retreat. That ended the big Indian fight in Pierre's Hole in 1832. But a great time had been had by all, except for the cornered Gros Ventre and the four trappers who foolishly had their way with Singing Bird.

Jacob and company did right proud in their trades with the various fur companies at the rendezvous, as well as they could anyway considering "this was the only game in town." They didn't get rich in the trades but managed to procure the needed materials allowing for at least another year in their beloved backcountry where they were still "kings with a kingdom yet to explore."

Then, Jacob and Martin were floored by a proposal forwarded by Ben as they all sat around the family cooking fire the following evening. Even prior to the incident with the four trappers, Ben had not been himself. He had been unusually distant as if wrestling with an issue larger than himself. After the incident with Singing Bird and the four trappers, his "issue" had returned and appeared to be an even bigger burden than before. Jacob and Martin both noticed his personality change and just waited for him to share with them what was sticking in his craw. That was Ben's way so both men respected him for it and gave him the space he needed.

As they sat around the fire that evening sharing another of Singing Bird's meals, Ben slowly said, "Singing Bird and I would like to travel with her people when they leave the rendezvous. They are heading east towards Pa-Ha Sapa. Over there, there are many Lakota bands they have associated with in the past and we wish to renew those friendships."

Ben poked at the fire with a stick, then continued. "Especially now since they are reduced in numbers such as they are. Once there, and her people settled, Singing Bird and I will continue on to the Knife River Villages, near the confluence of the Knife and Missouri Rivers, settle down and make that village our home. I still have many friends there and feel the time has come for me to stop wandering, make my place and raise a family."

Ben's eyes swept across the faces of Jacob and Martin. Singing Bird walked up to Ben and put her hand on his shoulder in finality. It was obvious he was her man and she was going with him. Then Ben continued onto another point that really caught Jacob and Martin cold.

"Both boys wish to go with us and remain as members of our immediate family as well," he said.

The issue of Ben leaving had really caught both Jacob and Martin by surprise. The issue of both young men leaving with them as well, struck an even deeper, more hurtful chord.

Keeping any emotion from his face as he knew Martin was doing, Jacob said. "Ben, both Martin and I always knew you wanted to return to the Knife River Villages, settle down and raise a family. If that is what you want to do, now is a good time. You have all you will need to make your way and your share of the trade goods will last you for several years. Traveling with Singing Bird's band will also give all of you additional security. Leo and Jeremiah are also becoming very good frontiersmen and their two rifles will be of help as well. And both you and Singing Bird still have the golden ingots from the Utes which will carry all of you for many years."

Jacob checked a glance at Martin, who nodded, then Jacob added, "If these are your wishes, then Martin and I support you and wish all of you well."

A glance over at the two boys confirmed, by the looks on their faces, that this was their wish as well. With the issue out and understood by all, the air then became heavy with awkwardness. It seemed no one had much more of interest to say. There was a lot of looking into the burning fire that evening for the answers it held. Those answers were not forthcoming and everyone went quietly to their sleeping areas earlier than usual that evening.

For hours, Jacob laid awake under the clear starlit night amid the constant buzzing of the ever-present mosquitoes. Just when things seem right in life, they always change, he thought. I wonder if this is how my dad and mom felt when they discovered I was leaving. Finally, sleep overtook him, closing his awareness to the world with the lonely howl of a wolf in the distance as a frontier nightcap.

20

BIG MEDICINE

JACOB AND MARTIN WATCHED BEN, SINGING BIRD, LEO and Jeremiah ride off with the band of Lakota early the next morning. The four of them stopped almost out of sight on the horizon, turned and waved goodbye once again. Then it was over.

Jacob and Martin spent the rest of the day getting ready to leave the rendezvous: shoeing horses, repairing broken packs, packing all their gear on the packs once they were repaired and saying goodbye to several old trapper friends. Before they completed the day, they had several hefty drinks back in the "lonely" of their camp from the gallon of whiskey they always carried for special occasions. This seemed like just such an occasion in which to draw from it rather deeply, and they did.

The following morning before daylight, the two men made ready to leave their camp in Pierre's Hole forever.

Word at the rendezvous from the traders was that
Captain Bonneville was en route to the Green River
Valley at that very moment to eventually locate near
Horse Creek for the 1833 Rendezvous. His route to that
area would take him via South Pass. It was rumored that
he was bringing over one hundred men, pack animals
and at least twenty wagons full of trade goods as he
planned an overwinter stay, to be more than ready to
trade his goods come the following July.

Like many trappers, Jacob and Martin did not know
the exact location where Captain Bonneville would set
up the rendezvous on Horse Creek. But like the other
Mountain Men, they knew the general lay of the land in
the Green River Valley which was south of their present
camp. Once there, it was just a matter of talking to the
local Indians or other trappers as to the rendezvous site.
Failing that, a bit of hard riding in the general area would
allow them to locate the trader's rendezvous grounds.
Even with the land almost empty of civilization, the West
still had its own set of "ears" and "eyes" for one to hear
and see. One just had to know where to look and how to
listen.

Jacob and Martin began their trek for new and
unknown beaver country to their south, following the
many Indian pony and travois trails leading from the
rendezvous. Both men liked the solitude of the West and
figured they would search out their next trapping area
based on the number of beaver sign and the lack of their
fellow man. They retraced their previous steps and jour-

neyed up over the Teton Pass and dropped back into Jackson Hole.

Mindful of the hated Blackfoot and chance encounters with Ephraim, they remained vigilant throughout the evening at their first camp. Early the next morning, they passed over Togwatee Pass as the sun rose over the mountains. The Grand Tetons bade them farewell as the morning sun's rays warmed their faces and the joys of the wilderness and all its grandeur greeted their eyes.

The next several days found them still heading south through the Wind River Range. From there they continued southeast through the Green Mountains. The high plateau country they crossed after leaving the Wind River Range was sparse of not only water but the beaver they sought as well. And any old beaver concentration areas they did discover had been heavily trapped previously.

They continued their trek southwest, following the Continental Divide and her waterways, still looking for sign of extensive beaver concentrations. These sought-after concentrations were not discovered until they entered a vast, wide valley crossed with numerous rivers, streams and beaver concentrations along the many willow-covered creek banks. They decided to make camp. From there, they would trap the abundant watersheds with their many promising tributaries.

They set their camp near a small cold spring in the heavy lodgepole pine dark timber. They first built a stout pole-corral for their horses. Then as Martin built a lean-to for sleeping, Jacob moved off into the timber and began cutting trees for their cabin. Soon Martin joined him and a week later, their winter cabin had been assembled. However, the structure was not anywhere near as grand as had been their previous cabin, a cabin that had been built with many more willing hands and grand ideas. Their current cabin however would provide cover and warmth from the coming winter's storms and was secluded enough to warrant little attention from the roving bands of resident Northern Arapaho Indians. A larger lean-to was built on the west end of the cabin for outside storage and their winter camp was complete.

Then they spent the next week cutting hay for their horses' winter use and setting it out to cure in the meadows adjacent to their cabin. Then it was off to the rolling surrounding lands to the north to make meat. When the two of them had first ridden into North Park, they had observed many extensive herds of buffalo. Intermixed with the wooly buffalo were abundant bands of pronghorn antelope, numerous moose along the streams, and elk and deer everywhere in between. It was truly a mountain paradise and not another white trapper was to be seen.

It was apparent the Arapaho had located in this pristine area as well, from their many tracks and tepee rings, making it incumbent upon the two trappers to be watchful. If not, they could get their "topknots" lifted by a tribe not known for their "friendly" towards many of the white men flooding into their ancestral lands.

For the next couple of days, Jacob and Martin contented themselves with the killing of locally abundant moose and mule deer. These were almost entirely jerked for winter's use.

With that done and stored in parfleches hanging from the ceiling beams, the men turned to serious meat gathering.

Numerous herds of buffalo ran on the sagebrush flats further to the north.

With two Hawkens apiece, along with their skinning knives, ample supplies of powder, primers and lead balls, they ventured forth. They crawled up over a small hill overlooking a herd of quietly feeding buffalo. Standing there in all his glory was a mature bull bison who was pure white.

"Big Medicine," as the Indians call him, thought Jacob as he unlimbered his rifles and shooting gear. Martin just lay there looking at the white animal in all his significance.

"Do we take him?" whispered Jacob to Martin, aware of the religious and cultural significance the plains and inter-mountain tribes attached to such an animal.

"He might bring us much in a trade," softly spoke Martin who, even though an Indian, was not imbued with the Plains Indian culture and the magical powers they attached to such a creature.

With that, Jacob laid his heavy Hawken on his crossed shooting sticks and took a bead on a spot behind the front shoulder of the white animal. *Boom* went Jacob's

Hawken as the animal lurched forward from the impact of the heavy, well-placed bullet. A bright spot of red now marred his shaggy gray-white hide where Jacob had aimed.

The rest of the herd started but Martin took out the lead cow before she made up her mind to flee the foreign sound. Soon the animals were in a confused "stand" as their lead cow and herd bull hit the ground with loud, dusty crumps.

Jacob and Martin each grabbed their reserve Hawkens and killed two more cow buffalo. They hurriedly reloaded both rifles, then again killed another cow per rifle. Then they quit shooting with six buffalo down.

For the next three hours, they cut out the best parts of the fallen buffalo and loaded the great slabs of meat onto the travois being pulled by their six packhorses. With that, they skinned out Big Medicine and threw his hide onto the last travois. The meat from Big Medicine was not considered fit to eat by the two men and was left for the numerous packs of wolves in the area. However, the wolves would have to hurry. The diminutive coyote and flocks of ravens, crows and magpies had descended on the bull's carcass like it was Christmas come early.

Two slow-moving hours with the heavily loaded horses finally brought the men back to their cabin. Slicing off chunks of the meat, Jacob threw them into a large cast-iron cooking pot. He filled it with water and some wild onions dug from a nearby rocky hillside and set it next to the edge of the fire to slowly cook. Then with their sharpest knives, they cut the remaining buffalo meat into slender strips and hung them over their newly built drying racks, and they constructed yet more drying racks to accommodate the volumes of meat. The men worked to set only about one third of the meat up on the drying racks before dark. The rest they hung from the trees to continue cooling down and out of reach of the larger meat-eating critters. Finally, hunger overtook the two men and they descended on the large iron cooking pot's good smells as only fresh buffalo meat gives. Soon the only noise to be heard was the eating of great chunks of meat and loud drinking of the hot, rich meaty broth from tin cups.

In one hour, the men had almost emptied the pot, so they refilled it with more water from their spring. Then more chunks of buffalo meat, salt, pepper, a handful of flour for thickening and more wild onions completed the repast soon to be. With that, the two men returned to the huge job of processing the meat. As a future winter treat, the meat being racked to dry was also sprinkled with salt and pepper from their vast stores of spices. Plus, by so doing, it helped to keep the flies off the meat while it dried.

By late the next day, all the meat had been cut into thin strips and hung to smoke and dry. Resting in shifts, the men arose every four hours to tend the smoking aspen fires and turn the meat. During one of those episodes, Jacob unrolled his white buffalo hide and staked it out on the ground in the filtered sunlight of the

pine forest. Getting out a scraper—something Singing
Bird would have done for him had she been there—he
scraped the remaining pieces of fat and meat from the
skin. Then he returned to the meat-drying racks to tend
the fires and turn the meat. Once the meat was cured, it,
too, was packed in parfleches for winter and hung from
the cabin's ceiling beams on wooden pegs.

Back on the sagebrush flats several days later, both
men prepared once again to make meat. Eight more
buffalo were killed and again the travois were loaded
until they could take no more. Only this time Jacob took
three buffalo skulls back along with the meat.

Once back at camp, Jacob cut open the buffalo skulls
with a hand ax and removed their brains. Jacob put the
brains into another large cooking kettle with some spring
water after he had mashed them into a pulp. Then every
time he and Martin had the urge, they urinated into the
pot of mashed buffalo brains.

Several days later, Jacob dug a hole and lined the
bottom and sides tightly with rocks and packed mud.
Then he placed the hide from Big Medicine into the hole
with the hair side down forming a large "U." After three
more days of adding their essence to the pot, the stinking
mixture was then stirred and poured onto the skin side
of the hide, covered and left to cure. In a week the
stinking hide was removed, taken to one of the nearby
creeks and staked down on a riffle. It was left in the creek
for two days with the water running over and under the
hide and the little fish tugging on the remaining pieces of

meat. The brain-and-urine kettle was left underwater in the creek as well to freshen out. Then the hide was retrieved and laid out to dry in the filtered forest sunlight on the lean-to roof.

One week later after being hand-worked with a smooth river stone, the tanned hide was as soft and supple as any trader would want. In addition, the creek waters had washed the hide clean to where the hair side fairly gleamed white in the light of day. It was now a truly beautiful hide to behold. Then, while Martin prepared for the trapping season soon to be upon them, Jacob cut and fashioned the hide from Big Medicine into long pullover winter capes for both he and Martin. With the fur side of that massive bull buffalo on the outside and the soft skin side on the inside, a nicer rain and snow protection garment never existed. The flap of the cape fastened in front by two sharpened notched sticks and both men were now prepared for the worst winter had to offer.

For the next two days, both men tore open a few of the many beaver dams along the Michigan River and set out their traps. Soon the traps were full of beaver captured as they had tried to repair the breaks in the dams. The men removed the large rodents' castoreum and, adding a mineral-oil base traded for at the rendezvous as an extender, had the necessary scent to lure the beaver to the traps. They built a smoky fire and hung the rest of their traps over the smoke to disguise the man scent as they cooked up the best parts from the beaver trapped for the castoreum. The beaver stew was a welcome repast for the men that night. It always seemed that a beaver-meat dinner prior to the advent of the trapping season was a good omen of things to come.

The next morning, Jacob set his last beaver trap as Martin sat nearby on his horse watching for any signs of danger. Then it was Martin's turn. Jacob took the reins of the packhorse and Martin moved to another large beaver dam on the Michigan to begin setting his traps. Jacob stayed alert because they had seen a lot of sign of the Arapaho in their vicinity and he was well aware from fur-trapper talk that as a tribe, the Arapaho didn't cotton to the presence of white men on their hunting grounds.

After Martin finished setting his traps, the two of them rode upstream for a few miles looking for other good beaver-trapping grounds. Beaver dam after beaver dam greeted their eyes. It seemed every body of water held a beaver colony as did every tributary to the river itself.

When they came back to the waters just trapped, they found every trap except one already held a beaver. The two men reset the traps and scented the lure sticks once again, then loaded the dead beaver onto the packhorse and returned the short distance to their camp.

Once at camp, a meat pot was started next to the fire and the men began skinning out the beaver. The castoreum was saved in wooden containers and willow was cut from the nearby stream to make the hoops necessary for stretching and drying the hides. Once "stretched" the hides were fleshed out one more time and then set out on the roof of the cabin to dry. The first morning's take had been good and the men hoped their luck would continue. Then the beaver carcasses had their ham and loin meat removed, chunked up and placed into the cooking kettle. The remaining carcasses were packed off from the cabin and placed in a ravine for the critters to eat.

The men awoke to a rainy morning the following day. Clouds hung low in the mountains and it was obvious to the weather wise that winter was soon to be their companion for many months. They heated up the partial pot of cooked meat from the evening before, then they feasted in a quiet fashion that had become a routine for the two men deeply lost in their thoughts. After break-fast, they saddled their horses and, taking the one pack animal along to carry the soon-to-be trapped heavy bodied beaver, they struck out for the upper reaches of the Michigan River. The rain was constant but the capes from Big Medicine not only kept them warm and dry, but also kept the ignition systems of their Hawkens tucked underneath ready to go at a moment's notice as well.

Jacob tended his six traps, happily finding every one of them filled with a large "blanket-sized" beaver. Then it was Martin's turn as he dismounted and walked along the edge of a beaver dam checking his traps. The first four of his traps, like Jacob's, were full of beaver and large ones at that. Martin tied those to the pack animal, re-set his traps and then continued upstream to his next trap. Unlike the others, it contained a still struggling beaver.

Just as Martin reached for the beaver, an arrow slapped into the creek bank just inches from his outstretched hand. Jacob whirled in time with Martin. The two of them observed at least thirty close-at-hand mounted Arapaho warriors staring hard at the invaders discovered on Indian lands.

The recent rains must have so dampened the vegetation that it muffled their approach, thought Jacob.

Both trappers quickly cocked their firearms. In a few moments our days as Mountain Men and lives as human beings are about to come to a violent end, if the looks on the Indians 'faces are any indication as to what is coming. Jacob quickly signed they were there in peace but not one smile cracked a single face nor did any sign of friendliness come to light. That's it! We're dead!

Jacob slowly adjusted his Hawken laying across the front of his saddle so he could kill the apparent leader of the band, if and when they made their charge. He knew that the move and his thoughts of defense were futile, but he was not going across the Great Divide without a good fight. The hardened look on Martin's face told Jacob it was apparent that he also realized today was a good day to die.

Then the band of Arapaho divided, with one bunch of horsemen moving quickly around behind the trappers and the other moving closer face-on. It was obvious the Indians were not happy with the trespassers and were just a set-trigger pull away from sending them into eternity.

Then it happened. An older Indian to the rear of the bunch of horsemen to Jacob and Martin's front started speaking excitedly. For a moment, his voice was the only thing heard over the softly falling winter rain. But as he spoke like a ripple of wind across the prairie grasses, the other braves stopped and began paying heed to the old man's loud ranting. Soon the horsemen began backing away from Jacob and Martin like they were a plague or a God of some sort. The fierce looks on their faces also turned from that of killing someone right now, to that of bewilderment and awe. Jacob sensed Martin taking advantage of the moment of concern among the Indians, for his friend moved closer to his horse if for nothing else than the cover its large body afforded. Indians hated to kill or wound horses in a fight. Maybe Martin feels he might at least get off a second shot before meeting his maker, Jacob thought.

The old Arapaho pulled his horse forward a mite and in a loud voice continued yelling at Jacob and Martin. Neither of the men understood a word of the Arapaho language so they couldn't figure out what the old man was saying. Jacob slowly raised his hand and bid them welcome in sign once again. Then he requested they speak in sign since he did not understand their language. The Indian continued yelling, ignoring Jacob's request to speak in sign.

Then Martin slowly moved to Jacob's side and said,

"Jacob, I think he is yelling because he is afraid of us for some reason."

Jacob realized Martin's possible wisdom, tried sign once again. This time the old man went to sign and what he had to say surprised both Jacob and Martin.

"Big Medicine!" he signed.

"Big Medicine!" he signed once again as the rest of the braves in his party continued backing their horses away from the trappers.

"You are wearing the power of Big Medicine around your necks," the older Indian continued to frantically sign.

Then Jacob understood what was happening. Both he and Martin were wearing their capes made from the white buffalo called Big Medicine by the Indians. As it turned out, they not only held the white buffalo sacred but were scared of its "medicine" or powers as well. With he and Martin both wearing the white buffalo capes, he figured the Indians must have figured the strong medicine from the white buffalo had transferred to them.

Jacob signed once again that they had come in peace, that they wished only to trap beaver and that Big Medicine had told them it was alright.

With those "words" the Indians really recoiled, backing their horses away from the trappers even further.

Then Jacob gambled with the moment at hand. Signing again, he advised the old man: "Big Medicine also told me to trade white man's goods with my Indian brothers."

The Indians were really now very perplexed.

Jacob then boldly kicked his horse in the ribs forcing him to walk up to the Indian who had been doing all the frightened yelling. The eyes of the old man spoke of the terror in his heart but he held his ground so as not to show cowardliness in the eyes of his fellow war party. As he stopped alongside the old man, Jacob noticed he never took his eyes off the white buffalo cape. Jacob smiled. He thought, *If I make any quick movement, it could cause the entire terrified band of Indians to flee into the forest in a heartbeat.*

Making the sign of peace once again, Jacob asked if his band would be interested in trading their furs for white man's goods as Big Medicine had requested.

The old man was having a tough time with the changing events and the closeness of the white magical cape but finally advised that his tribe was camped just a few miles away. And if the wearer of Big Medicine wished to trade, he would tell the chief.

Not wanting the Indians to know where their cabin and stash of goods and furs were located, Jacob asked if he and Martin could meet those who wanted to trade in the big meadow across the valley from where they now stood.

The old man nodded a frightened "Yes," still not taking his eyes off the white buffalo cape.

Jacob signed once again that they would meet those

who wished to trade tomorrow in the afternoon and they would bring items to trade for furs.

The old man nodded and then slowly reached out and touched Jacob's cape. He slowly withdrew his hand and looked at his fingers as if expecting his digits to be missing.

Jacob just smiled. *It was a very good thing that I saw and shot the white buffalo. If I had not done so, both Martin and I would be lying face down in the meadow at this very moment.*

Then with a yell that surprised the hell out of Jacob, the old man whirled his horse and the entire band of still terrified Indians disappeared into the rain-dampened forest without a backward glance or the click of a horse's hoof. Jacob and Martin just sat there looking at each other, realizing how close they had come to meeting their death—their rapidly beating hearts said it all.

Jacob and Martin quietly sat on their horses in the middle of the meadow the following afternoon. The two men agreed on the middle because if the Arapaho had changed their minds, Jacob and Martin would have a chance at killing eight of them with the Hawkens and horse pistols before being overwhelmed.

Both men held the reins to a packhorse loaded with trade goods from the last rendezvous: hand mirrors, steel rings to wear, blue and red glass beads, Green River skinning knives, kettles, beaver traps, a small amount of powder and shot were packed on one horse; the other was packed with whetstones, fish hooks, fishing line, brass tacks to decorate their rifles, flints and fire steels, sacks of coffee beans and several Hudson's Bay Company blankets. Jacob knew these items were a veritable bonanza of an easier life for a tribe not connected with a rendezvous or close to a trading post.

After a while, Jacob felt and realized they were now under scrutiny from many eyes hidden in the forest. He shifted uncomfortably under the heavy white buffalo cape and waited. Then from the north end of the meadow emerging from the trees came what appeared to be the whole damned tribe. They approached quietly at first and then, as they got closer, the Indians started buzzing with wonder and excitement. Jacob and Martin smiled at each other as they noticed many horses carrying furs.

Finally, a distinguished looking warrior rode up to Jacob in all his finery, all the while staring at the white buffalo cape. Without a word he rode alongside Jacob, boldly reached out and touched the cape. Then he rode over to Martin and did the same. With that, a sound of wonder rose from the hundred or so Indians gathered behind him in the meadow.

In sign, the apparent chief of the band asked Jacob, "Are you the one with all the powers from Big Medicine and do you have the White Man's items to trade?"

Jacob signed "Both my friend and I wear the sacred capes and we will trade if you and your people desire."

The chief turned to his people and said something in Arapaho. Those with pack animals loaded with furs moved forward.

Jacob and Martin dismounted and began laying out on a buffalo robe—one decorated with pieces of the white buffalo hide that was left over from the capes— their goods to trade. At first, no one wanted to approach the buffalo robe with pieces of white buffalo hide laid on it. Martin was the first to break the ice; he walked over and took the hand of a young Arapaho boy. Martin walked him back to the trade goods, reached down and took a piece of white buffalo hide to let him touch it. The young boy got a huge grin, then ran back into the comfort of the tribe. He at once was accosted by dozens of other Indians wanting to touch him. And with that simple gesture, the trading began.

For the next hour, Jacob and Martin traded their items for a small mountain of furs. Buffalo robes, river otter, gray fox, deer, beaver and elk made up the bulk of the trades. The pelts traded were not only rich looking but done with a quality the men had never seen previously except for those tanned by Cheyenne women. However, with each trade, the Arapaho trader had to reverently touch the buffalo capes worn by Jacob and Martin. It was a series of moving moments for not only the spiritual Arapaho but Jacob and Martin as well.

When the trading was done, the chief rode up to Jacob and Martin once again. He signed that Jacob and Martin were also Big Medicine. "You are welcome in the valley and will not be disturbed by any of my people."

Jacob could hardly believe their luck. A free pass from

Indian danger in the trapping Garden of Eden. Receiving safe passage was almost too hard to believe.

Jacob then signed, "Big Medicine is pleased with your words and if your people ever need help, they are to call on the two trappers for whatever is needed."

The chief signed his appreciation, turned and rode away. With him went the rest of the tribe but not without a lot of backward glances at the two men wearing the sign of Big Medicine.

Throughout that fall and early winter, Jacob and Martin hardly looked over their shoulders for sign of hostile Indians. When they did see the Arapaho hunting parties, they waved in a friendly manner. The waves of friendship were returned and then the Indians moved on as if still respective of the powers of Big Medicine.

Freeze-up found the two men more than satisfied with their trapping results. Between the trapping and trading with the Indians, they had over two hundred beaver skins, thirty buffalo hides, and another forty furs from the gray fox, mule deer, river otter, pine marten and elk. And yet, the spring trapping season of 1833 was still ahead of them.

One cold winter morning, Jacob and Martin oversaw a herd of buffalo from downwind that were unaware of their presence. Just as they were getting ready to kill a number of them for some fresh meat, they became aware of the sounds of many horses' hooves quietly coming up behind them. Turning, they observed about twenty mounted Arapaho warriors with women and horse-drawn travois moving up towards them. It was obvious they had been hunting buffalo as well. Jacob dropped back down the ridge to hide them from the quietly feeding buffalo.

Jacob signed to the leader of the party. "If you wish, my friend and I will kill some buffalo for our Arapaho friends. We have long rifles and can kill much more easily than you can with your flintlocks. Big Medicine has asked that we do this for our friends who are sharing the valley with us."

An instant smile crossed the face of Many Arrows Flying, the leader of the hunting party, and he agreed. With that and the Indians quietly sitting on their horses below the ridgeline, Jacob and Martin set to work. Boom-boom—boom-boom went the big Hawkens, and four cow buffalo dropped to the beat. They hurriedly reloaded all four rifles out of sight from the herd, and quickly dropped another four cows.

Within a short period of time, thirty buffalo from a "stand" graced the lightly snow-covered sagebrush flats.

Jacob agreed with Martin that there was more than enough meat for all, so they rose from their place of concealment, turned and faced the Indians as the buffalo thundered out of sight from the now-realized danger. Raising his hand, Jacob gestured for the hunting party to come forth and share the meat. That they did for the next four hours. Knives flew and soon the travois of Arapaho and trappers alike fairly sagged under the weight of the steaming fresh meat. There was much excited talk as they readied their horses to return, about thirty shots being fired and thirty buffalo lying on the ground. Truly there was Big Medicine in the two men.

The two hunting parties went their separate ways with a friendly wave of hands. Jacob and Martin rode to their cabin and the Arapaho rode to their campsite in the forested meadows along Willow Creek, some two miles distant. Jacob and Martin had a goodly share of fresh buffalo and the Arapaho had a hoard of meat that they acquired without firing a shot.

Come the spring of 1833, the two men went about their business of eradicating the beaver along the Michigan and Illinois Rivers. Soon they added another one hundred and sixty-seven beaver pelts to their hoard, and the beaver ponds in many areas became still and motionless except for the rise of a brook trout or from the flush of a pair of mallard ducks.

THE 1833 RENDEZVOUS

MUCH WORK WAS NOW NEEDED BY THE TWO MEN MAKING ready for the long trek north to the Green River Valley and the July rendezvous. Soon the furs were tightly packed, horses shod, and equipment repaired. The weather for travel turned pleasant. Rising before daylight on the given day to begin their trek soon found Jacob and Martin well on their way north. But before they left, Jacob took the time to carve his and Martin's name into the ridgepole of the cabin.

Four packhorses strung out behind each man, all heavily loaded with furs and equipment from the past trapping season. Both men had a lot to be pleased with and their smiles signaled that they were happy to be on the trail once again. Retracing their steps from the previous summer was made easier with the good weather and lack of hostile Indians to cause concern. However, it seemed every afternoon the skies would cloud up with black and violent thunderstorms, then the skies would open up and the rains would descend upon them. To avoid the danger of being struck by lightning on the open sagebrush flats, the men headed for the nearest small draw or a dry creek bottom and laid up until the worst part of the storm had passed. Soon the storms would move on and then the sage and other plants would come forth with many great fresh smells as only the cool high desert can produce. All of this made the life of a Mountain Man that much more memorable. At least for those who lived to enjoy it.

The two men traveled west up over the Continental Divide and headed for the Yampa River. Once on the Yampa, they headed north until they hit the Green River. Continuing northwest, they finally arrived in the Green River Valley, site of the 1833 rendezvous. Falling in with several other parties of trappers also heading to the rendezvous, they eventually ended up where the Green River and Horse Creek intersected. Several miles distant was a place euphemistically called Fort Bonneville, comprised of nothing more than a few log breastworks and some worse- for-wear log cabins. But it was there the American Fur Company and the Rocky Mountain Fur Company had both set up shop during that first week in July. However, because of the competition and the bad blood that soon followed, the Rocky Mountain Fur Company moved their location to the banks of the Green River five miles above the mouth of Horse Creek.

The American Fur Company on the other hand, moved its operations approximately five miles downstream to where the Green River intersected with Horse Creek. That left the much smaller St. Louis Fur Company remaining at Fort Bonneville.

Jacob and Martin set up their camp near the willows and under the cottonwoods on Horse Creek near its confluence with the Green. There were about one hundred trappers camped in the area with about another one to two hundred friendly Indians and their tepees. That number of Indians fluctuated daily, especially with the arrival and departures of nearby Snake Indians coming down from the mountains to trade as well. Soon the usual drinking, sporting events, squaw trading, shooting matches, food gorging and rampant hell raising spun its web around the traders on both sides of the table.

Jacob and Martin spent their time visiting with old friends like Jim Bridger and making new ones like those of Tom and Albert Potts. Both Potts brothers had been free trappers since 1820. They knew the country like the back of their hands and seemed to take a real liking to the younger Jacob and Martin. The four new friends compared tales and drank the vile drink the trappers called, "Trapper's Topknot Remover." Jacob and Martin also questioned those who had been to the new beaver trapping grounds to the north, west and south about the trapping potentials and friendliness of the local Indians.

Then came time to trade their pelts but a surprise was

in store for the men. After talking with representatives from the American Fur Company and the Rocky Mountain Fur Company, Jacob and Martin found that their buyers were downgrading almost every pelt and their trade item prices were higher than a dog's back in a three-way cat fight. Plus their members were advising that beaver plews were being replaced by silk top hats in the world of fashion, even though beaver-skin hats had been around and in fashion since 1600. It seemed in just a short period of time, beaver which had once sold in the eastern markets and Europe for up to six dollars a pound —a beaver skin properly processed weighed approximately one-and-a-half pounds—were now going for less than three dollars per pound. As a result, the fur companies advised they couldn't pay top prices like they had in years past. Ignoring that kind of depressing talk but keeping the silk top hat issue in the backs of their minds, the two men moved on to the St. Louis Fur Company hoping they would do better in their trades.

Jacob and Martin eventually contracted with the fur buyers from that company. Here the buyers were not quite as crooked and the needed trade items not as high priced. They were also seemingly unaware the beaver fur market had totally bottomed out, having left St. Louis before that information had arrived from the eastern markets.

Another surprise awaited the men as well. Both noticed that the trade in their buffalo robes they had traded from the Arapaho Indians brought even higher profits than those received for their beaver. This was something that gave both men pause when it came to thinking about their futures in the fur business. In the ensuing trades, Jacob and Martin did very well, so much so, that they more than replenished their needed items. In addition, they were able to acquire more trade goods useful for dealing with the Indians back on the trapping grounds. With their trades out of the way, the men had even more time to relax and enjoy their times and friends at the rendezvous.

But the good times were cut short by a rare and deadly incident that would likely be talked about for years afterwards. As was usual, many of the trappers drank more than they should have. Several of those men who had passed out along the fringes of the crowd found themselves subsequently bitten by a lone wolf frequenting the rendezvous. Then the wolf became more emboldened, approaching and biting several more trappers right in camp. This rare activity went on for about three days until the men realized the wolf was rabid and shot him. By then, over a dozen men had been bitten. Then those bitten began to show the signs of contracting rabies. Some growled and barked while others foamed at their mouths and couldn't speak. Several jumped off their horses while on hunting trips, foaming at the mouth and barking at their companions. Most affected trappers simply ran off into the timber and were never seen again. This event pretty much shut down the spirit and fun of the rendezvous.

Sitting in camp one morning, Jacob and Martin repaired their old moccasins and made several pairs each of new ones. That was soon followed with repairing the packsaddles, horseshoeing and the making of a pile of pistol and rifle bullets.

"Hello the camp," bellowed a familiar voice.

Both Martin and Jacob stood up in order to welcome their new friends. Tom Potts rode into camp with his brother, Albert, and both quickly dismounted. After greetings all around, Tom asked if they had anything good to eat.

"Nothing but a little bit of pronghorn," said Martin.

"Jus' so happens we have two hinds of an elk Albert shot a piece back. If you was to build a roaring hot fire, we could have some venison roasting on them there cooking sticks in short order," advised Tom with a grin of anticipation.

Soon the fire was going and slabs of fresh elk were roasting merrily away on the green cut willow sticks.

"Where the two of yer agoin' this fall?" asked Tom.

"Haven't decided yet," advised Martin "but somewheres north from here maybe."

"That be good," said Tom as he moved his willow stick holding the meat so it would be closer to the fire.

"Al and me have decided maybe to go north into the Hoback this go around. Or maybe even back into the west side of the Wind Rivers where the beaver are plentiful and the trappers aren't. Either way, that will put us close to next year's rendezvous."

"We trapped the Bighorn Mountains several years ago and did real good," advised Jacob.

"Ran into a little trouble with the Blackfoot but the risks were worth it," said Martin through a mouthful of sizzling hot elk meat.

Soon all the talk as to where to go was lost in the noises men make when they are hungry and eating something they liked. After finishing off the first round of roasted meat, more was sticked for roasting. While waiting for that to cook, the talk once again turned to trapping in the coming fall and winter season.

"Maybe the Hoback be too close," mumbled Tom, "and too full of our brethren." Al nodded thoughtfully at his brother's statement.

"What say the four of us hook up and go to the Wind Rivers for the new season? We know several places where the trapping is good and the competition will be little and only from the Snake Indians," suggested Tom.

"With the four of us working that area, maybe the Blackfoot will leave us alone and we could make a good haul," advised Al as he picked up on Tom's suggestion and looked all around the group for support.

"That would be fine with me," said Jacob.

"What do you think?" he asked Martin, who was wrestling with a gob of meat too big and hot for his mouth.

"Ummph," said Martin as he finally was able to wolf down the slab of hot meat. "Sounds good to me. Always could use the extra rifles. Not because of the Snake

Indians since they have always been friendly, but them damn Blackfoot and their killing cousins the Gros Ventre are worrisome when they decide to venture south on their raids. They make a man's blood run cold if they can approach a body whisper close," continued Martin.

The other three men nodded in agreement over Martin's historically wise words.

"Them Blackfoot and their friends can be a problem," said Tom thoughtfully. "But, the four of us are well-armed with not only the new Hawkens but all of us have extra rifles as well. That will put a lot of lead in the air with a passel of death at the other end should the need arise and we have a chance to shoot first. Then throw into that fracas our eight pistols at close range and we could put a hurt on anyone messin' with us." Tom had a serious tenor of meaning coming into his voice.

"Then is it decided?" asked Al. "If so, we can hook up and form our own fur brigade and trap the hell out of them Wind Rivers and their beaver," he continued with gaining enthusiasm.

There was a short pause and then all the men nodded in agreement. It was now decided that the four of them would sally forth to the western side of the Wind River Mountains and trap until the 1834 rendezvous—a rendezvous that according to Tom who had overheard the traders, would be on Ham's Fork of the Green. The next hour was then spent in less talk and more eating of the elk until all the eatings had been consumed with great relish.

22

POTTS BROTHERS, SNAKE SISTERS

TWO DAYS AFTER THE END OF THE 1833 RENDEZVOUS, THE four trappers were strung out with their mounts and pack strings heading for the Wind River Mountain Range. Since Tom knew the way to the trapping spot he had in mind, he led the band north up along the Green River until they reached the point where Beaver Creek joins the Green. There he turned the group east until they reached a large, twelve-mile-long lake. When they located a sheltered valley in between two long, heavily timbered ridges, the company drew to a stop.

Jacob's practiced eye quickly noticed an abundance of water and enough high-mountain grasses in the nearby meadow for their horses. Looking further, Jacob not only noticed that the location would provide shelter from the howling northwest winter winds but protection from prying eyes as well. There was also an abundance of firewood nearby and the beaver waters they had recently crossed were within spitting distance from where they now sat. A glance over at Martin and Al showed the same thoughts being calculated.

Tom said, "Let's light down. This looks like a great spot to drop our feet and rest our backsides a spell."

The men needed no further coaxing and soon unloaded their gear. First and foremost, the horses were unpacked, double hobbled and set out to take up some grub in the lush meadow. Then the men set about building a large lean-to for their temporary sleeping area. With that and a fire pit set into place in front of the lean-to for the warmth it would afford, the men set up shop.

Martin grabbed his bow and arrows and slipped off quietly into the dense stands of lodgepole pine and sage-brush flats at the edge of the meadow and was soon out of sight.

Jacob stacked all their packs in front of their lean-to to make a barricade for protection in case they got into a surprise fight with any local Indians upset over their presence. It shouldn't be a problem with the local Snake Indians. But those damn Blackfoot and Gros Ventre...thought Jacob. He let his thoughts drift off into nothingness as he finished stacking the packs and saddles in a protective barrier in front of the lean-to.

Al grabbed his Hawken and slowly ambled off down-stream from their camp to look for fresh beaver sign.

Tom, with rifle in hand, walked upstream to ascertain the beaver trappings in that neck of the woods as well.

Twenty minutes later, Martin came back dragging a nice rolling fat, four-point mule deer buck whose antlers were just coming out of the velvet. Jacob and Martin then built a meat pole set up between a couple of stout aspens near their lean-to. Soon the buck was hanging head down. As Martin gutted and skinned their dinner, Jacob scouted around for some stout green willow sticks that could be used in roasting the meat. In the process, he spooked a small herd of cow and calf moose out of the thick stands of brush adjacent to a large beaver pond. Jacob grinned at the abundance of game so near their camp and especially at the numerous signs of beaver and beaver houses in the watered areas.

This area has the possibility of being as good as the first valley we trapped in the Bighorn Mountains northeast of here, he happily thought.

When he arrived back at camp, Jacob soon had several large slabs of the mule deer's hindquarter and back straps merrily roasting around the fire. Martin, in the meantime, had staked out the deer hide in the sun and was busy scraping off the remaining scraps of meat and fat.

Yes, this area had great potential, thought Jacob with a grin.

Soon Tom and then Al returned. Both had wide grins beneath their massive beards.

"Beaver sign and beaver everywhere," advised Tom in a pleased tone of voice.

"I found the same as well," replied Al as he moved over to the fire and the cooking venison. Soon all the men followed Al's lead as he fell to the dinner provided by Martin. After finishing the first round of roasted meat, they fastened more to the roasting sticks and sat back and talked over the work that lay ahead of them before they could trap a single beaver.

"Tomorrow we had better start on our cabin," stated Jacob as the other three nodded in agreement.

"Better get a stout corral built as well before some Indian lifts our horses," mumbled Al as he picked the slivers of meat from between his teeth with the sharpened tip of his gutting knife.

"We have enough deer meat to last through tomorrow so maybe we can get an early start on the cabin and corral before we get doused with the afternoon rains and end up looking like a couple of wet beavers," suggested Martin.

The men grinned at the comparison, knowing what a summer thunderstorm soaking was like in the mountains, and nodded in agreement. The second set of roasting deer meat was now ready and the men fell to like they had not yet eaten anything that afternoon. Piping hot Dutch-oven biscuits accompanied that meaty repast. They soon disappeared, as did the second set of Dutch- oven biscuits. Then out came the men's pipes and the sweet smell of pipe smoke quickly filled the cooling evening air.

When the campfire was reduced to coals and the mosquitoes emboldened, the men retreated to their sleeping furs in the lean-to. Soon the faraway howl of wolves and a star-filled sky were the only signs that God was still awake.

The next morning, Jacob and Martin started cutting timbers and setting posts as they made a sturdy corral for the group's horses. Tom and Al continued doing nothing but cutting and dragging green logs to the area where the cabin was to be constructed. By that evening the corral was finished and a large pile of green logs had been stacked by the cabin site.

Jacob and Martin started construction of the cabin the following morning as Tom and Al continued cutting and hauling additional logs for construction. Their work started with scraping off the accumulated ground's duff then digging down a foot into the soil and packing a dirt floor outlining what was to be the cabin's exterior boundary. Next came the cabin's base logs which were the largest in size. After that, they measured and notched logs, descending in size, while log ramps to aid in the lifting of the logs onto the wall and a pair of pulling horses completed the work.

Soon the cabin's walls were six feet in height. Windows and doors were then cut, and shutters, shooting ports and log doors were constructed and placed. All the wood scraps were piled next to their central fire pit and used for cooking meals as the days and work progressed. By week's end, the men had their cabin. It was about twenty feet in length, fifteen feet wide and seven feet high on the inside height. It had the typical log, sagebrush and dirt roof. It also possessed two windows in front for the light they offered and two shooting holes per side on the walls. In short, it was ugly but hell for stout and built for warmth in the winter and coolness in the summer.

Another lean-to was constructed by the corrals and eventually filled with drying winter hay, cut and hauled from the meadow in huge armloads by the men between bouts of cabin making.

The next two days were devoted to cutting dead pine trees and dragging them to the camp area so they could be used for cooking and heat throughout the coming winter months. Since there was no mountain mahogany in the area—a species of iron hard, hot burning wood—a ton of aspen, cottonwood and willow was cut and stacked near the side of the cabin. Those woods were to be used for their Dutch-oven cooking, which needed non-resinous wood to prevent the cast-iron from sooting up.

Then the men went forth to the western foothills and sagebrush flats to make meat.

Twenty buffalo were shot and the next week was spent in smoking and drying the meat. Martin and Jacob then made numerous parfleches from their cured buffalo skins, filling them with the dried meat from the smoke racks. Moose taken from the waterways among the many willow patches were also harvested. That which was not eaten straight away by the always hungry trappers was jerked for hard times on the trail or during winter snowed-in periods. The moose hides were tanned as well because they made fine winter moccasins due to their thickness.

None of the men knew what the buffalo did in the winter as far as staying nearby or migrating out of the area once the deep snows came, so a concerted effort was made to make sure there was meat aplenty from the big animals before the anticipated heavy snows flew. They could always eat beaver meat, which they always agreed was very good, but there was just something to be said about a good "buffler" slab of hot meat cooked around an open fire with a slew of Dutch-oven biscuits slathered in wild honey. Then Al and Martin went forth, opened up a few beaver dams and procured the needed castoreum in order to start the serious business of fall and winter trapping.

Come the anointed day for the start of the 1833 fall trapping season when the beaver were coming into their prime, the men were up early. Jacob had great slabs of fresh moose back strap crackling away around the fire and the smell coming from his Dutch ovens proclaimed sourdough biscuits slathered with wild honey was soon to grace empty bellies.

The men finished breakfast and rechecked their equipment. Then they saddled their horses and placed packsaddles on two others. Jacob and Martin had decided they would trap the waters south of camp and Tom and Al the northern reaches of the valley. With a wave of the hand for good luck, the men quietly parted company and headed into another trapping season and the adventures it would bring.

That evening a tired but happy Jacob and Martin entered camp. They not only had twelve beaver plews across their pack animal, but a fresh hindquarter from a cow moose. The remaining hindquarter was left hanging in a shaded spruce out of reach of Ephraim about a mile distant. Shortly after dark, Al and Tom quietly entered camp. Their pack animal was heavy with twelve beaver carcasses but the looks on their faces was of an ominous nature. They dismounted and walked over to Jacob and Martin as if carrying the weight of the world on their shoulders.

"Lots of beaver from what we saw but we also have company. Blackfoot as near as we can tell and a pile of them. We found a place where they caught several Snake Indians trapping beaver several days back, butchered them and left what was left of their bodies to the varmints."

Jacob and Martin just listened but their earlier light-hearted entry into camp had now turned into something hard and cold.

"Think we all four need to work together for the protection it affords?" asked Martin.

There was a long pause as everyone looked to the more experienced Tom for answers.

"Don't rightly know," said Tom slowly. "First time I have seen Blackfoot this fer south so early in the year. Can't rightly figure out why. They have plenty game in their own backyard and don't need any of ours I reckon. I am also surprised the Snakes haven't discovered their presence and rooted them out. No matter. We must be on our toes or they will lift our topknots slicker than buffalo slobbers. Don't think we need to gang up as of yet because that will reduce our trappin's. Plus, the four of us would leave a world of fresh-shod horse tracks for them red devils to cross and backtrack. I figure we had better go armed to the teeth and only one man trap at a time. The other one best keep his eyes peeled and ready to fight," he thoughtfully suggested. "They will come out of nowhere and be as fierce as a she grizzly defending her cubs when they decide to attack, so we best be prepared. Another good thing might be to prime our pistols with buck and ball instead of just ball. That away we can flock shoot them if they come at us in a gang."

"With a little luck, maybe we can blind a few with the shot and finish them off at our leisure later," Tom mumbled as an afterthought.

Then the smell of fresh moose steaks cooking around the fire overrode their concerns regarding the bad news and soon all fell to chow like it was their last meal. However, all kept their rifles handy and their eyes peeled. Having the Blackfoot in country was no idle threat. All they could hope for was that they would move on into a different part of the country and leave them to their trapping.

Come daylight next morning, all the men around the campfire thoughtfully ate moose steak fried in bear grease, with bowls of hot cornmeal gruel sweetened with hard sugar, and tar-like coffee. When finished, words were not spoken as they separated with just a quiet wave of the hands.

This time, both sets of men really took their time working through a darkened forest which could be a friend as well as a foe. But once on the fringe of the beaver ponds, the edge of concern slowly disappeared as the traps set the night before were emptied of beaver and river otter, then reset.

The Potts Brothers took their work dead serious.

Al's practiced eye constantly checked the edge of the woods and patches of willows to the front and rear as his brother checked and reset his traps. When Tom finished, he mounted his horse, took his Hawken and repeated the same watchfulness his brother had just practiced.

Carrying his rifle and still keeping a watchful eye, Al began checking and then removing dead beaver and resetting his traps set the evening before. Slowly they moved up along the willows towards a finger of lodge-pole pine jutting out to the edge of the beaver pond. Tom took the lead and slowly rode into the pine finger that potentially posed a threat if someone was of the mind to use it as ambush cover. Al stood at the edge of the timber holding his Hawken as he covered his brother. Once on the other side, Tom motioned all was clear and for Al to come and bring the packhorse.

———

BOOM-BOOM—BOOM-BOOM—POW-POW, boom, boom, boom, boom, boom, boom broke the silence north of Jacob and Martin. They stopped instantly in their tracks and continued to listen, trying to discern what had just happened. The only sounds returning to their ears was that of a curious gray jay calling to his buddies. That was then followed with the loud call of a Clark's nutcracker high in a dead lodgepole pine and the ever-whispering wind through the trees.

Quickly remounting his horse from where he had been checking a trap, Jacob said, "Let's go!"

With that, the two men quietly moved through the forest to the north where they had just heard the mass firing of many heavy rifles and pistols. Half an hour later, Martin dismounted to look at a number of fresh horse tracks in the soft forest soil. A grimace soon followed on his weathered face. "Twelve unshod ponies following three shod horses. Looks like whoever they are, they cut Tom and Al's trail and followed."

Martin quickly remounted. The two men spurred their horses on to a faster but still cautious pace.

Twenty minutes later, Jacob saw something gleaming white through the timber next to a large beaver pond. They carefully working their way through the downfalls, then came upon a bloody scene. The "white thing" Jacob had spied was the naked body of Tom. He had been shot full of arrows and bullet holes, his heart and liver had been cut out and all the fingers on his shooting hand had been removed. His long brown locks of hair were also no more, leaving a bloody and gleaming white skull in their place.

Then Martin saw Al...or what was left of him. He had made it to the trees before the Indians had overrun his place of defense. He laid alongside a log, also stripped of all clothing like his brother and was mutilated. His head had been almost completely cut off and scalped. His body bristled with about thirty arrows along with two large purple and red bullet holes on both sides of his body. Rolling him over, Martin discovered that Al's chest had been split open and his heart had been cut out.

Both Jacob and Martin were appalled and angered at what they saw.

They rapidly cleared their senses for battle and glanced around to see if the danger still existed. Nothing but the quiet of the forest presented itself for view. It was obvious, however, some Indians had been wounded or killed in the ensuing action as well; there were several blood trails over the marks the hooves of the Indians' horses had made as they moved off. Both men began following the horses' tracks without hesitation. Regardless of the odds, their friends had been brutally killed and the killers had to be brought to justice.

Jacob thought, *Even if it means we're killed in the process, there'll be company in the killin'.*

Soon the men discovered hastily dug scrapes in the ground for three Indians' bodies. They were quickly confirmed as the dreaded Blackfoot by their dress and the markings on their arrows. That also meant that there were three less Blackfoot in the raiding party, leaving perhaps about nine. Just about the right odds, thought Jacob grimly.

A look at Martin's face revealed that he didn't care if there were a hundred. Someone was going to pay for what they had done to his friends no matter what the odds or outcome of the battle to follow.

That's one thing about Martin, Jacob thought. Once he gets his red up, someone or something is going to die.

After another careful three hours of travel, they came to overlook a scene of another deadly happening about to take place. In the creek's lush grasses below, thirty Indian ponies were feeding. They belonged to a peaceful band of Snake Indians. Off in a distance, on a flat under some cottonwood trees, there were fifteen tepees belonging to the horses' owners. A band of Snakes were camped, totally unawares that a party of dreaded Blackfoot were in their backyard with murder and thievery on their minds.

Martin pointed silently in a different direction. Not twenty yards from the two men, cleverly hidden in a large patch of willows, were the Indian raiders' horses, including those belonging to Tom and Al. Another twenty yards distant from the horses were nine Blackfoot Indians crawling up on the Snake's horse herd. They had already surprised the small Indian boy watching the herd from a distance and had quietly cut his throat. With the watcher of the herd dead, their way to the horse herd was almost free and clear. If they could spook the Snake's horses, return to their animals and then capture the loose mounts, the Snake could not pursue them except on foot. And an Indian on foot was no match for one on horseback.

As they continued slowly riding silently towards the deadly Blackfoot, Jacob and Martin became aware of another situation taking place in the creek. Two young women, probably in their late teens, were taking the time to bathe in the creek. Both Jacob and Martin, even under the stress of the moment, could not help but marvel at the naked beauty of the women. Then two Blackfoot warriors separated from the other seven and began crawling towards the unsuspecting women. With tomahawks in hand, their intentions were immediately crystal clear to the trappers. They would club the two women so they could not spread an alarm. Then the other seven would quietly move the horse herd back towards their staked horses, mount up and drive the Snake's horses out of the area, a real coup if they could pull it off.

Jacob and Martin quietly tied off their horses and took their reserve Hawkens off the pack animal. Normally they would not have carried their extra rifles but after Tom's words of caution the night before, carry them now they did. The extra firearms would come in handy in the events certain to follow.

The two Blackfoot Indians continued crawling through the willows towards the unsuspecting bathing women. Lying in the tall grasses unobserved, they waited until their seven partners were in position close to the

Snake's horse herd. Finally the signal was given when the seven could not sneak any further towards the horses without the women being removed from the scene first. Up jumped the two Blackfoot warriors and, in a matter of a few steps, they were upon the still unsuspecting women whose backs were turned to the onrushing danger. Both Blackfoot jumped into the stream and grabbed the women by their long hair before they knew what was happening. Then they jerked the women's heads back to prevent screaming and started to smash their tomahawks down on their faces. *Boom-boom* bellowed the trappers' Hawkens in quick tandem and the heads of both Blackfoot in the creek exploded, spewing blood and brains all over the two naked women. As luck would have it, both those Hawkens had only been loaded with ball, not buck and ball, allowing them to be shot accurately at long range. Screaming in terror, the women ran for the protective cover of the willows on the opposite bank of the stream.

Surprised at the shooting to their rear, the remaining seven Blackfoot turned to see what was going on. They decided to get up and run in panic towards their horses, allowing Jacob and Martin time to start reloading.

By now the Snake Indian encampment was alerted and their warriors streamed from their tepees with bows, arrows and rifles in hand. Looking all around, they did not see the running Blackfoot in the bushes by the creek until Jacob and Martin let loose with another barrage. *Boom-boom* roared the heavy rifles. Seconds later the reserve Hawkens let forth two more shots. At that range the men could not miss. Four of the seven running Blackfoot would never steal another horse or kill another trapper.

The remaining three scrambled up the hill as fast as they could towards their horses. The Snakes, upon seeing the fleeing Blackfoot for the first time, began shooting wildly. They were shooting but not hitting at that distance with their poor quality rifles and excited aim.

Just as the lead Blackfoot reached his horse, Martin stood up from his hiding place, shooting him squarely in the face with his pistol from a distance of three feet. The man was so close to Martin, his speed carried his body into the trapper, knocking him down.

The next two Indians, with tomahawks raised, moved to kill Martin as he was untangling himself from their dead companion. *Pow* went Jacob's pistol. The closest Indian dropped before he could swing his tomahawk. His partner, surprised now at the close presence of Jacob as well, turned to look and hesitated.

Martin, from his position on the ground taking full advantage of the Indian's hesitation, viciously sank his long-bladed knife upwards into the man's groin. An inhuman screech followed but it was not as loud and blood curdling as when Martin disemboweled him with another deft stroke of the same knife.

Still screaming, the man fell to earth on top of his intestines, wiggling in pain in the dirt. Within moments, he laid still in a huge spreading pool of bright red blood.

At that instant, the two trappers were swarmed by the revenge-seeking Snakes. Jacob and Martin held up their rifles overhead in a sign of peace and Jacob hurriedly signed that they came in peace to kill the Blackfoot about to steal the Snake's horses.

For a few brief moments, the anger of the Snake Indians was so great that many men's lives were now hanging in the balance. Then screaming and yelling came from the creek. The two women from the river were yelling to the Snake warriors. They continued yelling until the Snake men hesitated and finally lowered their raised weapons.

Jacob hurriedly began to sign to one of the Snakes about how their friends had been killed by the Blackfoot earlier in the day and how the trappers had set out to revenge the killing. Continuing, he told how they had come upon the Blackfoot after they had killed the boy guarding the horse herd and how the raiders tried to kill the two women in order to steal the horses. Then Jacob signed how their blood ran hot as they killed those guilty of killing their friends and who were now trying to kill the two women. Lastly Jacob quickly signed that they came as friends to the Snake and desired them no harm.

Based on what the women in the creek were yelling and the two men's peaceful moves, the fight went out of the Snakes and calm settled over the confrontation with Jacob and Martin.

With that, the Snake warriors descended on the dead Blackfoot, scalping and mutilating them in the process, the common practice among many Indians because it kept the dead with their missing parts from entering the Happy Hunting Ground. Jacob and Martin remained frozen in place as the Snake's anger was taken out on the nine dead Blackfoot.

When the Snakes returned, they were now led by what appeared to be a tribal leader. He turned out to be the chief of the band, a man named Nash-e-weta or He Grizzly.

In sign, the elder asked again what the trappers were doing there and how they had saved the two women. Jacob signed the whole story once again and the old man appeared not only to be satisfied but very pleased. The two trappers were then invited to the Snake's camp to eat and smoke the pipe of peace. Jacob and Martin agreed but not before recovering all of Tom and Al's horses, rifles, possibles, traps and knives. The remaining horses from the Blackfoot raiding party were divided up among the Snake warriors making them happier than all get out, not to mention wealthier than they had been just moments before the attack began.

Jacob and Martin went down to the camp loudly escorted by the Snake warriors. Soon several cooking fires were roaring with much meat being placed on roasting sticks and in cooking pots. Other items were also prepared by the squaws and soon a feast was in preparation for the two lifesaving guests. Feeling a little foolish, Jacob and Martin sat by one of the fires as the Snake children shyly approached the two men in order to touch the clothing of such great warriors and, by so doing, gain some of the white man's magic and strong medicine. Throughout the occasion, Jacob and Martin noticed that the two women who had been bathing in the creek before the shooting had started were now tending to their every want and need. Both women appeared to be sisters and about seventeen to nineteen years in age.

The men also noted to each other that, in addition to their good looks, they were very lithe and beautifully endowed.

Soon the eating and speeches commenced and Jacob and Martin were asked again and again to tell the story of how they killed the murderous Blackfoot, saving the lives of the two women and the valuable horse herd. Then a dance began with the warriors waving the bloody scalps of the Blackfoot in the air as they moved around a campfire in a ragged celebration of the event. The celebration went on past midnight over the wailing of the family members who had lost their son guarding the horses.

Finally, Jacob and Martin told their host that they needed to return to their camp in order to care for their horses still in the corral. The chief allowed the two men to leave but signed he must have some time to properly thank the men.

Jacob, realizing this was part of the Snake culture and not making a mistake like he did with the Ute chief before when he gave him the grizzly necklace, advised they would be happy to accept the chief's kindness at a later time. That brought a big smile to the face of the

chief and with handshakes all around the two trappers
headed back to their camp but not before going back to
the scene of Tom and Al's death.

Using their hands and sharpened sticks, they dug a
hole and buried the men in a single grave. Being that they
were brothers, Jacob felt that method of burial was
proper. Then the grave was covered with rocks to keep
the critters from digging the two men up and eating their
remains. Lastly, a roaring bonfire was built over the
rocks to foil any scents and further hide the bodies lying
below. Satisfied, saddened and drained of any further
emotions, they quietly headed for their camp.

They arrived at the cabin in the early morning dark.
They let their corralled horses out with hobbles so they
could water and feed. Then still emotionally drained over
the loss of their friends, they sat around a campfire
quietly staring into the flames. In so doing, they let their
thoughts go back to better times with Tom and Al.

Come daylight, both men were once again checking
and setting their traps. But in so doing, they remained
very alert to any other dangers that might be forthcoming. After returning to camp in the late afternoon with a
load of beaver, they commenced skinning and hooping
their skins. The best parts of the beaver were put into a
large cast-iron cooking pot with a handful of salt, pepper,
wild onions, red pepper flakes, some flour and water, and
soon a large stew was merrily boiling away.

Just as they finished hooping their last beaver, Jacob
was startled when he chanced to look up. Sitting there

quietly on their horses at the edge of the woods not thirty yards distant were twenty heavily armed Indian warriors.

"Martin," said Jacob to get his partner's attention as he quickly reached for his ever-present and always-at-arms-length Hawken.

Martin in one fluid motion did the same as the two men rose to face this latest threat. Only then did they realize the mounted warriors were from the band of Snake Indians they had met the day before. Lowering their rifles, Jacob strode forward and made the sign for peace. Chief Nash-e-weta did the same and soon the Indians and trappers were intermingling as old friends.

The Indians were invited to dinner and didn't have to be asked twice. Soon the twenty pounds of meat in the cooking pot was gone. That forced Jacob and Martin to stick chunks of beaver around the fire on cooking sticks for roasting to fill the rest of the Indians' empty bellies.

The chief remarked on the trapper's absence of fresh meat because of the recent battle and their lack of opportunity to replenish their stores. He turned and said something to one of his men. With that, the warrior quickly disappeared back into the forest on horseback.

Several hours later, the warrior returned with the two women from the creek incident who were now leading two horses each pulling a travois. Soon the women were cooking fresh meat they had brought from their camp.

It was about then that Martin made a decision relative to the celebration now about to unfold. He strode purposefully to their cabin, then returned with a gallon jug of whiskey from their own stores. It wasn't long before everyone was having a good time and as the whiskey ran out, the dinner cooked by the women was ready. Everyone fell to and soon the men were sitting around the fire with relaxed looks on their faces and full bellies. Then Jacob returned to their stores and brought forth two handfuls of smoking tobacco cuds. That lit up the faces of the Indians and soon the air was blue with the sweet-smelling James River tobacco smoke.

As the two squaws cleaned up the eating area, the chief rose to make a speech. In that speech he thanked the trappers for saving the two women and their entire horse herd from the hated Blackfoot. He also talked about the brave trappers and their straight-shooting rifles. Then he thanked them for the meal and advised that as long as he was the chief, they could trap all the waters in the valley as friends of his band.

However, Jacob and Martin, full of food and slightly warmed from the whiskey, were floored by the chief's next statement. The chief continued with the words that as a gift from his people for the trappers' bravery, they each would receive one of the women they had saved to be their wives.

Jacob and Martin were so stunned at those words that their faces must have showed great surprise. The chief, out of concern over the stunned looks, asked if the gift from his people was not good enough. It took a few moments for the men to speak but when they did, it brought instant relief to the face of the chief.

"Yes," signed Martin and Jacob at the same time.

Then an amazed Jacob signed, "The gift from the Snake is great and totally unexpected. A gift of such proportions is the greatest of honors."

"Good," signed the chief with a huge grin replacing his look of worry. "Then it is done. They will be your wives and, as such, my two daughters will be well cared for."

Jacob and Martin were still stunned and didn't know quite what to say or do, so they wisely kept their mouths shut.

With that, the band of Snakes made ready to leave after much good-natured back slapping and hugging. Once they mounted their horses, the chief signed good-bye and the Indians quietly disappeared into the night, leaving behind the two young women.

For a few long moments, the two trappers just sat there, lost at what to do with their change of fortunes. Then Jacob rose and headed for the women's horses and travois. He grabbed a load of items from one of the travois and headed for their cabin. He laid the items just inside the door, then headed back for another load. Martin followed Jacob's lead and did the same.

Once unloaded, the horses were unhooked from their travois and intermixed with the trappers' horses in the corral.

Then Jacob and Martin removed their sleeping gear from the cabin and laid it under one of the cabin's lean-tos.

Speaking in sign, Jacob indicated to the two squaws

that they were to sleep in the cabin that night for the protection it offered. Without a word, the women quietly rustled past the men and into the cabin. Jacob and Martin then headed for their sleeping furs under the lean-to and, placing their rifles next to them, drifted off into an uneasy but welcome sleep. Moments before they were two young and free trappers and now they had two Indian women to deal with and care for, and very beautiful women at that.

23

THE 1834 RENDEZVOUS

THE NEXT MORNING, THE TWO MEN WERE AWAKENED BY the women working around the campfire before daylight. Breakfast was ready and the women were waiting for the men to awake. Jacob and Martin washed off their faces and hands; Martin even attempted to comb his long mop of hair. As they sat on one of the log benches next to the fire, the men were served a wonderful tasting corn stew laced with chunks of smoked moose meat. The ladies made coffee far superior to that ever made by Jacob or Martin. The still surprised looks on the faces of the men were now mixed with appreciation for the new treatment and care they were receiving. It had been a long time since they had experienced some of the finer things of life and to their way of thinking, this had the makings of a good day.

When the men arrived back at their cabin later that

day with a large load of beaver, they were further surprised. The camp had been cleaned up and their sleeping furs had been lain over the corral rails to air out. There was a skinned-out doe taken with a bow and arrow by one of the women hanging from the meat pole and great smelling food was once again cooking around the campfire. Both men looked at each other in amazement still wondering how to handle the situation. Since dinner was not quite ready, both men, as if on cue, headed up into the hills surrounding their cabin and began cutting logs so another cabin could be built.

When Jacob had cut his first tree, he noticed the arrival of the woman he had come to know as White Fawn carrying an ax. Before he could say anything, she began removing the limbs from the tree just cut. A look over at Martin found the same event occurring with the other woman known as Running Fast.

Both men stood there in amazement until the women finished removing the limbs. With that, the men commenced cutting more trees as the women continued removing the limbs. With a load of timber cut, the men hooked up the horses and began pulling the logs into camp. This work was interrupted as the women gestured that dinner was ready.

As Jacob and Martin commenced eating, the two women began skinning and hooping out that day's catch of beaver. When they finished with the beaver chores, they returned to the campfire and then had their dinners as the two men sat there in surprise. Never had they experienced such hard working and yet pleasant-to-look-at women.

This pattern soon became a daily afternoon ritual after each day's trapping, until there were enough logs to build another cabin. Then the two men cut and built the second cabin while the women maintained camp, skinned and hooped the beaver, chinked the logs and assisted the men in whatever else needed doing in their extra time.

Over the next two weeks it became apparent that each woman had picked her man and both men were not displeased with their picks. Soon the men were learning the Snake language and the women English. When the second cabin was finished, White Fawn moved her belongings from the first cabin into the second. Jacob then moved his sleeping items from the lean-to into her cabin as well. Martin followed suit with his living items, moving them back into the first cabin with Running Fast.

As Jacob arranged his gear around the cabin, he was acutely aware of being watched. White Fawn's eyes followed him around the small room from where she stood by the door. Jacob could feel her anticipation, her fear, her excitement. Technically, they had been Mountain Man and squaw, husband and wife for weeks, but moving into one bed together, this marked their bonding.

Jacob avoided her eyes and busied himself by arranging and then rearranging his blanket furs on the bed. He knew what to do. The carousing at the rendezvous made it clear what men and women were

supposed to do. But that was different. The whoring of
uncouth men was what he had to draw from, but he
knew that it was not what he wanted, not for such a
beautiful and loving woman as White Fawn. He stopped
fidgeting, now that he realized he really knew nothing of
what men and women do to consummate a marriage,
nothing beyond the mere mechanics.

He turned and looked at her. White Fawn, in her
buckskin dress, simply waited for him. He thought of her
that first day, when he spied her bathing naked in the
waters while Blackfoot warriors plotted to kill her. At the
time, there was only thought of blasting a hole in a
murdering varmint's head to save the life of an innocent
woman, but as he pulled the memory back up in his
mind, something inside him stirred. Something hot,
something that took over his thoughts faster than
whiskey and twice as strong.

Lust.

White Fawn said something in the language of the
Snake. He held his lust in check, as the words, loving and
strange, flowed over him. She was of the earth, the wind,
the spirits of nature. He could not move with the crude-
ness of a Mountain Man. Instead, he stepped to her, with
the firmness of a warrior, a role he knew, one that spoke
of a desire to protect, not a desire to conquer.

Jacob took White Fawn's hand in his. "You are my
woman. This I swear to you, that I will keep you safe, that
you shall never fear the Blackfoot, the grizzly, or the
wolf, so long as I am with you. Not even the White Man

shall harm you." He caressed the jaw line of her face with a finger, and she pulled his hand against her cheek, pressing it into her face.

Jacob felt her spirit just below the skin. It flowed into his own. They touched, pressed and caressed, learning each other, letting one another's spirit flow together. They spoke in gentle words, each in a language the other did not understand, yet these were words as old as the earth, as easily understood as the sky. Jacob could not recall when they had disrobed, or when they had found themselves in the bedroll together, under furs and blankets. He only knew he wanted to learn more about her, to keep joining with her, to be closer than he had ever been to any person, inside her heart and her thoughts, as she was in his. He had discovered something stronger than lust, something nine times stronger.

Love.

It was hours later before Jacob could pull himself from his new bride. White Fawn lay quietly amid the furs, supple and beautiful and trusting. It took impossible strength for him to pull his eyes away, even more to actually leave the cabin for the late-morning mountain air—when had it become late morning? Had they been in bed for so long?

Martin and Running Fast had been waiting for him. They teased one another, while Martin would stop every now and again to teach her a word in English, and she taught him in Snake.

"Ahem," Jacob made his presence known. "Not like an Indian to let a white man sneak up on him."

Martin turned, and gave his childhood friend the biggest smile ever. The Delaware Indian scooped up Running Fast and whirled her about, then said to Jacob, rather matter-of-factly, but with much energy, "I have consummated my marriage, Jacob the White Man! This is my woman."

"That's good," Jacob replied, poking fun at Martin. "Perhaps you can give me a little bit of that meat and some coffee, and get back to whatever you were doing, and I can bring my woman some breakfast while I continue to consummate my marriage." The Wind River Mountains watched over them. The nearby creek gently reported its flow of water down the valley towards the large lake. Somewhere an eagle screeched. It was not like the men to lose a day without work, but this was their honeymoon with their new wives, and never had there been a more beautiful day in a more beautiful place.

Throughout that fall and into winter, the men trapped and their wives managed the camp. The men took Tom and Al's traps and ran those as well. Soon both pack animals returned to camp almost daily loaded with every beaver they could carry. And true to form, the hard-working women stayed ahead of the men in the skinning, fleshing and hooping duties. Soon their supply of beaver, river otter, muskrat and fox hides formed several small mountains in their cabins.

Fortune had again smiled on the two men as trappers.

And, if the price of pelts were worth anything that year, they would be able to replenish their supplies and gaily dress their women with just about anything in the way of apparel they desired.

Come the deep part of winter, the men quit trapping and settled down to await the spring thaw. Their work still continued, however. They were involved in such things as making new moccasins, repairing the old ones, casting more bullets for their rifles and pistols, and packing the furs into traveling bundles. The men also took the time to teach White Fawn and Running Fast to load and shoot the rifles and pistols accurately, in case the need arose in their absence. Those activities also included teaching the women the English language and learning that of the Snake. Lastly, when the weather was right, the men cared for their stock and made meat from the numerous moose and mule deer wintering in the valley near their camp.

When the spring of 1834 came, the men were more than anxious to resume trapping and add to their hoard of plews. Soon the ice was out and the men began once again the business of trapping. It seemed the beaver had greatly multiplied over the winter and the men begin catching large numbers of the furry rodent daily. Several times they brought in such loads of beaver that they had to stay home the following day to help their wives with the skinning and hooping duties.

Finally, the long-awaited moment after a hard spring-trapping season arrived and the furbearers had gone out

of prime. The men stopped trapping so they could have
their hides dried and processed before the journey to the
1834 rendezvous on Ham's Fork of the Green. The last
plews were finally packed into traveling bundles, more
bullets were cast for the rifles and items not needed for
the trip were cached since they would be returning to
this area after the rendezvous. The men then tended to
the livestock, making sure all were shod if needed and
the tack repaired for the long trip ahead. Lastly, two
moose were killed and made entirely into jerky for the
trip in case the hunting was poor along the way.

Come the day of departure, they made quite a caravan. Each woman rode her own horse and led two
others with travois carrying camp and sleeping items
along with a number of tanned buffalo hides. These
buffalo hides had been acquired from the Snake in trade
for North West fusils, powder, lead and Green River
knives over the quiet winter months. The men rode
their own horses, each of them leading four pack
animals heavily loaded with furs and some needed camp
equipment for the trip. Each woman carried a pistol
and by now knew how to use it, and Jacob and Martin
carried their Hawkens, two pistols each, and extra rifles
on the first packhorses in the line for instant retrieval.
They had done well once again. On the packhorses
were more than four hundred beaver plews, one
hundred muskrat hides, and another hundred fox, river
otter and mule deer hides. On two of the travois led by
their wives were nothing but tanned buffalo hides.

Suffice it to say, it had been a very good season for trapping.

For some several days on the trail, Jacob noticed that the two Indian women seemed to be conspiring in whispers. They would giggle and shoot the men sideways glances. Something was up, but when asked, White Fawn demurely looked away and would not answer.

One night, around a campfire, with the horses quietly eating the grasses in a meadow they had found, Running Fast told Martin "Come," and pulled him away by the arm to run off into the darkness nearby.

White Fawn sidled up next to Jacob on the rocks by the fire. "Jacob, you are good man."

"You are good woman." Jacob could see his wife struggling with English to tell him something.

"You are strong man. You bring good spirit to me."

Jacob was lost. "I am glad you are happy," he said.

"No! No, no no!" White Fawn's eyes began to well up. So frustrated was she to say what she had to say. She looked like she was making ready to sign, but instead pulled her dress up over her stomach. Jacob, confused by her timing, could not react. White Fawn reached for his · hand, then placed it on her stomach. Leaving the one hand there on top of his, she placed her other hand to his heart.

"Little person," she said.

Jacob rapidly pulled his hand back and jumped to his feet. "You're pregnant?" he stared deep at her, so intense was his question.

White Fawn stared into his eyes, afraid, unable to interpret his sudden actions, apparently. After a heartbeat, she quickly and nervously touched her belly. "Little person inside."

Jacob broke into joyous laughter and pulled White Fawn to her feet. "A baby!"

White Fawn giggled, the anxiety of telling her husband she was pregnant having been met with his pride and happiness. "Bay-bee?" she asked, as she always did when she was trying to learn a new English word.

"Baby. Little person." Jacob explained. "Wahh! Wahh!" he said as he tried to mimic a crying infant.

"Baby." White Fawn put Jacob's hand back on her stomach. "Ohmaa," to teach Jacob the Snake word.

Jacob pulled White Fawn close and tight. Then he began to dance a jig. "I'm going to be a father! I'm going to be a father!" Then, regaining his tough-man composure, Jacob said, "I can't wait to tell Martin."

"Martin make baby, too."

Jacob stopped, motionless. As he worked the new information into his skull, a loud Whoop! came from the darkness. It was Martin. Soon, Jacob's old friend came running back to the campfire, his wife barely able to keep up with her husband's grip. "Jacob! I'm going to be a father!"

"And so am I!"

———

THE COUPLES HEADED south along the New Fork River until it joined the Green River. Then, they followed the Green to Ham's Fork and finally arrived one beautiful afternoon after numerous days on the trail.

They soon discovered that the American Fur Company was camped near the junction of Ham's Fork and Black's Fork while the Rocky Mountain Fur Company was another seven miles up the Ham's Fork. Then they discovered that a man named Wyeth, a free-lance trader, was another five miles above the Rocky Mountain Fur Company on Ham's Fork. These scattered trading camps made for a lot of traveling back and forth during the rendezvous trading process.

White Fawn and Running Fast, never having been to a rendezvous, were wide-eyed at what lay before them. Surprise after surprise awaited the two because neither had ever experienced in their lives such an abundance of white man's things.

Jacob just had to smile at what their ladies were discovering upon arrival in each new trading camp, and he even caught Martin stifling a chuckle himself. One thing is for certain, the women sure do cotton to looking glasses, rings, bolts of brightly colored cloth and the many colored glass beads that are available in the camps.

The beaver plews were way down in price because the silk top hat industry was now more than ever supplanting that of beaver. Jacob and Martin traded very carefully for their needs in the coming year. Their many buffalo robes brought top dollar as did their river otter and fox pelts, especially since the two wives had done such an excellent job in skinning, fleshing and hooping the hides. As a result they got more than they needed in goods, including a fair amount of items to trade with the Indians throughout the coming year. Jacob and Martin also found themselves dressing up their wives in the finest "foofaraw" the beaver trade could supply. Many a trapper's head turned when those women rode by, making Jacob and Martin smile with pride even more so when they were offered top dollar for the women by other trappers. Their women had turned out to be excellent wives in every word and deed. Both men as well discovered themselves very deeply in love with their wives—and they, with them. No, these Indian women were not for sale.

24

GROS VENTRE

THE RENDEZVOUS WAS AS JUBILANT, DRUNKEN AND chaotic as in years past, but experience and a sharp eye kept the two Kentuckians and their new brides out of trouble. As rendezvous grew to a close, the word had spread that the next year's get- together would be in the vicinity of Fort Bonneville near Horse Creek, site of the 1833 rendezvous. Jacob and company retraced their steps back to the Wind River Mountains.

Back at the cabins, they found most everything as it had been left months earlier. For the next several months, they hauled winter firewood to camp and several buffalo hunts were held jointly with their wives' band of Snakes. Goods were traded with the Indians for their buffalo robes and they dug up their cached goods and equipment to make ready for the trapping season—

that and the care of the horse tack ate up the remainder of the men's time.

Soon it was time to begin trapping as the beaver started once again coming into their prime. On the day to begin trapping, the men hurried through a hearty breakfast of fried moose steak in bear grease, fried corn-meal mush and several steaming hot cups of coffee. Sitting there eating, Jacob ran through his mind the changes made to camp in the past months. Both cabins had been upgraded so they would be safer in case of attack by any roaming bands of Blackfoot. Those upgrades included a door that could be bolted and windows that could be locked and shuttered from the inside with shooting ports. An additional door had also been added to the rear of each cabin for emergency escape if necessary. An outhouse of rather stout propor-tions had been added nearby on the side hill, which precluded defecating just anywhere and later finding "it" on your moccasins. Also, being heavy with child, an outhouse made it easier for the women to relieve themselves.

Each woman now had a muzzle-loading, double-barrel shotgun over the door of her cabin and a Hawken rifle over the fireplace for defense, and knew how to use them. Plus, both women carried a horse pistol and knife at all times. And to the great satisfaction of Jacob and Martin, both women knew how to use such weapons and use them well. The lessons of Tom and Al's deaths at the hands of the murderous Blackfoot had been well learned and passed on.

Leaving that first morning of the 1834 fall trapping season, both men waved goodbye to their women and proceeded downstream, to a nearby valley full of ponds holding beaver lodges in such profusion it all but promised excellent trapping results. While Martin sat guard on his horse, Jacob set his traps. Then the men—used to the security ritual—switched places and Martin set his traps while Jacob watched over his partner. When they finished those activities, they tied off their pack animals in the dark timber out of sight from any prying eyes that might be in the country. Then the men headed further downstream to scout out new trapping territories for when the first area was trapped out. They hadn't gone a mile when they ran across many sets of fresh, unshod, horse tracks.

Martin examined the tracks. "As near as I can count, there are about twenty Indians here. I wish I knew which tribe. The tracks are pretty fresh, so we could be in some danger. Be quiet and we'll follow these tracks."

Later that day they ran across the mystery riders' encampment. Quietly looking on from a brushy ridge above the scene, both men quickly determined from the strangers' clothing that they were the deadly Gros Ventre, kin to the Blackfoot.

Jacob signed to Martin, "I see only young warriors. This looks to be a raiding party for horses and scalps. I will stay here, with the Gros Ventre, and you will leave quickly to seek help from the Snake Indian villagers, five miles upstream. With our combined numbers, we will attack this war party and kill as many as we can before they can hurt anyone in our valley."

Martin agreed. "The Gros Ventre have made camp for the night. Meet me here when I return."

"Once you bring the Snake Indian warriors, we will think of a plan of attack."

Moments later, Martin glided silently off into the forest towards the Snake's friendly encampment. Jacob, in the meantime, took to heavy cover, watched and waited.

———

FIVE HOURS LATER, Martin approached Jacob as silently as he had left him. Armed with his bow and arrows and his Hawken, he was accompanied at a distance by twenty-five heavily armed, fiercely painted and mounted Snake warriors.

Martin advised Jacob in sign: "I recovered the staked horses from the timber and took them to our camp. I told our wives of the danger. I brought back six North West fusils, powder and shot, which I gave to the Snake Indian warriors. The guns will fortify their resolve and guarantee their presence in battle."

Jacob nodded in agreement, then signed, "The Gros Ventre have bedded down for the night. They are all still near their campfire."

Martin gave Jacob a thumbs up and then they both scuffled off to where the Snake warriors were hiding below the overlook. Martin quickly informed Chief Nash-e-weta of the position of the Gros Ventre, then Martin, Jacob and Nash-e-weta began formulating a plan.

"I'll take ten warriors," Jacob signed, "and come in on the Gros Ventre from the side of their horse herd, over there. Martin will go with you and the rest of the warriors and overrun the camp from the far side, there. Once the Gros Ventre are surprised by the attack, they will naturally try to escape by running for their horses. As they come towards me, my group of warriors will kill as many Gros Ventre as we can with the rifles. Then we will all fight in battle."

"I will give the hoot of a great homed owl as a sign that the attack will start."

Chief Nash-e-weta agreed, and they clasped wrists.

Both parties quietly separated into the early evening's darkness. Jacob waited a short time for the others to get in place, then led his warriors silently down the hill and into position between the horses and the now sleeping and unawares Gros Ventre Indians.

Hoo-hoo—hooo, hoo-hoo—hooo came the call from Martin, and then all hell broke loose.

Jacob looked on at the Gros Ventre camp as Martin's group of warriors came running with a bloody war cry into it. The Snake warriors screamed, yelled and used their tomahawks with precision. The thudding reports of a tomahawk strike on a Gros Ventre skull were permeated by rifle shots. The Gros Ventre, caught unawares, started to rout. They began to run for their lives, to reach their horses. They ran directly at Jacob's hidden team, just as he had predicted.

Jacob's team of warriors watched him. They were eager to get into the fight.

"Fire!" Jacob shouted, and took aim and fired. The warriors lying beside him followed with their own volley. A barrage of thunder, a line of smoke and hurtling lead bullets met the onrushing Gros Ventre at close range.

Jacob reached for his pistol, while the rest of his team raised tomahawks and knives. They took advantage of the confused enemy to charge them and fight at arm's length. Jacob fired his pistol at one Gros Ventre, hitting him in the chest, and in one fluid motion before his opponent fell, he turned to another Gros Ventre warrior who was trying to run past and tomahawked him on the side of the head.

Then a white light of pain exploded inside Jacob's head before all went dark.

Jacob came to sometime later and looked into the fuzzy worried face of his friend, Martin. He blinked back the fog of injury and tried to figure out what had happened. He felt a burning sensation along the side of his head, just above his ear. Reaching up, he discovered fresh and dried blood from a long wound running the full length of the left side of his head. To the sounds of screaming and frenzied Snakes celebrating their great battle, Jacob tried to raise himself to a sitting position. He almost passed out from the pain, but Martin steadied him.

Soon his head cleared somewhat and between the two of them, they tried to make sense out of what had happened. None of the Gros Ventre running for their horses had fired any weapons, so the bullet that had creased Jacob's skull had to have come accidentally from the attack led by Martin's team. One inch closer to the center of the skull and he would have been a goner.

Jacob grabbed Martin's arm and rose on wobbly legs with a loudly ringing head—a reminder of the battle. Martin escorted him over to a downed tree, where he gratefully sat down. Jacob then witnessed a scene that only could occur in Hell or on the frontier: scalping, mutilation, and the removal of body parts and throwing of them into the fire by the Snakes. That was followed by removal of trigger fingers and eyes so the dead could not see who killed them. The desecration completely filled his still blurry vision.

Then along with the revelry at having killed so many of the hated enemy without a loss of life on their side, the Snakes moved to the Gros Ventre horse herd and divided up the spoils of battle. In the process, they discovered that two Gros Ventre had gotten away because there had been twenty riding horses in the herd and only eighteen Indians were dead on the battle site.

Two survivors got away. They'll return to their tribe and perhaps form another larger war party to return for revenge, thought a now grim-faced Jacob.

Come daylight, Martin grabbed his bow and arrows and quietly disappeared into the woods. Jacob and five Snake Indians awaited his return—which occurred around four that afternoon. Martin's grim face told the group he had not been totally successful. He had caught and killed one of the raiding party but the remaining Indian had fled the scene and had hidden his tracks by walking and swimming upstream in the area's many creeks and beaver ponds until he escaped.

Not a good thing, thought Jacob. Escaping Indians have a nasty habit of returning at a later date with another war party, blood in their eyes and revenge in their hearts.

The men left the Gros Ventre dead scattered about for the varmints, the ultimate disgrace for an Indian. The Snakes went back to their camp for a big victory celebration, and Jacob and Martin went to check and reset their remaining traps. The rest of that day and into the evening Martin did the checking, emptying and resetting of all their traps. Jacob and his still ringing, aching head was content to sit on his horse, hoping it wouldn't move too fast or start bucking.

Back at camp, Martin helped Jacob off his horse and into White Fawn's worried care. After she dressed the wound, they retired to their bedroll. She had dressed his wound well, but he was still in a great deal of pain. Come the next morning, however, Jacob felt a little better. He couldn't move too fast, but he felt good enough to eat some breakfast.

Martin left by himself later that morning to check and

reset their traps. To leave dead beaver in their traps would do nothing but advertise to the Indian world the trappers' presence. It would also provide beaver meals for the always-hungry wolves and bears. This would result in many lost, irreplaceable traps as well, if they weren't careful.

Mumbling for the rest of that day, Jacob worried himself sick over his friend being out in the wilds alone. For years, his trusted friend had always been at his side. It made him agitated not to be at Martin's side as well.

MONTHS LATER, winter was upon them in its full fury, and Jacob's head had long since cleared and healed. Aside from another long scar added to his body, he was fit as a fiddle. They had experienced another very successful fall trapping season and were now looking forward to the spring trapping in 1835 as well. However, they were always mindful of the Gros Ventre warrior who had gotten away during the fight. Would he come back leading others to avenge their earlier losses or had he died in the wilds attempting to return home? Those thoughts of a vengeful returning warrior and his friends were always on the two men's minds.

The one thing in their favor was the lateness of the season. Indians usually holed up come winter and did not like to travel because of its inherent difficulty and poor horse food. Usually. But come spring, that could be a horse of a different color.

Early one morning in late January of 1835, White Fawn woke Jacob up.

"It's the baby's time," she said with a grimace of pain. "Go get Running Fast to help me," she continued through clenched teeth. With that Jacob was out of the sleeping skins, dressed and out the door in a heartbeat.

Knocking loudly on Martin's cabin door, Jacob yelled, "Martin, I need Running Fast! White Fawn says it is time and I need your wife to help."

A rustling came from within and soon the cabin door was flung open. Martin stood there stark naked with a pistol at the ready and still half asleep. Seeing it was his friend and no one else, he told Running Fast, "Hurry, White Fawn needs you." Moments later Running Fast, heavy with child herself but still true to her name, ran by the two men and entered Jacob's cabin. For the next two hours, Jacob and a now-dressed Martin waited outside in the cold morning air by the roaring campfire. Then Jacob's cabin door opened and Running Fast came out holding something small in a tanned river otter pelt. Jacob went to her looking for any sign as to what was happening. Running Fast smiled and then removed the flap of otter skin covering the baby's face. Like all newborn babies, it was pink, wrinkly and ugly. But it was alive, appeared to be healthy and—

It's a boy!

Then, realizing there was another partner to this birthing team, Jacob bolted into the cabin and to his wife's side. She was smiling a tired but happy look. "You have a son," she said. "A son who will follow you in whatever you do for the rest of your life."

Ignoring his wife's comments Jacob asked, "Are you alright?"

"Yes," smiled White Fawn, "but it will be a while before you and I can lie together again. Your new son was very large and I tore a lot. But, it will be alright in time."

Running Fast brought the baby back into the cabin along with Martin. Martin built a fire in the fireplace and soon the cabin began to warm.

"What will you call the baby?" asked Martin.

Turning to White Fawn, Jacob asked what would she think if he named the baby "Jacob?"

White Fawn smiled and said, "That was the name I had picked out for him. After his brave and strong father." They both smiled as the younger Jacob started fussing and was returned to his mother's breast.

————

THIRTEEN DAYS LATER, Jacob heard a knock at his door late in the evening. It was Martin needing the services of White Fawn in the birthing process for his child. Within minutes of her arrival at Running Fast's side, Martin was a father. He, too, had a fine son and Running Fast was well from an easy birthing process, even though it was her first. She was sitting up and the baby was trying to nurse when Martin entered. Looking the child over, he then turned his attention to his wife. He was soon satisfied that she was alright and asked to hold the baby. Holding it for the first time, he smiled a large smile, even through the scar on his face caused by the Crow warrior during the battle on the Big Sandy. Then it struck him. The baby needed a name.

Looking over at his wife, Martin said, "What shall we name our son?"

"How about Martin?" she quickly replied.

Martin thought for a moment and then said, "Martin it shall be."

Looking over at Jacob and White Fawn, Martin saw a proud and pleased Jacob smiling through all his facial scars as well. Yes, "Martin" he would be.

The boys grew rapidly with the help of each of their mother's rich milk and care. Neither were very vocal but quiet like their dads and alert to every movement around them. They cried little and had appetites like the largest horse in the herd. With the new additions and the healthy mothers, 1835 was the start of another very good year.

CROSSED ARROWS

THE TWO MEN WERE RARING TO GO COME THE 1835 spring trapping season. The ice was out and the fear from the Blackfoot and Gros Ventre but a vague memory as the men now not only had a family but a new purpose in life. They had to protect and care for their new families and the best way they knew to do that was through successful trapping, and trap successfully they did. Day after day, the beaver and other animals trapped came back into camp hanging from the packhorses in plentiful numbers. Before long, they had more beaver plews than the year before and still they had some time to trap before the critters went out of prime. The trapping of foxes, lynx, wolves and coyotes had also been great, as had the trading throughout the winter with the Snakes for their fine quality buffalo, elk and deer hides.

Both men, however, being of "the soil" and understanding "The Way," began to be bothered with strange thoughts of the days and moments before them. Something unknown from the "spirit world" seemed to almost preoccupy their everyday thoughts and activities. Yet, neither man could put his thoughts to rest with any kind of satisfactory answers. Both men continued to discuss those most unusual feelings—almost premonitions— but after a time with little to validate those fleeting concerns, they soon were dismissed.

The feelings, in time, were quickly forgotten until one spring day; while out trapping, the two men crossed the trail of another large herd of unshod Indian ponies. Jacob and Martin crossed the tracks and then followed them for a short distance until dread in their hearts drew them up short.

"Our families!" Martin said to Jacob as he spurred his horse to a full gallop. Jacob followed, a heartbeat behind.

They quickly raced back to their cabins. Fortunately, the band of unidentified Indians had missed their trapper camp and had proceeded north towards the encampment of the friendly band of Snakes to which White Fawn and Running Fast belonged.

Jacob and Martin dropped off their beaver and pack animals at their cabins and retrieved their extra Hawkens. Then they made sure the women were safely in one cabin with the children and armed to the teeth.

With that, off they rode towards their Snake Indian friends. About one mile from their camp, one could hear light shooting in the distant winds that forever blew in their valley. They spurred on their horses to a faster but still safe clip and approached the Snake Indian camp with trepidation. As they rose over a small line of ridges, the two men discovered the horse herd that had made the tracks they had followed. Martin raised his hand and both stopped behind a thick stand of timber and dead-falls. Below them were three Indian teenagers left to guard the horses. All three of the boys were more interested in the ongoing battle to the front than to their backsides and, as such, were not aware of the arrival of danger.

The raiders were the dreaded Gros Ventre who were way south of their normal territory once again. Martin quietly slipped off his horse, took his bow and arrows and disappeared into the timber at a trot.

Jacob, on the other hand, grabbed all their Hawkens and moved silently towards the three Indians guarding the horses from the opposite side. Jacob crawled in behind another deadfall of downed pine trees, and unlimbered three rifles. He cocked their hammers and made ready. He then sighted in on the Indian furthest away from where Martin was sneaking, and he waited. The closest horse guard was intently looking over a small hill at the battle in the village below. He never saw Martin tomahawk him from —Martin's stealthy arrival even surprised Jacob. Martin then disappeared into the timber and the second Indian soon fell prey to an arrow in the eye.

The third Indian heard the commotion as his pal went

through the throes of dying, but he still caught the next arrow—partially deflected by a tree limb—in the belly. Screaming in pain, the Gros Ventre hobbled over the hill to warn his fellow raiders below, and warn them he did.

Soon the Gros Ventre, unnerved at what was going on behind them in the location of their horse herd, began scrambling away from the fighting in the village and back up the bank from whence they came. That was all the Snakes needed and they redoubled their fighting efforts. Soon the tide had changed and all the living Gros Ventre were scrambling for their horses with the surviving Snake Indians hot on their heels. The first two Gros Ventre who reached the hilltop by their horses died from Martin's well placed arrows in their chests. However, now they came on in such numbers, and Jacob knew that Martin could not shoot accurately or fast enough. They soon overran his shooting position and topped the hill.

The first one up caught a .54-caliber ball in the chest and staggered backward into his charging buddies. Jacob then placed a ball in the chest of the second Indian, who dropped like a pole-axed cat.

Five more came over the hill in a group and four made it to the horses. One of the reserve Hawkens had just had a rare misfire. The fifth Indian breathed his last, though, with Jacob's shot from his last loaded Hawken.

Three more Gros Ventre came over the hill but one was staggering with an arrow in his throat, shot by the ever accurate Martin. Before Jacob could reload, six of the Gros Ventre mounted their horses and rode off into the forest rapidly. Within moments, the Gros Ventre's horse herd area swarmed with angry Snakes, but not before Martin tomahawked the gut-shot Gros Ventre with the big mouth who had sounded the alarm when the trappers had attacked.

APPARENTLY, the battle had just been joined when the two trappers arrived. The gut-shot Gros Ventre had alerted his fellows to the danger from behind and that broke the back of the surprise attack.

Soon there was great celebrating as well as wailing coming from the Snake village. They had lost three men and one woman to the raiders. But from the litter of Gros Ventre bodies everywhere, the Snake were not caught completely napping this time. Not like the time before when the trappers had saved the lives of their future wives as they bathed in the creek.

Jacob and Martin hurriedly dismissed themselves from the celebrating, aware there were still six Gros Ventre on the loose. The last time they were seen, they were heading in the general direction of their cabins. They reloaded the Hawkens on the run, mounted their horses and sped for their cabins while the Snakes went crazy over the bodies and horses of their recently killed foes.

They stopped a hundred yards out and commenced sneaking on foot towards their cabins to make sure it was Gros Ventre-free. But just as they got to the area of the cabins, they saw the six remaining Indians openly charge Jacob's cabin, hoping to overrun the surprised inhabitants. White black-powder smoke rolled out from the cabin from two shooting ports and two Indians staggered and fell to the ground clutching their chests. The women had not been taken by surprise.

The remaining four Gros Ventre split up, with two running to each side of the cabin. There they began shooting into the cabin through the shooting ports with their rifles, bows and arrows.

Jacob and Martin ran to the cabin as fast as they could in a crazed state of mind. Their families were inside and there was danger on the outside!

Jacob and Martin instinctively separated and each took a side of the cabin. Jacob ran headfirst into an Indian trying to hurriedly reload his rifle. Jacob clubbed him so hard with his tomahawk that his head came clear off with the blow. For a moment, the Indian's body remained standing still holding his rifle. Then it quickly folded to the earth.

In the meantime, the second Indian, having seen Jacob's charge, hurriedly notched an arrow and let it loose at his new assailant. The hastily shot arrow missed—but Jacob didn't. Jacob's knife had plunged to the hilt in the Gros Ventre's guts. Not even slowing down, Jacob ran around the cabin hoping the women would not shoot him by mistake and in the process, charged right into Martin doing the same thing from his side of the cabin. Both men crumpled into a heap reaching for their weapons before they realized who they had run into.

The two trappers jumped up and yelled to the cabin's occupants. The front door flung open and standing there with the fowling piece at the ready was White Fawn. Inside one could hear the two babies howling at the top of their lungs over the noise of battle but sounding like they were unscathed. Running Fast stood by the two babies with her pistol in case someone overran White Fawn at the door. Sticking from the side of her right thigh was a Gros Ventre arrow that had been shot through a shooting port but, other than that deep flesh wound, all was well. Jacob and Martin simultaneously let loose a whoop of joy. It took many more minutes for their hearts to return to normal than it did for their efforts in finishing the battle.

After Jacob told White Fawn that her village was safe, she took over and removed Running Fast's arrow by cutting off the shaft and pushing it through the rest of the leg. Then she treated the wound and bound it with a clean bandage of cloth from her prized bolt of red calico.

———

SCOUTING OUT THE AREA, the two men became satisfied there were no more Gros Ventre in the vicinity. In the search, they discovered the six Indians' horses tied up in a clump of willows. They soon became additions to the trappers' horses in the corral. Taking their riding horses, they roped together the dead Indians and hauled their bodies to the far end of their meadow. For the next two nights, the wolves and a nearby black bear made meat.

Jacob and Martin sat down one evening shortly afterwards by the campfire. Beside each man was a cup of whiskey to help kill the pain of old war wounds.

Jacob chewed on his pipe. "You know, Martin, these incursions into our trapping area by Blackfoot and Gros Ventre, they're getting to be almost a bit regular. I'd never have figured they would stray so far south of their home range. And with such regularity."

"I do not mind fighting them, but it's our families I worry about," Martin added.

Jacob chewed on his pipe some more. "The trapping here has never been better. We have the Snake Indians nearby, and they've proven to be good friends and allies. The buffalo is close at hand, and certainly in large herds."

Martin nodded, and Jacob continued to ruminate on the valley's cornucopia of blessings. "The meadow is belly-deep in rich mountain grasses, and the water is as sweet as anything I've ever tasted. Isn't this our home?"

"You are right, my friend. It would be hard to leave under any circumstances."

They knew they had to make a decision as to whether or not to leave this country, but they were so in love with the valley. The only decision they made was to drain their cups of the searing whiskey and agree to discuss the issue another day.

Soon the beaver went out of their prime and the men

quit trapping. Plans were made to attend the 1835 rendezvous back at Horse Creek in the Green River Valley. Without second thoughts now that the Gros Ventre menace had seemingly waned, everything was put into order for the trip or cached to be used upon their return. Good days lay ahead on the trail and much was to be looked forward to in the coming rendezvous: the meeting of old friends, making trades for the coming year, showing off the women and now the kids, and a chance to see what had happened in the previous year in the civilized world. It was also a time in which one took stock of those who had wintered well and those for whom winter's cold was no longer a bother or of concern.

26

THE 1835 RENDEZVOUS

RETRACING THEIR FAMILIAR TRAIL FROM YEARS PAST, JACOB and company headed for the Green River Valley and the 1835 rendezvous in the Fort Bonneville area. Martin led the group and Jacob brought up the rear. Both men trailed four fully loaded pack animals, with six additional Indian horses trailing alongside which were to be used for trade. The two women carried pack boards with their babies, rode their own horses and led four horses each pulling a travois. Two travois were loaded with tanned buffalo hides and the remaining two were carrying much needed camp equipment for such a trip. It was an impressive caravan by two very successful trappers. They were successful due to hard work and the dead Tom Potts' earlier efforts at picking a very beaver-rich area in which to call home—a home in which neither he nor his brother were able to enjoy or leave.

Many days later, Jacob and company came into view
of the rendezvous site. More than one hundred Indian
tepees from the Nez Perce Nation dotted the plain next
to Horse Creek, along with many trappers' lean-tos
constructed in the adjacent creek bottoms. There were
also a number of trappers' tents and tepees in among the
Indians' camping site as well.

Jacob selected a campsite from a distance, one next to
the covering canopy of leaves from a giant cottonwood.
As he planned how to set the camp up, Jacob passed a
crowd of men gathered around a happening. Jacob
directed Martin to the campsite before it was claimed by
someone else, then stopped and looked on at the popular
event.

A white man was sitting on a loaded packsaddle with
his back to Jacob. Off to one side was another white man
standing. All at once the standing white man—Jacob
heard the name Dr. Marcus Whitman—began cutting on
the sitting man's back. Bright red streams of blood ran
down the very white skin of the sitting man; he moved
naught as the scalpel in the doctor's hand cut ever more
deeply into the shoulder area.

Moving in closer for a better look, Jacob discovered
the sitting man was none other than his friend, Jim
Bridger.

The doctor cut even more deeply through the knot of
hard shoulder muscles, then took out a pliers-like instru-
ment, reached into the bloody cut and pulled with all his
might. Bridger flew off the packsaddle from the force of

the pull as the doctor, in jubilation, held aloft a bent steel arrowhead in his pliers. Jacob heard one of the crowd say, "Three years! He's had that damn Blackfoot arrowhead in that damn shoulder fer three damn years! Can ya believe it?" Bridger returned to his feet and examined the bent arrowhead. Dr. Whitman also looked at the large metal arrowhead and just shook his head in disbelief.

Then he said, "Jim, it is a good thing this wound didn't get infected from the arrowhead."

Bridger just grinned and said, "Meat don't rot in the mountains," and with that a jug of whiskey was introduced from the crowd and passed all around in celebration of the successful operation as the doctor cleaned out and sewed up the still bleeding incision.

Bridger noticed Jacob sitting on his horse looking on. The older trapper walked through the respectfully parting crowd to shake his old friend's hand. "Good to see that you survived another winter with your hair," he said with a big grin.

"And the same to you, my friend. What was all the cutting and gutting for?" asked Jacob as he firmly shook Bridger's hand.

"Well, Doc there said he could remove the arrowhead and I let him. It had been getting bothersome lately, especially on cold or wet nights so I am glad to be rid of it." Bridger's tone sounded as if all that had happened was that he had just stepped on a bug. "Where you campin'?"

"Over by that big cottonwood," replied Jacob. "Come over and tip the jug with me and Martin. That will give you the chance to meet our Indian wives and our new sons," proudly proclaimed Jacob with a big grin.

"Be glad to. Maybe even show up to see how good them squaws are as cooks," Bridger replied with a grin and twinkle in his eyes. "How'd ye do this trappin' season last?"

"Very well, but don't know how much longer we will stay in the Wind Rivers. The Blackfoot and Gros Ventre are ranging farther and farther south into our trapping area and the Snakes don't seem to be able to keep them out. Lost Tom and Al Potts to them murdering savages in the fall of '33."

"Them was two good men. Damn! I guess it don't mean no difference how you die though, just so it is in the backcountry doin' what you love. Them Blackfoot had many good years on their own grounds and now it seems they is everywhere and with a meanness and blood in their eyes. By the way, the bottom is out of the beaver trade. Hope you caught more than them critters to sell. Otherwise, you will be on the debit side to the fur companies as many a trapper is now finding out if you don't watch yourselves." With that, Bridger handed Jacob the whiskey jug, who obligingly took a deep pull.

"Thanks, Jim. See you at camp if you have a hankerin' for some good food and company."

Bridger just grinned and slapped Jacob's horse on the rump, sending the Kentuckian off toward his camp.

For the next two weeks, Jacob and company made the rounds with the various fur companies at the rendezvous. Bridger had been right. The beaver market was all but gone. Silk had almost totally replaced the beaver in the top hat trade and now the buffalo hide was supreme. According to the traders, British merchants were buying buffalo hides as fast as they could get them. It seemed they were in some sort of mechanical revolution and needed the leather from the buffalo to make strapping to drive the wheels and pulleys of their newly developing machinery. Buffalo it seemed was thicker and stronger than cattle hide, which made better leather belts to run their machines. Thus, buffalo was all the rage and prices were doubled over past years' payouts for their hides.

Jacob and Martin received top dollar on their beaver hides because of the careful care their women had taken in skinning and hooping them. However, it wasn't as much as in past years and would not carry them through another year by itself. They also got top dollar for their mess of fox, river otter, lynx, coyote, wolf and buffalo robes—which turned out to be more than enough to carry them through another year.

Jacob and Martin used their credits wisely, to purchase more than they needed for recruiting their supply base of helpful Indians and for themselves to carry through another winter. Both men nevertheless could read the writing on the wall regarding the weak beaver trade.

"Maybe one more year and that will be it," Jacob told Martin. "And only then if we mix our trappings with a lot more fox, river otter, lynx, muskrat, elk, deer and buffalo hides."

"But the beaver trade and its problems are to worry about later," Martin replied. "Now is now."

The two men used their time to mingle among the trappers, drink some good and bad whiskey and renew old friendships. The ladies on the other hand, took a lot of their trade items they received from the men for doing such a good job dressing their furs and traded those with the Nez Perce camped at the rendezvous for tanned and supple bighorn sheepskins. A great time was had by all.

One day as Jacob and Martin mingled with old friends, both were suddenly roughly grabbed from behind in such a manner that their arms were completely pinned against their sides. Then both men were lifted up high into the air and tossed to the ground in a heap. Those trappers standing around who interpreted the aggressive actions as a prelude to a rough and tumble fight, started to scatter like a flock of sage grouse on the rise. The experience of having been in many fights previously and knowing what to expect next to avoid the danger of a follow-up, rib-cracking kick served Jacob and Martin well—they both rolled away from their attackers. Then they quickly leapt to their feet, turned and drew their knives in the same fluid motion. Two heavily bearded men of massive body size faced them. The assailants had big grins on their faces.

"Leo! Jeremiah!" Jacob and Martin exclaimed loudly at the same time.

In an instant there were four grown men clasped in each other's arms, all trying to speak at once. The surrounding trappers, seeing this was not going to be one hell of a fight but a friendly hurrah, gathered around to join right in. Soon several whiskey jugs were being passed around with the talk and merriment getting even louder and more animated.

Jacob and Martin could hardly contain themselves. Here were the two scrawny kids they had traded away from the Northern Ute Indians in 1831. Now both men were over six feet tall and built like bulls. And from the looks of their dress, were now very successful trappers. Questions flew back and forth between all four men like snowflakes in a howling November storm.

"How did you find us?"

"Where have you been?"

"How long have you been trapping?"

"Where have you been trapping?" and other similar questions flew back amid the responses until one particular question was asked...

"Where are Ben and Singing Bird? Are they here with the two of you?" asked Martin.

Leo and Jeremiah lost their smiles. After a quick look at each other, Leo said, "They are dead. All of us went and lived in the Knife River Villages as Ben had always wanted to do. In fact, we did right-proud hunting and selling buffalo hides to the riverboat trade while there. Then one day a paddle-wheel steamer came to the villages to trade. However, they had a number of men who were sick onboard and no one wanted to come ashore for fear of it spreading whatever they had to the Indians. However, some Indians sneaked onboard and stole some blankets off the sick men's beds. Several weeks later, a pox broke out among the Indians and soon almost everyone in the villages and surrounding country who came in contact with the villagers were dead or dying. It was smallpox, and it had come from the blankets that had been stolen. Ben and Singing Bird both died as a result. They didn't have any immunity like we did and it took them just a couple of painful weeks to join the Cloud People."

With those words, it became deathly quiet in the group.

Now I understand those feelings of dread that I've been having, Jacob thought. *Have Ben and Singing Bird been trying to let me know about the tragedy, speaking from beyond the Great Divide? Is there something they want me to do?*

Jacob looked at the boys, thinking of how they must have felt, wandering in the frontier after losing their parents yet again. *Yes, I know what what I must do, Ben!*

"Leo, Jeremiah," Jacob said, seriousness in his words. "We were once a family and we need to be a family once again." Jacob replayed in his head the rendezvous two years before when they had rescued the boys from Bull Bear and his band of Northern Utes, and the rendezvous from the year before, when Ben and Singing Bird had shared their dinner with him for the last time.

Jacob was deeply lost in his personal feelings for a

moment and then, realizing they still had the boys, he motioned them away from the group of drunken-and-getting-drunker gang of noisy trappers.

"We are camped over there in the cottonwoods under that big tree struck by lightning. Why don't the two of you grab your gear and throw it in with the rest of our family? We both married Snake women and now we each have a fine young son," continued Jacob, still saddened and stunned over the loss of Ben and Singing Bird.

"We would like to, but you see there are four of us now as well. We both have Lakota Indian wives," said Jeremiah slowly. "And as you know, Lakota and Snakes are lifelong enemies."

The men stood looking at each other for a long moment.

Then Martin spoke. "Our women are good women. Snake or not, they will welcome you and your wives once they discover the true nature behind our lives and how they are intertwined." Jacob nodded in agreement at Martin's wise words.

"Great!" said Leo.

"We will be happy to join you," said Jeremiah with a smile as broad as the mighty Mississippi. "In fact, those were the last words Ben spoke. He told us to find the two of you at the rendezvous, join up and become a family once again. That is why we came so far from the east. Now we are here, so are you, and we can be a company once again."

The men all looked at one another once again and

that soon led to all of them being in each other's arms in happiness once again. And in that moment, tears were openly shed by the four burly men over the loss of two of their beloved family to the deadly pox.

That evening, Leo, Jeremiah, Little Feather—Leo's wife—and Prairie Flower—Jeremiah's wife—joined Jacob and the rest of the family. Running Fast and White Fawn quickly realized their men had brought this family to join theirs and with good reason. As such, tribal and cultural feelings were laid aside from that moment on. Little Feather and Prairie Flower were younger than Running Fast and White Fawn and both of them were without children. As was quickly the case, Babies Jacob and Martin were willingly taken from their mothers and loved to death by the new adoring female members of the family, much to the happiness of their mothers.

Leo and Jeremiah on the other hand, were a little more proper when meeting Jacob and Martin's wives for the first time. However, both men took an instant liking to the women. It was almost like the boys had mothers once again. There was much celebrating around the campfire that evening and into the morning by the two reunited families. And it grew even more so when Jim Bridger joined in to see "if them squaws could cook."

After eating about ten pounds of fresh pronghorn antelope stew and flat bread at one setting, Bridger finally admitted the squaws could cook passably as he headed for a nearby tree to lay under and sleep off the good meal, one sloshed around with more than a little of the good grade of fiery trapper's whiskey under his belt and "in his snoot."

The next morning while the ladies got more acquainted and worked in camp, the men sat down to talk. They brought out the chewing and smoking tobacco along with a recently acquired jug of good trade whiskey and relaxed with their backs braced among the cottonwoods.

Jacob said, "We were planning one more year in the Wind Rivers because the beaver, otter, deer and buffalo are there in great abundance. The Snake Indians there are our friends and we do a large business in furs when trading with them. We have two very well built cabins and a good and healthy horse herd. The only problem we have are the occasional bands of raiding Blackfoot and Gros Ventre. They killed two of our friends several falls back and we need to be on our toes all the time or we will get our topknots lifted."

Jacob looked over at Martin for his input, who added, "Yes, we do have a great trapping area, especially for beaver. But like Jacob says, we have a problem with the Blackfoot and their kin the Gros Ventre. It is just a matter of time before they catch us 'not looking.' So as of this moment, our thoughts are pretty much somewhat open as to our selection of future trapping grounds."

"Why don't we team up?" asked Leo. "We are still excellent shots, our women shoot well, as we taught them as you taught us, and with the four of us, we can stand off just about anything."

Jacob just grinned. *Good old Leo. Still the positive thinker and a damn tough Mountain Man.*

Martin, ever the worrier, said, "That would be fine with me because there are more than enough critters in the valley for all of us. However, you would be exposing your wives to the same danger we are facing when the Blackfoot and Gros Ventre come raiding and the Snakes can't hold them in check or kill them afore they get to our trapping grounds."

Jeremiah quickly spoke. "No matter where we go in this land, it figures we are facing hostile Indians and it seems to be getting worse. There was a time when we white men were welcome. Nowadays there are bands of Comanche, Lakota, Northern Cheyenne, Blackfoot, Gros Ventre and others who just as soon as lift our hair as look at us. One place is just as good as another to die and any day in this great land is a good day to die."

The air hung heavy with Jeremiah's pregnant statement for a few long moments as the men thought about what he had just said.

Jacob broke the silence. "Then it is decided. We four and our wives will return to the Wind Rivers to trap beaver and this year shoot more buffalo. That way we can meet the changing demands in the fur market and continue living our way of life. But if the raids continue this year, we need to pull up stakes and move on. Maybe farther out west when the fur trade loses its shine. Then maybe lead the wagon trains that they say will come through the wilderness, hunt buffalo for them, raise horses or settle down and become farmers." Jacob paused. "And then we still have the Spanish gold as a backup in case we wish to settle down. The West is changing more and more every day. Even in the short time Martin and I have been here, it has drastically changed. We need to change with it or..." Jacob's voice trailed off into nothingness.

"Jacob," Martin said, "now is now. We go to the Wind River Mountains and work the wilderness, if everyone is agreed."

"I'm in," Leo said.

"Let's go ask the women," Jeremiah said.

The women listened to the logic. To the Indian women, Snake and Lakota alike, the violence of the Indian lands was commonplace, the providence of the Wind River Mountains was too good to pass up.

The decision was then sealed with a long pull on the whiskey jug by all the men.

Jacob and Martin traded the horses taken from the Gros Ventre in their recent battle to the Nez Perce and received an excellent price back in furs. Then taking those well-dressed furs from the Nez Perce, they traded them to the traders for more powder, lead, primers, coffee beans, sugar and Hudson's Bay Company three-point blankets. With those trades, they rounded out their needs and had some extra goods for trade with the Snakes upon their return to the trapping grounds. Leo and Jeremiah had done well in their trades as well and like Jacob and Martin, were now set for the coming year.

The following week was spent visiting friends, enjoying the fruits of the 1835 rendezvous and making ready for the long trek back to the Wind Rivers.

———

WHAT OF THE cursed Spanish gold? Bull Bear wondered.

Times had been good for his tribe of Northern Utes. His warriors had killed three of the Great Bears, without a single scratch. He had added three more sets of claws to the necklace he wore.

The bearskins would bring many of the White Man's goods to his people. More guns. More horses. He had traveled to the trading post with several of his people to trade the skins. The White Man Antoine Robidoux spoke in lies and half-truths, as the White Man always did, but Bull Bear was wise to his ways. Bull Bear would get the best trade for the skins, as he noted the envious eyes of a trapper also in the Ft. Uncompahgre trading post.

"I can give you blankets and tobacco," the wily merchant Robidoux had offered.

"Rifles. Horses. I am not interested in your blankets," Bull Bear responded.

The White Man laughed. "I can understand. Ever since the pox at the Knife River Indian Village, I have not been able to sell blankets."

Knife River! Bull Bear's attention caught on the name of the Knife River Indian Village, far far away. "What happened at Knife River?" Robidoux shook his head. "A boatload of trappers came to Knife River Indian Village. They had smallpox, bad medicine. Somehow, the Indians ended up with the trappers' blankets, which was infested with the smallpox. Killed almost all of them, I hear."

"What of the White Men called Leo and Jeremiah, who had been raised by Ben Bow and the Lakota squaw?"

Bull Bear always sought information about the whereabouts of Jacob and his band. He had sent one of his warriors to spy on the Mountain Man Jacob at the Rendezvous that day, and so he knew that the gold had been split four ways. News from the next year's Rendezvous was that the two boys his people had captured had left for the Knife River Indian Village with the one they called Ben Bow and Ben Bow's squaw.

Bull Bear's people now had good luck. He had no desire to ruin it by ever crossing paths again with any of the four who had split the cursed Spanish gold.

"You know white people from Knife River?" Robidoux asked. "A mite bit far fer yer circle of friends, I'd have thought."

The trapper, listening on, had something to say. "I heard of 'em. Ben Bow's boys."

"Yes, Ben Bow. What do you know of the boys?"

"I heard they were going to the Ft. Bonneville Rendezvous, to meet up with their old company."

Yes, of course, Bull Bear thought. With Ben Bow and the squaw dead from the curse, Jeremiah and Leo will have their part of the Spanish gold. If they have returned to Jacob and the other one called Martin, then all the gold is in one place again. All of the gold, and its curse, would be headed to the Wind River Mountains. Bull Bear's people had no reason to travel that far north into the mountains, but the White Man had a habit of pushing west. He would have to keep an ear open, if he and his people were to keep their good luck and not cross paths with the Jacob band.

27

THE CURSE OF THE SPANISH GOLD

THE REUNITED FAMILY LEFT THE RENDEZVOUS WITH Martin in the lead and the four women, with their babies on their backs and their travois colorfully strung out behind. Jacob brought up the rear of the caravan. Jeremiah and Leo rode on either side of the string of animals and humanity. If they were molested, then there would be hell to pay from the massed and highly accurate firepower carried by the travelers in the sometimes dangerous and troubled land.

But after days of uneventful travel, the group arrived back at Jacob and Martin's campsite. All the men tossed their sleeping gear into the lean-to that still held the remainder of last year's horse hay. The women and children settled into the two cabins for the extra protections they offered. Soon the camp was humming along as the men and women worked together.

Leo and Jeremiah decided there was not enough horse feed in the immediate meadow for all the group's horses to survive the long winter, so they took a walk to see if there was another like hay meadow nearby, which they found with a food-potential campsite less than a mile away. Soon the men had moved over to that site and began building two cabins for Leo and Jeremiah's families.

With the four of them working together, the cabins flew together as the women chinked the logs and built up the interiors with sleeping platforms and the like. As at Jacob and Martin's camp, winter hay was gathered and firewood logs hauled in for the coming months. Soon Leo and Jeremiah's camp site was ready for habitation.

A gala affair was held as the four families worked together to effect the move. Much food was consumed and even a little of the drink was passed around to further celebrate the activities. The family was once again together.

When the beaver approached their prime that fall, the two sets of trappers once again worked the beaver ponds and dams with their traps. Jacob and Martin continued to trap to the south of their camp and Leo and Jeremiah trapped to the north in Tom and Al's old stomping grounds. Soon the furs rolled in and both sets of trappers found themselves very busy and once again successful in their trade. Frequently, the families would join each other in making meat from the nearby buffalo herds or moose from the many waterways, and the times were good. In fact, so many buffalo were killed that the women seemed to be constantly cleaning and processing the hides. However, all realized the value those hides represented to their way of life and the backbreaking work was cheerfully performed.

That year the winter snows and bitter cold arrived late, allowing the men to easily continue trapping until the middle of January in 1836. Then winter came with a vengeance. For days on end, blizzards rolled unmercifully through the country.

The buffalo and deer moved out of the mountains down to the sagebrush flats but the trappers and their families still lived well. They had put together adequate provisions in the late summer and early fall and were hardly bothered by the elements. Plus, there was good news. Both White Fawn and Running Fast were once again pregnant. Jacob and Martin could hardly contain themselves. To be fathers once again and doing so well as fur trappers made both feel complete and very happy. It also made their old homes in Kentucky and the loved ones they had left behind in 1829 seem far, far away.

Winter hung on until late April that year. Finally, the men were able to wander out and effectively trap. However, for some reason, the beaver were not as plentiful as they had been in past years. Many times the men would find sick, starving beaver along the banks and soon realized something had beset the beaver and was killing them in large numbers. They soon deduced that the winter had been so harsh and late that many beaver had eaten all their food from their caches. Running out of food and unable to get any more because of the thick ice, they had begun to starve. Rolling with that punch, the men set more traps for the area's many fox, river otter, lynx and ever-present wolf. That change in trapping plans also included moving more frequently to the lowlands with the four of them killing even more buffalo for their hides and some meat. Soon the cabins began to house small mountains of furs ready for the 1836 rendezvous to be held in the Green River area.

Jacob and Martin's wives were beginning to develop bellies, announcing more "new trappers" were on the way. As for young Jacob and Martin, they were growing like weeds and were spitting images of their fathers.

———

THEY WERE HEADED FOR HOME. Martin took the lead, as he usually did, while Jacob led the packhorses. *This has been a very productive day*, Jacob thought. He looked back and counted again: ten large beavers, two gray foxes, and a mule deer buck that Martin had shot not too long ago.

I don't think I have ever seen a deer that fat before. "Martin," Jacob called ahead, in the soft voice that trappers in Indian country often used. "What do you say we have a hurrah tonight? This is quite a buck, and with all these pelts and the work we'll have to do to stretch them out, we could all use a little blow out."

"Like a birthday party," Martin said. Both men's

twenty-third birthday came within days of one another, and today was Jacob's day. "Guess this buck makes a pretty fair birthday present."

"I don't think I can give you anything nearly as nice," Jacob said.

"Typical white man," Martin joked.

Black Eyes watched from the darkened woods. I remember you, White Man! Anger seethed through him, his heart burned with vengeance.

The one who leads the pack string, he is one with the land. The way the man sat in the saddle gave him away, even though he talked like a white man. We must be careful of that one. I remember now, he has the eyes of an eagle and the strength of a lion. He must have been the one to track me and my brother the day after we attacked the camp of Snake and their White Man friends.

Black Eyes remembered. He and his brother had been tracked relentlessly, no matter how they tried to hide their trail. He remembered his brother, run down with an arrow through his head.

Black Eyes let the image brand his determination. He and his brother had been wet, cold and hungry, yet had been hunted like animals. It was a vision of disgrace that Black Eyes was determined to take to his burial scaffold. He recalled the fear of an arrow ripping through him at any moment. He recalled the terror from every crack of a twig as he retreated northward for many days. He recalled the dread of facing his father and the tribal leaders with news of his brother's death and the defeat of the raiders.

He recalled how the tribal council delivered its judgment, that Black Eyes had dishonored the Gros Ventre people with his cowardice. He should have stood against their enemy and avenged his brother's death.

But I survived to return. Today, I will stand and avenge my brother. Today, I will bring honor to my people!

Black Eyes looked left and right, to see if there was more of the enemy. There was not. Black Eyes gave the signal.

———

MARTIN SENSED DANGER! A danger that gave him a feeling like he never had before. *Boom-boom-boom!* Three hidden rifles in quick succession. White smoke rolled out from the dense cover at the edge of the trees bordering the meadow.

Martin flew out of the saddle as the heavy lead loads from the hidden rifles smashed and tore into his body. He was dead before he hit the ground.

Jacob, surprised at the sudden unseen onslaught from the edge of the timber, quickly swung behind the packhorses and, in one practiced move, grabbed his extra Hawken off the packsaddle.

Gros Ventre Indians streamed yelling and screaming from their cover in the trees, heading straight for the trapper's pack string. As they closed, two of the horde split off and ran for Martin's body, clubbing it with their tomahawks as it laid motionless on the ground. Then out came an Indian's knife, which scalped Martin in one fluid motion before Jacob could protect the body of his friend from mutilation.

Rage took over as the fear of dying left his body. The first Indian to tomahawk Martin died with Martin's scalp still in his upraised hand. The impact of the speeding bullet from Jacob's first Hawken blew out his heart and closed that warrior's black eyes forever.

"Goodbye, my dear friend and brother," muttered Jacob as he got down to the killing business at hand. Boom. The first Indian of the savage charge coming towards Jacob flew backwards under the impact of a chest shot from the reserve Hawken. *Pow*. A second Indian, close at hand, folded instantly from a head shot issued by Jacob's horse pistol. As Jacob hurriedly reloaded his pistol, the Gros Ventre charge momentarily wavered and then stopped in confusion.

However, that confusion only lasted a moment; the mad charge commenced once again. This time, Jacob did not have enough time to remove the ramrod from the barrel before the howling Indians were once again upon him. *Pow* went his nearly reloaded pistol, and the ramrod drove itself through the skull of the next closest Indian.

Jacob's riding horse reared and bucked almost out of control at the savage onslaught. Stepping off on one of the horse's back-arching bucking jumps, Jacob shot

another Indian in the face with his second pistol. A tomahawk swung from close range by another assailant. It
missed his arm but knocked the pistol from his hand.
Jacob quickly grabbed his own tomahawk from his waist
sash. The Indian who had knocked away the pistol hit the
ground with a screaming bounce when Jacob's tomahawk
sunk out of sight in his face.

Jacob turned to run for the cover offered by some
nearby willows. He began hurriedly reloading his
remaining Hawken as the Gros Ventre forcefully plowed
through the terrified and still bucking string of riding
and packhorses.

Zzip...thunk. A steel-tipped arrow slammed into the
middle of Jacob's back, just like that of his father years
earlier back in Kentucky. Jacob plunged forward into the
willows. He felt the searing pain as the arrow skipped off
the side of his spine and plunged deeply into his lungs.
The pain was so intense, that Jacob instinctively struggled to reach the arrow to tear it out. Finally realizing he
was struggling in vain trying to reach the arrow's shaft,
Jacob staggered forward and finished reloading his
Hawken.

Desperately grabbing the Hawken's comforting steel,
he staggered forward trying to cock the weapon. He
turned slightly to confront his assailants, and he became
aware of the fast-approaching darkness at the edge of his
eyes and the strength flowing out of his arms.

Jacob saw an Indian running towards him only a few
yards distant with an upraised tomahawk. He struggled

to raise his beloved Hawken. One last desperate attempt to raise his rifle. He helplessly felt it slip from his weakened hands.

Thwack. The steel-bladed tomahawk viciously split Jacob's skull.

————

CURLY BEAR LET out a primal scream as he snatched the fancy White Man's rifle from the hands of the falling, mortally stricken trapper. This was triumph. As the leader of the raiding party, this was a great honor.

His twenty Gros Ventre warriors echoed his victory scream. There was a mad dash for the trappers' horses and equipment as each warrior scrambled for spoils of victory.

But this is not over. Black Eagle, our chief has been killed, and Black Eyes, the sole survivor of these men's cowardly massacre of our people, has also been killed; killed while avenging his honor and his brother's life. Curly Bear spat. *Yes, we have more to do.*

Curly Bear watched as the Gros Vetnre warriors quickly cleaned out the area. He gave his warrior team the signal to go back to their horses, picketed well out of sight in the heavy timber. They raced back.

The trappers are out of the way. We should have no more resistance.

————

WHITE FAWN AND RUNNING FAST, upon hearing the shooting to the south, froze in stoic terror. That frequency of shooting meant only one thing—Indians were in a fight with their men. Both women hurriedly scooped up young Jacob and Martin and hid them in the outhouse under a buffalo robe with desperate instructions to remain still and out of sight. Then the women ran to their cabins, grabbed every available firearm and then joined each other. They locked themselves into one cabin. In the near distance to the south, they could hear the pounding of many horses' hooves, and they were rapidly coming their way.

A large force of fiercely painted Gros Ventre stormed from the woods and boldly streamed into the clearing in front of the cabins. In a heartbeat, two were blown clear out of their saddles, quickly followed by two more as the women let loose with blasts from their fowling pieces through several shooting ports. Totally surprised at the fierce defense, the Gros Ventre milled in confusion in front of the cabin as two more were lifted from their saddles by the two big Hawkens being fired through the firing slots by the desperate women.

Now totally dismayed at the death and destruction spewing from the cabin, the raiding party scattered and lit out for cover, only to return to the cabin from all quarters on foot. They stormed the cabin and smashed through the front door. Two more Indians died from the blasts of pistols as White Fawn and Running Fast, knowing what was ultimately in store for them, extracted the highest toll possible. Both women were then clubbed to the floor, as the remaining thirteen Gros Ventre tore the cabin apart.

In their frenzy, the raiders took everything of value, including the furs and firearms; the items not of interest were tossed in the clearing in front of the cabins. Then the women were hauled from the cabin and one at a time savagely raped by everyone in the raiding party. Seeing the naked women were with child—and trappers' babies at that—the Gros Ventre continued their rapes, forcing screams from the two now badly bleeding and hated Snake women. However, unknown to the Gros Ventre, one of those seeming screams from White Fawn was in the tongue of the Snake, for the two children to remain still and not leave the outhouse. Finally, in so much pain, both women passed out. Then both women were mercifully stabbed to death and mutilated to the point of being almost unrecognizable by the frenzied Gros Ventre.

———

WITH SO MANY killed from the raiding party by the trappers and their women, Curly Bear could now hardly go back to his tribe and declare a victory. *To lose one warrior was bad enough, but to lose fourteen of the original twenty-seven would be viewed as a failed war party no matter the number of horses or goods they brought back. I will be looked upon as a failed war chief!*

In an act of total madness, the women's bodies were

tossed into the cabins and everything from the hand of the hated white man that was of little value to the raiding party was scattered all over the ground. Then both cabins were set ablaze.

No one bothered the outhouse for obvious reasons.

———

LEO AND JEREMIAH stood at the edge of a stand of timber a short distance away, in utter anguish.

When they had heard the shooting to their south, they suspected trouble, and so they had stopped trapping and had ridden hell-bent for leather towards the sound of battle. They had arrived a short distance from Jacob and Martin's cabins, but had drawn to an abrupt halt as they observed the battle ending.

They both stifled an onrush of tears of anger. To try and intervene, now that everyone in the cabins were dead, would be foolish. All that would probably do is get themselves killed and their wives as well once their trail was backtracked.

In extreme anger and frustration, the two men watched the remaining Gros Ventre take the horses out from the corral, load them with goods taken from the cabin and leave. Leo also noticed that Jacob and Martin's riding horses and pack animals were with the Gros Ventre raiding party. That could only mean one thing...

———

AN HOUR after the raiding party had left, Leo and Jeremiah cautiously emerged from the trees. They followed the raiders' tracks and saw the raiders were fast leaving the area before the Snakes could discover the decimated band and take advantage. With only a few braves left, they were now in danger of not being able to safely ride through the vast territory of the Snake Indians and go back home to their territorial lands far to the north.

The two brothers returned to Jacob and Martin's campsite. They backtracked the raiding party to whence they came before attacking the cabin. They quickly discovered Jacob and Martin's badly mutilated bodies. They dug a grave and placed both men into the same grave.

Jacob and Martin had been together for their entire lives and Leo felt it best they be buried together like the brothers they were. Then a cairn of rocks was placed over the gravesite, but to avoid any further detection of themselves by any other raiding parties, no fire was built to hide the scent of what lay below.

THE ROCKS WILL HAVE to do at keeping the wolves and grizzly bears from digging up and eating the bodies, Leo considered.

Leo and Jeremiah returned to the burned-out cabins. Leo was amazed to see little Jacob and Martin standing by the open door of the outhouse with terrified, wide-eyed looks. Both men, overjoyed at their survival, bailed off their horses and scooped up the youngsters. The two toddlers recognized the men and just snuggled in their uncles' muscular arms, unaware they were now without parents.

After the kids calmed down, Leo gave little Jacob to Jeremiah and went over to the ashes of the cabins. He discovered the bodies of White Fawn and Running Fast in a still smoking and charred pile. Leo openly cried as he carefully dragged the two women over to a nearby old cache hole and placed them in it. Soon the smoking and charred bodies lay beneath the comforting damp soils of Mother Earth.

Leo made one last swing through the area in front of the cabins. He discovered two partially opened and discarded parfleches. In them were numerous golden ingots and several handfuls of silver and gold coins.

"Leo, those are just like the golden ingots Ben and Singing Bird gave us before they died!" said Jeremiah, looking on.

Leo just nodded.

The two brothers picked the treasure up and placed the parfleches on his and Jeremiah's pack animals.

Leo said, "We will keep these riches for little Jacob and Martin so when they grow up, if they want, they can become farmers. They can buy some land and settle down without having to go into this deadly game of trapping and trying to keep one's topknot all at the same time. That would have made Jacob, Martin and their wives very happy." Leo had to push the words through the tears freely cascading down his weathered face. He grieved for his once lost but found and then lost forever family.

Leo clenched his teeth. "We can do nothing more here and now have our own families to think of. And that now includes these two," he said, nodding towards the children.

With that, the two men remounted their horses and carried the two little ones back to their own cabins. With heavy hearts, they shared the terrible news with their wives.

The following morning, the area around Leo and Jeremiah's cabins was abuzz with activity. Both men had enough of living among the northern tribes of Indians and the constant danger it always seemed to bring, especially with wives and the children their wives had taken for their own. They were taking their pelts and moving back towards some sort of civilization.

With Leo in front and Jeremiah in the rear of a long pack and travois string, they left the area once full of happy moments that had now turned into blackened, hurtful memories. They passed the graves of White Fawn, Running Fast, Jacob and Martin, to say goodbye one last time.

Goodbye, Leo thought. *I swear in Jesus's name, I will raise your son to be a good man who will live in the West. I will take them somewhere where death is not always nearby, but they will live in the West.* He began reciting Psalm 23: "The Lord is my shepherd; I shall not want...

Jeremiah joined him, quietly...

"He maketh me to lie down in green pastures; He leadeth me beside the still waters."

Leo considered the view of the lake that commanded the valley, and the assorted, now unpopulated beaver ponds nearby.

"He restoreth my soul; He leadeth me in the paths of righteousness for His name's sake."

Leo let his tear-laden gaze turn to the Wind River Mountains, the jagged top of this valley of...

"Yea, though I walk through the valley of the shadow of death, I will fear no evil; for Thou art with me; Thy rod and Thy staff, they comfort me."

Leo turned to look back at the destruction they were leaving: the freshly dug graves, the scorched timbers of the cabins, the abandoned bodies of the Gros Ventre. Then he looked to consider his family, with his new ward and son, young Jacob.

"Thou preparest a table before me in the presence of mine enemies; Thou anointest my head with oil; my cup runneth over."

Leo turned forward again, and settled himself into his saddle. He finished the psalm with a stronger voice, with the feeling that the circle of life had again turned another revolution.

"Surely goodness and mercy shall follow me all the days of my life; and I will dwell in the house of the Lord forever."

A lone wolf howled off in the distance, soon followed

by howls from the rest of the pack almost as if saying goodbye to others like themselves. A fitting end to those who lived like the wind and disappeared into the soil of the wilderness, like the lonely howl of the wolf against a chilly November night sky.

28

SERVED COLD

Leo and Jeremiah, ever mindful of the raiding party's close proximity, kept their little band to the cover of the trees and brush-lined creeks. Even though the Gros Ventre raiding party had been reduced in numbers in the battle with Jacob and Martin and their wives, they were still plenty dangerous. Both Leo and Jeremiah carried .54-caliber Hawkens and two single-shot pistols each as standard protection. They also carried a readily available second rifle across the pack on the first animal in each of their horse strings. Additionally, each wife carried a pistol and knife and knew how to use it. However, if attacked, they would still be at a disadvantage against the Gros Ventre raiding party's superior numbers, so no chances at discovery were taken. When the boys had backtracked the raiding party earlier, shortly after the battle, they observed that the raiders were heading north.

"By going almost due west, any chance of running into that passel of killing Gros Ventre is pretty slim," Leo told the others.

But towards evening with Leo still leading the group, they cut across the tracks of about a dozen Indian horses and shod packhorses. Leo had earlier found a horseshoe from one of Jacob and Martin's packhorses and there was a horse in the group of tracks without a right front shoe.

Leo stopped with a racing heart. He quickly looked in every direction expecting to be ambushed at any moment.

Jeremiah pulled alongside and quietly said, "What is the matter?"

Without a word, Leo pointed to the ground in front of his horse without taking his eyes off the surrounding landscape.

"Jesus! What are they doing way out here? The last time we cut their trail, they were heading due north and from the looks of it, as fast as they could."

"Must have run into a passel of Snake Indians to the north and figured they best head west to lose them and then head due north once they were out of danger. Less Indians in their way that way," said a grim-faced Leo.

"Now we got them in our backyard and agoin' our way. What do you think?"

"They won't be thinkin' pursuit by anyone way out here," Leo said slowly through a set of tight lips and narrowed eyes.

They turned to look at each other. It was obvious

Jeremiah was now thinking along the same deadly lines Leo was, like that of a maddened sow grizzly.

————

CURLY BEAR SAT QUIETLY STARING into the small crackling fire. His war party had started out with such high expectations. True, they had a rich load of furs, six of the newest Hawken rifles, over a dozen captured horses, and other valuable goods from the trappers to show for their efforts, but he had lost too many warriors in the process.

To go home now with such losses would be to go home in disgrace, he grimly thought.

Yet he had to get home and away from his enemies, the Snakes. Earlier in the day, after the fight with the trappers, his raiding party had traveled north towards home. In their haste to get out of enemy territory, they had observed a large war party of Snake warriors in their path who appeared to be hunting his little band.

They had slipped away unseen, but he knew that traveling north through country heavy with bands of aroused Snake Indians would now not be the safest way home. It would have been the shortest route but was not possible with the Snakes up in arms and blocking their way.

No, we will head west until we get to the sagebrush plains at the fringe of the Snake territories and then head north once again. A longer route but safer.

Freshly roasted venison aroma began to crowd out his worried thinking. Neither he nor his warriors had eaten since the morning of the big fight with the trappers and their wives.

Hot meat will be good for everyone, he thought as he reached for a smoking piece of venison cooking away on a willow stick over the crackling fire. The venison was that which had been provided by the two trappers from the earlier hunt on the day of their deaths.

————

THE FIRST TWO Indians hardly made a sound other than a soft gurgling noise as Leo and Jeremiah cut their throats clear to their spinal columns. Kneeling there in the quickly spreading blood pools, each man held his dying Indian still until there was absolutely no movement left to arouse his remaining sleeping companions. With a quick look at each other in the dying fire's last light, both men silently moved forward once more towards two other sleeping mounds wrapped in blankets around the fires.

Leo and Jeremiah grabbed each Indian by his mouth and nose to preclude any struggle or sound. The Indians' heads were pulled violently but quietly back as Leo and Jeremiah's knives sliced clear to the vertebra of their necks. Blood spurted from the gaping wounds, spraying both brothers as they held the quietly struggling Indians. By now covered with blood as they were, both men looked hideous. Their looks in no way however captured what they felt in their hearts as they crawled silently from one unsuspecting sleeping Indian to another. Soon there were only three Indians left alive out of the original thirteen.

Once he reached the last three Indians, Leo decided to use his tomahawk because his knife handle was so slippery with blood that a good grasp could not be guaranteed. After Leo pointed to his tomahawk, Jeremiah got the message and went for his own tomahawk in his waistband. Two solid bone-crunching thwacks soon followed and the remaining Indian, the last of his raiding party, awoke with a start. He awoke faced by two bloodied white men on their knees holding two pistols on him from a distance of just a few feet.

As he looked at his dead comrades and realized it was all over for this world, the Gros Ventre Indian began to sing his death song. Both brothers rose to their feet with the realization this was the Indian seen leading the band of killing savages at the trappers' cabins. With that realization, Leo felt his heart beating quickly and then hardening even further.

The brothers tied the Gros Ventre chief to a tree next to a rekindled fire. Then Leo scalped him while he was still alive, eliciting primal screams. Both ears and his nose were then cut off and tossed into the coals of the now blazing fire. As the Indian screamed in abject pain, Jeremiah grabbed each of the Indian's hands and one at a time spread the fingers alongside the tree. Then, with a vicious swing of his tomahawk, Jeremiah cut off all the Indian's fingers and thumbs. The Indian screamed in unholy pain, begging the White Man to end his life in a language neither man understood. Both men, however, were still not through.

Wolves circled the small campfire as Leo gathered up all the rifles, pack animals and furs. He roped together the riding horses. Jeremiah kicked out the remainder of the fire leaving only a few coals.

With the pungent smell of so much blood in the air, the wolves went into a feeding frenzy. They darted into and out of camp savagely mauling several of the Indians' bodies lying at the edge of the dying firelight with each venture. Soon, horrendous fights and flesh-tearing sounds rent the quiet night air. The only other noises were that of an Indian tied to a tree softly moaning his death song and the sounds of many horses' hooves slowly moving away from this, the newest dark and bloody ground.

After riding several hundred yards from the bloody scene, Leo heard a scream like that of a mountain lion, a sound that defied description...or was it the sound a human makes when he is being torn to pieces while still living by hungry wolves?

The two men soon joined their concerned wives and children who were hidden in the dark timber. Nothing was said by the women of the bloodied clothing worn by their men. Camp was made, everyone soon fed and then they went to their sleeping skins for some much-needed rest. Tomorrow would bring another day and the start of a new life in a country known for its intense beauty and equally intense violence.

The toddlers slept all that night, quietly and well, all through the night in a land covered over with a blanket of stars.

EPILOGUE

BULL BEAR WELCOMED THE TRAPPER INTO THE CAMP OF the People of the Great Bear. It was a typical trading session. The White Man, Jean-Luc, wanted furs and had heard that Bull Bear's band had done well in collecting grizzly and brown bearskin furs. He was ready to trade, and he had brought whiskey and horses.

But this was their second meeting. Bull Bear had let the trapper trade the White Man's goods for the furs. But then, this White Man, Jean-Luc, had begun asking his people about the yellow metal, if they knew where to find it in the mountains. Bull Bear sent for the trapper, and two warriors had brought him into Bull Bear's tepee.

"Why do you ask about the yellow metal?" Bull Bear asked the trapper.

"I believe that this metal, which is more valuable to our people than furs, is hidden within these mountains. I have seen some in a stream." The man called Jean-Luc reached into a fold in his buckskin shirt and produced a tiny pebble of malleable yellow metal, not much larger than a piñon nut. "I found this on the other side of the mountains. I want to know if you have ever seen metal like this."

Bull Bear jumped to his feet when he saw the gold nugget in his tepee. He took a step back and grasped the Great Bear claw necklace that had kept them safe from the curse of gold. This was not one of the Spanish ingots, though, that had carried the curse.

Bull Bear stepped cautiously towards the trapper, to look closely at the tiny nugget in his hand. "Does this metal bring death and sickness?"

The trapper Jean-Luc threw back his head and laughed. "Oh, yes. This makes White Man crazy with desire to own it. White Man will kill and die for this. They call it Gold Fever, and that is why I tell no one that I know there is gold in these lands."

Bull Bear smiled. There was more gold, and the Spanish had discovered it.

"There is more of this, but I do not know where."

"You've seen gold? Here?"

"No, not here. In Spanish camp, many years ago. They had much gold. Tell me, do you know of the trappers they call Jacob and Martin, with two other men they call Leo and Jeremiah?" Jean-Luc put the nugget away. He cocked his head, apparently confused by the shift in conversation.

"Yeah, they disappeared into the mountains. Horse wreck, maybe, or Blackfoot. Ain't seen 'em at rendezvous for a long time. They were in the Wind River Mountains, last anyone heard. Dangerous country."

It was then that Bull Bear realized the curse of the Spanish gold had struck once again. "Leave, and take your gold, White Man. We do not want the metal that makes men crazy, and we do not want you here anymore." Bull Bear gave the signal to the warrior at his side to take this man out of camp.

What of the cursed gold? Bull Bear wondered. Now I cannot tell where the gold is, now that the curse has taken the Jacob band. The curse will follow anyone who finds the Spanish gold, and perhaps we will cross paths with the Spanish gold. Perhaps, the curse will return to us.

Bull Bear spent the rest of the night listening for evil spirits in the wind and clutching at the claws of the Great Bear that he wore around his neck.

A LOOK AT CURSE OF THE SPANISH GOLD, BOOK 2

In 1829, Jacob and Martin left Kentucky to become Mountain Men, trappers of the Rocky Mountains. The rugged mountains that lay beyond America's frontier remained mostly unexplored. In those days, when beaver were plentiful and the buffalo roamed freely, the killing was good. The two young men would also find that life would be hardscrabble in the high frontier. They would face grizzly bears and hostile Indians. And they would risk horse wrecks and mountain storms to trade their furs each year at "rendezvous." Crossed Arrows is the story of two adventurers who lived hard in the earliest days of the Wild West.

AVAILABLE NOW FROM TERRY GROSZ AND WOLF-PACK PUBLISHING

ABOUT THE AUTHOR

Terry Grosz earned his bachelor's degree in 1964 and his master's in wildlife management in 1966 from Humboldt State College in California. He was a California State Fish and Game Warden, based first in Eureka and then Colusa, from 1966 to 1970. He then joined the U.S. Fish & Wildlife Service, and served in California as a U.S. Game Management Agent and Special Agent until 1974. After that, he was promoted to Senior Resident Agent and placed in charge of North and South Dakota for two years, followed by three years as Senior Special Agent in Washington, D.C., with the Endangered Species Program, Division of Law Enforcement. While in Washington, he also served as Foreign Liaison Officer.

In 1979, he became the Assistant Special Agent in Charge in Minneapolis, Minnesota. Two years later in 1981, he was promoted to Special Agent in Charge and transferred to Denver, Colorado, where he remained until his retirement in 1998.

He has earned many awards and honors during his career, including, from the U.S. Fish & Wildlife Service, the Meritorious Service Award in 1996, and Top Ten

Award in 1987 as one of the top ten employees (in an agency of some 9,000). The Fish & Wildlife Foundation presented him with the Guy Bradley Award in 1989, and in 1993 he received the Conservation Achievement Award for Law Enforcement from the National Wildlife Federation.

Unity College in Maine awarded Grosz an honorary doctorate in environmental stewardship in 2001. His first book, Wildlife Wars, was published in 1999 and won the National Outdoor Book Award for Nature and Environment. He has had ten memoirs published since then— For Love of Wildness, Defending Our Wildlife Heritage, A Sword for Mother Nature, No Safe Refuge, The Thin Green Line, Genesis of a Duck Cop, Slaughter in the Sacramento Valley, Wildlife on the Edge, Wildlife's Quiet War, and Wildlife Dies Without Making a Sound (in two volumes) —and his Mountain Men Novels — Crossed Arrows, Curse of the Spanish Gold, The Saga of Harlan Waugh, The Adventures of the Brothers Dent, and The Adventures of Hatchet Jack.

Several of Grosz's stories were broadcast as a docudrama on the Animal Planet network in 2003.

Terry Grosz lives in Colorado.